I0788777

Stop my
Bleeding
Heart

Stop my Bleeding Heart

A CONTEMPORARY FAIRY TALE RETELLING

VICTORIA ANDERS

Stop My Bleeding Heart

Copyright © 2021 by Victoria Anders

No part of this publication may be reproduced, distributed, or transmitted in any form or by any means, including photocopying, recording, or other electronic or mechanical methods, without the prior written permission of the publisher, except in the case of brief quotations embodied in critical reviews and certain other noncommercial uses permitted by copyright law. For permission requests, email the publisher at stephanie@alt19creative.com.

ISBN: 978-1-955256-05-6 (paperback)
ISBN: 978-1-955256-02-5 (hardcover)

Published by:
Alt 19 Publications
Tampa, Florida

OTHER BOOKS BY VICTORIA ANDERS

MY LIFE SERIES
My Life as Kelsey
My Life as Noah
My Life as Marlee
The Last Hurrah
Saving the Garland Inn
To Find You Again

MERRYVILLE HIGH SERIES
Unwrap My Heart
Unleash My Love

MAGIC MIRROR
ON THE WALL,
WHO IS THE FAIREST
ONE OF ALL?

THEME SONG FOR
Stop my Bleeding Heart

Bloodstream
by Stateless

interlude 1

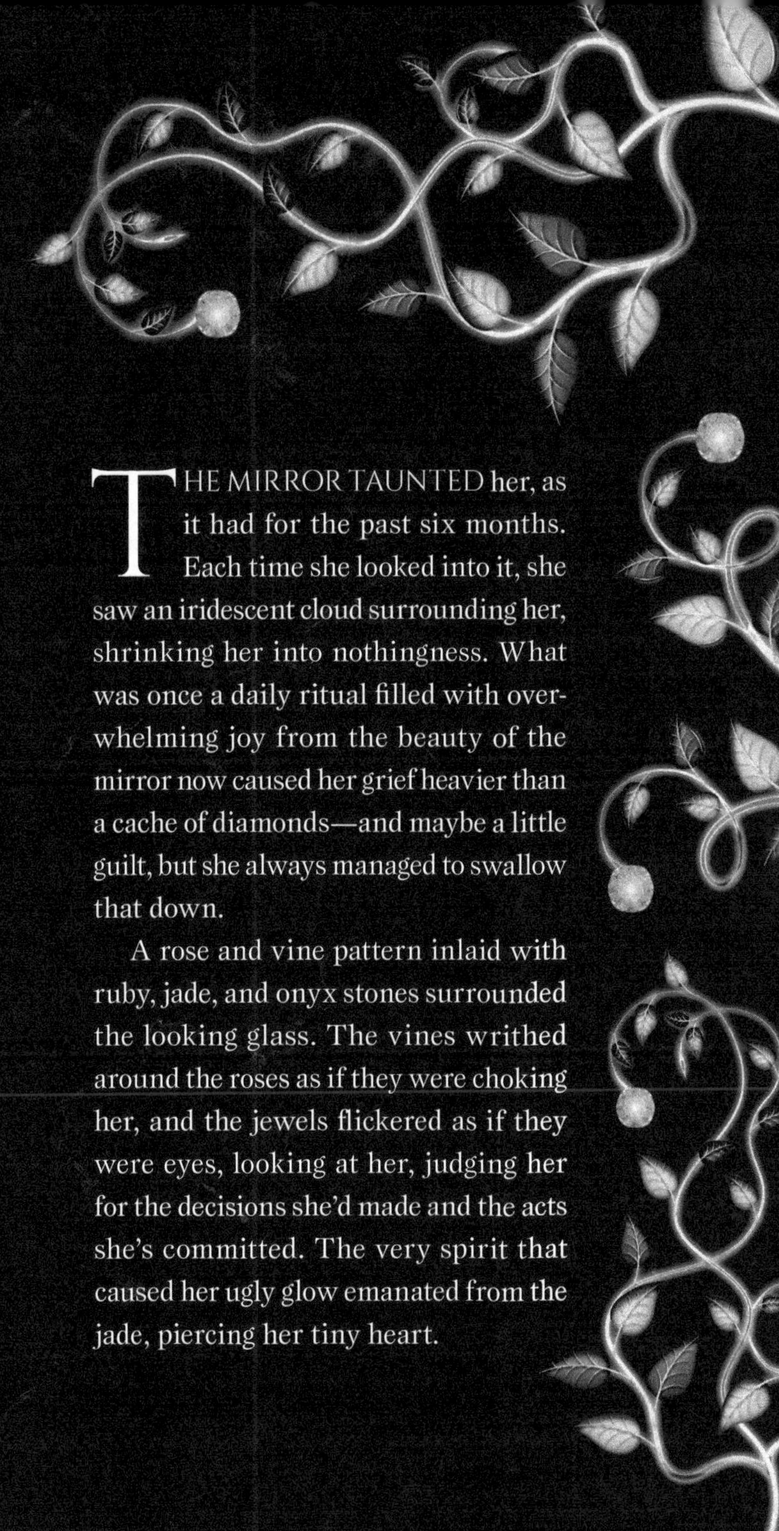

THE MIRROR TAUNTED her, as it had for the past six months. Each time she looked into it, she saw an iridescent cloud surrounding her, shrinking her into nothingness. What was once a daily ritual filled with overwhelming joy from the beauty of the mirror now caused her grief heavier than a cache of diamonds—and maybe a little guilt, but she always managed to swallow that down.

A rose and vine pattern inlaid with ruby, jade, and onyx stones surrounded the looking glass. The vines writhed around the roses as if they were choking her, and the jewels flickered as if they were eyes, looking at her, judging her for the decisions she'd made and the acts she's committed. The very spirit that caused her ugly glow emanated from the jade, piercing her tiny heart.

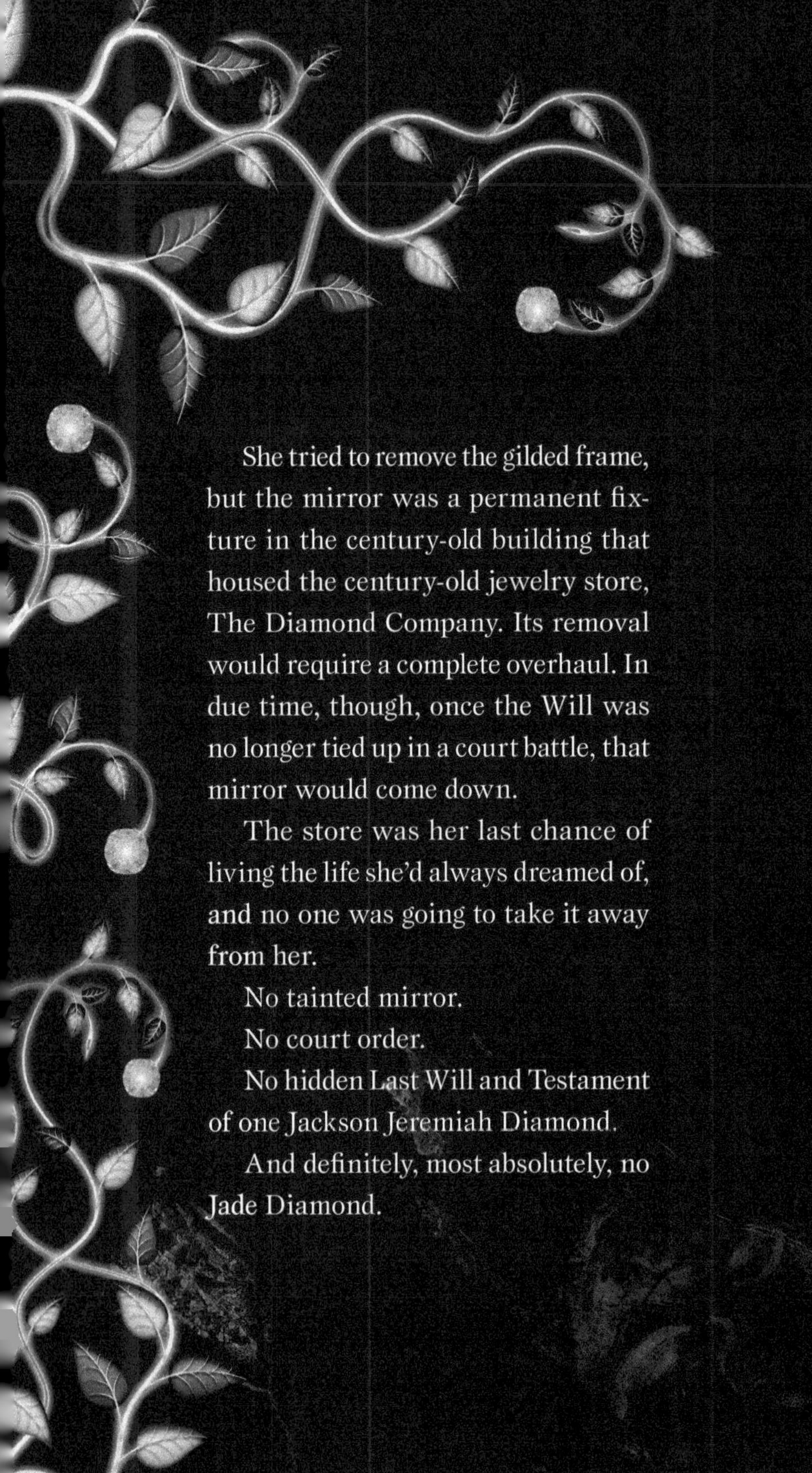

She tried to remove the gilded frame, but the mirror was a permanent fixture in the century-old building that housed the century-old jewelry store, The Diamond Company. Its removal would require a complete overhaul. In due time, though, once the Will was no longer tied up in a court battle, that mirror would come down.

The store was her last chance of living the life she'd always dreamed of, and no one was going to take it away from her.

No tainted mirror.

No court order.

No hidden Last Will and Testament of one Jackson Jeremiah Diamond.

And definitely, most absolutely, no Jade Diamond.

jade

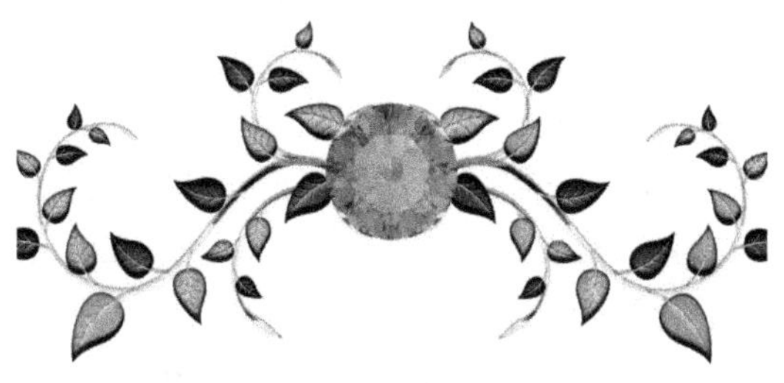

CHAPTER 1

I T SUCKS WHEN a birthday ritual ends. It sucks even more when the reason the ritual ends is death. The death of a loved one.

The death of my father.

When I wake up on my eighteenth birthday, I don't expect the island of French toast in a sea of real maple syrup, smothered by a mountain of whipped cream, and topped with red trees made of strawberries to fill the landscape.

I may not expect it, but I wish it would happen. It'd be possible, *if* someone cared like he had cared.

But *she* doesn't care.

She's not my mother. I call her miss vain, not to her face though. She'd backhand me in a second if I dared call her that. She asked me to call her Mrs. Diamond on the day my dad died. Her real name is as unimportant as my existence is to her.

She was always there physically and had been since my twelfth birthday when my dad presented me with my annual birthday breakfast feast. She even sang happy birthday with my dad on my sixteenth. Off-key and only a single verse, but it was the thought that counted.

Or was it?

I'm sure it was more out of her own vanity. After that day, she'd no longer have to drive me anywhere. Her stepmother duties were officially over in her mind.

Until he died.

Then that *legal guardian* title came into play.

Part of me died with him. All that's left is a hollow shell that resembles me. I lost interest in everything, including my life-long love of art. I haven't picked up a drawing pencil or paintbrush since his death.

The rickety stairs creak and groan as I make the climb from my spider web-filled room in the damp basement.

I used to have the biggest room in the Victorian-style house that's been in the Diamond family for over a hundred years. But miss vain decided the walls needed to be torn down and the three bedrooms on the second floor needed to be joined into one gigantic master suite with an oversized tub and an even more oversized shower. We won't even talk about the oversized closet filled with designer labels and red-bottomed Louboutin heels in every style.

The old shiplap walls were consolidated into a box of splinters and replaced with gold, diamond-patterned wallpaper. It happened so quickly that I only had a chance to save and hide a few family heirlooms from the rooms before it all disappeared.

What came as a shock to me—although after the years of her hatred, I'm not sure why I was shocked—was when she told me we could no longer afford the private school I had attended since kindergarten.

Starting senior year as the new girl at Merryville High School is something I'm still recovering from today. Sure, the hot quarterback is my new boyfriend, but as the weeks turn into months since my last day at my former school, my old friends seem to have forgotten me. I'm now known as that girl whose dad was tragically killed.

I pause at the top of the stairs, listening and sniffing, hoping the smell of warm, eggy bread and hot sugar will overpower the musty basement odor, but the mildewed scent still clings to the air. The slight hint of her flown-in-straight-from-Colombia coffee brewing tells me miss vain is up and ready for her daily battle with the thorn in her side, also known as her stepdaughter, also known as Jade Diamond, also known as me.

Happy birthday to moi.

"STAND UP STRAIGHT," miss vain says, disgust heavier than normal as my back instinctively straightens. "Go back downstairs and brush your hair. Your eyeliner is uneven. And for *Ruby's* sake, change your damn clothes. You look like you went through a paper shredder."

I hate when she takes my mom's name in vain.

Telling her this is what the public school kids wear is pointless. She'll go on a rampage, saying I shouldn't have spent money on a new wardrobe of jeans and tees and just wore the prim and proper private school uniform—or forked out extra money on silk suits in a gossamer rainbow of colors.

But, unluckily for her and totally against her wishes, I control my own money and buy what I want. She may control the house. She may control the store. She may somewhat control me, being my legal guardian, although today that on-paper prison sentence miraculously ends. But she doesn't control my bank account. I didn't work at the family jewelry store since I turned fifteen for nothing.

Worked, that is. She made me quit—fired me is more like it—after my dad died, telling me I needed to have fun my senior year. More like she needed me out of her bleached blonde hair, which she wears pulled back in a bun so tight that her cheeks and eyebrows slant to a 90-degree angle.

It sucks 'cause I love that store. It's in my blood. It was supposed to be my future. But now, it's her future. Unless a silver-winged angel comes down and plucks another Will from a super-secret hiding place.

It's pointless to dream. My blood needs to find an alternative path to take, preferably as far away from her as possible. I just need to hang in there for the seven months until graduation.

Then I'm free.

Every day, I tried to plant a seed, adding water and soil, coming out of the earth bit by bit. But her constant beratement on everything I did, everything I wore, everything I felt, has left me ripped from the dirt like a weed.

She will no longer impede my ability to bloom.

She pours her expensive coffee into the Father-of-the-Year mug I bought for Father's Day when I was fifteen, then grabs her keys and pauses at the backdoor. "I won't be home tonight. Make yourself one of my frozen meals for dinner."

I fake a smile and say, "Thanks," then mumble, "don't let the door hit you where the real sun doesn't shine." Luckily, her fake-tanned ass doesn't hear me. Otherwise, I'd go to school with a bruised cheek.

THE HUNTER GREEN: Woke up late. Won't make it. Meet at school.

I try to swallow the disappointment, but it's stuck in my throat. Hunter's never late. My luck is he's late on my birthday. And he didn't even say *happy birthday* in his text.

The windows of Hattie's Diner display laughing faces of fellow Merryville students as they finish their breakfasts before heading off to school. I should be strong and head in by myself to order my birthday French toast, but time has eluded me while waiting on Hunter.

My stomach growls like a bear as I pull out of the parking lot. A gas station chocolate milk and three-day-old strawberry and cheese pastry will have to hold me over until the dreaded Merryville High lunch.

If there's one thing I miss the most from my old school, it's the daily gourmet meals from an award-winning chef.

"Come on, Jade," I say aloud then sing, "*it's your birthday*. Positivity from this moment forward for the rest of the day, where you'll be as far away as possible from miss vain. Okay?

"Okay," I say in response and put an actual smile on my face.

Hunter will be at school, leaning against his neon green mustang with his gorgeous smile, holding a dozen

red roses. He'll smother me into a hug then seduce my senses with his magical mouth. His enormous hands will take my face and cradle it gently as he says *I love you* for the first time. I'll tell him I'm finally ready, and he'll sneak into the basement late this evening.

And it will be the best birthday ever.

When I pull into the lot at school, Hunter's leaning against his car as expected, but he's not holding roses or any other kind of flowers, and he's not wearing that smoldering grin. When he sees me, his eyebrows draw in and his posture stiffens.

My heart opens the dam and bleeds. It's what it does when tragedy is about to strike. It's a natural instinct I was born with, knowing when something bad is about to happen. Sometimes, it's a false alarm, but most times, it's dead on.

The first time I remember it happening was when I was five. My mom had been in the hospital suffering from what my dad always told me was a bad heart. I missed her like crazy and only got to see her on the weekends. One day, I wanted to see her so bad that I told my daddy my heart was bleeding and he needed to take me to the hospital because I had a bad heart too. I remember it pounding so hard I thought it would come out of my chest.

He didn't take me to see her. And he always said that was his biggest regret. The next day, my mom died at the age of thirty-two from heart disease.

After that, my daddy ambled around like the walking dead, only ever smiling at me. He gave me a good life and tried to be happy, but his heart hurt as much as mine did for years.

Then miss vain came along. My dad was blind to the way she treated me, as she did a good job of hiding it when we were all together. We'd go shopping as a family, and she'd pick out things for me. Doting on me as if I were her daughter. Then we'd get home, my dad would head to work, and she'd take everything back, returning it to the store for the cash. I tried to grin and bear it because my dad deserved happiness and miss vain seemed to make him happy.

But she didn't make me happy. She made me miserable, and my heart bled all too often. She convinced my dad to cart me off to boarding school. After three days, I ran away, eventually being picked up by a cop. My dad stood up to her after that, and I was back at Blue River Prep in no time.

Then, on the day my dad died, I woke up with damp sheets twisted around my body, a pounding headache, and a heart that beat so hard I was gasping for air.

I tried to breathe through it, thinking it was because of a mid-term I had in math. But I couldn't shake it off. So, when I was escorted to the Principal's office during fifth period, I knew something was wrong.

When my heart bleeds, I've learned to listen.

I put my car into park and take a deep breath. "Calm, Jade. Maybe he just had a fight with his stepdad."

Hunter crosses his ripped arms over his Merryville Knights football tee that clings tightly to his sculpted pecs. He glances around the parking lot, not once meeting my eyes.

"Hey there, sexy," I say, trying to cut the tension with a provocative voice.

He unfolds his arms and holds them out as a stop sign, halting me in my tracks. His eyes are shadowed from a bad sleep.

"Don't, Jade. Look, it's been fun and all, but I need to focus on football and school. We can't do this any-more." He turns and walks away. He pauses, and I swear he's going to turn back around and tell me he made a mistake. Instead, he shakes his head and takes off jogging through the double doors.

Happy birthday to moi.

MY HEART HASN'T stopped bleeding all day. Word quickly got around that Hunter dumped me, so my day was full of fake-pity and whispers as I walked zombie-like through the halls of MHS.

By the time I put distance between my car and school, the tears of tragedy I know so well begin to pour.

How can someone so young face so much heartbreak?

I love Hunter. At least, I thought I loved him. He was my first real boyfriend. Granted, we had only been dating for two months, but we'd spent so much time together outside of football games and practice. Because of everything I've gone through since my dad died, I've thrown myself into him, needing some sort of relationship to give me hope.

I was finally ready for him to take my virginity, after several false attempts on his part, only I hadn't told him yet. He'd been pressuring me, telling me how much he liked me.

Is it because I'd made him stop Saturday night as he was rolling on a condom? I shouldn't have stopped him, but my heart did that negative pumping thing, telling me I needed to halt.

I couldn't get the vision of the condom breaking and me with a very pregnant belly out of my head. I had trouble breathing then. I wanted to enjoy my first time, not keel over from a massive panic attack.

I knew it had upset him, but I thought I calmed him down by pleasing him another way. I guess it wasn't enough.

When I pull into my driveway, I'm relieved miss vain's car isn't here. She told me she'd be gone; I just didn't believe her.

I want to curl up into a fetal position and cry myself to sleep in peace with no one banging away at something upstairs, making dust fall from the ceiling.

Tears blind my vision when I reach for the door handle.

"Stupid, Jade. Pull yourself together, at least until you get inside." I insert the key and attempt to turn the deadbolt, but it doesn't budge. I pull it out and reinsert it then wiggle it back and forth.

It's stuck.

I walk around to the back to see a stack of tote boxes and suitcases by the back door.

"What are you getting rid of now, miss vain?" I say to no one. "Some more old Diamond family photos? Or perhaps my grandmother's teapot collection that was stuffed away in the attic?"

The deadbolt on the back door shines as the sun falls below the tree line. Did miss vain change the locks today? She does that on occasion due to her crazy-ass paranoia.

I lift the welcome mat, hoping to reveal a new key. Only there isn't one. But there is a torn piece of paper with the letter *J* written in purple ink.

The heart bleed begins to rush as I flip the note over. The tears continue to fall, faster even. I hold on to the porch railing to steady myself.

It's your 18th. Find a new place to live.
You are no longer my problem.

Happy *fucking* birthday to moi.

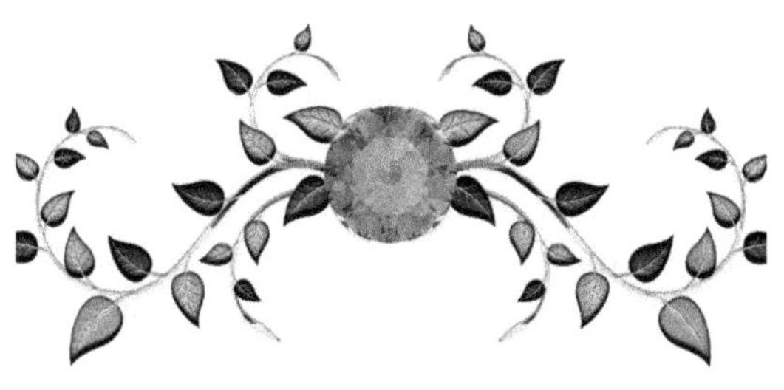

CHAPTER 2

THE PROBLEM WITH changing schools your senior year is that you haven't developed strong enough friendships with anyone who you could call and ask, *hey, can I come stay with you until I solve my homeless problem?*

If Hunter hadn't ripped my heart out today, I'd be heading back to school, waiting on football practice to end. He'd let me stay with him, even if he had to hide me from his stepdad. His mother liked me, so she would've been okay with it. I would've finally done the deed, and we'd live happily in sync, at least until we both went off to college. Maybe I would've followed him to State, and we'd have spent our nights together, rotating dorm rooms.

After loading the tote boxes and suitcases into the back seat and trunk of my car, I headed straight to the jewelry store, ready to battle the vicious queen. But a sign hung in the window saying the store was closed

for inventory. Not a soul inside. Driving around town to all her favorite spots yielded no results.

Revenge would have to wait for another day.

I was defeated.

I was exhausted.

My heart was out of blood, but somehow, it kept on bleeding.

One call and I knew where to head.

Instead of finding solace in Hunter's arms, I'm driving three hours away to another state and my only option.

My aunt's horse ranch in nowhere Kentucky.

THE SUN HAD been set two hours by the time I pull under the wrought iron sign for The Diamond Ranch. What I'd hoped would be a therapeutic drive turned out to be two close accident calls, thanks to driving out of the city in the middle of rush hour, and three emergency stops to the bathroom, thanks to a queasy stomach and three Dr. Peppers to keep me alert. I wouldn't have made it at all if it wasn't for the angry chick music busting the speakers of my little blue BMW.

If it wasn't so dark out, I'd silence Bea Miller and choose a deep focus playlist to enjoy the last five minutes of the trip. White wooden fences would frame the rolling green hills. I'd stop at the wooden bridge

over the creek to enjoy the picturesque view, letting the country air cleanse my distraught lungs.

Instead, my shoulders are the most tense they've been the entire journey. The unfamiliar blacktop drive has no lines to keep me on track. The moon, barely a crescent, provides more shadows than light, thanks to the white oaks that line the fence. I turn *Like That* to barely above a murmur and focus on the path before me.

Finally, the blue, wooden two-story house with white trim and a cupola overlooking the 100-acre ranch comes into view, lit up in all its grandeur. Two covered walkways leading to two stables extend out from the sides of the house.

The ranch is one of the most well-known horse training and boarding facilities in the area. On the left side, the Dogwood stable mainly houses horses that belong to the family. The Magnolia stable, the main boarding barn, is on the right.

I roll my shoulders to release some of the tension. It's been too long since I've been here. I used to spend summers with my cousins, Malachi and Mica, skipping stones in the fish-filled pond and riding horses on the miles of trails, until we were ten when Malachi's horse got spooked by a snake and he fell off, breaking his femur. Since that day, he's stayed clear of the horses.

He's two months younger than me, and we've always been close, chatting or texting each other at least once a week. Once we both hit high school, our contact

dwindled to about twice a month. I haven't talked to him or my aunt, Janet, since my dad's funeral, except for a *hello, how you doin'* text here and there.

She and my father had a falling out when he married miss vain. What used to be equal shares of the Diamond properties split between the two of them were restructured, with my dad taking 100% ownership of the jewelry store and my aunt taking all of the horse ranch. And now, the ranch is the only remaining legacy that belongs to an actual Diamond, even though her married name is Turner.

I park my car in the circular drive right in front of the house. My aunt sits in a rocking chair on the porch that wraps around the entire first level outside, floor to ceiling windows on every side.

She stands and meets me at the bottom of the front steps. Her dark hair is the same as mine. Her gray eyes are the same as my dad's. A comforting yet haunting reminder. Oh, how I miss him.

I swallow hard and bite back tears then crumple into her open arms, letting it all come out in a low, tortured sob. It's been too long since someone who truly cares has held me. If I can't be in my own home with my dad anymore, this is definitely where I need to be.

Why didn't I see that right after my dad died? My aunt offered for me to come live here. I let the false sense of security miss vain was giving me the week after my dad died get in the way. How that quickly changed. I

thought I could tough it out with each blow she threw at me. I should've known by how often my heart bled.

"Oh, sweetheart, I'm so sorry for everything." She holds me at arm's length and wipes away the hot tears rolling down my cheeks.

When I called her, I said little other than the wicked stepmother kicked me out now that I'm eighteen. It's nice to know that I don't need to explain or give her all the details. She knows the woman is evil and will probably leave it at that.

I don't want to spend another minute thinking about miss vain.

She doesn't exist in this world. Only in tales of evil stepmothers.

Aunt Janet places her hand on my lower back and guides me up the porch steps, directing me to a rocking chair. She stands over me, tucking my hair behind my ears and lifting my chin. "You want a drink? Sweet tea? Water?"

I manage to get out, "Sweet tea," and she leaves me on the porch as I weep loudly while rocking back and forth. My eyes stayed dry most of the trip, but now, I can't close the gates. The dam releases and it's a flash flood.

A boy yells out from inside the house, "Janet, I think one of them wild cats is out there again." His voice cracks, too young to be Mica or Malachi.

"Shh, Reid," my aunt says. "It's not a cat. Now run along and watch television with Carson and Sam

before Anson and Mica get back from the stables and make y'all watch something scary. You have an hour before bed."

My aunt has always opened her home to foster kids throughout the years. She probably has the house crammed full.

Deep sobs rack my insides. I try to breathe and focus on the sounds of the ranch. An owl hoots in the distance. Crickets and katydids buzz and crackle. Horses neigh.

When Janet makes it back out with a tray holding two tall glasses of tea and a plate of chocolate chip cookies, my body has stopped the full-on tremors and settled into the occasional shiver. She hands me a glass and a cookie, then we sit in silence and listen to the night's orchestra.

My voice comes out scratchy when I say, "I shouldn't have come here. You sound like you have a full house already." I gulp down my tea, attempting to soothe my throat.

"Now, Jade. You need to be here. I wouldn't want you anywhere else. You need family right now. Half of these boys would sleep in the stables if I let them. I found one that way, actually."

A whimper escapes as my body shudders again. "How many are living here now?"

"Five. Seven counting Malachi and Mica. All boys."

It's a four-bedroom house. Luckily, all the bedrooms

have a bath connected, but where will a girl fit in with seven boys? If I took over one of the bedrooms, that would leave seven people sharing two rooms.

She waves a hand at me. "I know what you're thinking. And don't go there. I need another female here. All this testosterone gives me a headache."

I shake my head. "I don't want to be a burden." I should've called one of my dad's old employees. Mr. Regal got the boot the same time I did. I've known him and his wife my entire life, and they don't have any kids. They would've taken me in.

She drinks her tea while maintaining a contemplative expression. Finally, she says, "Families are burdens, but they're the best kind of burdens." She sets her half-empty glass down on the side table. "Besides, Boyd finally retired last year, so the apartment above the Dogwood barn is available. It just needs a bit of cleaning and painting."

The thought of sleeping in the barn all alone frightens me a bit. But I'll take what I can get. Luckily, having moved into the basement at home made me put on my big girl panties real quick. I'll beg Malachi to walk me to my room every night.

Janet takes the empty glass from my grip and sets it beside hers on the wooden table. She then caresses my hands, sending vibes that radiate warmth throughout my body. "And no, I'm not going to make you sleep in the barn. Malachi and one of the older kids can move out

there. No worries. We'll start sprucing it up tomorrow. For tonight, though, you can sleep in Malachi's room. He's been camping at the lake with friends over fall break and won't be back until around noon tomorrow."

A rumble starts low in the distance and builds until it rips through the night. My aunt stares out at a single light that bounces up and down along the long drive, getting closer and closer. "Well, I thought they were staying at the lake tonight. You might have to sleep on a couch."

"I'm fine with that." I doubt I'll sleep very much anyway.

A motorcycle pulls into the drive, turns right, heads to one of the stables, then comes to a stop under the breezeway. The rider removes his helmet. His black hair falls out in waves. Baby scruff covers his chin.

Malachi. It feels like forever since I've seen him, even though it's only been six months. He's taller and ripped. I knew he was getting serious about football, but I didn't realize he was that serious. The boy has been lifting.

He makes his way to the front porch, staring at the ground with a somber face. He must be having a bad day, like me.

"What in the world are you doing on that death machine?" Aunt Janet says, her voice much heavier than when she just spoke to me.

"Not in the mood, Mom," he says, walking right past us on the porch. "Not feeling well. Going to bed."

"Is everyone coming home then?"

"No, it's just me."

He goes to open the screen door but pauses, dropping his hand from the handle. He takes a few steps backward and looks at me. The glower on his face disappears and a big cheesy grin replaces it.

"Jade? What the hell are you doing here?" He walks over, lifts me from the chair, and smothers me into a bear hug. From the way his body shakes, I think he needs this hug just as much as I do.

Aunt Janet clears her throat. "Jade can sleep in your room tonight then. Tomorrow, we have work to do in the stable apartment. You're getting booted from the house and Jade is going to take over your room."

Malachi sets me down and looks at me, his eyes filled with joy. "You're going to live here?"

I nod, afraid to speak. My emotions are out of control.

Aunt Janet was right. I need to be here. With family. There's no place I'd rather be.

"I'm going to take a shower then hit the sack." He wraps an arm around my waist and lays his head on my shoulder. "You look like you could use sleep."

"Yeah—" my voice wheezes. I nod my head, not trusting myself to speak.

He taps my shoulder and adds, "I'll see you upstairs in a bit."

Once Malachi leaves, we settle back into the rocking chairs. After a comfortable silence, Janet starts to speak

then pauses for a minute, her eyes dart back and forth. "I'm calling the attorney tomorrow to see if there's any update with the court. She doesn't deserve any of that. There is no way your dad left her everything without any consideration of you. It's just not possible. You were everything to him." She stands then pulls me up from the chair and places her hands on my shoulders. "I will not let her win. Now grab what you need tonight out of your car then get upstairs and get some rest. We have a busy day tomorrow."

THE SOUND OF running water comes from Malachi's bathroom. I quickly change into a tank top and a pair of shorts then slip under the covers on the neatly made twin size bed.

My head sinks into a fluffy pillow, and an aroma of forest and earth tantalizes my nose. Whoever Malachi's roommate is, he sure smells heavenly. Pulling the navy comforter over my head, I close my eyes and take in the scent.

My eyelids feel like they weigh a hundred pounds, and I quickly drift off into that state between awake and asleep.

A weight pressing down on the bed pulls me from the haze. I uncover my head to see Malachi sitting beside me, hair dripping.

"You wanna talk about it?" I ask.

"Not really." He smirks and adds, "You wanna talk about it?"

"Not really."

"But we will." Holding out his little finger, he says, "Pinky swear."

My mouth twitches with amusement at all the memories that flood me. We made a lot of pinky swears as kids. I wrap my pinky around his. "Pinky swear."

He squeezes me. The same warmth that I received from his mother washes over me. "I'm glad you're here. I really need you right now. I'm sorry for not keeping in touch. I—I just didn't know what to say to you after everything."

I scrunch my eyes shut and nod, trapping the emotions in my throat. Malachi turns the bedside lamp off and crawls into his bed.

In no time, his soft snores take over and I try to lull myself to sleep. My aunt's words won't stop playing on repeat. *I will not let her win. There's no way your dad left her everything without any consideration of you.*

I used to think that, but as time passed and no other Will was uncovered, I lost hope. My dad must have cared more about miss vain than me.

I jolt awake to a pitch-black room. Long, strong arms are wrapped around me, rubbing on my belly. A hand moves upward, grazing my chest, then tugs my hair. I pop the hand. Malachi has always been a sleepwalker.

"Go away, Malachi," I mumble. "You know I don't like people messing with my hair. We'll talk tomorrow."

"Goldilocks, I'm not Malachi," a husky voice whispers in my ear.

I sit up straight and scream.

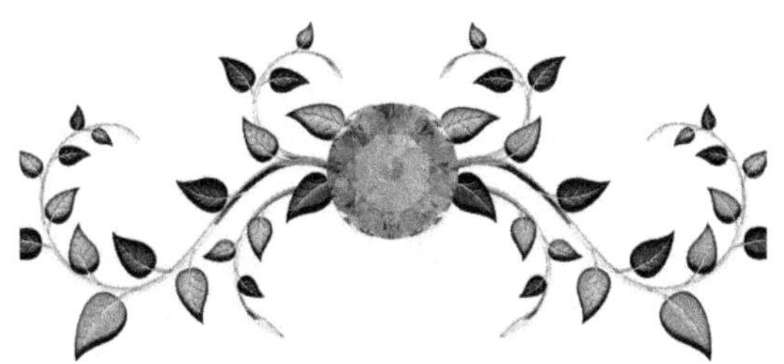

CHAPTER 3

MY HEAD PULSES with fear. I'm on the verge of passing out. I stand on the bed and frantically move my arms up and down and kick my feet around, giving the intruder a nice pounding, thankful Hunter loved to watch televised fights. I never thought the moves would come in handy.

A string of curse words are sprinkled with a few *ows* and a *that's my nuts*, but I don't stop releasing all that I have. And it's a lot. The traumas of the day still fresh on my mind.

It's therapeutic, beating the crap out of an intruder. At least, I hope I'm beating the crap out of an actual intruder and not one of the many fosters my aunt has taken in. I didn't meet any of them before heading to bed. Aunt Janet said we'd save the introductions for the morning.

The figure disappears, and I have to catch myself from falling off the bed.

Light fills the room, casting Malachi in an amber glow. He's sitting up in his bed with his hand on the lamp, his eyebrows drawn together. The intruder is curled into a ball on the floor with his arms protecting his head.

Malachi looks at me then stares at the ground. He throws his head back on his pillow and roars with laughter.

The human ball's voice is muffled when he says, "Is it over?"

"Bro, I thought you wouldn't be back until tomorrow," Malachi says between deep gasps of air.

The ball unfolds and keeps on unfolding. His bare, long limbs extend up and out like a pine tree. Slender yet stout and only clothed in gray boxer briefs. His hazel eyes hold a deer-in-headlights look and blood trickles from the corner of his shapely mouth.

"Since when do you let girls sleep in my bed?" he asks, swiping his hand over his busted lip.

Crapola, Jade. Couldn't you've asked what he was doing before you went all MMA on his ass?

One head pops into the door opening, followed by two more, then another, and lastly one that I recognize pushes through, and the room is suddenly full of seven guys in varying stages of teenage. They all stand around, half naked in a gradient of gray underwear.

Nice way to make an introduction. You really know how to make yourself at home.

Malachi's reached the point of hyperventilation in

his chuckling episode; his face is as red as a strawberry in the month of June.

"Care to explain why you're in my bed, Goldilocks?" the not-intruder asks as he runs a hand through his wavy, brown hair. "This isn't the home of the three bears." The non-busted side of his lip curls up into an arrogant smirk that I find oddly appealing. "I guess Goldilocks isn't the proper name. Snow White also slept in a bed that wasn't hers. And you look just like her."

"I guess that makes you one of the seven dwarves then," I say, timidly taking the hand he's holding out to help me down from the perch of his bed.

He hovers a good ten inches over my five-three frame. "Look around." He releases my hand and waves his arm around the room. "We're hardly dwarves."

All eyes are on me when I scan the room. And he's right. The shortest one stands two inches taller than me. I'm the only dwarf in this room.

"What's going on in here?" Aunt Janet says as she squeezes into the room.

Not-intruder dude places his arm around my aunt and says, "Well, Janet, imagine my surprise when I found the lovely Snow White here in my bed when I crawled into it." His voice holds a compassionate tone when he addresses my aunt but quickly turns patronizing when he says *lovely Snow White*.

"Found? More like felt up," I say, annoyance heavy in my voice.

"Yeah, sorry about that. I thought you were Chi." His lips twitch into a show of amusement, not quite smiling.

Janet looks at her watch. "Well, it's still the middle of the night, but since everyone's here, might as well share the news." She sidles up beside me, standing an inch shorter, but her confidence makes her the tallest person in the room. "Everyone, this is my beautiful niece, Jade. She's now living with us. Jade, meet Sam, Reid, Anson, and Carson." She points at each of the younger guys as they each salute. She then taps the not-intruder on his lean, muscled chest. "And it seems you've already met Onyx."

Onyx? A nervous energy builds from within. I've never heard that used as a name. He meets my furrowed brows and frown with his own face of indignation.

"Now, all you boys, put some clothes on." She fans her hands at all the boys then leans in and whispers in my ear. "And Jade, you might want to put on a bra."

I cross my arms over my chest as I feel blood snake up my neck to my face. Note to self: Try not to wear clothes that help tell everyone when it's chilly.

"Let's all go downstairs for a well-past-midnight snack," Janet says, her voice back to full volume. "Onyx, you can apologize to Jade for feeling her up by making your world-famous pancakes." She smacks him lightly on the back and exits the room.

"And what does she have to do for giving me a busted lip?" he yells out after her.

"Absolutely nothing," she hollers back.

"Of course not, Snow White is a precious little princess." A mischievous look comes into his eyes as his tongue lingers along his busted lip.

His pupils freely roam over me, making me wish I had on more than a tank top and night shorts, yet also making me wish I didn't have on any clothes at all. Or maybe that's that nervous energy still building like hundreds of butterflies in my stomach at knowing his name is Onyx.

Conflicted. Friend, foe, or something else entirely? Just because he isn't an intruder doesn't mean he's not a foe. He may be friends with Malachi, but that doesn't make us instant friends. Just because his name is Onyx doesn't mean we're destined to be together. Just because my mother has a ring made with onyx and jade doesn't mean he holds my attention.

He gently pushes me aside and opens a drawer in the dresser behind me, grabbing a pair of athletic shorts.

I reach down and swipe my pink bra from the top of my open suitcase then rummage through until I find my lilac sweatshirt with princess written across the front in gold and covered in purple rhinestones.

He takes a step toward the bathroom, but I beat him to it and shut the door in his face. If he wants to call me princess, I'll show him a princess.

TEN MINUTES LATER, I'm sitting on a barstool at the expansive kitchen island with my uncle, my cousins, and the other boys.

Onyx places four large cast iron skillets on the stove. The blue flames flicker alive then dance along the edges of the pans. He retreats into the walk-in pantry as my aunt pulls ingredients out of the stainless steel fridge then sets them on the stone countertop.

Janet sits down on the end, next to my uncle, and referees a yelling match between the two youngest, arguing about who has to give the horses hay and water in four hours. The youngest boy loses—Ray, maybe? I need flash cards with faces and names if I'm ever going to figure out who is who.

Overwhelmed at the scene before me is an understatement. I've been an only child my entire existence. Quiet time has been a way of life. For the next seven months, if I decide to stay here until graduation, I don't think quiet time will exist. Bickering, laughter, and rowdy banter continue to fill the room. The only person quieter than me is Malachi, his head laid down on the countertop next to me.

Onyx cracks an egg in each hand with ease; the gooey insides drip into a bowl. He quickly whips up the batter and pours it into the skillets from a good foot above. No one besides me pays him any mind, even though he's acting like he's the star of a cooking show. I feign boredom by picking my fingernails and faking a yawn.

Internally, I'm intrigued. What's his story? Why is his name Onyx? And how did he learn his way around the kitchen? Since my dad died, my skills are all about ordering food via phone app. The hardest part is choosing which option might stay down, seeing as my appetite left when my dad died, then waiting for it to be delivered.

He effortlessly flips four pancakes, each the size of my head, onto four plates. He drops pats of butter into the skillets and pours the remaining batter into the hot pans. His gaze narrows on me when he turns and slides one of the plates in front of me.

"Syrup?" he asks with raised eyebrows.

I nod. "You expect me to eat all that?"

He shrugs. "If you don't, I'm sure one of the dwarves will finish it for you." He slides another plate in front of the resting Malachi, causing him to jerk up.

I nudge Malachi. "Want to half this with me? I'm not that hungry."

"Sure," Malachi mutters as he pushes his plate to his brother.

"How do they compare to Grandma Diamond's?" My grandmother would fill us with the best pancakes in the world every day of the summer when we were kids.

"Even better," he says, with a spirit-lifting smile.

I crinkle my nose. "No way!"

"Yes, way," Onyx says, plopping down the jug of pure maple syrup in front of me.

I lather the cake with the liquidy goodness. Onyx leans forward with his elbows on the countertop and rests his head on his hands. Ignoring the irresistibly devastating grin that crosses his face, I take a bite, hoping it tastes like dirt.

But it doesn't.

Malachi's right. It's even better than Granny Di's. The fluffy, buttery goodness almost brings a smile to my face.

"Not bad," I say.

Onyx scoffs. "Not bad? What's wrong with your taste buds, Snow White?"

"It's Jade," I say, setting my fork down with a clank against the plate. My mouth waters and begs me to take another bite, but I deny it. Onyx, looking defeated, turns his attention back to the stove.

"What kind of name is Jade?" the youngest boy asks. His voice breaks and *Jade* comes out as if a bullfrog said it.

"Reid, don't be rude," my aunt scolds.

I sketch a mental flashcard. *Reid:* brown-eyed, blond, youngest, and not that much taller than me. His voice sounds like a poorly played clarinet. Clarinets need reeds.

"Jade is a gemstone, usually green," I say matter-of-factly. "It was one of my mom's favorite stones." Her others being onyx and ruby, the latter her namesake.

She designed a ring my dad later crafted with a three-carat ruby wrapped in a gold vine with onyx

and jade leaves. I've been looking for that ring since my dad died. The only place I haven't checked is at the jewelry store, in the hidden safe tucked away behind the mirror with a similar look as the ring. I've resigned to never see it again.

"Onyx is a gemstone," pancake dude says, placing a piping-hot pancake in front of Reid.

"Yeah, but Onyx isn't—" Reid stops mid-sentence when Onyx looks at him with a taut and derisive expression.

"Don't be telling secrets, towhead," Onyx says.

Reid's eyes roll. "I'll keep my mouth shut as long as you get the ketchup and mustard out of the fridge."

Onyx curls his lip and wrinkles his nose. "Why do you always have to ruin my masterpiece?"

As he disappears behind the fridge door, I quickly take another bite of the pancake. It melts in my mouth; my taste buds thank me. I get three bites down by the time he sets the condiment bottles in front of Reid. He returns to manning the stove.

Reid slathers his pancake in red and yellow goo. "Now that Jade is living with us, what day will be her day to scoop horse poop from the stables?"

"Yeah, which day will be princess's day to shovel shit?" Onyx adds.

Aunt Janet arches an eyebrow and tsks, "Language. If you don't watch that mouth, you'll be shoveling horse shit all day every day."

Onyx matches her smirk with one of his own as he plates the remaining cakes. He sits down across from me with the biggest pancake of all, slices through it, and shovels a piece bigger than my hand into his mouth. Chewing, he says, "So, *Jade*, what brings you to the home of the seven dwarves at the Diamond Ranch in Maybee, Kentucky?"

Aunt Janet gathers the empty plates of the first round of eaters, mine included, no thanks to Malachi and his one bite. He's back to sleeping with his head on the countertop. After placing the dishes in the sink, Janet taps Onyx on the shoulder. "Eat with your mouth closed, and let's not worry about why she's here. Anson, do the dishes."

Mental flashcard two. *Anson:* about six foot, maybe sixteen years old. Green eyes with reddish-brown hair and a sprinkle of freckles across his nose and cheeks. *Hanson? Manson? Dancin'?* I got nothing. I'll forget who he is tomorrow.

"I expect everyone to be in the Dogwood stable in the morning at seven sharp," she continues.

Reid whines. "But that's like in four hours. Can't we sleep late? It's our last official day of fall break. Then the weekend. Then school is back in session."

"Nope. Lots to do over the next few days before school starts back. We're moving Malachi and Onyx into the second-floor apartment. And Jade will take

over their room. We need to clean, paint, and decorate, so everyone can feel at home."

Onyx wraps his arm around Janet's shoulder. "So, let me get this straight, Snow White here doesn't have to shovel shit, doesn't have to apologize for busting my lip, *and* she boots me out of the house to sleep with the horses."

Joy bubbles in Janet's laugh. "Didn't you sleep with the horses for weeks before I found you and offered you a bed?"

He runs his fingers through the little wave of his hair that partly covers his ear and turns his head, obviously to hide the pinkening of his cheeks.

Janet claps three times then shoos Onyx. "Okay, everyone. Hop to it. Back to bed."

His eyes, like green-polished jade wrapped in gold, glimmer at me. "Well, princess, do you mind if I sleep in my own bed one last time?"

"I'll crash out on the couch," I say before adding, "It's the least I can do for busting your lip." I keep my eyes hard and my mouth even harder.

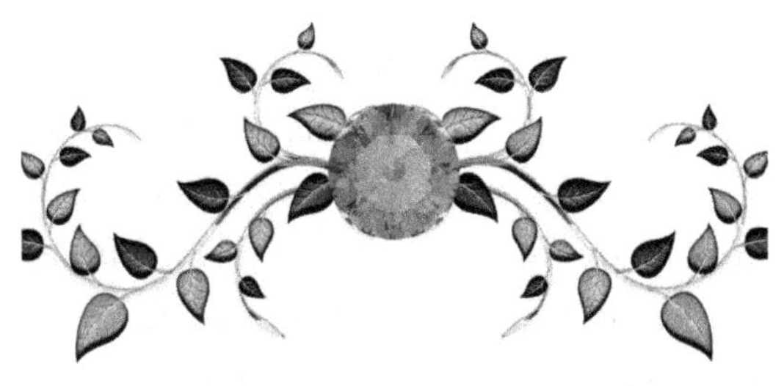

CHAPTER 4

AFTER SUCH AN emotional day, I was shocked that I slept as well as I did—until pancake dude woke me. His excuse that he thought I was Malachi makes me wonder what their relationship is really like.

Do they secretly snuggle at night?

I don't know enough about Onyx to make any assumptions. With Malachi, I've always wondered. He's never come out, though. If the two of them are, maybe it's a good thing I'm booting them to the barn where they can have alone time without worry.

The grandfather clock in the hallway chimes six times, one more since the last time I counted, and two more since the time before that.

It's mocking me. It's telling me, *Jade, look, I know you're tired, but sleep will continue to evade you because your mind is too much of a jumbled pile of shit.* I'd almost be back to sleep and the damn thing would send that reminder every bleeping hour. If it didn't originally belong to my great-great-grandma Diamond, I'd push it over and kick the living crap out of every gear, spring, pendulum, and whatever the hell else is in there.

After the household late night breakfast, everyone went back to their rooms for a few more hours of shut-eye. No wonder pancake dude wanted his own bed. He knew if he took the couch, that bloody clock would keep him awake.

Thanks, dude.

Realizing sleep is a lost cause, like everything else, I slip on jeans, my princess sweatshirt, and a pair of sneakers then head out into the dawn.

My favorite place in all of Diamond Ranch is a little pond about a ten-minute walk from the house. Last time I was here, the path to the pond was overgrown. Today, it's worn down, making it easy to find the rickety, wooden dock that stretches a quarter of the way over the water.

A chill runs the length of my spine as the cool wind whips my hair around my face. The temperature has dropped a good twenty degrees overnight. I sit on the edge of the pier facing east, a perfect view of the sunrise that will happen within the hour.

Remembering the last time I watched the sunrise from this location causes the tears to flow. My dad and I were here for my grandmother's funeral. We sat in

this very spot every morning for the three days that we stayed.

Crisp, early morning air fills my lungs as I go through the mantras a therapist taught me not too long after my dad's funeral.

Rule one: Don't analyze. Toss up the thought stop sign when you're obsessively thinking. You can't go back in time to undo something. It's beyond your control. One day, I'm going to get a tattoo to symbolize a stop sign to help me remember this.

Rule two: Accept the situation and move on. Stupid therapist. Doesn't she know how hard it is to not think about it? To not continue to say over and over, *if only?*

Rule three: Be and stay in the present moment. That's hard to do because of the present moment reminder. I shouldn't have come down here.

Rule four: Find the beauty. Sure, I have the best memories of my dad. But there's no beauty in not being able to make new ones with him.

Rule five: Talk about the loss. It's been six months, yet I still can't talk about it without totally breaking down.

Honestly, I don't know why I still cling to her advice. The first thing she told me was that my heart wasn't really bleeding, that it wasn't some sixth sense warning me something terrible was about to happen. It was a case of everyday anxiety that could be solved with drugs.

She tossed a trial bottle of pills at me then went on about how feeling anxious after a death is normal, and she'd question my status as a human being if I didn't have a certain level of anxiety. When I got home that day, I took that bottle of pills straight to miss vain's medicine cabinet and placed it next to all her crazy pills.

The sound of a twig snapping teases my ears. The hairs on the back of my neck rise. Is there a wild animal? Bears and mountain lions have been spotted in this area. Is Aunt Janet going to find my carcass picked clean in a field? I tremble as fearful images build in my mind.

A wooden board groans as the dock shakes. I have nowhere to go but in the water. Before I can jump off the edge, a husky voice says, "Hey, this is my spot."

I gasp and turn to see Onyx walking toward me in the morning twilight. "Fucking hell, you scared the shit out of me," my voice quivers then gets louder. "And for the second time today. Let's not make it a third. You might kill me." I place my hand on my chest and push, hoping to put my heart back in its place.

His brows pull together, and he gives me a soft, honest smile. "I'm sorry," he says, resting his hand on my shoulder. "I didn't mean to scare you, again."

I fight a battle of personal restraint to grab his hand from my shoulder and shove him into the water, but his eyes gleam with interest. He's probably wondering who the heck this sad girl is that has come to invade his home and displace him to live with the horses. So instead, I shrug his hand off.

He drops his hand by his side. "Do you mind if I join you? I can't start my day without watching the sunrise from here."

I gesture to the spot beside me then bring my knees up to my chest and wrap my arms around my legs. "You get up this early everyday?"

He sits and lets his long legs dangle over the dock. "Yeah, if not for football practice then for stable duty."

Football. Hunter's handsome mug flashes in my mind, and the curveballs that have been thrown my way over the past twenty-four hours bring on an avalanche of tears on top of the ones that were drying up.

Fuck my fucking life.

Onyx wraps me in a side hug. This time, I don't push him away. The strength to fend him off is non-existent.

"I'm so sorry for scaring you," he repeats. He releases me then rummages in his jeans' pocket, pulls out a scalloped-edge handkerchief with blue and purple embroidered flowers, and gently blots my cheeks. Who in the world carries a handkerchief anymore?

His hazel eyes with sweeping lashes search mine. I know what he sees. I've seen my reflection, full of remoteness, for the past six months every time I look in the mirror. I blink away, not wanting his compelling orbs to find their way through the dark and unfathomable trenches.

"You didn't scare the tears out of me," I say. "They were already there."

He stops cleaning my face and hands me the handkerchief. "I'm only loaning you this. It's the only thing I have left of my grandmother's, so treat it like a rare diamond." His voice is velvety but carries multiple layers of humor.

I run the piece of thin fabric over my face. I will not be responsible for losing the last artifact that belonged to his grandmother, so I deposit the family heirloom back in his hand. "Thanks."

He graciously bows his head then returns to staring at me as if I'm an alien he's trying to study. "What's your story?"

I lift my chin defiantly, meeting his soul-searching gaze head on. "What's *your* story?"

He lets out a great peal of laughter. "Who says I have a story?"

"You live at my aunt's house. People who live here usually have stories."

"It's not an interesting one."

I turn my head to watch ripples in the water. "Sure," I say. "Do you know what's up with Malachi?"

"Trying to figure that out myself."

"So, no girl problems?"

"None that I know of."

I glance in his direction. "Or *guy* problems?"

He knits his eyebrows together and gives me a hard stare. "You think he could have guy problems?"

I shrug. "It's possible."

He picks at a hole in the knee of his jeans. "Huh."

"No lovers' quarrel between the two of you?"

His head darts up quickly. "You think I'm gay?"

"I don't know you from Adam. You did try to snuggle with me in the middle of the night thinking I was Malachi."

He covers his face with his hands. "Chi left the lake in a weird way. Even asked to borrow my bike to get home. That was just me trying to cheer him up."

"You try to cheer people up by mauling them?"

"I didn't maul you."

"Okay, whatever."

"And I'm not gay by the way."

I couldn't care less whether he's gay or not.

After a few moments of awkward silence, I have to get this guy talking again or the floodgates will open with vengeance, forcing me to give him my downhearted life story. "You come here and watch the sunrise everyday?"

"Every day starts with a sunrise. Why not start your day with one? It marks a new beginning."

I follow his gaze into the distance, toward the sliver of blinding yellow that appears on the horizon. The rays lift, and a sense of unexpected peace washes over me. I've never looked at a sunrise that way. Today's a new beginning in so many ways. I need to treat it like one.

Onyx glows with appreciation as he watches the sun perform its morning stretch. After the orb shows its full body and creates a beautiful reflection on the pond, he turns his attention to me. "Do you ever smile?"

I pick at the green polish on my nails and gnaw on my lower lip. "You need a reason to smile."

He stares at me with an odd twinge of disappointment. "I disagree. The act of smiling alone makes you feel better. It's scientifically proven."

"What are you? The happiness guru?"

He stands and offers his hand to me. "Yes! Yes, I am. And my mission this weekend is to get you to smile. Now, let's go find your aunt before we piss her off for being late."

I let him assist me in standing, then I drop his hand like a hot potato. "I hope you like impossible missions."

"No mission is impossible. Tom Cruise always succeeds."

"Oh, and you're Tom Cruise?"

"I'm better." His smile is one of confidence and not conceit.

"Yeah, sure."

"Oh, you want to bet, huh? Okay, by the end of this weekend, I'm going to have your face hurting because you've been smiling too much."

"Good luck with that."

Today may be a new beginning. But that doesn't mean it'll be worthy of a smile, especially one on my face. A smile means you have something to be happy about. What's so great about being a friendless, homeless orphan who just had her heart broken?

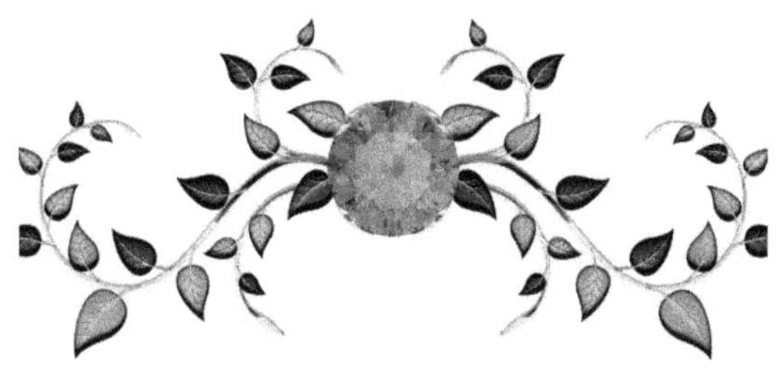

CHAPTER 5

THE WALK TO the Dogwood stable is silent except for Onyx picking clumps of red berries off of passing bushes and tossing them one at a time against the trunks of trees sporting leaves of red and gold. Occasionally, a berry gets a good bounce and knocks into another tree like a pinball. Mindless, but it keeps my thoughts from wandering, and I'm thankful for it.

We arrive at the barn at the same time the other guys arrive from the house. The navy, tin roof sparkles under the early morning sun as Onyx opens the blue door marked by a white *X*. A peppery leather smell mixed with grass seeps up my nose, almost putting a smile on my face thanks to the happy memories the smell evokes.

I walk the length of the foam flooring made to look like wood, passing by horse after horse behind the metal

bars of their stalls. I stop at the empty stall with the name *Cinnamon* burned onto a wooden plank tacked to the door. Malachi follows behind me. I look at him, questioning.

"She died six months ago," he says.

I wince. "Same time?"

"When we got back from the funeral." He pinches his lips as his eyes become a stormier gray. After tapping my shoulder, he leaves me and walks to the end of the stable where a flight of steps leads to the upstairs apartment.

I trace the name on the sign of my dad's favorite mare. She lived well past the normal life of a horse, but it's just another addition to the list of what I've lost recently. A single tear rolls down my face. I wipe at it before anyone notices.

Onyx comes up from behind me, pulling out his grandmother's handkerchief again, and brushes my cheek with it. So much for catching it in time.

"She was amazing, wasn't she?" he says.

I nod, afraid my response would come out as a wail.

He pulls an apple out of a bucket hanging from a post and hands it to me. "Nutmeg here is just as awesome."

I hold back what would be a sardonic laugh, afraid Onyx may take it as a smile. Nutmeg is the reason Malachi stays far away from the horses. He's also Cinnamon's offspring and was a prized racehorse in his early years. Only one word can describe Nutmeg, and that's feisty, whereas Cinnamon was a gentle giant.

I set the apple in the palm of my hand and hold it out. Nutmeg's giant mouth swoops in, snatching it away. He chomps on it, causing slobber and bits of apple to fly out, covering my hand in goo and drool.

"Yeah, he's a bit of a messy eater." Onyx wipes my hand with his grandma's hanky. That thing comes in handy.

Nutmeg lowers his head, allowing me to pet his snout. His black mane flows down his shiny chestnut brown body.

Janet's voice rings from upstairs, causing me to pause. "We don't have all day folks. Get your butts up here."

Nutmeg nudges my stilled hand and stares at me. I rub his nose again and gently say, "I'll visit you later." He bobs his head up and down. Looks like Nutmeg is a little like his mama in his adult years.

We make our way to the stairs, and Onyx extends his arm for me to go first. When we reach the top, he passes me to stand next to Janet. He holds his hands over his head and claps, the sound filling the living space containing a holey plaid couch, a wooden coffee table covered in drink ring stains, and a tube television that belongs in a museum.

"Look alive, folks!" he says, adding, "we don't have all day."

Janet laughs and shoves him away. "This is what's going down today." She turns over a large white board that was leaned against the yellowed wainscotting. Tasks written in varying colors decorate the board. Each color represents a name that's mapped out in a key.

Onyx dramatically scratches his hairless chin, his chiseled jaw jutting out to the side. "Um, I think you missed a name."

"Nope," she responds. "I didn't miss any names."

He narrows his eyes at me and mouths *princess.*

I want to stick my tongue out at him, but again, I'm afraid he'll take that as a win in getting me to smile. Instead, I give him a dramatic eye roll.

"Jade and I are going shopping," my aunt says in her authoritative tone. "Plan on us being out all day. Every last one of these items needs to be crossed off." She taps on the list of about twenty tasks, ranging from clearing out every room in the apartment to relocating boxes and files to the Magnolia stable office. Onyx mimics her every movement as she goes through the list, resulting in hysterics from everyone but me.

She tosses a black dry erase marker to him. "Think you can handle being in charge?"

"Of course," he says, then he points to all the guys. "Any funny business out of you and I'll grab a whip from the tack room."

"Oh, please," Reid says, "you're the one that'll be doing the funny business."

Onyx wraps him up in a soft headlock and musses

his hair. "Only authority can perform in funny business, funny guy. And you aren't the authority."

Janet leads me toward the stairs. "We'll be home by dinner with pizzas and furniture. Then plan on a late night of painting." She nods her head at Malachi. "Come attach the trailer to the truck."

JANET AND I spent the morning in Maybee, searching through the discount and second-hand stores. After finding nothing that spoke to me or her, she threw in the towel on the little town and drove an hour away to Lexington where we found everything we needed and more.

We're on the drive home and I'm beat. I need a nap—Janet said we're not going to bed tonight until all the painting is done. With ten people tackling it, we'll manage. However, my lack of sleep catches up to me, and I pass into a dreamless slumber. I wake as she exits the highway about ten minutes from town and twenty from the ranch.

The drive through the rolling hills of horse country is peaceful. It's the first time I've experienced silence in the past eight hours.

My aunt kept my mind from jumbling most of the day with picking out paint colors, furniture, bedding, and decor for my new room as well as the guys's new

apartment. It was the first time in six months that I channeled my creativity.

It felt refreshing without feeling like I was drowning.

And it helped me get through the painful parts of the day—the constant reminders that Janet is my dad's sister. Similar personalities. Similar speech patterns. Similar sarcasm. But those painful parts were some of the most enlightening as my aunt is a problem solver, just like my dad.

I never knew she was so involved in the court battle of my dad's will. She's the one that contested it, which I knew, but she's also the one that has been providing evidence to the case, which I didn't know. The big blow of miss vain kicking me out of my childhood home left the attorney speechless. I've rarely spoken to the lawyer about the case and had no hope that anything would come out of it. Today, a faint glimmer showed through the dark tunnel.

I also learned that my aunt has been hounding the police to reopen the investigation into my father's death. I thought it was an open-and-shut case, thanks to it all being recorded on security cameras. It was a robbery gone wrong. A gunman came in and demanded my dad to open the safe, which he did. The thief kept on asking my dad to open the other safe. I guess he didn't feel the millions of dollars worth of sparkling jewels was enough. When my father said there isn't another one, the criminal shot him then

dropped the gun out of shock. Miss vain picked it up and killed the robber.

The thing is: There was another safe—the old one hidden behind the mirror. Normally, my dad doesn't keep things in it because it's too hard to open. No one even knows about it except me, my dad, and Janet.

It's like the robber knew there could be another safe. Could that mean something?

Before meeting Janet, my uncle Kevin was a police detective. I listened to her speak to the Merryville Police for thirty minutes on her and Kevin's speculations of what happened. They think miss vain was involved somehow and want the police to look into it further.

After stopping at the local pizza joint for six large pies and five pounds of chicken wings, we pull under the Diamond Ranch sign with plenty of sunlight remaining to take in the majestic countryside.

The tranquility of the drive is short-lived when we cross over the tiny wooden bridge, my dad's favorite spot to fish. Pain hammers at the base of my skull. The daily living nightmares from the past six months surface and whisper for me to jump in the creek and never resurface.

Could miss vain really be involved in my father's death? Is she really that cold? To me she is, but I always felt like she truly cared about my father, and his death hit her almost as hard as it did me. Granted, she recovered a lot quicker than I did.

I shake the dreaded demons away and fill my mind with positive images from today. The white bedspread with the rainbow colors of charming paint strokes. A purple throw pillow that says *I will fill my heart with hope.* A yellow and pink wooden sign with a Ronald Dahl quote that says *If you have good thoughts they will shine out of your face like sunbeams and you will always look lovely.* Maybe the happiness guru from this morning inspired my decor choices for my new room.

"You think they got everything done?" I ask.

Janet turns down the radio blaring a song about the *Boys of Summer,* one of my dad's favorites and apparently hers as well if the lyrics she was belting out are a representation of her most loved song. "I'm sure they did. Onyx, although he likes to act goofy, is really good at completing tasks."

"But, does he get it done right?"

A smile reaches her eyes before she speaks. "Better than right. He has more drive than Malachi and more brawn than Mica. He's a year older than you and Mal. Been through a lot."

"Oh, I thought he was still in high school." What did he mean this morning about getting up early for football practice?

"He's a senior. His parents kept him out of kindergarten, so he fell a year behind."

"Are all the other guys in high school?"

"All but Reid. He's in eighth grade."

The pleasant thing about starting at a new school this time is already knowing six people. All guys, but I'll take what I can get. Surely, one of them will let me sit with them at lunch. My first week at Merryville had been pretty embarrassing during lunchtime until I caught the attention of Hunter.

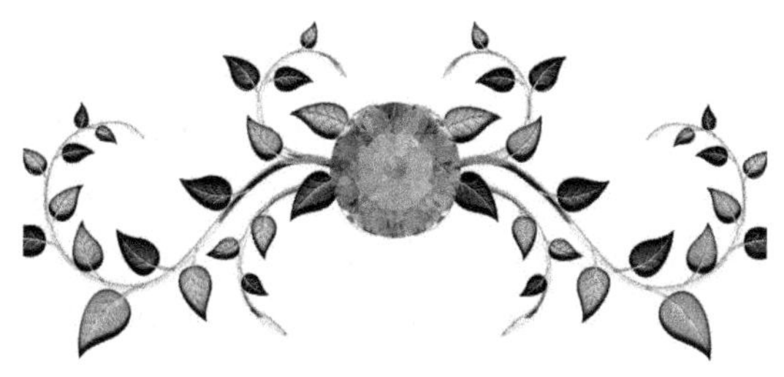

CHAPTER 6

J ANET PULLS THROUGH the circular drive and parks in front of the house where some of the boys rest on rocking chairs and the others on the front porch steps. All with a bottle of Gatorade in hand. And all half naked, yet again. And all laughing at whatever Onyx is saying.

He leans against the porch railing at the bottom of the steps, looking a bit more sculpted in the afternoon light than he did last night. Sweat glistens off his brawnilicious abs that lead down in a *V* to his narrow hips. He's in dust-covered jeans and has a red t-shirt hanging out of his front pocket. His work boots untied and spread open, revealing black socks with yellow smiley faces.

His gaze, shadowed by his hair peeking through a backward baseball cap, meets mine, making me wish the truck's windows were tinted. He lifts his eyebrows and shines his flashbulb eyes.

Why am I staring at him?

Just because I'm broken doesn't mean I can't gawk at something so pretty. And boy is he pretty in a devilishly handsome way. A touch of ruggedness skirts around his smooth skin. The way he carries himself with a commanding air of self-confidence and has everyone laughing their asses off.

Everyone except me, that is. My numb soul refuses to budge.

However, if he keeps it up, his warm and brilliant smile might melt away the frozen tundra that holds my lips in a downturned state. At least temporarily. I don't think I will ever fully thaw.

Look where my ogling got me with Hunter. The last thing I need is to jump into another relationship, especially one in which my aunt might not approve because I live with the guy.

Relationship? Where did that come from? I haven't even been here for a full day, and he's already ruffling my feathers.

You know you'd like him to ruffle those feathers even more.

Get a grip! I'm totally losing it. Just because Hunter dumped me yesterday doesn't mean I need to latch on to the first person that gives me attention.

I snarl at Onyx, as if I hadn't been admiring his tall, athletic physique and planning out our future, then hop

out, grab the pizza and wing boxes from the back seat of the massive truck, and head straight toward the house without another glance in his direction, ignoring those thought-provoking eyes the same color as my name.

AN HOUR LATER, the contents of the truck and trailer have been moved to the covered concrete pad next to the Dogwood stable where the work vehicles are usually parked.

Onyx looks over the towering stack, touching packages of sheets, bedspreads, and decorative pillows. "Did y'all leave anything in the store?"

"Just stuff that could've gone in your room," my aunt responds.

He pauses at a piece of framed artwork with layers of black, white, and silver veined with gold, painted to look like sliced agate. "You mean my closet? I'm going to christen it my clos-room."

"I'll have you know that I've lived in that room twice in my life. Once when I was fresh out of college, and the second time three years ago when we renovated the house. You should be happy you're getting that and not Cinnamon's old stall."

He rubs his hands together and speaks in a wicked tone. "I'm going to love my little clos-room."

She smacks him on the back of the head. "It's big enough for a dresser and a full size bed. You'll have more space than you do now."

Wrapping his arm around her shoulder, he squeezes and whispers, "I'm extremely thankful and overwhelmed by your generosity."

She returns his hug and whispers back, "You've worked hard for it. And I appreciate you."

If I wasn't standing right beside them, I wouldn't have heard it.

At first, I thought I was going a little overboard in picking out things for Onyx's room, but Janet agreed to everything I found. It seems he has a special place with my family. I was worried he wouldn't like how I chose to decorate, but something tells me he'd actually be happy with a ratty blanket on a bed of hay in the stable. He appears to be the walking definition of grateful.

"Okay, listen up," Janet starts. "Let's split up and get everything painted tonight so we can move furniture in tomorrow."

"And where are we going to sleep?" Malachi asks.

She opens a pack of roller covers and separates them amongst three metal paint trays. "I thought you could camp out. Build a fire, roast s'mores, and sleep under the stars."

Malachi takes the supplies from his mom. "Ugh, I camped out for five days. My bug bites just stopped itching."

"I'm fine with it." Onyx grabs a paint roller from a bucket and rolls it over Reid's back. "The Orionid meteor shower is just getting started."

Malachi rolls his eyes. "Enough with the meteor shower, star guy."

Janet hands me a tray and roller cover. "Jade, you can sleep on the couch again."

Onyx swishes the paint roller as if it was a magic wand. "Aw, pretty princess can't sleep outside."

"When she decides she wants to bust your lip again, I'm not going to stop her." Janet shoves the last paint tray and set of roller covers in Onyx's direction.

I take a step closer to Janet and speak loudly. "I can sleep outside. I'll sleep outside." I've done it before—I can do it again. I'll lather myself down in lemon eucalyptus oil to keep the bugs at bay. Although, the cold front that went through last night seems to be doing that job.

Janet claps and everyone stands to attention. She's trained these boys well. "Alright, folks, let's stop wasting time. Jade, distribute the paints."

I pull my hair back and secure it with the elastic tie that I keep on my wrist, for emergencies. "Okay, Mica, you and I will paint my room in this color." I hand him a can of paint the color of orange sherbet.

"Malachi, I thought you'd like this color. Janet said you and Reid can team up." He looks at the seafoam green swatch taped on top then nods his head in approval.

"And Onyx, this is yours. And you get to paint your closet all by yourself." I hand him the can of silver shadow paint and quickly move on.

"It's a clos-room," he interrupts, giving me that teasing smile.

"And the rest of you will help Janet and Kevin paint the kitchen and living room of the apartment. The cabinets get this color." I hand off the blue-gray paint to Sam. "The top parts of the walls are to be painted this color." I hand the gray-beige paint to Anson. "And the wainscotting gets this color." Lastly, I loop the holder of the navy paint can around Carson's awaiting hand.

"Oh, and once you're done with the walls, paint all the trim this color." I hand each team a can of pure white paint. I then clap my hands and say, "Now, get to it." I almost smile so they'll realize I'm joking around, but I catch myself again. Onyx will not win this smile bet.

Luckily, they all realize I'm kidding as they each give me a salute and head in separate directions with grins on their faces.

"I'LL DO THIS WALL." I point to the wall the heads of the beds were pushed against. "If you want to do that one." I point to the front wall with the window. "That way, by the time we finish the last two walls, maybe these will be ready for the second coat."

Even though my aunt forked out for the high-end paint, I'm sure these dark green walls will take two layers to cover.

"Sounds good." Mica spreads the drop cloth over the wooden floor. "I'd like to listen to music while we work. Do you want me to wear headphones or set up a speaker for both of us?"

"It depends," I say, tapping my finger on my chin. "Do you still listen to that country crap?"

"Of course. I *am* a cowboy. There's no other music that passes through these ears." An easy smile plays at the corners of his mouth as he covers his ears.

I give him a fake choking face. "Headphones then."

"I'll be right back. Need to grab my Beats."

He leaves me alone to rummage through my backpack looking for my earbuds. I'd rather talk while painting to help keep my mind occupied, but Mica has never been much of a talker, at least with me. Whereas Malachi and I would spend all night talking about anything, everything, and absolutely nothing. I can't wait until we get back to that point again, hopefully tonight. I have a feeling Onyx can carry on those same conversations as well.

I probably should've asked Janet to have Reid help me instead of Mica. My guess is he's as much a talker as Onyx. Although I'm not sure what eighth graders talk about these days.

A huge exhalation of pent-up breath releases from my mouth. I don't need a distraction. I don't have to talk. Minus the time I've spent with Hunter the past two months, I've been alone a lot. What's a little bit of thinking going to hurt? I can't imagine I can physically produce anymore tears. I was pretty numb today when Janet briefly mentioned the Will situation and the murder investigation.

I need to make this painting session productive, not only with color on the walls but adding a little mind channeling. I'll put on a deep concentration playlist and flip through my brain to see if anything stands out as a sign that miss vain was involved in my dad's death.

I'd be breaking *rule one: Don't analyze*; but maybe in doing so, it'll help me in moving toward *rule five: Talk about the loss*.

Mica returns with headphones on. I open the paint can and pour the orange creamy goodness into the plastic liner of the metal paint tray. With a roller in hand, Mica loads up the nappy cover and begins slopping paint on his first wall.

I push the roller through the color in the tray then smooth it onto the wall. The color reminds me of an orange creamsicle.

There was this little ice cream parlour in downtown Merryville my dad took me often as a kid. They sold those orange push pops.

Dad would always ask if I wanted a scoop of chocolate ice cream in a sugar cone. I'd always stomp my feet, ball up my fists, and say, "You know what I want."

He'd laugh and respond with, "Oh yeah, you want a scoop of cookie dough in a waffle cone."

We'd go back and forth until he'd pick me up and swing me around, smothering me with kisses. He'd then say, "I know what you want, my little orange creamsicle."

By the time I finished my push pop, he'd always say that I got more on my face than I did in my mouth. I'd tell him I painted it on my face to save it for later. He'd joke and say we should paint my bedroom walls with all the push pops in the world.

Rule four: Find the beauty.

My walls will hold that memory. And they'll be beautiful.

Time for a new rule.

Rule six: If you're going to break rule one by analyzing, start with rule four: Find the beauty, then move on to analysis.

Capture the beauty in something physical, whether it be finding a token to represent a moment, writing down the memory, or painting a wall to capture it. Maybe one day, I can pick up a paintbrush, colored pencil, or my drawing stylus to sketch on my iPad once again.

Now, it's time to *analyze.*

I take a deep breath and hold it then release it in small spurts. As I paint over the evergreen wall color, the scene changes. The school secretary, Mrs. Crenshaw, interrupted my fifth period math class just after Mr. Rossi handed out our midterm exam.

"Jade Diamond?" she asked. Mr. Rossi pointed at me. "Can you come with me, please?"

"Uh-oh, someone's in trouble," my friend Blakely said with a smirk.

I'd only been in trouble once at school—for cheating in history. I had written notes on my arm because I couldn't remember the correct numbers of all the various amendments. I was an artist, not a memorizer. Mr. Upchurch, my American history teacher, caught me. After that, I studied my butt off and became more of a memorizer, implementing a color method to help me study. I'm a very visual person.

Anxiety had already taken hold of me thanks to the heart bleeding issue I had that morning after a poor night's sleep. That walk from the social studies hall to the main office with a silent Mrs. Crenshaw was excruciating. A police officer was standing by the front desk waiting for me.

"Jade Diamond?" she asked.

I remember giving her the stare down, wondering what I did wrong to have a cop asking for me at school. I nodded after a minute, realizing I had to confirm who I was. Otherwise, she might take me out in handcuffs.

"You need to come with me." She walks out the door.

I didn't follow. I couldn't follow. My feet suddenly became immovable, stuck to the ground. I felt like I was enclosed in a huge, glass container of sour cherry jam,

sticking to all the mushy fruits that kept drowning me, pushing me down to the bottom of the slime.

"Jade?" Mrs. Crenshaw said in a honeyed voice. "You need to go with Officer Wilson."

The next thing I remember is being at the police station, sitting in a room with four chairs and a table. Miss vain was pacing the room, mumbling stuff that I couldn't make out or didn't try to make out. She hadn't said anything to me. My face felt clammy and my head was pounding. Words kept playing on repeat in my mind, only I hadn't heard them or I didn't remember them being spoken. But they had been. *I'm sorry, your father is dead.*

I don't know who said it. It was a male. A cop, I guess. I can't recollect what he looked like. I don't even know if miss vain was with me when they told me. I was only seventeen at the time. Surely, I needed an adult with me when they broke the news.

How can I analyze when I can't even look back on the details of that day? Are they in this chaos-filled brain of mine, locked away deep in the dark recesses? Maybe I should look into a hypnotist.

I shake my head and realize thinking while on this painting job isn't going to help. I've been covering one small area over and over. Mica is halfway done with his wall. I start a playlist with loud, angry music at maximum volume and load up my roller again.

Time for another new rule.

Rule seven: Only analyze when you have nothing else to do.

I press the brush to the wall and roll up then roll my way toward the bottom. A light pencil design catches my eye. A tiny laugh escapes as I read it. Thank goodness he's not around to catch the smile.

Onyx Finch was here. Alive. And well. All the past troubles are behind. Focus on the present. The now. You have grown wiser, young padawan. Continue to overcome.

A silhouette of what looks like Yoda with a lightsaber frames the right side of the words. I snap a picture of his mantra, whether to save for myself or have evidence to show him that he's a crazy person then cover it with my happy-memory paint.

MICA FINISHED UP two coats on both of his walls and left me alone to myself. After tuning on a happier vibe playlist, I begin to paint the last section of my last wall. Happy paint needs happy vibes.

"Boo!" a husky voice sounds, making me jump and paint orange sherbert over the white baseboard.

"Dammit," I say, baring my teeth at him. "You weren't supposed to scare me, *again*."

Onyx grabs a rag sitting on the dropcloth and wipes the baseboard clean. "I won't apologize this time. Because the look on your face was so worth it."

I shoot him a bird. "Fuck off, young padawan."

My bitchiness doesn't wipe the huge grin off his face. Maybe he sees through my front better than I do myself. "I guess you found my message."

Taking the smallest paintbrush out of the variety brush pack, I write *Jade was here* across his forearm. "And I thought you didn't have a story."

"I'm a complex guy." He grabs the paintbrush from me and loads more paint on it.

"What are you doing here, messing with my concentration? I only have this tiny bit left." I hold my hand out and air circle the six square foot area.

He grabs my arm, turns it over, and writes *Onyx was* on my foreman. "Mission smile," he says, then draws a smiley face instead of writing *here*.

I take the brush from him, wipe away the smiling mouth, and paint a frown. "Another failure."

"There's still more time left to succeed. By tomorrow, you'll be laughing so hard you snort, then you'll laugh because you snorted." He takes hold of my wrist again and runs his finger over the frown, causing the paint to smear while sending a chill down my spine.

He then grabs a roller, coats it in paint, and finishes my wall. With his back to me, I let go a tiny smile.

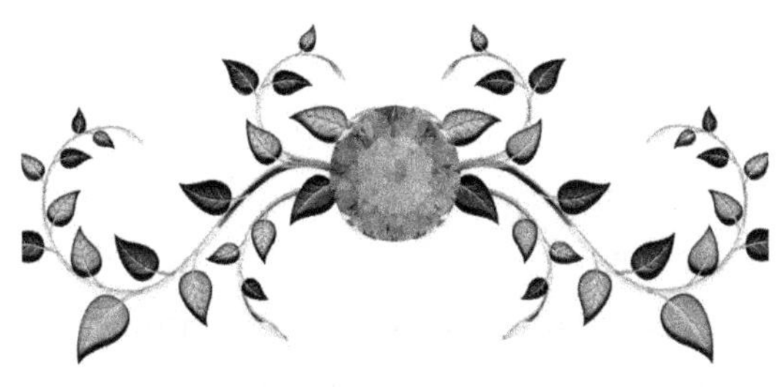

CHAPTER 7

"**W**HAT ARE SHOOTING stars?" Reid asks as he loads four marshmallows onto a stick.

Reid, Carson, and Sam decided to camp out as well. Malachi retreated to Reid's bed after claiming he was being eaten alive. Funny, considering I'm not, even though I forgot to lather myself in oil and bugs usually love to feast on my pasty-white skin, leaving itchy red bumps from head to toe.

"Space rocks," Onyx replies. He tosses another log into the fire pit. Little sparkles travel in the air and dance around.

Reid shoves his stick in the heart of the fire. "Space has rocks? I thought they were meteors."

Onyx takes the bag of marshmallows from Carson, grabs one, and pushes it on a stick. "Meteors. Rocks.

Whatever. Space has a lot of things banging around up there. Some things get knocked into our skies."

He holds up the bag in my direction and raises his eyebrows. I shake my head. Two s'mores are more than enough for me.

Reid pulls a flaming mound of marshmallows from the fire then jiggles it around to shoo away the flames. "Then why do they move? Why don't they stay in place like a star?"

"They come hurtling through Earth's atmosphere so fast, they burn up. Stars move even faster, but we don't see their movement because they're so far away."

"So, shooting stars are space rocks that come to Earth?"

Onyx blows at the marshmallow on his stick to cool it. "Basically."

Reid grabs two pieces of chocolate from a paper plate. "Then what happens when they reach the ground?"

Onyx squashes his black marshmallow between two graham crackers and a piece of chocolate. "Most never reach the ground. But those that do are meteorites. If you ever find one, you'll be rich."

"I hope I find one then, one day."

"Me too, Reid. Me too."

Reid's eyes dart across the sky. "Look! That one looked like it hit the ground near the pond. Can we go look for it?" He squishes the four marshmallows from his stick between the two pieces of chocolate.

I cover my mouth to hide the smile that tugs at my face from watching him shove his entire concoction in his mouth all at once. White cream and chocolate stains his lips and checks.

Onyx taps my sleeping bag with the clean end of his stick. "I see that Snow White."

Opening my mouth wide against my hand, I say, "You see me yawning?"

"M-hm. Sure. That was a smile."

"No, it wasn't."

"She smiled at me earlier." Reid says. He's caught onto Onyx's little game of try-to-make-Jade-smile.

Onyx gives me a wide-mouthed gasp. "She did? Then I win. Why did she smile at you?"

"'Cause I told everyone you left to take a shit. You always take your craps at night before bed, and I heard that one you let go before you walked away. I also smelled it."

"I thought we talked about keeping secrets, especially bodily function secrets."

Reid's eyes spiral like a perfectly thrown football. "Oh please. You always make sure everyone knows when I fart."

"It doesn't matter. If she smiled then I win the bet."

"Actually, the bet was, and I do quote, 'by the end of this weekend, you're going to have my face hurting because I've been smiling too much.' One, it's not the end of the weekend. Two, my face isn't hurting. And

three, Reid is the one that made me smile, not you." I purse my lips together to prevent the smile from bursting through. It's becoming difficult to keep a straight face around him.

"Oh, burn," Reid says, licking his finger and extending it in the air while making a sizzling sound.

And the rest of the weekend goes the same. Reid would do something that made me smile, and he'd rub it in Onyx's face every time.

I do have to give it to Onyx, though. He really tried. Saturday morning, I woke with his mug in my face. He had painted a faux mustache that curled onto his checks with ash from the fire remnants. He then acted out a story, with body motions and no sound. Reid was laughing so hard, tears flowed from his eyes. But I held it until I went to the bathroom and let it out with no one around.

The hardest time to hold the smile back was not one of the times he was being a total goofball, but when it was just me and him, putting together his *clos-room*, which looked large and spacious thanks to the paint.

He was like a kid in a candy store, oohing and aahing over every last item I brought to his room. The painting of the agate he admired earlier. The geode bookends, the black-and-white striped comforter that feels like silk, and my personal favorite, the collection of vintage cameras, some his and some we found while

shopping, that fit perfectly in three old Coca-Cola wood crates we attached to the wall behind his bed. It looks much cooler than a regular headboard, and I'm glad Janet told me he had a thing for old cameras.

But I bite my cheeks and hold the smile in, even then not wanting to give him the victory. He's right though, by the end of the weekend, my cheeks will hurt, but only because I keep on biting them.

SUNDAY NIGHT, I'M stretched out on my new bedspread that covers my amazingly comfortable bed that's crowned by a denim headboard with white tufted buttons and a row of white piping.

For the first time in six months, I feel at home. I feel at peace, somewhat. I feel like I've walked the path toward happiness just a tad.

And I'm drawing again. Something small that means something, and once I'm done, I doubt I'll do it again, at least, not for a while.

After emptying all the totes that miss vain packed away rather haphazardly, I came across art project after art project. I now have an entire wall dedicated to my former self. I debated putting any of it up, but all the pieces fit the happy vibe I've got going on in my room. So, I thought, why not?

My art style was on the whimsy side, and I wrote out inspirational quotes with hand drawn flowers, rainbows, unicorns, and dogs. I no longer needed to keep them hidden away in bins. I had an entire bare wall that needed to be decorated. And decorate I did.

The wall inspired me to pull out my iPad and stylus to sketch. I'm working on the tattoo that I hope to get soon. It's an interpretation of my mom's ring. It will serve as a sign to think constructive thoughts only. The ruby center will represent a stop sign. If I can analyze my father's death constructively, I don't need to stop. But if I can't, I need to. I think that should go for everything in my future life. The tattoo will be a reminder.

"Boo," the husky voice says. I don't even flinch. He's cried wolf too many times this weekend, I've become numb to his boos, his ridiculous antics, and his Cheshire cat grin.

Onyx steps in and circles, eyeing all four walls. He stops at the personal wall of artwork. "Wow, this is amazing."

I stand and admire it with him, taking in my years and years of artwork with happy thoughts and mantras. It builds and I can't hide it. I don't even try to hide it.

My smile.

Onyx pulls out his phone and snaps a picture. He shows me and says, "I got you."

He really didn't. I got myself. But I'll let him have this small victory even though my cheeks aren't hurting.

interlude 2

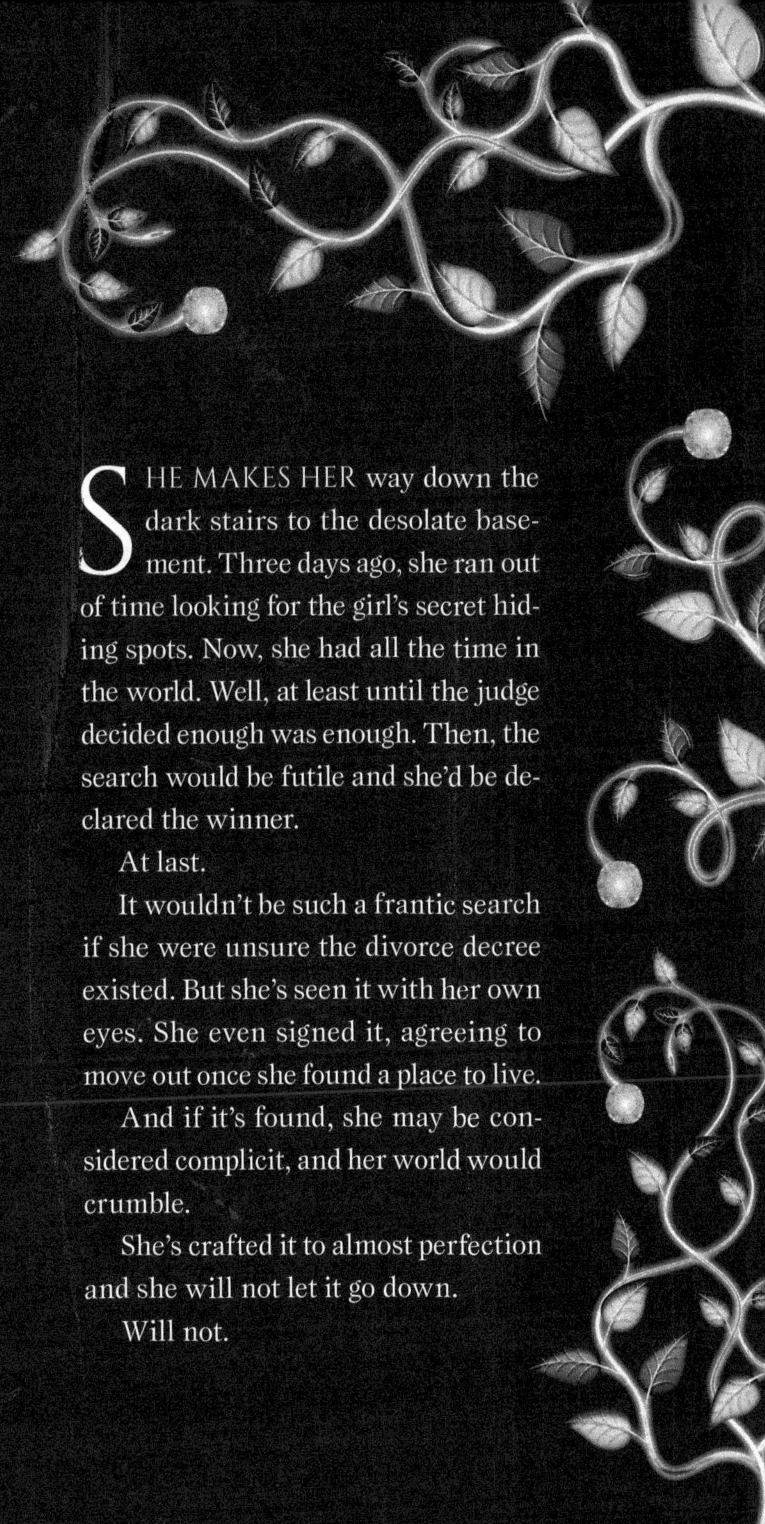

S HE MAKES HER way down the dark stairs to the desolate base-ment. Three days ago, she ran out of time looking for the girl's secret hid-ing spots. Now, she had all the time in the world. Well, at least until the judge decided enough was enough. Then, the search would be futile and she'd be de-clared the winner.

At last.

It wouldn't be such a frantic search if she were unsure the divorce decree existed. But she's seen it with her own eyes. She even signed it, agreeing to move out once she found a place to live.

And if it's found, she may be con-sidered complicit, and her world would crumble.

She's crafted it to almost perfection and she will not let it go down.

Will not.

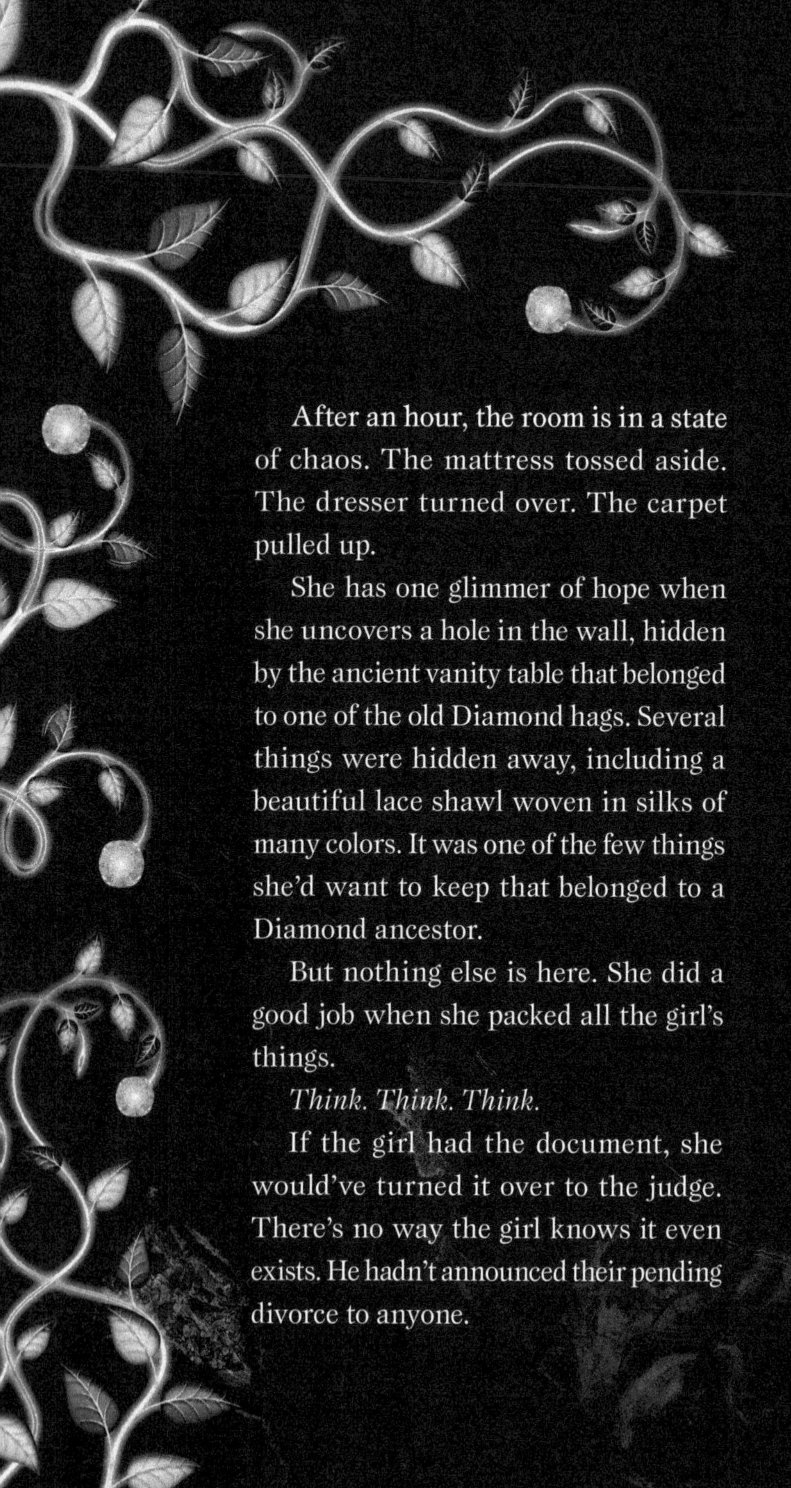

After an hour, the room is in a state of chaos. The mattress tossed aside. The dresser turned over. The carpet pulled up.

She has one glimmer of hope when she uncovers a hole in the wall, hidden by the ancient vanity table that belonged to one of the old Diamond hags. Several things were hidden away, including a beautiful lace shawl woven in silks of many colors. It was one of the few things she'd want to keep that belonged to a Diamond ancestor.

But nothing else is here. She did a good job when she packed all the girl's things.

Think. Think. Think.

If the girl had the document, she would've turned it over to the judge. There's no way the girl knows it even exists. He hadn't announced their pending divorce to anyone.

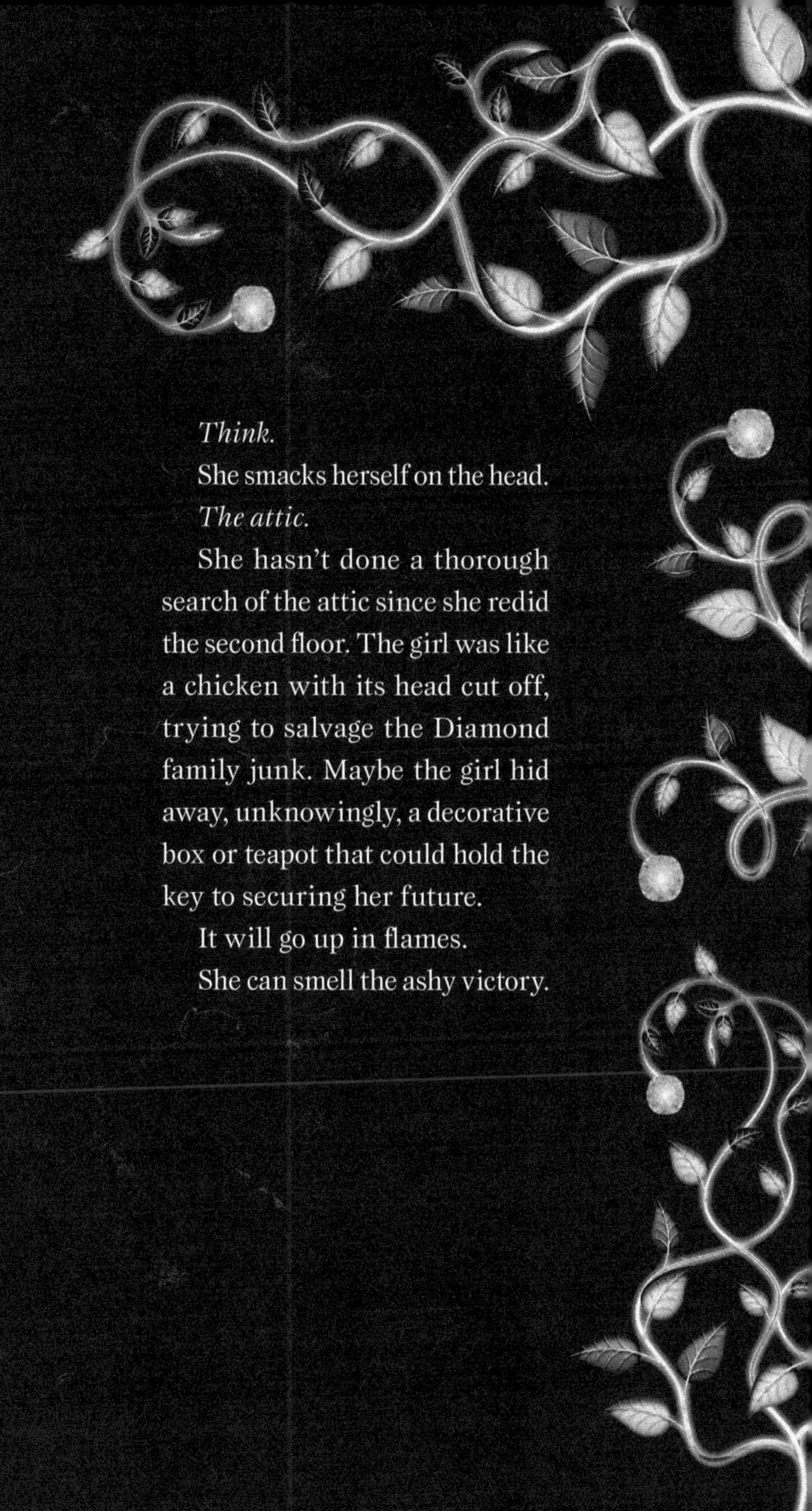

Think.

She smacks herself on the head.

The attic.

She hasn't done a thorough search of the attic since she redid the second floor. The girl was like a chicken with its head cut off, trying to salvage the Diamond family junk. Maybe the girl hid away, unknowingly, a decorative box or teapot that could hold the key to securing her future.

It will go up in flames.

She can smell the ashy victory.

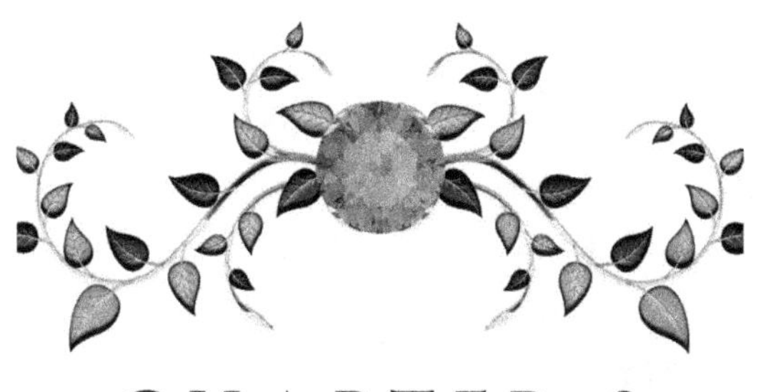

CHAPTER 8

J ANET PARKS IN the *guest* parking spot in front of my new high school. "You nervous?"

I take in the beige brick building with a large black metal emblem of a bear flanked by green hanging signs that say Bradley County in yellow.

This time last year, I was a happy Junior at Blue River Prep with a group of friends I'd had for years. Friends that were involved in so many activities, we didn't hang out much outside of school functions. Between art and the jewelry store, I didn't have a lot of freetime myself.

Blakely was the star soccer player, spending her weekends traveling all over the south for various soccer games and tournaments. Irelynn was an amazing gymnast. She missed a lot of school due to travel and had just received word that she'd be moving away her

senior year to live in a compound where she'd focus on gymnastics all the time in hopes of making the Olympic team or at least get a scholarship to an SEC school for gymnastics. Trinity was a dancer and, since making the varsity dance team at Blue River, had already started straying from our little foursome.

I'd been dreading senior year at Blue River. Although I was sad to think I wouldn't return to the school I'd gone to since kindergarten, I was somewhat relieved. I would've been mostly on my own, which was no different from attending Merryville High.

So, no, I'm not nervous about Bradley. I have Malachi, who has gone to school here since kindergarten. I know Onyx and all the other guys.

I'll be okay. Okay for me anyway. When you're numb, it doesn't matter where you're at or what you do. You can't feel much of anything.

The only thing that matters is finishing those last several classes I need to graduate.

But then what?

I have no clue.

A year ago, my goal was to follow in my mom's footsteps and attend the Savannah College of Art and Design in Georgia. She was a senior studying jewelry making when she met my dad. He was a guest speaker for a career class. Despite the ten-year age difference, sparks flew brighter than the welding equipment she used to craft the jewelry piece that caught his attention.

Six months later, she was at his doorstep in Merryville asking for a job, and six months after that, they were married. He didn't care that she had a bad heart.

"Jade?" my aunt says, pulling me from my inner thoughts.

What did she ask again? Oh, am I nervous? "No." It's an honest answer; I'm not nervous. It's another stepping stone in finishing up my youth and preparing me for my unknown future. Maybe being here will help me solve my issue with not knowing what steps to take. Maybe being here will help me find a path that leads to happiness again. If that's even possible.

"Well, that's good," Janet says, patting my hand. "Let's get you registered then."

We walk through the front doors as students start trickling in, all eyes glued to me. New girl, yet again, but I wasn't going to hide out in the library to avoid their lingering gazes. I'd put up a strong front backed by Malachi and Onyx. Something tells me Onyx would be a loyal friend if I let him be one.

Maybe I can allow that a little. He does find ways to make that frozen tundra melt.

The office is separated by the hall in an encasement of glass windows on three sides. A little bell tinkles as we open the door.

A portly lady with little ringlets framing her face of bright, pink cheeks click-clicks her little heeled feet from the back of the room to the main counter.

"Janet, I see you found another stray." Pink lipstick stains the woman's teeth when she smiles.

"Not a stray this time, Francis," my aunt says, plopping down the folder containing my school records. She called the office of Merryville on Friday and demanded they email everything, so I would be able to register today. I kind of hoped I'd have a few days off waiting around, but not with my no-time-goes-wasted aunt supporting me.

"This is my niece, Jade. She's a senior and now living with us. Here are her records." She slips the folder under the lady's chubby fingers decked out in silver rings, only her thumbs are left without any ornaments.

"Jade, this is Principal Miller, but the kids call her Francis."

Francis picks up the folder and reaches for the phone on the desk behind her. "Ed, I have a new student for you." After a pause, she says, "I'll send her back." She hangs up the phone and returns to the counter with the folder in hand. "Head on down to guidance, and they'll get you squared away."

Janet picks up the folder and turns on the heels of her cowboy boots. "Thanks, Franny. See you at poker tomorrow night."

Francis lets out a belly laugh and yells as we exit, "You should just hand over your nickels now, Janet."

My aunt turns down a few hallways. I'm instantly lost. We left the ranch while the boys were finishing

up breakfast. I should've made Malachi come with us to hold my hand and be my personal tour guide.

A gray-haired man greets us at the entrance of the guidance office. "Another one, Janet?"

"This one's a little different," she responds. She hands him the folder. "Jade, this is Mr. Norman. He'll get your schedule squared away. Ride home with Mica since Malachi and Onyx have football practice. I have to go meet someone about a horse." She gives me a quick hug then leaves.

Now that I'm here, and without my aunt, the panic bubbles start building in my stomach. I'm not nervous. I can do this. I'm not going to freak out. I lift the sleeve of my pink and navy argyle sweater and trace the red stone woven with black and green vines that I sketched with Sharpies on the inside of my forearm.

This is easy, Jade. You've done it once already this year. But this time, you have people you know who won't desert you.

"Have a seat, Jade," Mr. Noman says, directing me to a plastic chair next to a black table topped with two sleek computer monitors. He sits in the office chair behind the desk and spreads out the contents of the folder as the bell rings to start off the school day.

After ten minutes of typing at a frantic pace, he lifts his glasses to rest on top of his head, causing his peppered hair to spike in all different directions around the gold frames. "You'll need to pick out two electives

to take as we don't offer any replacement business classes for what you were taking at Merryville until the spring." He looks at the computer while jotting down a list. He slides a blue piece of scrap paper in my direction with three choices.

1) Future Farmers of America
2) Culinary Arts
3) Art

That's it? Three choices and I have to pick two of them? No thanks to number one. I don't want to learn how to plant corn or milk a cow. Living on a ranch will be enough introduction to the world of farming.

I can handle cooking. I could use that life skill. Maybe I'll stop burning water.

But art? No painting, ceramics, or digital media? Just plain old art? I took art in elementary school. Isn't there another choice?

Art has been a part of my life since I can remember, up until six months ago. I swore it off after my dad died. Even though I drew my future tattoo last night and again on my arm this morning, I'm not ready to venture down that path again. I suffered a minor panic attack that I had to power through before I could pick up my Apple pen.

Requiring myself to create art on a daily basis is not what I'd call a safe healing passage. I need baby steps.

Drawing the tattoo was a baby step. Hanging my art pieces on the wall was a baby step. Art class would be gigantic leaps that I'm just not ready to take. No thanks.

But being elbow-deep in a pig pen is not something that sounds remotely interesting.

I mumble two and three as my breath becomes jagged and my palms sweat.

He types more data then prints out a schedule and marks numbers on a map. Looking at the school laid out on a sheet of paper eases my mind. It looks like an electrical pole with one main hallway that acts as a main artery topped off with several smaller hallways. The gym is in a separate building near the football field which also holds the cafeteria and several classrooms, three of which Mr. Norman labeled in red with a one, two, and three.

He hands me the map and schedule. "Enjoy your first day, Ms. Diamond. If you have any questions, don't hesitate to stop by."

Nodding, I make my way outside and follow the yellow, highlighted route to number one on my schedule.

I don't need to read the number above the door to know I've arrived at my Health class. Colorful signs cover the door with phrases such as *Got Condom?*, *Just Say No*, and *Your Body, Your Territory*. There's even a cartoon diagram of how to use various birth control options properly.

They created health class to embarrass the crap out of us with topics that have been hounded in our brains more than enough the past four years. It's a requirement though; I need it to graduate. So bring on the torture.

I quietly open the door and slip into the room.

Great, the door leads me to the back. The teacher's obviously a coach, because one, what school doesn't have a coach teach health, and two, he's dressed in green warm up pants with yellow stripes down the sides and a yellow polo featuring a bear and *Bradley Football* embroidered on the left side of his chest.

"Pay attention to labels," he says, flashing a red laser light on the whiteboard displaying a picture of a food label. "Lots of unsuspecting food items that are supposedly good for you have ingredients that you may be unaware of."

I clear my throat lightly, hoping to get his attention. Only a few heads turn toward the back row to stare at the new girl. Coach goes on about the secrets behind natural flavors and how they're not natural at all. I clear my throat louder this time and raise my hand, causing all heads to turn to the back of the room.

"Yes, can I help you?" he says.

"Um," I mutter. Heat fills me from all the beady eyes staring in my direction. I walk down an aisle toward the front. My sneaker catches the edge of a denim backpack and I start to stumble. A strong arm wraps around my waist and catches me before I faceplant on the tile floor.

The husky voice of my savior permeates the room. "New student, Coach. Trying to make a grand entrance but failing. Or should I say falling?" He snickers.

I want to turn around and smack that sexy grin that I know is on his face right off.

"You can release her now, Onyx, unless you want to share your seat with her," he says, motioning for me to come to the front of the room. "I'm Coach Brown."

I shrug away from Onyx's grip and walk to the front of the room, handing the coach my schedule. He glances at it then returns it to me.

"Tell us your name."

Ugh. What do teachers do this?

"Jade," I whisper as I shuffle my light blue, slip-on Vans across the floor.

"And Jade, do you have a last name?"

"Diamond."

"And where do you come to us from?"

"Merryville, Indiana."

"Pick any seat, but there's only one available," he says, laughing at what I think was meant to be a joke. "And everyone, say, *Welcome to Bradley, Jade.*"

An orchestra of voices shout out my greeting. Onyx waves and smiles from ear to ear, modeling the empty seat at his two-person table. I slump into the vacant chair, wishing it came with a blanket to hide my head under.

Onyx swipes the schedule from my hands and nods as he reads it. He hands it back and whispers, "I've got you 'til third period."

"Wasting no time hitting on the new girl, Onyx?" Coach Brown says.

"You know me, I'm always on the prowl. Need to leave my mark so no one else messes with her." He wraps his arm around my shoulders; it feels like a dead-weight. I don't shrug him off—I'm relieved I know someone in my first two classes.

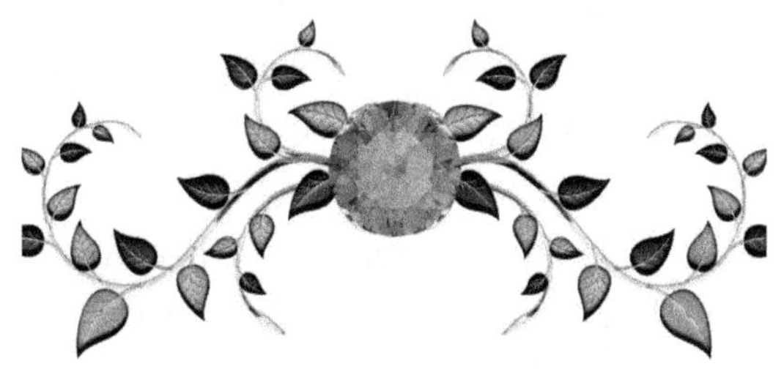

CHAPTER 9

THE NICE THING about walking the halls with Onyx, besides not getting lost, is no one pays me any attention. Girls, clothed in cheer gear, bat their eyelashes at him and call him *O-Baby*. Guys fist bump him, call him *Magic*, and say *Go, Bears*.

He's not dressed like the other guys in their letterman jackets and Bradley Bears tees. He's in a wrinkled Yoda t-shirt that says *Do or Do Not, There is No Try* paired with holey jeans and a black, leather jacket with silver angel wings on the back.

Not everyone has love for him though. A few guys that wear black leather jackets, similar to the one he has but without the wings, call him *sell-out Ollie*. He ignores them, not even giving them a glance, and doesn't respond when I ask what that's about.

He and Coach Brown had several back and forth banters throughout class, causing Coach to rush through his last four slides on food preservatives.

In culinary arts, the cooking teacher—Mrs. Sweet, I can't even make that shit up—was practically falling over herself when she tried the brownies Onyx made.

Needless to say, he seems to not only have a special place with my aunt but with all of Bradley County High School as well. I haven't determined, nor have I asked, what football position he plays. He's too skinny to be a quarterback or a defensive lineman. But hey, what do I know?

"That hall, then down a flight of stairs to the basement," Onyx says, pointing to a dark, weirdly-glowing hallway that supposedly leads me to my third period art class.

I think it's leading me to hell. And my face obviously says what I think.

He pushes the wrinkles out of my forward. "It's actually a really cool walk. Take a look around. I'll see you at lunch. Tell Miss Hannigan I say hello."

I take a step into the hallway black-lit with stars, mountains, and waves of neon blue, pink, green, yellow, and orange. Even though the paintings are stationary, I'm moving through the surf. My head spins and I don't feel grounded. It's like being on drugs but without the drugs, though I don't know what it feels like to be on drugs—other than the pain killers I took for a few days after I had my tonsils removed in eighth grade.

A sign that says *Watch Your Step* hangs at the end of the hallway. Bulbs flicker like flames down the

stairwell. And the walls are covered in photographs, mostly black and white, mounted on metal.

One photo catches my eye—it's one of the few that's in color. The flaming light bulbs flickering above add even more drama to the photo. It's of the dock at Diamond Ranch at sunrise. No doubt about it; I'd recognize it anywhere. A small signature in black ink is in the corner. *Prince.* Maybe one of Janet's previous fosters.

At the bottom of the steps is a fierce-looking, cartoon-style illustration of a bear wearing a number twelve Bradley County football uniform. *This way to the dungeon* is painted as if the bear clawed it out of the wall. It's signed by a *T Becket.*

Maybe my heart can find its way back to art being around all these talented artists.

Feathery piano music greets me, along with a woman about the same age as my aunt. She stands beside a desk and a chalkboard that has an illustration of a bear, this one in plain white chalk saying *Miss Hannigan's Art Dungeon.* The teacher's in a long, flowing, flowery dress with soft-pink ballet slippers. Blonde curls frame her weather-beaten face.

"Welcome to the dungeon." Her smile makes her eyes squint. "You must be Jade."

I nod and hand her my schedule as a handful of other students file in behind me.

The hexagonal room is definitely not a dungeon. Although there are no windows, every inch is bathed

in a faux sunlight thanks to the rows and rows of track lighting covering the ceiling. Wooden tables are scattered in groups of two with a tower of drawers between them. Cabinets, sinks, open shelves, and artwork cover most of the walls. One wall has a door and is painted to look like a barn with a sign that says *pottery* over the frame. The last wall is all black and has a faint outline of a door with a knob that's painted white, the only other decoration is a small sign that says, *Shush, we're developing.*

And the smell. Oh, the smell. A mixture of aromas that makes my nose twitch. So familiar yet so foreign. Some good, some bad. It's dirt mixed with wet paper, turpentine layered with oil and chalk.

Mrs. Hannigan rummages through her desk drawer and pulls out a single gold key on a loopy keychain. "What media do you like to work in and what's your style?"

Maybe this isn't basic art. "Um, acrylics, pencil, metal, I guess, mixed media? Anything really." My art style has always been whimsical but that was when I was a happy-go-lucky teenager. When the only thing providing me angst was my wretched stepmother. If I could put a brush or pencil to paper now, I'm sure it might lean more toward dark and gruesome. I'd wind up adhering broken pieces of anything and making slashes in the canvas. The teacher might send me to see Mr. Norman so he can *council* me and lead me to the light.

She places the key, along with a red folder covered by a sticker that reads *senior art,* in my hands. "This class is senior art portfolio. In December, at the end of the semester, we host an exhibit in the theater. You can take whatever time you need in class and outside of class. This room is always open. The only requirement is to have at least five pieces to display at the exhibit. It's best to pick a theme and stick with it."

Relief hits me. Thankfully, I won't be spending all semester relearning the principles of design.

She points to the cabinet behind her desk and holds up the key. "Your bin is number six. Store your finished art or pieces in progress there. If you need a bigger space, we have a storage shed back behind the pottery barn."

She walks me over to an empty seat next to a guy who has the top of his table propped up into an easel. A white sheet of paper hangs from the clip, and his hand glides over the smooth surface, drawing sharp, black lines with a felt-tip pen.

"This is your seat." She pulls the metal stool out for me. "Feel free to spend today coming up with a couple of theme options for your portfolio. If you want to discuss your ideas with me, don't hesitate to come chat. I'm here as a muse, not as a teacher. But I will teach if you need a lesson on anything. And I'm always available for a critique."

I nod as she walks back to her desk and sits in a wooden chair painted in a rainbow of colors. The stool scraps the tile floor as I scoot myself under the table. My neighbor's hand zig zags across the paper at the sound.

"I'm sorry," I whisper.

He glances downward as a shy smile covers his face. Shaking his head, he turns in my direction. "It's okay."

Air rushes out of my lungs as his eyes shimmer at me. It's like I'm looking at The Hunter Green.

He's beautiful. If a guy can be that. And he's definitely that, as was Hunter.

His eyes are deep set, narrow, and the color of the deepest parts of the ocean. Brown hair with blonde streaks are coiffed into a faux-mohawk. His body tells me he's an athlete, yet his style tells me he's an artsy intellectual. He's dressed in a simple, navy tee and dark jeans with no tears or holes, his feet decked out in tan loafers. His station is just as neatly presented as he is.

And I can't break the hold his gaze has on me. His sun-kissed skin makes me look even whiter than a ghost. Even if I spent all summer in the sun, I couldn't get anywhere close to his golden hue. He glances away and gives a faint chuckle as a pink color floods his cheeks.

Shaking my head to break the trance, I mumble another apology.

"Really, it's okay." He yanks the paper from the easel and crumples it into a ball then tosses it with a perfect arc into the wastebasket behind me. "It wasn't going in the right direction anyway. You saved me from wasting time. My brain is still at the lake on fall break."

I nod, feeling my own cheeks trying to match the color of his.

"I'm Tad Becket." He holds out his large fist.

T Becket. The frightening bear at the entrance. Wow. He's beyond talented.

I bump his hand and say, "Jade. Jade Diamond."

"Nice to meet you, Jade. Jade Diamond."

A giggle releases from my mouth without me realizing. Where the hell did that come from? Has this Hunter Green clone turned me into a giddy school girl? His lip curls into a knowing smirk, obviously conscious of what he's doing to me.

For the rest of class, Tad's eyes go from me to a blank sheet of paper then back to me. We're full of brief and awkward eye contacts, uncomfortable small talk, and weird silences, yet I'm intrigued by this cartoon-drawing, shy guy. At least I think he's shy. One minute he's suave and the next his ears glow scarlet.

He's a fathomless mystery that I want to unfold.

The bell rings, and he stands placing his pen set in a drawer. He stares at me for a good minute, sending me on a trip through the late afternoon sky. I have to fight the overwhelming need to touch him.

"What's your next class?" he asks.

I look at my schedule even though I know I have lunch next. I need a tiny break to breathe again after his piercing gaze. It's like his eyes touched every internal part of my being. I try to remind myself that this is how

I responded to Hunter, and look where that got me. But I refuse to listen. Then again, this guy may look like Hunter, but he doesn't have the arrogant attitude on display at all times like Hunter. "Lunch."

"Me too. I'll walk you."

We're the last to leave the dungeon and I pause right outside the door, pointing to the bear. "You do this?"

He looks at the piece and gives a proud smile. "Yeah. His name's Charlie."

"Charlie? Why Charlie?"

"I don't know. I just thought he looked like a Charlie."

I guess I was expecting a more creative answer, like Charlie is a football legend here or his favorite NFL player has the same name or even because he loves the comic strip *Peanuts*.

He quickly climbs the flickering flame-lit stairs, passing all the amazing photography without a glance. I admire the dock at Diamond Ranch from *Prince* again then hurry to catch up. He slows in the glowing hallway, pointing out an orange cat hiding in green grasses that skirt the dancing water. "And this is Kitty."

I don't bother to ask why Kitty, afraid he might shatter the mystery that surrounds him.

He pauses at the end of the luminous corridor. Rubbing the back of his neck, his eyes turn down at the floor as he says, "Can I ask you a question?"

"Ask away."

"It's senior night at the football game on Friday. And I play. It's tradition that we walk out with a senior escort to the middle of the field where we meet up with our parents." His sapphire eyes, caught up in a hurricane, finally meet mine when he adds, "So, I was thinking in art, since you're new here and a senior, I'd like you to be my escort. If you would."

His cheeks flush crimson again, which is a relief. Tad may look like Hunter, but he's definitely not the arrogant, pompous ass that is Hunter. At least, first impressions tell me he's not.

Hunter didn't have a shy bone in his body. The first time he talked to me, he said, "You're going on a date with me tonight."

My heart bleeds a tiny bit at the thought of being Tad's escort. Not uncomfortably though. More like butterflies are fluttering around with wings tipped with tiny needles. I rake my bottom lip with my teeth, pushing the feeling aside. "Yeah, sure. That'd be great."

"Awesome," he responds.

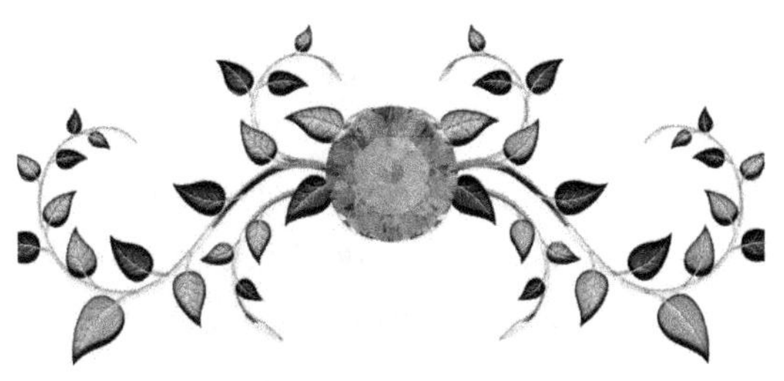

CHAPTER 10

THE MINUTE TAD and I step out of the art passage and into the traffic that is a Bradley County High hallway, Tad transforms into someone totally different.

He turns into Hunter.

He turns into that arrogant, pompous ass that lifts his chin, walks with a strut, and bumps his fist with all the other muscle heads—probably the ones that acted like Onyx was a god earlier are doing the same with Tad.

It makes me wonder who is the real Tad? The artsy shy guy, the outgoing football player, or maybe someone else altogether?

He points to an empty table and slides into a seat. "We sit here."

We as in me too? I'm not sure about this. I need to find a familiar face. The heart bleed flows again, and

I'm afraid I'm not going to like my newest friend. He'll unsurface too many Hunter memories that I'm trying to forget. If I stay, I'll fall into the rabbit hole and be transported back to Merryville High where all the football jocks talked vulgarly about the cheerleaders as they pranced around in their short skirts. I'll be back in the middle of belching contests and food fights.

Before I can retreat to find Onyx or Malachi, strong arms wrap around my waist and lift me up, making me squeal like a pig.

"Put me down, you goon," I scream.

Onyx laughs but does as I command. "I see you met Tadpole here." The two boys do a bro-hug-handshake-fistbump dance.

"I don't know about a Tadpole, but I did meet a Tad," I say, feeling comforted by Onyx's presence as the heart bleed slows.

He wraps his arm around Tad's shoulder. They stand about the same height, but Tad has a good forty pounds on Onyx. "It's Tadpole. You must call him that."

Tad shakes his head and taps Onyx on the chest. "My name is not Tadpole, and only Ollie here calls me that."

Onyx's jaw hardens as he taps Tad on the chest in response. "And no one calls me, Ollie." Both of their chests fill with air, as if they're male cats getting ready to rumble over the lioness who's just walked into the den. Hopefully, it's not over me.

They both start laughing and punching each other in the gut, allowing my shoulders to drop the tension.

Malachi shows up and separates them. "Hey, no playing without me."

Tad jumps back in defense but his body eases as he and Malachi perform the same secret dance that Tad and Onyx did.

"I see you met my cousin." Malachi pulls me into a side hug. "How's your first day been?"

Tad's eyes dart back and forth from me to Malachi. "Cousin?" I try to ignore the huge lump that I can visually see slide down Tad's throat. Like it's just as bad I'm Mal's cousin as if I were his sister. Maybe Tad doesn't date siblings—or cousins—of his friends.

"Yeah, cousin. She's living with us now. Mom made Onyx and I move out to the stables for her."

"Oh, please." I say, punching him in the shoulder to relieve the tension that continues to work its way up and down my body. "You guys are living it up. You have your own kitchen and living room. Not to mention that big screen TV. Your mom almost didn't go for the new Playstation."

"You want to trade?" Malachi asks, adding, "although I'd need to repaint."

Onyx comes up behind him and wiggles his eyebrows at me. "Yeah, you wanna trade with Malachi?"

Ignoring him, I say, "I'm hungry. Show me what this place has for grub."

I think I might be okay here at Bradley. Sitting with two handsome guys and my cousin at lunch is way better than hiding out in the library like the first couple of days at Merryville. I just need to figure this Tad guy out. Why is my internal warning going off with him?

TWO GIRLS SIT at the same table when we return with trays full of everything the lunch ladies had to offer, thanks to Onyx insisting I try a little bit of this and a little bit of that.

"Jade, this is Delani." Malachi waves his hand to a tall girl with purple, braided pigtails pulling a glass container of salad from her hot pink backpack. *Delani.* That name is familiar.

She smiles and says, "Welcome."

"And this is Pepper. But don't get her talking. Otherwise, she'll never shut up."

Pepper has a *peppering* of freckles across her nose. She's a gorgeous, auburn-haired girl with full lips that would never need a lip injection like miss vain. She flicks Mal a bird. "It's nice to meet you, Jade."

"You too," I say, giving both girls a genuine smile in return.

Onyx sets different food items in front of me, insisting I taste everything. Finally, I settle for fries and an apple then pass everything else to him.

Tad gives me awkward glances a couple of times, causing me to worry that my first date at Bradley may back out on me thanks to being Malachi's cousin. And maybe I want him to back out with all the yellow caution signs flashing in my heart. He stays quiet most of the lunch period. When he does talk, its usually to Malachi or Pepper, proving my theory that he's no longer interested. Pepper and Onyx carry on most of the conversation.

"Oh, look what Eli gave me over break." Pepper pushes her hair back behind her ears.

Delani turns Pepper's head to inspect the sparkling earrings. "Those are beautiful. Are they real?"

"He said they were. Two carats of real-ness. Well, I guess four if you put them together."

"Dang, girl."

"Please," Malachi spews. "Eli couldn't afford a half a carat. Let alone four. I bet those are fake."

Delani's eyes spiral when she says, "You're just jealous, Mal."

He tilts his head and smirks. "Hardly. Ask Jade. She's a diamond expert."

"Just because her last name is Diamond doesn't mean she's a diamond expert." Onyx laughs at himself.

"But she is," Malachi says. "She used to work in a jewelry store."

Pepper's eyes light up in my direction. "You used to work in a jewelry store?"

I nod.

"How cool. Would you be able to tell if these were real?"

"Uh, maybe." From here, I can tell they're fake by the way the light reflects a rainbow of colors off of them. If I had earrings that were real diamonds and that big, I wouldn't be wearing them to school. We're talking about a twenty thousand dollar value. My guess is Eli paid twenty dollars tops.

She takes one out and holds it across the table. I take my time inspecting it, turning it over and holding it up to the light, trying to determine whether I need to be honest or not. I don't want to ruin the possibility of a budding friendship, but I don't want to lie to her in case she finds out another way. So, I go with em-bellished honesty.

"They're a nice fake." I place the earring back in her awaiting hand and give her a soft smile.

"Told you," Malachi says.

The bell rings and students start to scatter.

"What's your next class?" Tad asks.

"Um, math."

"Mrs. Swanson?" Pepper questions.

I look at my schedule then nod.

"You're with me then." She loops her arm through mine, dragging me out of the cafeteria and down the hall. "I'll show you the way."

Is she the revengeful type? Is she going to take me outside and kick my ass for telling her that her boyfriend bought her fake jewels?

She leads me into a classroom with posters of varying angles and math formulas. "I can't believe Eli," she says, pointing to an empty desk next to her. "I was going to break up with him, but then he gave me these. And I was like, I can't because his gift was so sweet. But now, I sure can. He better hope he's not at my house waiting on me when I get home. This lie was the final nail in the coffin. He's so full of shit. I don't care if they're not real. I refuse to be with a liar."

I let out a sigh of relief. Sometimes, even when fake jewelry is involved, it pays to be honest.

CHAPTER 11

GRABBING A PILLOW and my iPad, I head up the old ladder just outside my room to the tiny space of the cupola to take in the night sky. When I stayed here during long childhood summers, Malachi and I often slept here. The space seemed so big then. Now, to sleep up here, we'd have to curl into balls as if we were rollie pollies.

Facing west, I stare at the night sky in hopes of seeing more meteors. Having always lived close to bright city lights, I've never spent time staring at the stars before. Seeing all the fireballs during Saturday night's campout was enlightening. Just sitting here now and looking at all the visible stars in the country sky takes my breath away.

Onyx said the Orionid meteor shower will peak later in the month. He also provided several other interesting tidbits about meteors including that some cultures believe shooting stars are human souls traveling between heaven and Earth.

Saturday night, I had a dream that my dad visited me in my basement room of our old house. It couldn't have been real, seeing as I was at the ranch and sleeping outside. But it gave me hope that he's watching over me somehow, in some shape or form. The only words I remember him saying in the dream were *not to forget the three things.*

Every night before bed, Dad and I always shared our three favorite things about that day. Since his death, I haven't once stated them. Good days have been hard to come by. But because I'm striving for happiness once again, writing down my three positives of the day will be part of my new night time ritual, in honor of my father.

It kind of goes back to when Onyx said the act of smiling makes you feel better. Maybe the act of writing down my favorite things will help me realize that I've got a lot to be happy about.

I open the notes app on my iPad and draw a vine on the outer edges of the page then write the date. What three things do I want to memorialize for today? I easily survived my first day at Bradley. After meeting Tad during art and the girls at lunch, I had someone I knew in every class. I even have a *date,* if you can call escorting Tad on Friday night a *date.*

So three things.

In swooshy letters, I write down the names of my three new friends.

Tad, Pepper, and Delani.

Tad was in my psychology class right after math. I debated all throughout lunch whether he'd still want me to escort him after finding out I was Malachi's cousin. He told me he was looking forward to Friday night when he showed me the location of my last class—English.

A big relief, once I stopped listening to the Mayday calls my heart was sending out. The warnings have got to be because of the similarities between him and Hunter. He's definitely proven that he's not the ultimate douche that Hunter is. Hunter controlled conversations, said inappropriate things that made my face live in a state of flush, and walked around with a swagger like he's God's gift to women. Tad seems to have a lot more of a reserved swagger. But still a swagger.

I was even more relieved after walking into my last class of the day and seeing Pepper's and Delani's faces light up. They motioned for me to sit near them and whispered to me the rest of the class, pissing off the teacher.

The only person I don't have a class with is Malachi. We didn't have time to catch up over the weekend, and with football practice in the afternoons and the full house in the evenings, I don't know when I'm going to be able to spend time with him and learn what has him so moody.

"Boo," says the husky voice that I've become more familiar with than Malachi's. This time, he gets me, and I bump my head into one of the ceiling rafters.

"Damn you," I say as Onyx's head pops up through the ladder opening.

He squeezes his lanky frame into the small space, answering my previous question of how would Malachi and I fit up here now. *Really tightly.*

"Why are you invading all my most favorite spots?" he asks. "First the dock and now up here."

"Oh, sure." I rub the spot that's starting to form a knot. "You can join me. Go right ahead. There's plenty of room for two."

He replaces my hand with his own, kneading my noggin. "Did I do that?"

With wide eyes, I nod.

"I'm sorry," he says.

"I'll live."

He stops the head massage and picks up my iPad. I yank it out of his hands and turn the screen off.

The corner of his mouth tips up. "Writing love letters to all your new BFFs?"

I roll my eyes, but my heart warms at my three things from today.

Life can totally change at the blink of an eye. Sometimes it takes you down so far, you don't know

how in the world you're going to claw your way back up. And sometimes, you just want to give up. But then, one simple decision can help you climb from the deep without the need for talons. You're a balloon, being inflated. Suddenly, you're in the low clouds, barely above the surface, but able to breathe again.

"What are you doing up here?" I ask.

"I can't go to sleep at night without coming up here," he admits.

"You can't start your day without watching the sun rise from one of my favorite spots. And you can't go to sleep at night without coming to another one of my favorite spots."

He elbows me gently. "Sounds about right."

"Then we need to create a schedule to rotate. Your dock days will be my cupola days and vice versa. I'm tired of you scaring the shit out of me."

Pinching his nose, he says, "I was wondering what that smell was."

I slap him on his hard chest, hurting my hand more than I hurt him.

He throws his arm around me and leans us back against the east window. "How about we enjoy the spaces together. You bring coffee in the mornings, and I'll bring hot chocolate in the evenings."

"No."

"I like my coffee black. Do you like marshmallows?"

I relax into his hold. "No."

"Okay, no marshmallows for the weirdo."

A bright light streaks across the sky. I close my eyes tightly and make a wish. *Help me continue to heal.*

He squints at me. "What'd ya wish for?"

I poke him in his side. "It didn't come true. You're still here." I wouldn't want him to go away. He brings a sense of peace, like he's giving me air to inflate my balloon.

His smile widens as if he knows I really want him here. "How was your first day at Bradley?"

"Good, actually."

"What made it good?"

"Well, it was nice seeing someone I at least somewhat knew in all of my classes."

"Is that why you wrote down Tad, Pepper, and Delani on your iPad?"

I lift away from his arm and turn to face him. "Kind of." I shake my head. "It's silly."

"What's silly?"

Can I tell him why? I think he'd understand that I'm grateful for what I've received today. Friends are gifts, and he's one of those gifts. Had I started the three things a few days ago, he would've been included on a list at some point.

I squint my eyes and tap my forehead. "My dad and I used to end each day by sharing our three favorite things that happened that day. I haven't done it since he died, but I thought it was time I started that again."

His smile slips and his brows crinkle. "I'm sad I'm not on that list." It's the first time I've ever seen him not look 100% confident.

I turn on my iPad and create a new page with another vine frame and yesterday's date. I title it *my three favorite things from the weekend.*

Onyx brings his scrunched face closer to watch as I write, almost touching his forehead to mine. A little performance anxiety builds as I mull over what to include without being too revealing.

1) Onyx liked the decor I picked out for his room.

2) My new room. It beats the musty basement hands down.

3) Sunrises at the dock. It's always better with company.

He leans back and a smile finds its way through his mask of uncertainty. "Your dad sounds like he was a good man. I'm sorry about his passing." He taps my hand three times then rests his on top of mine.

"Thanks," I whisper.

"I remember when Malachi and Janet went to the funeral. I didn't put two and two together until just now, when you mentioned him."

I bite my lip until it throbs, holding down the lump that's trying to rise in my throat.

"Did you enjoy the haunted hallway on your way to art?" he asks.

Thankful for the change in subject, I force the lump down and give a meager smile. "I did. Do you know of someone that used to live here who liked photography? There was a stunning image of the dock hanging on the wall signed by a *Prince*."

He ignores my question, asking, "What are you going to do for the art exhibit?"

"How do you know about the exhibit?"

He shrugs. "How was math with Old Lady Williams?"

"Oh, her room reeked." It smelled like a cross between a kennel, baby powder, and dirty diapers. At first, I thought it was someone's BO and I was worried it was my own. Pepper caught me sniffing my shoulder and laughed, letting me know it wasn't me. "Do you have her?"

He shakes his head. "How was Mr. Worley's English class?"

"I got in trouble for talking to Delani."

"Yeah, he's an asshole."

"He targeted me. Pepper talked even more and was way louder. She only got a stern look. Not the tongue-lashing I got."

"Pepper's the princess of Bradley."

"Why's that?"

"Why didn't you ride home with Mica?" he fires again.

The annoyance Onyx sometimes brings is on full throttle. I shoot him a penetrating look. "Are we playing twenty questions? If so, you need to answer my questions when I ask."

The corner of his mouth twists with exasperation and amusement. "Me ask. You respond. Why didn't you ride home with Mica?"

"You're frustrating." I see how he's going to be. All take and no give. "Delani and Pepper invited me to hang out with them after school. Didn't want them to have to drive me all the way home, so I came back to school to ride with you guys."

"Did Pepper talk your ear off?"

I push my hair behind my ears, revealing that they're both still there.

"Funny. Will you be my escort for senior night at the football game?"

It comes out so fast, I have to rewind what he said in my head. *Will. You. Be. My. Escort.* My heart flips and I regret saying yes so fast to Tad. I also hate telling people no, but I can't escort two different people. "I'm sorry. Tad asked me that same question today."

"As in Tadpole?"

"As in Tad."

He squints his eyes as if I'm covered in a foreign language he doesn't understand.

"Is something wrong with Tad asking me?"

"No. Just didn't expect it. I thought he was into someone else."

"Who?"

He shakes his head. "I was way off."

"You should ask Pepper. She broke up with Eli today over the earrings." We went to her house after school and he was there waiting for her. He was whining and pleading his case while she remained as cool as a popsicle. She sent him on his way with the earrings he gave her.

Onyx quirks his mouth to the side and scratches his head. "Why did you tell her they were fake?"

"I wanted to be honest. Should I have told her they were real?" She didn't seem bothered by my honesty at all. In fact, she seemed pleased, like she wasn't used to people being honest with her.

"Did you know Tad and Pepper used to date?"

"I did not." I hope it doesn't bother her that I'm escorting Tad. Maybe I should cancel on him and escort Onyx instead.

"Yep. And Delani and Malachi dated during the same time. Freshman and sophomore years."

That's why Delani's name was familiar. Malachi used to talk about her all the time.

"And who did you date?"

His laugh comes out like he's a donkey. "No one and everyone."

"Player Onyx."

A yawn escapes, making my jaw pop. "I'll leave you to enjoy your spot alone. I'm going to bed." I scoot over him to reach the ladder.

He places his hands across my upper arms, my lips hovering just inches from his, pausing me. "I like my coffee black." His voice is coated in a chocolate seduction. My heart flips again.

"You're incorrigible." I pull away and laugh off the heat coursing through my body.

"There's that smile," he says with a wink.

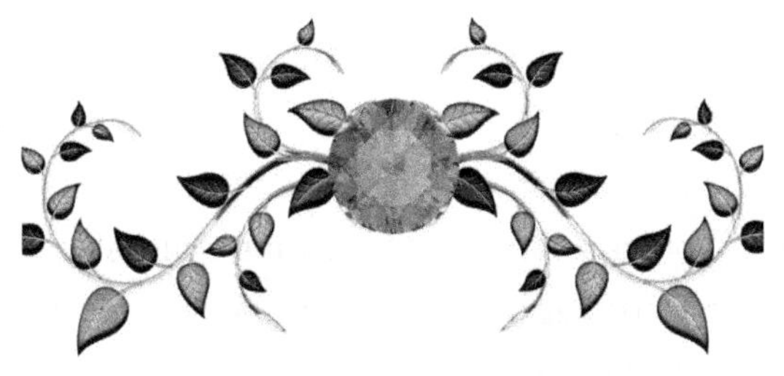

CHAPTER 12

A SHIVER RUNS THE length of my spine as I take a peek outside from the warm comforts of the gym. The stadium is filled to capacity as the Friday night lights shine, illuminating the green field.

Why did I let Pepper talk me into wearing this short dress? It's emerald green and satiny, and it even has cool pockets for my phone. But it's sleeveless, and it's freezing. And where is she? She was supposed to meet me here ten minutes ago. The pre-game ceremony begins in five minutes.

Aunt Janet walks in the door of the gym closest to the field and pushes a black leather jacket in my direction. "Onyx said you looked like you were freezing."

The rich, earthy, and slightly minty smell emanating from Onyx's coat fills my nose. We meet every morning for sunrise. Tuesday, I failed to bring the coffee, but he was prepared and brought four options with him

in a fast food carry container—two blacks, one that was more cream than coffee, and the one that I chose with a nice, medium caramel color. That evening, he arrived in the small space of the cupola with two mugs of hot chocolate. I asked him for marshmallows, to which he rolled his eyes but pulled out a small bag from his sweatshirt pocket.

When I arrived here, at the family farm, I thought my friendship with Malachi was what was going to get me through. So far this week, it's been my friendship with Onyx that's helped me the most, followed by Pepper and Delani.

Since Monday, Malachi has been even more moody and he barely looks at me, or anyone else. He eats with the family at dinner, only because Janet forces him to, then he hides away in his room for the rest of the evening, telling me to go away the one time I'd attempted to visit him.

Onyx told me he'll get over it. Then I asked, get over what? To that, Onyx just shrugged his shoulders. He seemed to be just as perplexed about the situation as I am.

At least it's not me. Malachi's shunning everyone, even his own mother. I was privy to a yelling match between the two of them just this morning.

Janet's eyes dart across the gym toward the entrance from the parking lot. She lets out a huff and mumbles under her breath, "What's she doing here?"

She leaves me alone and cuts off a haggard lady

dressed in black leather pants and a denim jacket. Her long, wavy, brown hair lays in strings, framing her sunken face.

After a few moments of heated back and forth, the lady nods then holds her head down, as if in shame. She turns and leaves. Before the door closes behind her, Pepper and Delani sneak in.

Delani's in a short, orange dress with puffy sleeves that interestingly matches her purple hair. She never seems to have a care in the world, especially when it comes to her appearance, which I greatly admire. I spent too much time under miss vain's *everything must be matchy-matchy* wing. Pepper is even more put together than I am in a navy dress with a lace bodice. Unlike me and Delani, she opted for heels. Have fun walking in the grass with those, girl.

"Pepper," one of the moms says, "it's been a while." The lady is dressed in an exquisite navy suit, reminding me of something miss vain would wear. It's a humorous contrast to Janet's wrangler jeans, cowboy boots, plaid shirt, and brown leather jacket. She is sans cowboy hat—I wonder if that was at Malachi's request.

Pepper returns the woman's hug. "It's so nice to see you Mrs. Becket." Pepper motions for me to join them. "Have you met Jade?"

"No, I haven't." Mrs. Becket smiles and takes my hands with hers. "So, you're the pretty girl that's escorting my son."

After school on Tuesday, I hung out with Pepper again while Delani was at volleyball practice. I was concerned that I was stepping on her toes with Tad. She assured me they were long done, having broken up amicably well over a year and a half ago, and she couldn't care less if I went out with him. I can't say we're dating because tonight is the only thing we've planned.

I've yet to figure him out, though. I can't tell if he's a great big mystery and I've barely scratched his surface, or if he's all surface and no substance, therefore, no mystery. He's a mixed bag of personalities and doesn't say a lot. He shows no emotion, not even in art.

"Attention, everyone," Principal Frances yells out in her southern twang. "Parents, get ready to line up on the field alphabetically. Girls, take a rose and go find your player. And no, the rose isn't for you, it's for the player's mom."

Pepper grabs three roses, hands one to me and one to Delani, then wraps her arms through ours and drags us out the door.

"Shit, I should've worn flats," she says as we step on the field and her navy heels sink into the ground.

Delani rolls her eyes. "Told ya."

"Yeah, yeah. You can't make a fashion statement without heels."

Delani waves over her attire and holds out her purple Conversed feet. "Says, who?"

"And Jade, why do you have on Onyx's jacket? It doesn't really go with your dress."

I wrap the jacket tighter. "Because it's forty degrees

outside. I don't care to make a fashion statement." And I'm rebelling against the tyranny of my ex-stepmother's fashion wrath. *Wow.* It's been a while since I've thought about the witch. Out of sight, out of mind.

She laughs. "What am I gonna do with you two? Try not to pull this crap next weekend for homecoming."

"Uh, I'm not on court. I'm not dressing up again," Delani says.

"I mean for the dance."

Delani shakes her head violently. "I'm not going to the dance."

"Yes, you are. We'll all go stag if none of these boneheads ask us."

"I'm not going if Malachi asks me. He can be his moody, dateless self."

Glad I'm not the only one who calls him moody. He didn't even ask Delani to escort him. Pepper arranged that during lunch on Wednesday when she found out he was escortless. Though it seemed more like she was trying to find an excuse to force Delani to go dress shopping with us that afternoon.

Along with the twelve other girls who are serving as escorts, we make our way to the far side of the field where the players stand, dressed in their football uniform.

Onyx winks at me then whispers as we pass, "You look good in my jacket."

I playfully shove him into Malachi who turns and walks away, dragging Delani with him.

"Where are we going?" she asks.

"Let's go line up," he mutters.

Pepper walks Onyx away, leaving me to stand with Tad.

"You look nice," he says, even though I haven't felt him really look at me. And why does *nice* always rub me wrong. It's like when someone says they're *fine*. They're really not *fine*. So, does *nice* really not mean *nice*?

"Thanks. You think you guys'll win tonight?"

He shrugs. "Maybe."

"Who are you playing?"

"Pitts County."

And that's how it's been all week. I've learned that if I want him to talk, I have to pull things out of him.

"So, what position do you play?"

"Quarterback."

"Oh." *Quarterback.* Meaning he's in charge and probably in the zone right now. I shouldn't bother him with the small talk. Hunter would never hang out with me on Fridays before the game. Something about hype time and the need to work it up. I was a distraction he couldn't have before game time.

Coach Brown claps over his head several times. "Start lining up."

"We're second behind Keaton Abbott," Tad says. He holds out his arm and looks at me, like really eyeballs me from head to toe, like he did on Monday, no part of me feels left untouched. "You do look really nice." His blue eyes shimmer and shoot me all kinds of questions, even though he remains silent.

I loop my arm through his and return his gaze, happily grabbing onto his bicep to steady me. It's the first time we've touched since meeting. I melt a little as my heart goes pitter-pat. Behind it all, there's an inkling of heart bleed that I brush aside.

Does he even realize how freaking sexy he is? So far, it's strictly by looks though.

I want to know if that brain matches the outside appearance. I want to carry on conversations about absolutely nothing and about the meaning of life with him, like I do with Onyx.

"Can I ask you a question?" he says. I've learned Tad doesn't come out and asks questions. He first asks if he can ask the question, and it's not very often that he asks anything. It's a little annoying, and it always makes me a bit anxious.

"Shoot," I respond.

He finally breaks eye contact and stutters a bit when he says, "Is there something going on between you and Onyx?"

Is he jealous?

"No, why? I mean, we live together. That would be super inappropriate."

Well, for the past week, I've had a couple of hot dreams about him. Unlike Tad, Onyx is confident and knows he's hot, and he's constantly flaunting himself in my face, usually trying to make me laugh. I can't help but to be in awe of the sharp lines of his jaw and the way he moves his powerful, lean body with easy grace. The way his green eyes of amber veins and brown rims light in a golden and emerald glow.

We're just friends. Good friends at that, well on our way to becoming best friends, possibly. If I can learn to open up, which I'm getting better at; he needs work in that department as well. The only conversations neither of us touch are about our pasts.

We always play the twenty question game, but it's Onyx who does all the pumping for responses. I've given up asking because he usually skirts around giving me an answer on the tougher questions. I've shared with him the simple reason of being kicked out for why I moved to the ranch. But that's all I've shared. He has yet to offer me the reason why he's there.

"Good." Tad's voice sounds relieved.

"Why do you ask?" I'm trying to put together the Tad puzzle, but none of the pieces seem to fit together.

"You have his jacket on." The muscles of his forearm harden beneath my hand.

"Only because I was cold."

"I would've given you my jacket to wear. I mean, I'll give you my jacket to wear." The unsureness in his voice wrecks me a little. Does he just lack self-confidence? Onyx needs to give him lessons.

"Like right now?"

"No, like later tonight, after the game." He turns

to look at me again, his eyes probing. "Want to go to Hawks after the game?"

I run my finger along his arm, causing his hairs to stand at attention. "Yeah, that'd be great, but what's Hawks?"

His eyebrows raise as if in surprise, but he gives me an irresistibly devastating grin that I haven't seen before. "It's this burger joint just outside of town toward the highway. A bunch of us usually go after a game."

The announcer welcomes everyone to the field as a special moment passes between Tad and me. At least, in my mind it feels like we've crossed over a bridge.

He's serving me more clues in his mystery. He's on the shy side. The confident side of him only makes a visit when he's around other football players, excluding Onyx and Malachi. Maybe he's starting to feel more comfortable with me, seeing as this is the longest conversation we've had outside of discussing art-related topics.

We're announced and he tears his eyes away from me with cheeks full of fire, or maybe that's just the cool air whipping around our faces. We're blowing smoke like chimneys as we exhale the frosty air. He leads me to the center of the field where his parents wait. His dad's eyes meet mine for a second, then he glances away with a smug look. He presents his mother with the rose before we shuffle to the sideline to allow the next senior their time to shine.

My gaze finds Onyx standing with Pepper; two more seniors to go then it's his turn. That's when it dawns on me, and a feeling of regret for not escorting him sweeps over me. He has no one to meet on the field. I asked him a few days ago what happened to his parents. He didn't give me an answer, but the hollow look in his usually solid eyes told me what I needed to know.

His smile and laughter tells me he's not bothered by it tonight, but that's another thing I've learned this past week. He's good at masking his feelings. I feel like I'm a pro at it, so I can spot it when someone else is doing it.

Finally, his name is called. Out of the corner of my eye I see Janet leave her spot in line and walk to the center of the field. Of course, leave it to her to ensure he's taken care of. I can't tell if he's tearing up from here, but I see the emotions on his face. He hugs her and they walk together, arm in arm, toward the sideline. Janet then leaves and circles back in line for Malachi.

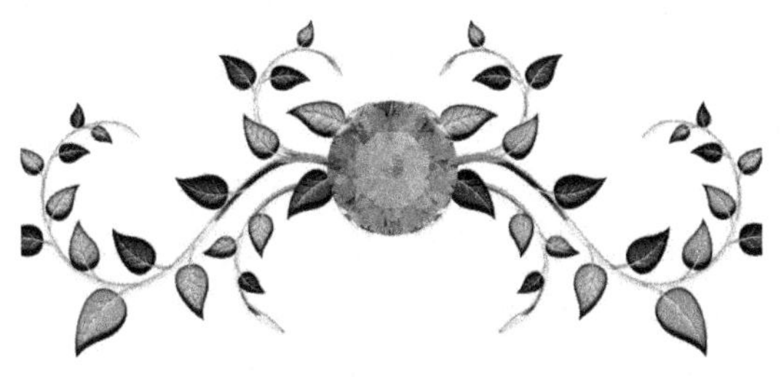

CHAPTER 13

I NEVER WATCHED MUCH football before Hunter came along. I did my best to learn as much about it as I could since it was such a big part of his life. He taught me all about it, signing me up for *Hunter's Take on Football 101*. According to Hunter, there are four key positions.

The quarterback, obviously. I only have Hunter and the quarterbacks he played against to compare. Hunter is exceptional, and that's why he was being heavily recruited and hoped to commit to play football at State.

Tad? I was impressed with his leadership on the field. I didn't expect that based on what I've observed of him this week. He has a good arm. He works well in what Hunter called the pocket, but if that collapses, he's frantic in trying to escape the pressure. The guys that are supposed to protect him failed him repeatedly. He was taken down three times before getting rid of the ball and threw two passes to the opposite team.

Another position that's key is the guy who goes down field to catch the ball—the receiver. Usually there are two. Malachi is one of Tad's receivers. And he was off. Tad threw him so many good passes. It was like his hands were coated in oil; the ball slipped right through them every single time. Delani was speechless. Apparently, it's not the norm. He and Tad are known as the dynamic duo on the field. We sat near my aunt, and I had never heard so many curse words come out of her mouth before.

Then you have the running back, which apparently Bradley County doesn't have because their running game sucks.

If Bradley County played Merryville, I hate to say it, but they'd get bulldozed. Like smeared on the ground with blood and dirt everywhere—demolished.

The only reason Bradley won was that last key position. Hunter says most people think it's not that important; he disagrees and after tonight, I finally understand why.

Onyx's field goal in the last few seconds of the game is what put them up by one. One point to win the game and it was because of the kicker. During kickoffs, Onyx pinned the opposing team so deep, they rarely made it out after the first few drives.

I can't help but to laugh. After the way the other players treated him all week, I thought he was going to be one of those glory positions, always catching passes or running for touchdowns. He's the kicker! But a damn

good one. He also led the team huddle before the game started and at the end of halftime, totally pumping up the players. No wonder they bow to his feet at school. He's a natural motivator.

After the game, Pepper and Delani leave to claim a table at Hawks. I wait on the boys in the parking lot at the entrance to the field. Onyx comes out first, then Malachi. They head on to Hawks after I insisted Onyx could leave me by myself. After I'm the only one left hanging around, I start to wonder if Tad sneaked past me, forgetting he asked me to ride with him. Finally, he walks out of the field house, dressed to perfection, not a sign of wet hair like most of the other players.

Primp much?

"Thanks for waiting on me."

"You're welcome."

We walk to his truck and drive to Hawks in silence. He pulls into a parking space and turns off his truck.

He hands me his letterman's jacket. "You can give Onyx his jacket back."

"Won't you be cold?"

He shrugs but tugs on his Bradley County football sweatshirt. "This is pretty warm."

I wiggle out of Onyx's jacket and put on Tad's. Vanilla and pastries infiltrate my nose, washing away Onyx's earthy scent. The extreme difference in smells is somewhat comical. Like the earth mover versus the mama's bakery boy.

Tad evacuates the truck and I hesitate for a moment out of habit. Miss vain always said guys should open doors for you every time. Hunter was good about opening doors. And anywhere I've gone with Onyx this week, he's always been quite the gentleman. Tad walks and pauses in front of the vehicle while shoving his hands in his sweatshirt.

So much for that. It doesn't upset me; I'm not the dependent type. I don't need to have my door opened for me.

I follow him inside where he passes high fives to the rest of the football players then slips into a booth in the back of the restaurant next to Malachi. Delani and Pepper sit opposite of them, and Onyx is in a backwards chair at the end of the booth. I hand him his jacket then glance around, hoping to find a seat nearby. The restaurant is packed; no empty seats in sight.

"Sit here." Onyx stands and turns the chair around.

"We can squeeze," Pepper says, squashing Delani against the window. Onyx flips the chair back and straddles it again.

As I sit down next to Pepper, my knees brush against Onyx's long legs. He grabs my legs and sets them across his lap then hands me a menu.

"What's good?" I ask.

"The patty melt is to die for if that's your kind of thing," Onyx says.

"I'm not really that hungry. Are the fries any good?"

He nods. "You can have some of mine."

The waitress takes our orders then brings our sodas.

The conversation is a repeat of how the week went at lunch. Onyx and Pepper talk while everyone else throws in a tidbit here and there. Only tonight, Malachi doesn't say anything and Tad has his lips sealed. It's four girls and a guy talking about what went down on the football field. Delani tries to probe Malachi for why he was out of whack during the game. He closes his eyes and lays his head against the window.

When the burgers and fries are delivered, the conversation ceases.

"Take a bite." Onyx shoves half of his patty melt in my face.

"You know that has onions on it," Tad says with a scowl.

I'm okay with onions. But is he saying that because he plans on kissing me tonight and doesn't want me to have onion breath? Like I'd want to kiss him after he didn't even offer me the open seat.

I take a small bite to appease Onyx. The burger smothered in caramelized onions and melted cheese soothes my taste buds. "I don't recall ever having a patty melt but I now have a new favorite thing. That's freaking yum."

"It's disgusting," Tad mutters.

Onyx waves him off. "You've never had one."

After asking for an extra plate, Onyx gives me half his patty melt and fries. Tad doesn't offer me any of

his food. Silence ensues as everyone chows down. I finish off the food in no time, surprised by my appetite.

Tad crumples his napkin on top of the lettuce, pickle, tomatoes, and onions he removed from his cheeseburger and slides his plate to the center.

"What's the plan for the homecoming dance next weekend?" Pepper asks as she dips a fry in mayonnaise. *Weird.*

"I was going to ask Jade to go with me," Tad says, not even looking at me.

WTF? *Hello! I'm right here.* I wave my hand around, but he doesn't notice. Onyx lets out a stifled chuckle.

Malachi shoves his plate to the center of the table then waves his hands at Tad. "Let me out."

Tad stands and Malachi slides out of the booth. He rifles through his wallet and drops a twenty on the table. "I'm going home." He turns and leaves.

Another *WTF.* I was supposed to ride home with him.

Pepper turns to Delani. "Seriously. What's his problem?"

Delani shrugs. "Why is it my problem now to figure out what his problem is? We've been broken up for well over a year. And he's the one that broke up with me. Don't know. Don't care. "

"But you know him better than anyone."

She juts her chin toward me and says, "Not anymore."

Onyx takes my feet from his lap and puts them on the ground. "Scoot over, Tadpole." He waves his hand

in front of Tad's face that's frozen with blank eyes and a dropped jaw. "I'm sure the girls don't want to be shoved in like sardines."

Onyx holds his chair out for me then moves in next to Tad who shakes away whatever thought had him stuck.

"So, homecoming?" Pepper brings up again.

"I'm out," Delani says.

"I'm going with Jade," Tad says.

I want to yell out, *Excuse me?* but I bite my tongue. I'm still new here and not ready to reveal my snark, despite his rudeness.

Pepper points at Onyx. "Then that leaves you and me."

"Okay," Onyx replies with a face of indifference.

"The four of us can go together then," Pepper adds.

A waitress with pink stripes scattered throughout her white hair returns with our tabs, smacking her gum as she says, "I'll take these when you're ready."

I try to give Onyx money for the food but he refuses. After heading outside, I stand beside Tad as Delani and Pepper head to Pepper's red Civic. Onyx stands next to his motorcycle.

"Oh, I guess you need a ride home," Tad says and walks to the driver's side of his truck.

I scrunch my forehead and walk to the passenger door as Onyx lets out a little laugh. "You can ride home with me. I have an extra helmet."

I almost hop on his bike. But I need to figure out what the deal is with Tad. Is he just going to assume that I'm going with him or is he going to actually ask me? "I'll see you there," I say as Onyx slips on his helmet.

The silence on the drive home is mind numbing. I'm sitting here in Tad's letterman jacket, apparently going to homecoming with him if saying he's going with me counts as an ask, and he can't even speak to me.

Finally, as he pulls under the Diamond Ranch sign, I break the silence. "So, you want to go to homecoming together?"

"Yeah."

Okay. That went well.

I lean my head against the window and stare out into the vastness of the ranch, wishing this driveway was shorter. At last, he pulls into the roundabout in front of the house.

"Thanks for the ride home." I get out and close the door, willing myself not to slam it.

The passenger window rolls down and he leans over to say, "Hey, Jade? Can I ask you something?"

I turn around with an incredulous face. "Sure."

"You want to meet me tomorrow at Sadie's Ice Palace?"

"'What's that?"

He laughs. "You don't know what Sadie's is?"

"Um, no. I just moved here. I don't know anything about this town." I can't keep the sarcasm out of my

voice but Tad's goofy grin tells me it's flown over his head.

"Best chocolate ice cream in Maybee."

Well that's not saying much.

"I'll be there around four tomorrow if you want to meet me," he continues.

"Sure."

He rolls up the window and leaves.

I stomp up the stairs, unsure of what tonight was. Malachi's voice comes from the farside of the porch where he's rocking on the porch swing, a gentle yellow glow from the window lights his hard jaw. "So, you and Tad a thing?"

I'm not in the mood to discuss what Tad and I are, especially since I have no clue. "No."

"Well, you're wearing his jacket."

"Is that supposed to mean something?"

"It means you guys are a thing."

My nerves throb. I want this conversation to end so I can go upstairs and go to bed. "Shouldn't he ask me to be a thing and not just assume we are by giving me his jacket?"

"That's just the way things work around here."

"That's pretty stupid. I mean, he didn't even ask me to the homecoming dance. Just announced it. Why would I want to have a *thing* with someone who barely talks to me?"

He regards me with a speculative stare. "Be gentle," he says, his voice layered with emotions.

I let out a long, exhausted sigh. "What do you mean by *be gentle*?"

He stands and leans against the porch rail, crossing his arms. "He's interested in you."

"He sure has a great way of showing it."

"Look, I've known him for a long time. He can be a little slow. Just don't chew him up and spit him out."

My lip curls up in disgust. "Is that what you think of me? That I'm some fast-paced, rabid animal leaving a path of destruction everywhere I go?" The unnecessary bitterness spills over into my voice as I continue. "You've barely talked to me since I've been here. And now, you can't even talk to me to see how I'm adjusting. Instead, you're berating me because you think your best friend is too fragile for me. Well, guess what? I'm the one who's actually some delicate egg. So stop trying to crack me." Tears tremble in my eyelids.

He closes his eyes and pinches the bridge of his nose. "That's not what I meant."

"You know what? Leave me alone. We used to be best friends, Mal. But now, I don't even know who you are."

I turn and walk through the front door as hot tears roll down my face.

Malachi calls out, "Wait."

But I head upstairs without a pause. If he cares, he can come to me. I've put in effort this week to reconnect. He's the one who's refusing to plug in.

VICTORIA ANDERS

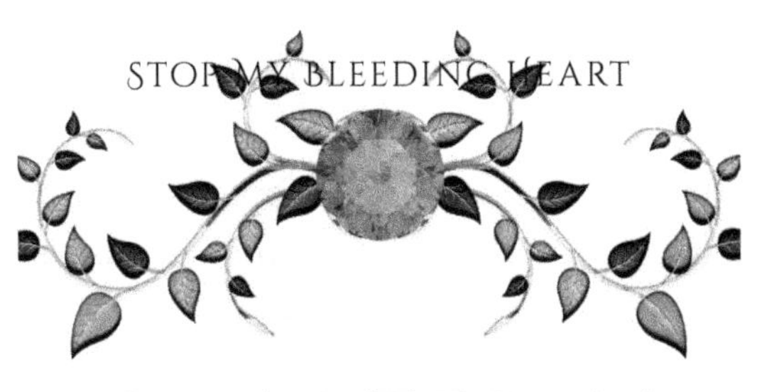

CHAPTER 14

AFTER WASHING MY face and changing into a pair of shorts and a tank top, I plug in my phone that went dead while I was waiting for Tad after the game to juice it up enough so I can play some mind-numbing game before my eyelids become too heavy to hold. I should be writing my three things from the day, but I'm wallowing in self pity. I can't even begin to think of anything that I want to commemorate from the day.

Once my phone powers on, several text notifications pop up, including one that makes my stomach turn.

First Tad's weird behavior, then Malachi's misdirected apprehension, and now this.

THE HUNTER GREEN: Wow.

I didn't realize you were so

fragile. Seriously moving just because I broke up with you?

I know I should cool off before responding but I can't. I start typing a response as another one comes in.

THE HUNTER GREEN: State offered me a scholarship today. I feel like a ton of bricks have been lifted from my shoulders. Just wanted you to know that...and I miss you.

JADE: If you think you had anything to do with me moving, then you don't know me very well.

Hunter wanted that scholarship so bad and he worked hard for it in the months I knew him. I really am happy for him. I swallow my bitterness down and shoot him off another text.

JADE: And congrats on the scholarship. You'll do great there.

Why am I even messaging him? My mind still replays his cold-hearted breakup on the second worst day of my life. Am I trying to torture myself? I need more time to erase the pain, but instead, I'm fueling it.

Two seconds later, he responds.

> **THE HUNTER GREEN:** Then why did you move?

> **JADE:** Hag kicked me out on my birthday.

Hunter didn't know the full story of my life, but he knew that my dad had died and that I didn't have the best relationship with my stepmother. We were kindred spirits when it came to stepparents.

My phone rings. Hunter's devastatingly handsome face pops up. *Ugh.* Tad looks so much like him. My fingers twitch. Should I answer it? It rings three more times then goes silent. A message follows two seconds later.

> **THE HUNTER GREEN:** Pick up.

It rings again and I do as he commands. Maybe out of curiosity? Maybe because my heart still hurts from his rejection? Maybe because I like to torture myself?

"Hello?"

"Hey, sexy." His sultry statement sends a warm shiver down the length of my spine.

"What do you want, Hunter?" My voice comes out with layers of anger like a dagger slashing at his name.

"I deserve that."

"I'm in bed and want to go to sleep."

"What are you wearing?"

I grit my teeth then say, "I'm tired."

"It's only eleven. Since when do you go to bed before one a.m.?"

"Enough of the small talk. What do you want?"

He's silent for a few seconds but then, "I'm sorry," comes out in a rushed mumble.

"For what?"

"For getting scared and bailing on you." His misery is so severe it's like a physical pain.

I release a breath into the speaker. That sound always annoyed him unless it was a breathy release from getting hot and bothered over the phone.

"Let me make it up to you," he says. "Go out with me tomorrow night. We'll go to Canal Walk, find a spot to have dinner, take a gondola ride, and figure us out."

The words thrill me, but they also frighten me. "There is no us," I whisper.

His tone is tender, almost a murmur when he says, "Please, Jade, I miss you."

A pulsing knot twists from within. I *won't* fall into his trap. "I'm too far away, now."

"Where did you move to?"

"Kentucky."

"What part?"

"North of Lexington."

"Why?"

"My aunt lives here."

He lets out a long breath. "Meet me in Louisville then. We can get a hotel and spend the night together. And work it out."

Still reeling from Tad's behaviour and Malichi's accusation, I almost consider breaking the ice cream date and leaving Maybee behind for the day. But I can't go there with Hunter. He'll want to do more than just sleep, and in my lowly state, I'll give in only to later regret it.

"There is no us," I say. "You made that clear a week ago with your shitty ass breakup."

His speech slurs. "I need you, Jade. And not to have sex. I'll be a good boy."

He's drunk. I'm shocked—he always claimed to avoid drinking during football season. Drunk dialing at its finest. Knowing this makes it easier to not cave to his wishes.

Deflecting, I ask, "Have you been drinking?"

"Just a little celebratory drink."

"A little? Sounds more than just a little."

"Okay." The rattling sound of cans crushing together comes through as he counts. "One, two, three, four, and this one makes five."

"How about this then. If you remember this conversation in the morning, call me and maybe I'll consider meeting you sometime. But not tomorrow. I already have plans."

"Oh, I'll remember." His voice is low and purposefully seductive.

"Good night, Hunter."

Before he has a chance to respond, I hang up.

The nerve! Who in the hell does he think he is calling me like this, barely a week after he broke up with me. If he misses me, why was it so easy for him to end things that day? On my birthday of all days.

I slam my head back into a pillow. A knock on my door pulls me from the current misery and reminds me of the previous misery I had just before coming to my room. "Go away, Malachi. I'm tired. If you want to talk, we can talk tomorrow."

The door opens and Onyx peeks in. "I gave up waiting on you after the seventh shooting star." He holds up a mug piled high with marshmallows. "It's kinda still warm."

I sit up and lean against the headboard. "Come in."

He sets the cup on my bedside table then waves his hands. "Scooch over."

I slide to the middle of the bed. He sits facing me and wipes the tears from my face. I'm so numb that I didn't even notice they were falling.

"What's got you gushing like Niagara Falls?" he

asks. Although his question is meant to make me laugh—which it does—his face is full of strength. A serene peace as his eyes wrap me in their energy.

"Life," I admit.

My phone chimes, signaling another text. Onyx's eyes dart to the screen before I have a chance to react. I don't bother picking it up and reading it. I'd bet my car it's Hunter bumbling like the drunk idiot he currently is.

"I see." Onyx's lips quirk into a bemused smile. "Boy trouble. I didn't realize you have three boyfriends. And you call me a player."

I can't help laughing aloud; it's tinged with a bit of hysteria. "Three boyfriends? And here I was crying because I don't have a single one."

"Oh, but my dear princess, you wore two jackets of your suitors this evening. And now, The Hunter Green is saying he really does miss you. He misses your eyes. He misses your lips. He misses your mouth around his—"

"He did not!" I yell, grabbing my phone from the bed. The embarrassment quickly turns to annoyance when I read Hunter's text. I slam my head against the headboard, making it jar the wall.

"Watch out, Hulk. Don't tear the house down."

"Stupid jerk," I mumble as a suffocating sensation tightens my throat. I gulp hard as the hot tears slide down my cheeks.

Onyx wraps me in his warm, friendly embrace. "Hey, I'm only kidding with you. Not about the text obviously. What can I do? I don't like to see you upset."

I shake my head as I drench his AC/DC tee.

"Talk to me, princess. You've become my best friend in only a week. Let me help."

I pull away. "I'm fine. Just too much all at once. I'll get over it."

"Let me guess. You have a boyfriend you left behind. And then Tad presented you with his jacket and now you're all torn between Tad and this *The* Hunter Green."

He points to my phone again which lights up with another I miss you text followed by please stay with me tomorrow night. I promise I won't pressure you. I didn't break up with you because you weren't ready to have sex. I had a bad fight with the stepdad that morning and I took it out on you. I'm empty and lost without you.

"He must be something special if you have him in your phone as *The* Hunter Green," Onyx says.

"He was. But not anymore." I pick up my phone again and type out a text. Onyx watches me.

> **JADE:** I'm turning off my phone now. Don't message me again until you're sober.

"Ah, a drunken booty text." Amusement flickers in his eyes as they meet mine. "Those are the best."

I swipe to my contacts and delete *the* from Hunter's name then turn off my phone. Hunter's the one who put his name in my phone like that on the first day I met him.

"Oh, princess is getting serious. She's downgrading Hunter, taking away his title."

A smile tips at the corner of my mouth.

Onyx winks. "That's the smile I like to see."

"Thank you. You always make me feel better."

He brushes a strand of hair behind my ear that fell from my loose bun. "No more tears, okay? This Hunter dude obviously isn't worth them."

I nod. I won't shed another tear over Hunter. A large part of me wants to meet him just to tell him that it won't work out. An even bigger part wants me to see him grovel at my feet. A tiny part wants to be in his arms and covered in his kisses.

His face adopts a sullen look. "So, you and Tad, ah?"

I glance at the green letterman's jacket hanging on my desk chair. "I don't know. He's barely talked to me. Is it really a thing when a guy gives you his jacket, he's asking you to go out, to be a *thing*?"

"Around these parts, yep. And Tad is a man of few words, sometimes even on the football field. Those are the games we usually lose."

"If he wants to have a *thing,* he needs to learn to talk to me so I can get to know him and figure out if there's anything even there. I mean, he's hot and all, but I need mental stimulation as well."

He chuckles—it's a dry and cynical sound. "Mental stimulation? Did *The* Hunter Green provide you with that?"

"He's no longer *The.* And yes, sometimes he did." Kind of. When he talked passionately about his interests. Having lost all my interests when my dad died, I didn't have a lot to bring to the table. I was nice and attentive to what he liked to do and picked some of his interests up myself. He got mad at me when I beat *The Last of Us Part II* before he did because I was really good at being stealth and using a combat move that he could never pull off.

"So, what happened? You guys break up because of the move?"

"No. He broke up with me before I found out I was moving. The same day my stepmom kicked me out but before." My eyes trace the orange paint strokes on my comforter. "Last Thursday. My eighteenth birthday."

Onyx's eyes bug out. "The day you moved here was your birthday?"

I gnaw on my bottom lip and nod.

"Well, I'll be. Happy late fucking birthday to you." Sadness clouds his features, even though a smile stays.

I break out into a manic fit of laughter. Welcome to Jade's world. A yawn breaks the hysterics. I shove Onyx off my bed. "Now leave me alone. I'm going to bed."

He leaves, and I break out my iPad to write one thing for the day.

Onyx made me laugh and
forget about my troubles.

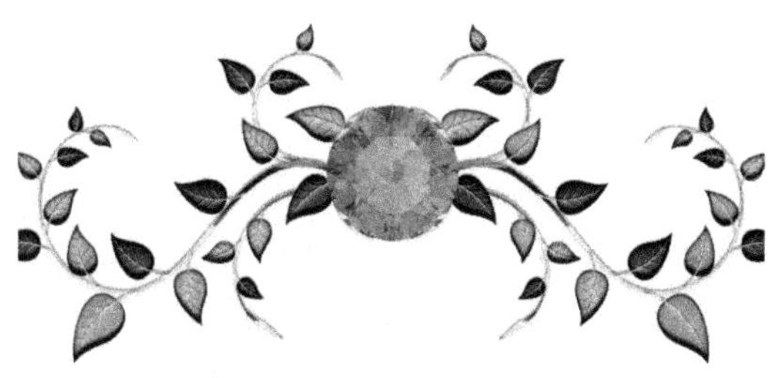

CHAPTER 15

TO MEET OR not to meet Tad for ice cream. I've been mulling over that question all morning long. Well, all afternoon long. I'm usually not this late of a sleeper, but I had a fitful sleep, waking up every hour. Finally, at about seven this morning, I fell into a hard slumber and didn't wake up until a few minutes after twelve.

I've stayed in bed, only to vacate after a few hours to take a shower and get dressed and ready, in case I decide to meet Tad. I have just under an hour before I need to leave. I'll feel guilty if I don't go since I told him I'd be there. I don't have his cell, so I can't text him that I'm not coming.

I could easily get his number from Mal or Onyx, but part of me wants to meet him. I'm still hoping there's a mystery to unravel, but I don't believe there is. Maybe there is a bit more depth to him that I just need to unearth. Mal said he was interested in me. I need to see if I can be interested in him.

In art, I spent the week watching him draw as I attempted sketching ideas for my exhibit. Mrs. Hannigan probably thinks I have no artistic ability at all. Every time she comes by my table, I'm erasing something on my iPad. Inspiration hasn't hit me yet. I have just over two months to find it.

Tad's incredibly talented in his cartoon style of drawing. However, I've learned he has no interest in any other art form. I tried to get his opinion on a couple of ideas I had for my theme, but he offered a shrug with no advice and went back to refining the googly eyes on a drawing of an animated frog.

"Knock, knock." Janet's voice sounds from the other side of my door.

"Come in," I say.

She comes in and sits down on my bed beside me. "How you doing, kiddo?"

"I'm alright."

Her eyes search me. "You sure?"

A suffocating sensation tightens in my throat. Déjà vu sets in. It's like my dad is sitting here on the bed with me, questioning why I had a bad day, searching me with those same gray eyes. I swallow hard and attempt to bite back the tears. But I fail.

Janet wraps her arms around me and lets me bawl, rocking me back and forth. Minutes pass and the body

shakes ease. She squeezes my cheeks. "You know I'm here anytime you need a hug. Anytime you need to talk about it. Okay?"

I nod and one last sob releases.

"I spoke to the lawyer again. Still no update. I also spoke to the Merryville police. They're considering reopening the investigation."

I nod again. Will this ever get easier to talk about?

"Do you want me to keep you updated?"

I weigh her question. Part of me just wants to forget. "I honestly don't want to think about her at all."

She grabs a tissue from my nightstand and swipes it over my eyes. Thank goodness for waterproof mascara. "I'll only tell you something if it's big. Okay?"

"Okay."

"You got a minute to come to the kitchen? I need your help with something."

"Of course." Although I don't know how much help I can be in the kitchen. I overcooked the hard boiled eggs in cooking class this week, leaving a thick, green sulphur ring around the yolk. My partner, some girl who fawned over Onyx the entire period, told me they cook for twelve minutes on high after the water starts to boil when I was supposed to turn the stove off once the water reached a boil then let the eggs sit for twelve minutes.

After checking the time, I grab my keys, purse, and a jacket then follow Janet into the kitchen.

The entire household, excluding Malachi, surrounds a beautiful, two-tiered cake iced in white with veins of gold and green streaked throughout. A portion of each tier is cut out and filled to look like an emerald geode. A gold cutout that says *Jade is 18* sits on top with a long, green candle. Onyx lights it when I enter, and it emits gold sparkles.

An unharmonious chorus of *Happy Birthday* begins, making my heart warm. Not a single person wished me a happy birthday last week.

Janet hugs me once the animal calls die off. "I'm sorry that I didn't wish you a happy birthday. I planned to call you that evening but then you came here and it totally slipped my mind."

I hug her back and say, "No worries. It was a whirlwind of a day."

Onyx cuts the cake and hands plates to everyone, giving me the first slice. The elegant exterior clashes with the party on the interior. It's a white cake with strawberry filling and a whipped buttercream cream frosting that tastes like my dad's french toast.

"Oh my," I say, licking my fork clean as Onyx watches me. "This thing is the bomb."

He takes a bite then, with his mouth full, says, "I've been wanting to try this recipe. You gave me an excuse when I found out your birthday was last week."

"You made this?"

He nods.

"Like decorated it and all?"

He nods again.

"Wow. Do you want to go to culinary school after graduation?"

He frowns and shrugs.

Janet claps her hands. "Okay, kids. Time to exercise the horses."

Everyone but Onyx and I moan as they leave the kitchen.

"I'll be out there as soon as I clean up," Onyx calls out. "Leave Nutmeg for me."

"Thanks for this," I say.

"You're welcome."

"And you really should consider going to culinary school. Or just skip that altogether and open a restaurant or bakery. Damn, boy. You can cook and bake." He's made dinner several times this week, from lasagna to ribeye steaks with loaded baked potatoes—everything has been delicious. How he has time to cook such elaborate dinners along with football practice and stable duties is beyond me.

He gives me a smile that doesn't touch his eyes. Instead, something flickers far back in them as if masking a secret. "Where you heading off to looking all princessy, princess?"

"I look princessy?" I glance down at my attire. Tight, black jean overalls with holes in the knees and a plain white tee underneath. Throw on the green

leather jacket and I look like I'm a member of a biker gang that farms snakes.

"You always look like a princess." This time, his smile takes over his face and his eyes.

"I'm meeting Tad at Sadie's for ice cream."

"Ah. Don't get the chocolate. I swear she puts a laxative in the mixture."

I laugh, remembering Tad said the chocolate was the best in town. "I won't. I'm an orange sherbet kind of girl."

"Is that why you painted your walls that color?"

"That's part of the reason."

He gathers the empty plates and tosses them in the garbage can.

"What are you doing tomorrow?" I ask.

"Whatever Janet needs."

"I have a favor. Can you go with me to Louisville? I'm meeting Hunter at a mall for lunch. I don't want to go by myself. You can hang out at the mall while I meet with him. There's also a movie theater. I'll get you a ticket to watch whatever you want, so you won't be bored."

"You decided to meet him?"

"Yeah, I really need closure."

"I'd do anything for you, but I'm not letting you buy my movie ticket. I can afford to buy one myself."

"That's not what I meant. I don't want you wasting your day for me, so I want to make it worthwhile."

His eyes sparkle like the candle on his cake. He starts to say something but the timer on my phone goes off, telling me I need to leave to meet Tad. He clamps his mouth shut.

"Thanks, Onyx. I'm off to meet Tadpole now."

His face contorts into a cross-eyed, goofy-grinned cartoon character. "Anytime, princess."

He follows me out the front door and leaves me at my car. He continues on to the Dogwood stable, skipping. Skipping! He turns around, catching me watching him, then winks.

One of the times I woke up overnight, I turned my phone back on to eleven messages from Hunter. I knew if I didn't meet him and come to some resolution with him and *us*, he'd continue to message me until I did. Persistency is something he's good at. So I caved and said I'd meet him Sunday for a few hours.

I don't think he'll be too thrilled that I'm bringing someone. I believe that having Onyx there, even though he won't be hanging out with us, will keep me from caving to the charms of Hunter Green.

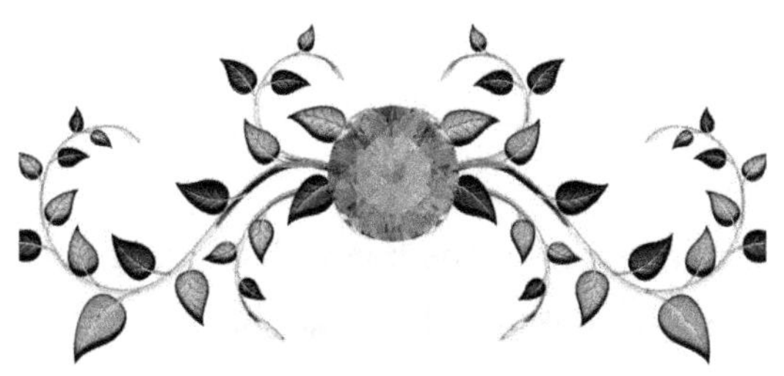

CHAPTER 16

I CIRCLE THE MAYBEE courthouse and find the little ice cream shop on the corner of the square just as Onyx said I would. I don't see Tad waiting outside. And I don't see his truck either. Maybe he decided to bail. Or he's just late.

I'm right on time, so I park and wait.

After ten minutes, I go in only to find him sitting at a booth with a bowl of chocolate ice cream. Not a soul in the shop other than the girl working—well, doing something on her phone behind the silver counter without even acknowledging me when I enter.

"There you are," he says. "I was about to text Malachi for your number."

I slide into the seat across from him. "I was waiting outside. I didn't see your truck."

"I walked."

"Oh, you live near here?"

He nods.

"Cool."

"Um, if you want ice cream, you'll have to go to the counter."

I turn and look at the board displaying a long list of flavors. "Oh. Okay. I'll be right back."

After ordering, I sit back down across from Tad with a single scoop of orange sherbet atop a sugar cone.

"What's that?" he asks.

I raise my eyebrows in question. "You've never had orange sherbet?"

He lifts his upper lip in disgust and shakes his head.

I shove the cone in his face, channeling my inner Onyx. "It's delicious. Try it."

He flinches back and shakes his head. "No thanks."

I shrug. His loss.

"You're not wearing my jacket." His eyes drop down to the retro-style laminate table top.

"Yeah, about that. Um. What did you mean by giving me your jacket?"

He lifts his shoulders then drops them. "You know."

He hasn't responded to my heavy sarcasm all week, so I go with the innocent approach. I smile sweetly and talk in a semi-baby voice. "No, I don't know. I'm a city girl, I'm not used to how things are here in Maybee. I found out that being given a jacket means that we're a thing. But that's not the way things work where I'm

from. It usually just means that you thought I was cold." I point between the two of us and add a little more grown-up to my voice. "If we're a thing, I want to be asked out."

He drops his spoon in his bowl and a wave of confidence that I haven't seen on him washes over his face. It's like my giving him permission opened up a whole new world. He reaches over and grabs my free hand from the table's surface, sending a few tingles racing up my arm. He stares at me hard with those aquamarine eyes. "Jade, I think you're pretty and would really like you to be my girlfriend."

A giggle escapes. Suddenly, I feel like I'm transported back to third grade when I received a note from Wilson Yunich, asking me to be his girl with two empty squares, one labeled yes and the other labeled no. Malachi's *a little slow* repeats in my head.

"Well, where I'm from, we go out on a couple of dates to get to know each other then determine whether we'd fit as boyfriend girlfriend."

"Okay. This is a date then."

Hardly, I want to say. In my book, asking someone to meet up somewhere isn't really a date.

As if reading my mind for the first time, he adds, "Will you continue this date by going down the street with me and having dinner at Stevie's pizza?"

"Then it's a date," I say with a timid smile.

AFTER A DINNER of plain pepperoni pizza cooked to a crisp, the mystery has been solved. Cartoons, video games, and football fill the mind of Tad Becket. Once I discovered those topics, I was able to have decently flowing conversations with him. That was thanks to Hunter's love of all three, making me realize he's even more like Hunter than I'd assumed. The main differences of the two are personality, confidence, and overt sexual innuendos. And Hunter is definitely not slow when it comes to girls.

We walk back toward the ice cream shop where my car's parked. He was about to leave me and head home after we left Stevie's, but I told him that the boy should walk the girl back to her vehicle on a date. I loop by arm in his, even though he didn't offer. Something tells me I'll need to be the initiator in this relationship.

I'm doing him a favor by teaching him dating 101. When he heads to college, if he doesn't have a few basic dating skills, he's going to be a lonely person. I need to interrogate Pepper as to what went on in their dating life. They were together for two years. Was he always this way?

A flashing neon sign blinks at me from an alleyway. "Is that a tattoo shop?"

His bicep tightens around my hold. "I think so. Why?"

I pull him down the path. "I want a tattoo."

He snarls at me. "Why?"

Realizing that tattoos may be too risque for Tad, I take another glance and recall the name to memory, so I can inquire about getting one later. *Prince's Tattoo Parlour.* I wonder if it has any relation to the *Prince* photographer at school?

After a few more steps in silence, Tad asks, "You'd really get a tattoo?"

"Yeah, in honor of my mom and dad. My mom died when I was five and my dad earlier this year." I'm able to get it out without a quiver in my voice or a lump building in my throat.

"I'm sorry."

"Thanks." We arrive at my car. "And thanks for walking me to my car."

I stand on my tippy toes and plant a soft kiss to his cheek. "Thanks for dinner. Have a good night. I'll see you at school on Monday."

He grins with no trace of his former animosity at my wanting a tattoo. "Can I ask you something?"

"Ask away."

"Will you come to dinner at my house tomorrow night?"

Family dinner already? "I have plans," I say with my bottom lip puffed. "I'm driving to meet a friend in Louisville. Maybe another time."

"My mom cooks a big meal every Sunday, so come next Sunday. And we have the homecoming dance on Saturday. Then maybe you'll wear my jacket again."

At least he gets what I was saying—that he has to work toward a relationship. Woe me Tad Becket. Woe me. Your looks do it for me. Now maybe your brain will too.

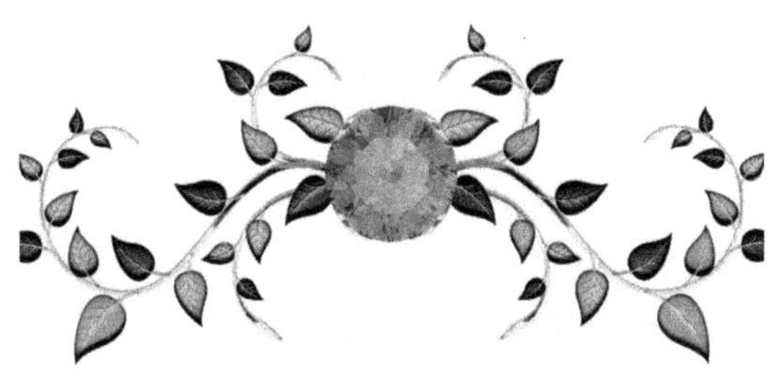

CHAPTER 17

"I'D LOVE TO drive your baby if you'd let me," Onyx says when we walk out of the house on Sunday morning. His eyes twinkle as they beg me—the look I often get when a guy asks to drive my car.

I press the button on the remote to unlock the doors. "How about on the way back? Driving there will distract me."

"Can we ride with the top down?"

My jaw drops at his question. Boys just don't get it. "Uh, hair." I point to the waviness I so meticulously crafted this morning.

His smile's smug when he says, "Oh, right. Couldn't look bad for *The* Hunter Green, now could we."

I open my door and slide into the leather seat. "We can on the way back." I pop one of the hair ties that's wrapped around the gear shift. "That's why I keep a supply here. And no, I don't have to look good for

171

Hunter. But I do want him to remember me at my best when I tell him there's no chance of getting back together."

"Cold."

"Hearted," I add.

He quirks up his eyebrows when he says, "Snake?"

I laugh then turn on the ignition and hand him my phone. "You're in charge of the play list. My only rule is absolutely no country music."

"I can handle that." He clicks on his seatbelt. "How did you score this kind of car? I mean, you're a princess. And this is definitely a princess car. But most princesses I know—Pepper—drive little four-cylinders like hers. Not this sporty six-cylinder that probably goes faster than any car I've ever driven before."

This car is the one thing that came from miss vain, but not as a direct gift from her, even though she played it that way. My dad bought her a brand new car, even shinier and sportier than this one which meant I got this older, but still amazing, BMW hardtop convertible. "It was a hand me down from my dad when I turned sixteen."

"Well, happy fucking birthday to the little princess."

A week ago, if he had said that to me, I probably would have bawled my eyes out and never wanted to speak to him again. But if I've learned anything about Onyx this week, most everything he says is 95% bullshit and 99% sarcastic. Sarcasm is my first language, thanks to my dad.

The hour-and-a-half drive goes by quickly, and I don't have time to think about where I'm heading. Onyx keeps me occupied flipping from song to song. He finds some of my playlists amusing but lingered a bit too long on my more sensual selection featuring Labrinth, Missio, and Banks. He played *Bloodstream* by Stateless three times in a row, making me channel my old infatuation with Damon from *The Vampire Diaries*. I don't need to get all steamed up before meeting Hunter. It might not go in the right direction, so I force Onyx to flip to my angry chick music playlist for the last twenty minutes of the drive. That always brings my talons out.

At ten to twelve, I pull into a parking spot in front of the steak restaurant Hunter picked, conveniently located next to the movie theater.

I hold my breath and slowly exhale. It's been eleven days since I last saw Hunter. I'm not over him, not in the least bit. But I need to be.

He doesn't need to be tied down by a girlfriend that lives over three hours away. I'd have trust issues if we tried the long-distance thing, thanks to him always being horny as hell. And once he finds out that I live with seven guys, especially one as hot as Onyx, he might have a fit of jealous rage. It would be too difficult to make things work, and I don't think it's worth it. Like he told me those eleven days ago, it's been fun and all, but we need to move on.

Onyx pulls me from my inner monologue and taps on my hand resting on the gear shift. "You okay?"

"Yeah."

"You might need an escape clause. How 'bout instead of me going to the movies, I'll ask to be seated a couple tables away. You can signal me if I need to come save you."

"That's not necessary. Go enjoy your movie."

"Tad might whine if I go see the latest Marvel without him. And nothing else really interests me."

"Really, Onyx. I'll be okay." Then I feel and hear it. The vroom-vroom of Hunter's souped up mustang vibrates throughout my entire body. He parks a couple spaces from me then gets out and walks toward my vehicle.

Onyx eyes him. "Nope. Definitely not going to the movies. I won't let this douche pull you back in. Not going to happen."

My heart seizes when Hunter passes my vehicle and gives me his devastatingly handsome grin. "Okay, yeah. That might be a good thing." I grab a hair tie from my gear shift and slip it on my wrist. "I'll put my hair up if I need you to come save me."

Hunter tries to open my door but it's still locked. "And Onyx?"

His emerald and gold eyes fill me as his brows raise. "Thanks for this."

"I'll always be here for you, princess."

I unlock my door and step out. Hunter wraps me in his arms, his large hand slipping under my shirt, searing the small of my back. He nestles his head in my hair and whispers into my ear in his spine-tingling voice, "I've missed you so much."

My mind seeks to get free but my heart wants to latch on.

Onyx's, "Ahem," causes the mind to win, and I twist in Hunter's arms, arching my body to separate from his strong hold.

Hunter entwines his hand with mine as his attention falls to Onyx. "I didn't realize you were bringing someone with you," he says.

Onyx holds out his left hand, making Hunter drop my hand to shake his. "Onyx Finch. Bodyguard of the princess. I live with her. I have my eyes on her 24/7." He says it with such a straight face, I can't contain the laughter. Only Hunter doesn't laugh with me. And neither does Onyx.

Hunter stands taller, hovering two inches over Onyx, and puffs out his chest. "Hunter." He holds Onyx's hands for a few seconds in a definite power struggle.

Finally, Onyx releases and says, "Don't mind me. I'm just here for the show." He points to the movie theater sign and walks in that direction.

Maybe he changed his mind about playing the savior. "I'll text you to see where you're at when it's time to leave," I call out.

He waves but doesn't turn around.

Hunter's eyes follow Onyx until he disappears at the front of the theater. "Seriously? You brought a watchdog?"

"It's not like that."

Hunter's nostrils flare. This could turn ugly real quick. I'm here for closure, not a fight.

I'm used to taking down his quick temper. I run my hand along his sharp jawline. I know I shouldn't, but he needs to be softened. "My aunt didn't want me to come this far by myself. My cousin was busy, so she sent Onyx. He's a foster kid that's been living with her for a while. He's a big goofball. Perfectly harmless." I'm a horrible liar, but Hunter's shoulders relax. I grab hold of his bicep and tug him toward the restaurant. "Let's go eat. I skipped breakfast so I'm a little hangry."

We're seated in a booth near the bar area. After we order, I see Onyx being seated several booths away. He waves and mouths, "I got you."

I bite my bottom lip to hide the smile.

"What?" Hunter asks.

I guess I didn't hide it enough. "It's really good to see you. How have your past two football games gone? And what about State's offer?"

He tells me about the two beatings Merryville put on their opponents the past two games. He beat his previous record of passing yards in a game which resulted in him capturing the overall school record. He

already has the school and state record for touchdowns. He then goes on about his full ride scholarship until the food arrives.

After the waiter clears the plates and returns with the check, Hunter reaches over and clutches my hand, rubbing his thumb along the lifeline of my palm. "I'm so sorry, Jade. You told me you loved me and I freaked a little. I didn't break up with you because of you halting us that one night. Nor did I do it because of the *L* word. Please don't think that. I got in a huge fight with Dan about my grades and everything just spiraled that morning and I had to lose the one thing that I thought I could. But it turns out, you were the best thing I had going. And it took me a few days to figure it out, only you were gone."

I squeeze his thumb.

"Tell me what I need to do to make this better," he continues. "I've been miserable without you."

I pull my hand away. This will be too hard with him touching me. "I don't think we're strong enough to survive a long-distance relationship, especially not our senior year of high school when we're meant to have fun and make mistakes and live it up." Geez. I sound like Onyx. "Maybe next year, I'll wind up at State and we can see if something still lingers." It's still a slim possibility.

His entire face drops. "What would've happened to you had I not broken up with you that day?"

The undeniable truth slips from my mouth. "I would've been in tears waiting by your car when football practice was over, looking to you for help and shelter."

He shakes his head, knowingly. "And you'd be staying with me right now."

I nod, somewhat relieved that he was just as involved mentally in the relationship as I was and not just physically.

"But instead, I forced you away."

I nod again.

He stands and sits next to me, gently pushing me over to the far side of the booth. Grabbing my clenched hands from my lap, he peers at me intently. "Jade, please. We can make it work. Now that I have the scholarship offer, Dan has completely chilled out. Football season will be over in less than two months. Once that's done, I'm sure I can talk Dan and my mom into letting you stay. We can finish high school and you can come to State with me, like we talked about before."

Why did he have to come over here and sit with me? I can feel the sexual energy that makes him so confident wrap around me, seeping in through my pores. The elastic tie wrapped around my wrist begs me to use it. Onyx would be over here in two seconds flat and halt this madness.

But I don't want to call for help. I want to do this myself.

I tilt my head down and close my eyes to block the eagerness I see in his. "Hunter, please don't make this so damn difficult. Right now, I'm where I need to be."

He leans his forehead against the side of my head, his lips brush lightly against my neck, making my heartbeat throb in my ears. "Please, Jade."

I turn my head, cutting off access to my neck. "I can't."

"And you'll go down in history as the girl that got away from me." His whisper is laced with sex, and my resolve almost fails. *Almost.*

I laugh, feeling honored that I'd be that girl for *The Hunter Green.*

He moves away from me, allowing me to breathe again. "So, why'd you meet me here today then? Why not save time and just tell me this over the phone?"

"Had you reached out to me last Friday, I would've given you a different answer, and I would've found a way to come back. I was so shocked and heartbroken. But I'm with family now. That's where I need to be."

I take a deep breath of fresh air that's Hunter free. "Since I left, I found out I'm still reeling from my father's death. I became aware that I was masking my healing process by being with you. And now I'm dealing with it all over again. And I need to deal with it, otherwise I'm never going to feel alive again. So, I met with you today because I needed closure. And

I'm sorry." Admitting this gives me a sense of peace and satisfaction.

"Don't be sorry. I'm the one who's sorry. And thanks for being honest." After dropping cash in the check holder, he slides out of the booth and holds out his hand to me. "I need to jet so I can go home and sulk. You can call your bodyguard and tell him the show's over."

I turn him around and point to Onyx who salutes. Hunter nods his head in that direction and I follow him over to Onyx's table.

He holds his hand out and gives Onyx a friendlier handshake. "She's all yours. Take care of her, please. She's very special."

"Oh, I *will* take care of the princess," Onyx says. I don't know if Hunter can read it, but I've learned a lot about Onyx's facial expressions this past week. His face holds a calculating expression. He takes Hunter's words as a challenge.

"Hey, you know how you're always talking about the kicker being almost as important as the quarterback?" I ask.

Hunter nods.

"I finally get it thanks to Onyx. He's way better than Carson. You'd love him if he played at Merryville."

"Right on." He holds his fist out for Onyx to bump then turns and hugs me, brushing his lips against my cheek. I return his embrace, knowing it would be our last.

He can't get out of here soon enough. When he turns to leave, his eyes are watery.

I watch as he leaves. Suddenly, I feel like I'm on safer ground, but I pause to reflect the moment as his tall and bulky figure exits the restaurant. I'll always remember him as being the first guy I ever told *I love you* to.

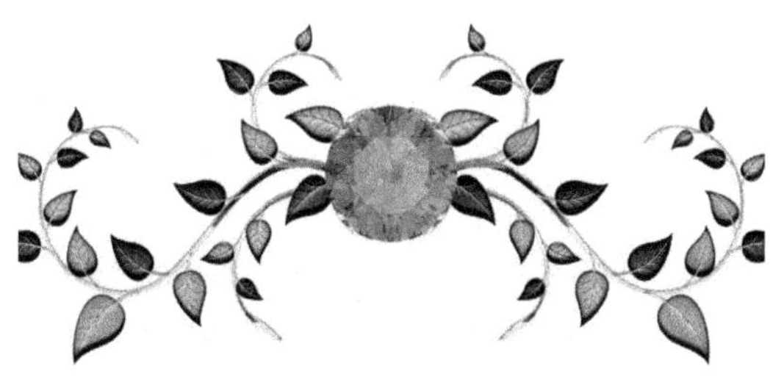

CHAPTER 18

ANDS WAVE IN front of my face. "Earth to Jade," Onyx says in a robotic voice.

I don't know how long I've been standing here, staring at the door. Blinking away, I slide into the seat opposite of Onyx.

"I thought I was going to have to go over there and separate you two. He was getting way too close for comfort."

"I held strong." Proud isn't strong enough of a word for how I feel right now. I fought a huge battle of personal restraint. His touch. His scent. His presence. I was consumed. But his easy dismissal that day was stronger.

My thoughts break when the waiter drops off the check.

"Actually," Onyx says, sliding the folder back to the waiter, "can we have one of those chocolate thunder thingies. It's her birthday, and we're here to celebrate."

The waiter pushes the check back to Onyx. "Sure thing. On the house."

After the waiter leaves, Onyx places his elbows on the table and leans toward me. "What went down over there?"

I give him a quick recap. The waiter comes over with a crew of other servers and a huge brownie topped off with a scoop of vanilla ice cream. A mound of whipped cream holds a single candle.

They start singing *Happy Birthday*. Onyx orchestrates the folks in the bar to join in. By the time the song's over, my face is burning red and my ears ring from the noise. I think Onyx managed to get everyone in the restaurant to sing.

"You didn't tell me that your ex is Tad's doppleganger," Onyx says as we head back to my car.

"I know, right? And the fact they're both quarterbacks. It's weird. But those are the only similarities."

"Yeah, Tad is definitely not a douche."

"Hunter's not a douche."

"Yes, he is. He drives a Mustang, his t-shirts are too tight, and he wears loafers. That's the classic definition of a douche."

"Whatever. Tad wears loafers."

"That's because his mama dresses him."

"Seriously?"

"Yup."

Onyx follows me to the driver's side and holds out his hand.

"Oh, yeah. I promised you could drive."

"And you promised we'd go with the top down."

I pull my hair back into a ponytail as I walk around to the passenger side. I'm thankful the temperature has warmed a good bit since Friday night.

Onyx backs out of the parking space. "I feel like we need to go do something. It's only one o'clock and Janet gave me the entire day off to come with you."

"Hey, you think that little tattoo parlour in Maybee is open on a Sunday?"

He grimaces as if he just downed a spoonful of cough syrup. "Prince's?" The word heavily rolls off his tongue.

"What? Don't tell me you think tattoos are beneath you like Tad does."

"No, I actually have a tattoo. They're definitely not beneath me."

"You have a tattoo?"

"Yeah. Isn't that what I said?"

"What is it?"

"Maybe I'll show you one day," he says. His mouth turns up into a deceitful grin as he winks.

There's a lot of innuendo in that wink. "Where is it?"

He circles an area just below and to the right of his waist line. My cheeks flame. Does he really want to show me one day? It's so close to...

"You want to get a tattoo today?" he asks.

Having faced Hunter and holding strong against his command, I feel empowered. "Yeah."

"Do you have any hidden tattoos? I saw you half naked on the night we met and didn't notice any. And yes, I was looking."

"No, I don't have any yet. And I wasn't half naked. I had on a tank top and shorts."

"Uh, booty shorts and a tight top that revealed your stomach. Trust me. I remember."

I roll my eyes.

He returns my eyeroll. "Why don't we find a tattoo parlour here in Louisville? Look for one on your phone."

Thirty minutes later, I'm sitting down with Onyx by my side, sketching out a drawing of my mother's ring for Fat Freddy, who's skinnier than Onyx, at Chaos Ink just outside of Louisville. The walls are painted teal and covered in skulls and cartoon characters in bright colors. Seats that look like dental chairs are scattered throughout.

"That's really cool," Onyx says, staring at my drawing. "Is there a meaning behind it? A tattoo should always have meaning."

I rake my teeth over my bottom lip and nod. "It's inspired by a ring that my mom designed before she died that my dad made. He said he'd give it to me on my eighteenth birthday. I never could find it, so I think my stepmother sold it. At least this way, it can be a part of me."

"There's no better meaning than that."

AT 10 P.M. sharp, Onyx brings my nightly dose of hot chocolate with a mountain of marshmallows to the cupola. It's strange to think that I've only known him for such a short time, and I'm already closer to him than I am with Malachi.

I haven't spoken to Mal since our little tiff on Friday. I haven't even seen him around the ranch. I'll give him another week of ignoring me, then I'm going to do something about it. We're family. I want to be there for whatever's going on with him, to help him through it. He just has to talk to me and let me know what's going on so I can help.

Onyx pulls me from my thoughts. "What's on your mind, princess?"

We've already beaten the Malachi talk to death. "Notta."

"Just air?"

"Yep, just air."

"How's the tat?"

I flip my wrist over and admire the artwork. It's still red around the edges and looks a little bruised, but the red stone sparkles as if Fat Freddy dusted it with glitter. "Beautiful."

Onyx grabs hold, turns the flashlight on his phone, and inspects it. "You said it was based on a ring. Tell me more."

I open my iPad and tap to my photo gallery, flipping until I come across a photo of the ring. "My mom's health was failing, and she couldn't handle working with her tools. But she could still draw."

Tracing the vines wrapped around the ruby, I continue. "And in my family's jewelry store, there's this mirror that's old and gaudy but absolutely beautiful. She sketched this design based on the mirror and my dad made it for her. He finished it just a week before she died."

He takes the iPad and zooms in, admiring the intricate details. "The big stone's a ruby?"

"Yeah, that was my mom's name."

He pans around more, then pauses and holds the iPad barely an inch from his face. "Did he use Onyx and Jade for the leaves?"

"Yep."

He hands me back the iPad, and a devilish look comes into his eyes. "Interesting."

"Not really, considering they were, along with rubies, her favorite stones. She loved the way the black, red, and green played off each other. She always said you need the onyx in the design so it doesn't look like a ring meant to be worn only at Christmas time."

"And you think your stepmom sold the ring?"

"Maybe. There's only one place I haven't looked for it. That mirror I was talking about has a really old safe behind it. My dad rarely used that one because it was

temperamental. But sometimes he'd hide presents that he bought for my stepmom there. She didn't know about the safe. For some reason, I think it may be in that safe."

"So, why not ask your stepmom to let you look?"

I manage a choking laugh. "Um, I don't think that will ever happen. She kicked me out, remember? Hasn't bothered to check on me, not even to see where I'm living."

A blank stare passes over his face as he tugs his bottom lip. "Since you used to work in the store, can't you get in somehow?"

"She fired me then changed all the locks and security codes."

"What about other employees? Maybe they aren't loyal to her."

"She fired everyone at the same time and hired new folks. I have no ability to access it."

"Wow."

"Yeah."

Onyx grabs my iPad and opens my drawing app. He writes the date and attempts to draw a vine around the edges. It turns out looking more like barbed wire. It's become a habit that I can't leave the cupola until I write down my three favorite things.

He hands me the iPad and smiles knowingly he's going to be on my list. Every night, I have to include at least one thing about him. He makes sure of it in the actions he takes to get me to smile each and every day.

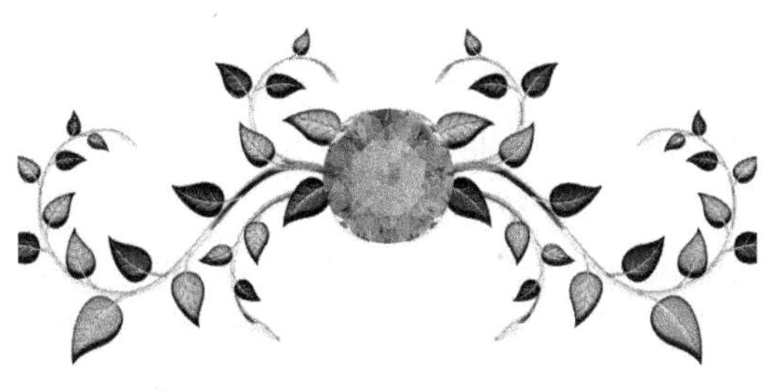

CHAPTER 19

"**B**LOT." PEPPER HOLDS a tissue to my lips and I press down lightly. "Let me admire my masterpiece." She holds up her phone. I quickly pout, jut out my chin, and smolder my eyes for the picture.

"Now both of us," I say. We squeeze together for a round of goofy and smiley selfies as Katy Perry's *Roar* plays in the background.

Onyx yells from somewhere down the hall. "Stop dancing and let's go. We need an hour at Tad's because his mom thinks she's the paparazzi. Pepper will miss her grand, red carpet entry in her sparkly little crown."

"Ugh." Pepper picks up her plastic homecoming queen crown and throws it to me. "Put this hideous thing on me."

I bring my hand up to my mouth to stifle the giggles. She and Tad were elected Homecoming King and

Queen during halftime at last night's football game. Tad seemed to have gained a big head about it. Pepper on the other hand, although she's appreciative of her peers voting for her, is over the high school popularity game.

Pepper has everyone fooled, even Onyx. She's far from the princess that everyone seems to think she is. We spent the day riding horses along the trails of Diamond Ranch with Onyx and Mica. She's a cowgirl at heart and would trade in her heels for cowboy boots and her crown for a cowboy hat, albeit they're both covered in rhinestones. Considering how she scolded Delani and me at Senior night for not wearing heels, I was shocked.

I love it when I'm able to peel back the layers of others like they're onions. Pepper and Onyx continue to surprise me at how many levels they have. I wish I could say the same about Tad. He's more like a banana—soft in the center.

But him and I have chatted a lot this week. And he's held my hand on the way to lunch everyday, even though he quickly drops it when we arrive. I've stopped sitting right next to him at the table, too, preferring to sit closer to the girls and avoid Malachi's wafting attitude. We also finally exchanged phone numbers, but he has yet to text me.

It feels weird talking about him with Pepper, so I avoid it.

I place the crown on top of Pepper's head and pull out a few auburn tendrils to frame her heart-shaped face. "How's that?"

She glances in the mirror. "As good as it's going to get."

"Oh, please. You look like an actual queen."

We step out of the bathroom to find Onyx sitting on my bed in a black suit, a green tie loosely wrapped around his neck. His eyes roam the lengths of both of us in our matching sequin and velvet dresses. Pepper opted for red whereas I went for green. We even found a purple one for Delani, but she refused to come.

Onyx stands and runs his tongue slowly along the top and bottom of his lips. Discretion is not his forte. "Okay, princesses. New plan. We're leaving Tad at home, and you'll both be my dates. I'll be the luckiest man on the planet."

Pepper taps him on his bicep. "It's a good thing you're a *Prince*."

Onyx narrows his eyes and frowns. She shrugs her shoulders and begins gathering up her things that are scattered around my room.

I step in front of him and tug on the tie. "Why aren't you fully dressed?"

Scarlet stains his cheeks. "Uh, I don't know how to tie a tie. I couldn't find Malachi and the only person I could find was Reid, but he has no clue how to tie a tie."

I pull the wider part of the tie about twice as long as the thinner side. "You know there's probably a million YouTube videos for this."

He purses his lips. "I tried."

His eyes burn holes in my face as I wrap the wide part around the narrow part, pull the wide part through the loop then through the knot. I tighten it then straighten it. His muscles flex as I run my hands down the tie to smooth it out.

"Cool," Pepper says. "How'd you learn to do that?"

I take a step back to avoid the feel of Onyx's cool, minty breath in my face. "Eleven years of private school where I had to wear one every day. Now let's go so Pepper doesn't miss her chance of walking the red carpet."

She shoots me a bird as I tug on both their hands and head downstairs.

Onyx drives Pepper's four-door car to Tad's house after he loses the battle of wanting to take mine. Pepper and I refuse to crawl into the back seat in these tight, bodycon dresses.

As Onyx promised, Mrs. Becket's a photographer busy-body, taking fundreds of photos from every an-gle in every pose. And, she doesn't take photos with her phone. She takes them with a big camera that she keeps on switching out the lenses. She even asks Tad to kiss me, to which he only gives me a quick peck on the cheek. Lastly, she asks Tad and Pepper to pose

together with their crowns while Onyx and I take a seat on the porch swing.

Tad has on a red tie that matches Pepper's dress perfectly. He looks so comfortable around her. Joking and laughing. Part of me thinks I should feel jealous, but I don't.

"Who broke up with whom?" I whisper to Onyx.

He follows the direction of my eyes. "Pepper. You're the first person he's asked out since they broke up."

The jealousy slips in a little. Maybe he isn't 100% over her, and I'm just a rebound date. I shake the thoughts away before they grow out of control.

Onyx wraps his arm around my shoulder and squeezes. "You okay?"

"Yeah. Do you think he's over her?"

He stares at the two for a few seconds. "I've never thought about it, really. She's definitely over him. But I don't know if I can say the same about him."

Tad's looked at me a couple of times the way he's looking at Pepper. But the fact that he drops my hand when we walk into the cafeteria, where she's usually at, makes me wonder.

Onyx leans over, pushes my flat ironed-straight hair back behind my ear, and whispers, "You always have me." His laughter is a light-hearted sound when he pulls back.

Sometimes, I can't tell when he's joking and when he's not.

AFTER THE FIRST hour of the homecoming dance, my hair's in a loose bun and my body's coated in a layer of sweat. Who knew both Tad and Onyx liked to dance—and are actually somewhat decent at it.

I've been to a number of high school dances before, including Merryville's homecoming dance where we stayed for a whole thirty minutes. Just long enough for Hunter to make his king appearance. That was the Saturday night we almost went all the way. It seems like a lifetime ago. Definitely not just three weeks, at least.

The music stops and we sit down at a round table covered in a white, paper table cloth. Onyx grabs four water bottles from a nearby cooler and brings them over. The gym looks like it always does. No decorations. No banners. The only differences are the big DJ booth with speakers taller than myself and the mob of students in varying levels of casual dress. Only a few have on the fancier garb.

Principal Francis's squeaky voice blasts throughout the gym. "Can I get our king and queen out on the dance floor?"

All night, Tad hasn't danced solely with me. But they haven't played any slow tunes either. The overhead lights dim, and a sparkle of flashing lights start up. Ed Sheeran's *Perfect* reverberates through the ceiling rafters. Tad stands and holds out his hand to Pepper.

"Oh, jeepers," she says, rolling her eyes. "Why are they playing our song?" She takes his hand and they walk out onto the area designated as the dance floor.

I gulp the bottle of water, happy for a cool down, as I watch them dance. Tad's a bit of an awkward slow dancer, taking baby steps and turning in circles. Pepper looks like she wants the moment to be over. Maybe he's tried to get back together with her, and she wants nothing to do with it.

The song blends into another slow one, and Tad releases Pepper and motions for us to join them on the dance floor.

He gathers me into his arms and holds me snugly. It's tighter and closer than he held Pepper, which puts me at ease.

His hot breath warms the side of my face when he whispers, "In case I forget to tell you, you look really pretty tonight."

"Thanks, you look pretty good yourself."

He kisses my temple, causing me to melt into him as Shawn Mendes tells us to *Never Be Alone*. In this moment, there's nothing else going on in the world except Tad and me.

The song blends into the piano beginning of *Bloodstream*. The hairs on my neck begin to rise, as they always do.

"I need water," Tad says.

"But I love this song."

"I'll dance with you princess," Onyx says. He grabs my hand as Pepper and Tad leave us on the dance floor.

I try not to dissolve into a bowl of jelly, but it's hard not to when Onyx leads me around with his strong embrace. You couldn't shove a penny between our bodies. He whispers the words to the song in my ear, sending warm chills all over.

"Malachi," a voice screams out. "Slow down."

I turn to see Delani in sweats and a t-shirt running across the dance floor in Tad and Pepper's direction. Onyx grabs him by the waist and halts him.

Malachi tries to wiggle free but Onyx holds him tighter. "Chill, wild one."

"He's drunk," Delani whispers.

Onyx leads him over to the table with Tad and Pepper and shoves a water bottle in his face. "Drink up. Franny's watching you. Do you want her to call your mom?"

That seems to calm Malachi down. He slides into a seat and drinks slowly. Delani sits down beside Pepper, and I join her.

"He drove to my house completely wasted," Delani says. "Then hopped back into his car and said he was heading here. I forced him to get out. I didn't know what else to do so I gave in to what he wanted and brought him here."

"You drove drunk?" Tad asks.

Red veins streak across Malachi's glossy eyes. "What do you care?"

Onyx flips him on his chest. "Not cool, asshole. You could've killed someone or even yourself."

As if finally realizing what he's done, Malachi's face drops.

"Jade, get Malachi's keys and pull his car around to this door." Onyx points to a side door near the parking lot.

Delani hands me the keys. "I parked right out front."

I leave and pull the car around to the side door where I find Onyx hovering over a puking Malachi. I put the car in park and open the back door.

"Your aunt's really cool about a lot of things." Onyx says. "But drinking isn't one of them. Let's hope she's already in bed, or she may lay it in on all three of us."

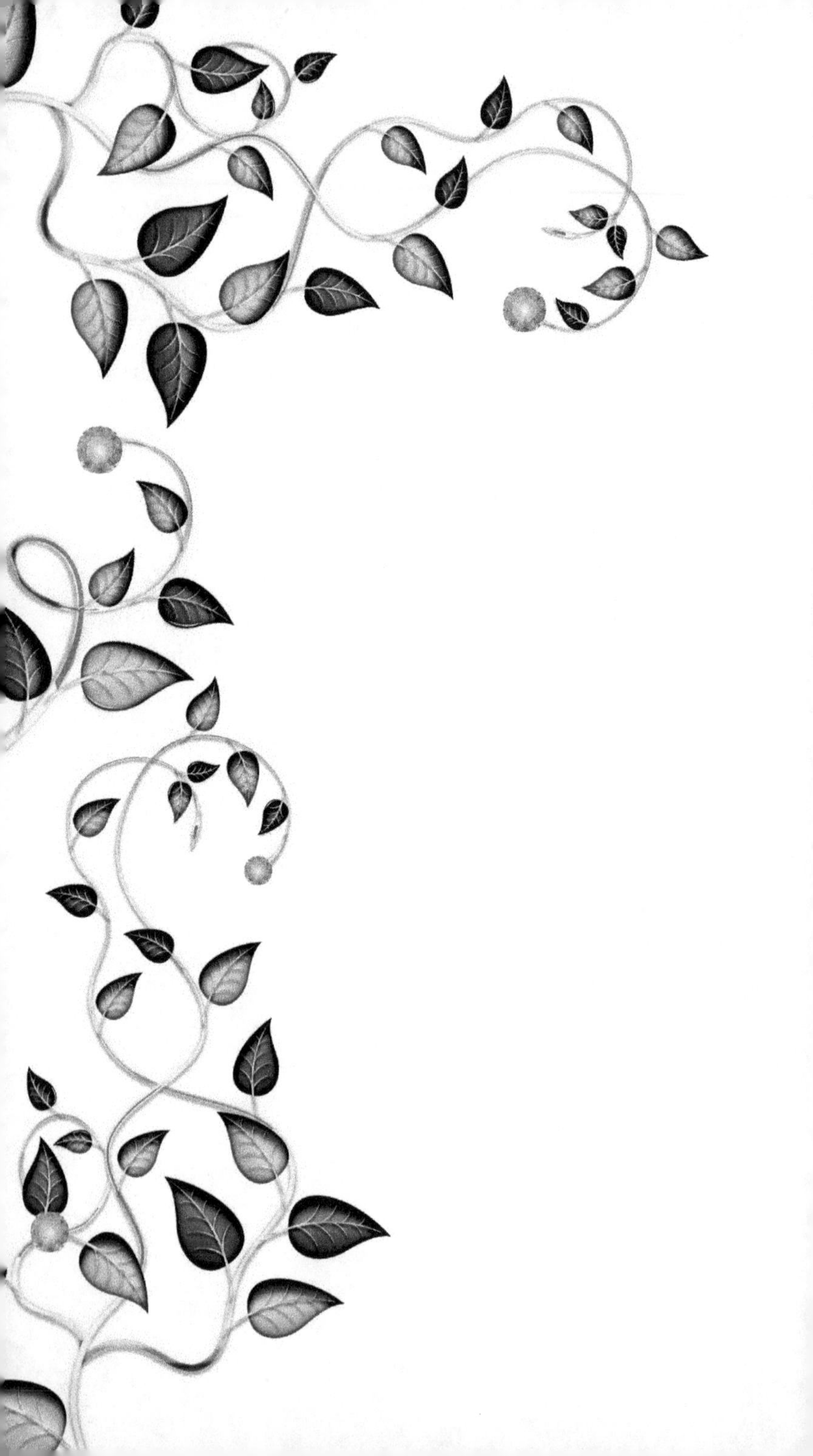

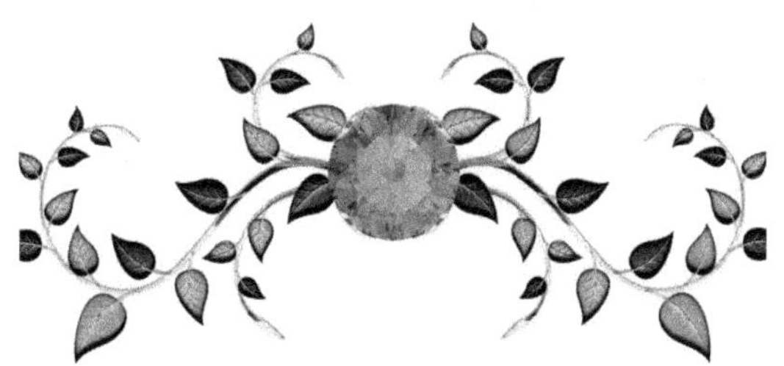

CHAPTER 20

ONYX'S HANDS TIGHTLY grip the steering wheel on the drive home as Malachi's passed out in my lap in the backseat. His features are relaxed for the first time since I'd arrived in Maybee. It's a glimpse at what my cousin once was, and hopefully still is.

When we get to the bridge, Onyx flips the headlights off. The only light comes from the dashboard, illuminating his face in a pale, blue glow.

"I don't see how you're doing it," I say to break the silence that's been lingering in the vehicle since we left the gym. "I can barely make this drive at night with the lights *on*."

Onyx starts to say something but only a scratch comes out. He clears his throat. "Familiarity," he responds with a hard edge to his voice.

"Does Mal drink often?"

"Occasionally, but I've never seen him this drunk."

The lights are off on the first floor of the house, except for the porch light, when we roll past the circular driveway. Onyx parks on the far side of the Dogwood stable.

I gently shake Mal. "Hey, cuz. We're home. Let's get you upstairs and in bed."

No response. Panic climbs my throat. I don't have a lot of experience with drunks. Is he even breathing?

Onyx opens the door I'm leaned up against. Luckily, Malachi's weight keeps me from tumbling out.

My voice quivers. "I can't wake him."

Onyx shakes him like he's a bottle of Italian dressing then slaps his cheeks. "Chi, get your lazy ass up. I'm not carrying all two hundred pounds of you up the stairs."

"Fuck you, Onyx," Malachi murmurs. "I'm not even close to two hundred pounds."

Now that he's spoken, I can breathe again.

"What've you been drinking tonight?" Onyx asks.

Malachi sits up from my lap and laughs. "My two best friends, Jose and Jack."

I slide out of the car. Malachi follows me and staggers out, landing face first on the gravel path.

"That's gonna hurt tomorrow," Onyx says as he helps Mal up. His lip is dripping blood, and his cheeks are streaked with fine, cat-like scratches. "And try not to puke again until we get you upstairs."

I glance around to make sure no one has spotted us. Onyx parked in a way the view from the main house is cut off.

Onyx wraps his arm around Malachi's waist and helps him up the steps to the apartment. I follow behind them, and all I can think is Mal's going to tip over and we're all going to tumble down the stairs. Luckily, Onyx's grip is firm, and we make it to Malachi's room where he falls face first again, his legs dangling off the bed.

Onyx twists them onto the bed, turning Malachi over on his side. "Grab the trash can out of the bathroom."

When I come back, Onyx is sitting on the floor in front of the bed, clenching his hands in and out of a fist.

I kneel down and grab onto them. "You okay?"

"No, I'm pissed. How could he be so selfish? Getting drunk is one thing. But driving? He knows better than that."

After a squeeze, I release his hands. "Nothing we can do about it tonight."

He tugs at the tie around his neck. "Get this thing off me, please."

I loosen the tie then pull it over his head.

"Thanks."

"You said he drinks occasionally. Have you ever noticed any triggers? Like maybe more hostility between him and Delani?"

203

He shakes his head. "It's usually him and Tad drinking when Tad's parents go visit his sister."

I slide down beside him and lean my head on his shoulder. "Tad has a sister?"

"He has three sisters."

Just goes to show what little I know about the boy. "I guess I need to learn to ask more questions with him."

Onyx lets out a tiny laugh, more out of courtesy than amusement. "Two of his sisters are in Lexington at UK. The other got married over the summer and moved to North Carolina."

"So, he's the baby and the only guy."

"Yep. And a total mama's boy."

That was made obvious tonight before the homecoming dance. She kept straightening his tie, smoothing out his jacket, and messing with his hair between every picture.

"Do you join them when they drink?"

"Nope. It's not my idea of a fun-filled Saturday night to sit around and drink from Tad's parent's liquor cabinet. If there's a party, I'll go but I'm always the DD."

There goes another layer of Onyx's onion. Caring and compassionate. A loyal best friend.

Malachi lets out a low moan, or maybe it's a snore.

I lift my head and position myself in front of Onyx to keep my eye on Mal. "You don't drink at all?"

"Nope."

I don't know why, but this surprises me. Onyx is

a fun-loving guy who's often the center of attention. High school stereotypes would tell me he likes to party.

"Why not?" I ask, wanting to peel back more layers.

His shoulder's slump and he drops his head between his knees. After a minute, he murmurs, "My grandparents were killed by a drunk driver two years ago. I used to drink, but I haven't had a drop since that night."

"Is this the grandma with the handkerchief?"

He lifts up and reaches in his pocket, pulling out the floral napkin. I take it from him and dab his misty eyes. He leans his head back down between his knees. I hope he isn't hiding his head in shame at showing his emotions. It's about time someone else besides me cried around here. Although I feel the tears welling in my own eyes at his openness. This is a raw Onyx that I haven't been privy to yet.

I rub the tight muscles of his neck, kneading them until they soften.

"Damn. You've got some magic hands, woman."

"That's what Hunter used to say."

He lifts his head again and the wetness has subsided. "Oh, I bet he did." His playful smirk is on full display.

I toss his grandmother's hanky in his face as my phone chimes from my purse.

Onyx reaches my bag before I can. "Oh, it's Hunter. Right on cue." He pulls out my phone and glances at the screen. "Nope. It's Tad. He says he really wanted

to kiss you tonight." His eyes spiral as he tosses my phone into my waiting hand.

I read the message to confirm. "How am I supposed to respond to that?"

"He should've asked how his best friend is first." My phone chimes again.

> **TAD:** Please come to dinner tomorrow night.

> **JADE:** What time? And Malachi's passed out by the way, if you were wondering.

> **TAD:** 6.

> **JADE:** See ya then.

I stand and set my phone on Malachi's bedside table then rummage through his drawers to find a t-shirt and a pair of boxers.

Onyx neatly folds his grandma's handkerchief and tucks it back in his pocket. "What're you doing?"

"Getting out of this dress, but I'm not leaving him alone tonight."

In the bathroom, my finger serves as a toothbrush, and the pine-smelling soap serves as a face wash. When I enter Mal's room, Onyx has created a pallet on the floor out of his comforter. His head's on a stack of pillows and black lines peek out of the athletic shorts hanging low on his waist.

"Is that your tattoo?" I ask.

He nods.

"Can I see it?"

He shakes his head. "Like I said, maybe one day I'll show it to you." He lifts his eyebrows in a suggestive manner.

I grab a pillow from Mal's bed and throw it at him.

He catches it easily. "You need to learn to be more spontaneous, princess. You're so easy to read."

I flip on Malachi's lamp and turn off the overhead light. I crawl over Mal and say, "Good night, Onyx."

He flips the lamp off. "Good night, princess."

THE WORST SMELL hits me when I wake up. Malachi's open mouth is a foot away, spewing the sewage odor in my direction.

I crawl over him and out of his bed, careful of my footing knowing that Onyx is on the ground. But the morning light peeking through the window shows me he isn't.

On Mal's bedside table, a bottle of aspirin with a sticky note attached to it reading *take me* sits beside a bottle of water with another sticky that says *drink me*.

Malachi rolls over and opens his gray eyes still veined in red.

"How do you feel?" I ask.

"Like hell."

I hand him the pills and bottle of water. "Talk to me."

He tosses the pills in his mouth and drains the water. Finally, he says, "About?"

I sit cross-legged on his bed. "What's going on with you? Why did you drink so much last night? And why the hell did you drive like that?"

With squinted eyes, he says, "I drove?"

"Yeah. To Delani's. I don't know where you were before that. She drove you to the dance."

He rubs his face. "I don't remember."

"Mal, that's serious. What's going on?"

His flat, unspeaking eyes prolong the silence. He lets out an exasperated breath and holds out his pinky. "Pinky swear."

I wrap my tiny finger around his large one.

His blink causes a single tear to roll down his face. "I'm gay."

"And?"

"And what?"

"I don't know. I mean. You've been all moody and shit. So, you're gay. What's the big deal?"

He throws his head back onto his pillow. "Jade, things are different here in Maybee than they are in the big city. Honestly? I just want to get the hell out

of this place. Being gay in a small town like this, it's not normal. "

"Normal doesn't exist, Mal. If it did, both my mom and dad would be alive and I'd be living a normal life. Instead, I've been putting up with my asshole of a cousin the past two weeks only to find out he's suffering from something he could've shared with me weeks ago when I first got here."

"I was going to. I really wanted to share it with you."

"Then why didn't you?"

"It's complicated."

"How?"

He shakes his head.

"Come on, Mal."

"Look, there's someone that I liked and I thought he liked me back. But it all fizzled. So, yes, it's a bit more than just coming out, it's about dealing with *that*."

I wrap him up in a hug. "I know now. I'll help you through it. And just to warn you, Onyx is really pissed at you."

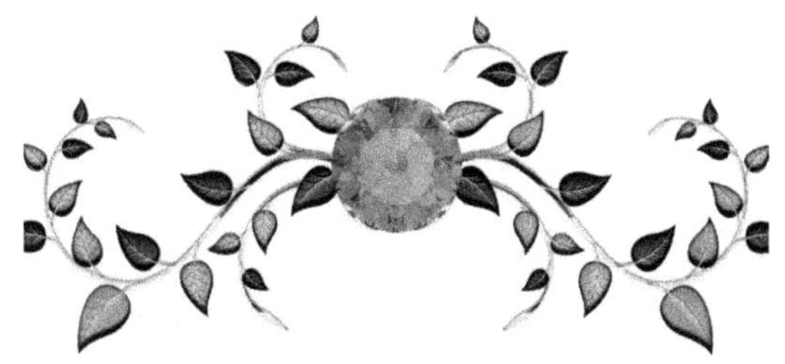

CHAPTER 21

AFTER SPENDING ALL day with Malachi, I leave for Tad's house for dinner.

I didn't ask Malachi many questions, and he wasn't forthcoming with information, but we did hang out like we used to. Playing video games and eating too much sugar. Chatting about nothing and everything, except the obvious.

Onyx stopped by on a break from his stable duties and bitched him out for driving. Malachi apologized, but Onyx didn't accept it and stormed out. I followed him out to talk him down, but he wasn't in the mood.

Now knowing about his grandparents' deaths, I can't say I blame him. Hopefully, he'll meet me in the cupola at ten tonight like he does every night. I don't want my relationship with Malachi to affect mine with Onyx.

I'm glad to have my cousin back, and I wanted our time together to continue. But Tad kept on texting me sweet things throughout the day like *I can't wait to CU*

2nite and *U looked so pretty last night*. He also shared that his house was smelling so good from his mom's dutch oven beef stew that she started preparing right after breakfast. How could I turn down a meal that takes all day to cook?

When I arrive at Tad's, he's sitting on the porch steps of an exquisite two-story white house dressed in a pair of khakis and a button up shirt. I guess I should've dressed a bit fancier than my light-washed, high-waisted jeans and black sweater. I do have on heeled black boots. Maybe that'll count for something.

He's at my door by the time I unbuckle my seatbelt. I grab the glass vase of orange roses, sunflowers, and gold and rust mums from the box in my passenger seat. Bringing a gift to your host is something worthwhile that I learned from miss vain. She may not have done much for me, but she did teach me good etiquette.

Tad opens my door and says with a question on his face, "You brought me flowers?"

I look at him in amused wonder. Sometimes, he's so clueless. "They're for your mom."

"Oh, good. She'll love them."

He awkwardly gives me a hug either thanks to the largeness of the bouquet or that he's still not comfortable with me. "How was your day?"

"It was really good. Malachi and I hung out all day. It's the first time we've done that since I moved here. And boy did he suffer from a hangover all day."

His expression is that of complete unconcern about his best friend as he leads me inside.

Just as with the outside, the inside is decorated in a display of red and yellow leaves and orange pumpkins. Everything is in perfect order without a speck of dust.

The house reminds me of my old home. Traditionally but beautifully decorated—a tad too fancy, as if it's on display for one of those home tours.

I follow Tad to the open kitchen where Mrs. Becket stands in front of a large stove, stirring the contents of a gray dutch oven.

"Hello, Mrs. Becket," I say. "It smells amazing in here."

"Thank you, Jade," she responds. "I'm glad you could make it."

"These are for you." I hand her the vase. My first thought when I saw this arrangement was it would be perfect. But seeing the interior of Tad's home makes me feel like I should've gone with a larger, grander one.

"Thank you. These are beautiful." She takes them from me and sets them on the center of the kitchen island, a massive piece of white marble veined in gray. "Tad, escort Jade into the dining room then go get your father. It's ready."

"Is there anything I can do to help?" I ask.

She ladles the stew from the pot into a white turren. "Oh, no, dear. But thank you."

Tad holds his arm out as if a true escort, following his mother's instructions to a T. I loop my arm through

his and walk with him into the next room where an eight-person dining table stands below a sparkling chandelier almost the size of my car. He holds a chair out for me then leaves me alone.

Everything feels familiar, but it's choking. It's like miss vain's stamp is on every surface. When she moved in with us, she slowly changed everything about our home. After my dad died, her changing pace went into rapid speed until no glimpse of the former house remained, except for the exterior.

I suck in a few calming breaths and count to ten, ridding my thoughts of the step-witch. Tad returns and sits next to me, placing his napkin in his lap. I should probably tell his mama that he's bad at opening doors for girls. I think she'd be embarrassed of it.

His dad enters in a white shirt and tie and sits on the far side from us, acknowledging me with his smug smile and a slight tilt of his head. The table is way too big for just a four-person dinner. The breakfast nook in the kitchen was much cozier. Why couldn't we eat in there?

Tad's mom serves us and we eat quietly. Glasses clink on the table, spoons clang against the ceramic bowls, mouths slurp the rich and hearty broth. I'm thankful when Mrs. Becket clears the dishes to halt the awkwardness, again denying my assistance.

Mr. Becket sets down his cut crystal glass of amber liquid. "So, Jade, Junior tells me you're new at Bradley. Where did you go to school before?" Tad's a junior?

I fold my cloth napkin and place it on the table. "Blue River Prep, then Merryville High in Indiana."

"What brought you here to Bradley?"

Mrs. Becket returns and interrupts. "Thomas." A harsh glance passes his way.

"It's okay," I say. "Long story short. My dad passed away, leaving my stepmom everything. She kicked me out on my eighteenth birthday, and I moved in with my aunt." I've reached the point that the harsh truth doesn't cause the tears to fall.

He squints his eyes. "Is your aunt Janet Turner?"

I nod.

"I'm so sorry about what happened to your dad. Your aunt sought my advice, and I referred her to an attorney in Indiana to assist in the matter. What's the latest on the case?"

"The Will's still stuck in probate. My aunt spoke to Mr. Eaton a few weeks ago, but he didn't have an update on the case."

He shakes his head slowly. "I'll follow up with Mike to see what else we can do, for your sake."

I'm too startled by his assistance to offer anything other than, "Thanks."

"What are your plans after graduation?"

"Um, I don't really know. I originally planned to go to art school to study jewelry design. I wanted to work with my dad. But things change."

"Oh, you're an artist like Junior?"

I nod. "I met Tad in art. He's super talented. My style is a little different from his though."

"The Diamond Company is a well-known jewelry brand all over this part of the country. It sounds like you could make a fine living in jewelry design. I'm not so sure Junior can with the cartoons he draws."

I'm about to defend Tad, even though I know I shouldn't, but Mrs. Becket interrupts. "There's a plate of cookies on the island in the kitchen. Why don't you kids take them downstairs and watch a movie?"

Tad rises quickly and I follow, happy to have the inquisition come to an end. Although, I'm relieved to know that I have another partner to help me with my legal matters.

We head downstairs to a theater room with eight plush, leather recliners in front of the largest television I've ever seen.

Tad rubs his forehead as if smoothing out a headache.

I pull his hand away and massage his temples.

"That feels good." His lids slip down over his eyes.

"Are you okay?"

"Yeah. Just hate when the topic of my future comes up."

I drop my hands from his forehead to the sides of his neck below his ears. After a minute, I say. "Turn around."

He turns around, giving me full access to his back and shoulders.

I roll my knuckles up and down either side of his spine. "What are you planning to do after graduation?"

"Anything to get out of this hell-forsaken town," he says, slumping his neck over.

"Are you going to pursue art?"

"Yeah. My dad is pissed that I don't want to pursue law and follow in his footsteps. Did you want to work with your dad or was it on his insistence?"

"I wanted to. My mom was a jewelry designer too."

"Cool." An unspoken torture is alive and glowing in his eyes when I turn around and sit next to him. It's eerie in contrast to his spoken word. There's something there, something I didn't expect to see. Maybe Tad does have more depth to him. His thumb strokes my hand. "Can I kiss you?" His whisper is laced with pain.

I lean toward him, wanting to take away whatever agony he suffers at the hands of his dad. His lips brush against mine, soft and calculated. It's over before I can register any feeling.

When he pulls away, his mouth spreads into a thin-lipped smile. "Saturday night, there's a Halloween party at Duncan's Corn Maze. You want to go with me?"

I mold myself into the recliner, feeling the disappointing kiss as a huge knot in my chest. "Sure."

"It's a costume party. I already have a costume for it. Something I've been planning since last year's party. You want to see it?" Excitement takes over his gloomy expression.

How can I deny his infectious enthusiasm? "Of course!"

He pulls me up from the recliner and weaves his hand in mine, dragging me to another room of the basement. I feel like I've stepped into the workroom on *Project Runway*. Sewing machines line a windowed-wall that overlooks the backyard. Bolts of fabric stand neatly on their shelves. Dress forms are covered in half-finished works. A mirror that covers part of a wall from top to bottom is flanked by big bulb lights.

"My sisters are really into fashion design," he says. "Their skills come in handy when you have an idea for a costume." His hand proudly waves toward three mannequins in the corner that are dressed in authentic-looking Iron Man suits, as if they were taken straight from the wardrobe department on a Marvel movie set. Each one slightly different in coloring and bulk. "They helped me with sewing the base of the suits. I did the rest with a 3-D printer."

"Wow. Maybe you should think about costume design. Why do you have three?" I run my fingers over the hard armor. Maybe there's a bit of depth to Tad after all.

His proud smile brightens even more at my compliment. "Malachi and Onyx. Maybe you could go as Black Widow or Captain Marvel. That way, we'd kind of match."

"I'll find something."

"You want to watch a movie?" he asks.

"That'd be great."

"THANKS FOR INVITING me over," I say as I click the remote to unlock my car.

"Thank you for coming. I enjoyed your company." He leans down and kisses me for the second time this evening. It's soft again, but not calculated. I part my lips to test the waters, to attempt to swirl up something, to give him permission. He responds with warmth and sweetness, but it's over all too quickly.

Thoughts of Hunter's lips plague me on my way home. His kisses always lit me up whether they were simple, closed-mouth pecks or passion-filled ones that set every nerve on end. He hasn't texted me since we met a week ago. I'm not going to break down and text him, no matter how much my lips crave the way he kisses. Maybe I can train Tad to kiss like that.

I make it home right at ten and head to the cupola where Onyx waits with mugs of hot chocolate. I settle in beside him and sip the deliciously creamy, chocolatey goodness topped with whipped cream and chocolate shavings, letting it warm my taste buds. Even his cocoa tastes amazing, as if he'd gotten it from Hattie's cafe in Merryville where Hunter and I frequented for breakfast.

"Thanks," I say. "How'ya feeling this evening?"

His eyes are empty and his mouth is downturned. Onyx just doesn't look right without a smile on his face.

He shrugs.

I know Malachi brought back painful memories for him. And it hurts to see him so bothered. I want to be here for him like he has been for me. I want to be able to turn that frown upside down like he so often tells me he's going to do when my face is stuck in a scowl.

Wrapping my arms around his neck, I bring his head to my heart. "I'm sorry." He relaxes into my hold as I run my fingers through the wavy ends of his hair.

Channeling my therapist's mantras, I say, "Tell me about them."

"They were the only people who ever cared about me."

"My aunt cares about you. I care about you."

He lifts his head, his eyes pierce me. "You care about me?"

"Of course. You're my best friend."

An easy smile tugs at his lips. An Onyx smile. "I spent most every weekend at their house. My grandmother taught me how to cook."

"Do you use her pancake recipe?"

"Yep, she made them for me every Saturday morning."

I stretch my legs out in the small space. "What else did she teach you to make?"

He tries to stretch out too but his legs are too long. Instead, he brings his knees to his chest and wraps his arms around them. "Biscuits and gravy, fried chicken. They'd take me to the Outer Banks every summer to visit my grandpa's family. We'd go shrimping then she'd make shrimp and grits. That meal was my favorite. We'd freeze some of the shrimp and bring them back home, but the meal wasn't quite the same as it was when it was fresh."

"Well, we'll have to go to the beach and go shrimping, so you can make me her famous shrimp and grits."

"I'd like that."

"What was your grandpa like?"

He chuckles then says, "He was a grumpy man, but funny. He never really knew what to do with me until I started watching all the Star Wars movies with him. He loved Yoda, and we'd speak Yoda to each other. Yoda speak we would. And my grandma would put him in his place. My bike belonged to him as did my jacket."

"The leather one with the silver angel wings?"

He nods. "He was in this motorcycle gang. My grandma would go crazy when he spent too much time with his boys."

"She sounds like she was an amazing lady."

"She was. How was your evening?"

I drum my fingers on the wood floor. "It was okay. I got to see your Halloween costume."

"Isn't it awesome?"

"Yeah it is. Tad kissed me."

His eyes narrow at me. "Why're you telling me that?"

"Isn't that what best friends are for?"

"Okay then, channeling my inner best friend with this question. What was it like?"

I shrug. "It was okay, I guess. It wasn't like kissing Hunter."

He wraps his arm around my shoulder and pulls me into his chest, kissing the top of my head. "No Hunter talk. And no Tad talk. Let's just sit here and watch the stars."

And so we sit in comfortable silence until I fall asleep. He wakes me around one when my body's stiff from being curled up next to him.

"Did you fall asleep too?" I ask as we head down the ladder.

"Nope."

"Then why didn't you wake me earlier?"

"You looked too peaceful, for once."

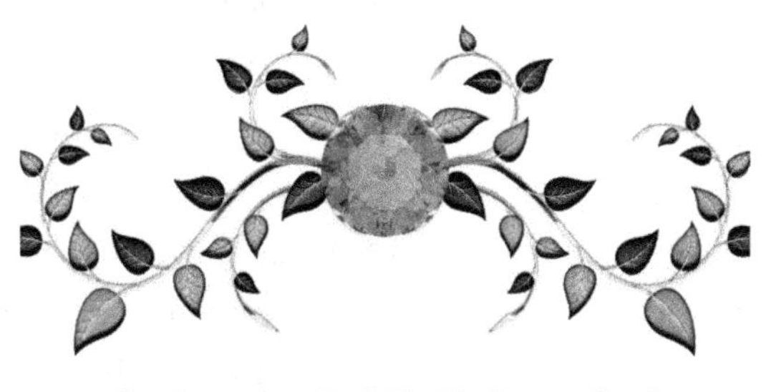

CHAPTER 22

I SNEAK THE GARMENT bag into my car, hoping that Onyx isn't anywhere in sight. He's been trying to sneak a peek at my Halloween costume since I got it. Luckily, I make it out of the drive without him catching me.

Pepper, Delani, and I went to a costume shop in Lexington after school on Wednesday in hopes of finding Marvel costumes to match the guys. Pepper found a Captain Marvel and Delani found a Black Widow.

The minute I saw the Snow White dress, I knew it would be the perfect costume, even though she's not exactly in the Marvel world. Too bad I couldn't backtrack and make everyone else go as dwarves. Even though he now meets me around school at every possible chance just to give me a kiss, I doubt Tad would've given up his Iron Man costume to be a dwarf.

I've been wearing his jacket every day, too.

I'm trying to be into him. He's so freaking gorgeous. Anytime he looks at me, I melt. But when he kisses me, I solidify. His lips are just too sweet. And I want something sweet, but there needs to be a little spice in there as well. Maybe we just haven't had enough practice yet, seeing as all his kisses have been quick. It's just such a drastic contrast to how Hunter was, when I felt it deep within my bones.

It still feels too awkward to bring it up with Pepper. And Onyx, anytime I mention it, he zones out. I guess a best friend relationship with a male is a bit different than one with a female. The only piece of advice he gives me is just to go for it. Stop waiting on Tad to make the *devour-me* move.

A rift still exists between Onyx and Malachi. Pepper tells me this is normal. Tad or Malachi will do something to piss Onyx off, usually something immature, and he'll stay mad at them for a while. But, we're all going together to the Halloween party at the corn maze tonight, so he can't be too mad still.

Tad's truck and a car I don't recognize are parked in Tad's driveway when I pull in at four in the afternoon. His sisters are in town just for the event, so he asked me to come early to meet them. His parents went to visit his other sister in North Carolina for the weekend, and everyone else is coming by around seven before heading on to the corn fields.

I shift the garment bag to my other hand then knock on the door. After a minute, I ring the doorbell but no one answers. I set the bag down on the porch swing and rifle through my backpack for my phone. Tad picks up on the first ring.

"Hey, Jade."

"I'm at your front door."

"Oh, okay. Um. Come around back. We're in the basement."

I walk around through a vine-covered archway to the back. I can only imagine how beautiful this yard is in the spring and summer. It's covered in ornamental trees and bushes. Fall flowers bloom all around. Adirondack chairs surround a firepit.

Tad waits at the sliding glass door. He's barefooted in holey jeans and a fitted Captain America tee, showing off his sleek, powerful build.

He slides open the door, takes the garment bag from me, and drapes it over a couch.

"I've never seen you dress so casually. You look good when your mom doesn't dress you," I tease.

He smirks as his face flushes. "Are you saying I don't normally look good?"

"You always look good, but this T-shirt does something for me." I run my hand up his taut abdomen to his chest. It's a solid, unyielding wall.

"You saying I should've went with a Captain America costume? It would've been a hell of a lot easier to make."

Wrapping his arm around me, he brushes his lips against mine. It's another sweet kiss, but I need more.

My hand tugs his short hair at the base of his neck as I press my lips more firmly against his. He responds with more intensity. It's deeper and rougher, almost savage, and I immediately want to track back to sweet.

A girl clears her throat from behind us then starts singing, "Bow chicka wow wow."

"Sorry for the audience." He laughs then releases me. "Jade, this is my sister Callie." Another girl enters the room. "And this is Ava."

Callie looks like Tad, only with long hair.

Ava, the brown-eyed blonde, picks up the garment bag from the back of the sofa. "Is this your costume?"

I nod.

"Can I take a peek?"

"Of course."

She unzips the bag to reveal the long dress with the blue bodice and yellow skirt. "Oh, you're going to fit right in with us as part of the princess crew. This is gorgeous."

"Thanks. They didn't have a cape for it though."

Callie inspects the white standing collar and fluffs out the puffy sleeves. "Oh, we can make you a cape and add a couple of details to this in plenty of time, if you want."

"Really?"

"Yeah."

Hours later, Callie and Ava not only have made a red cape but have jazzed up my dress with sequins. Tad helped by sewing on red bows. It didn't stop there—they styled my hair and perfected my makeup, treating me like a doll and making me a shoe-in Snow White. The three of us make a nice Disney princess collection with Callie as Belle and Ava as Cinderella. I'm glad I couldn't find another Marvel costume. I'd much rather be a princess than a superhero. And Onyx will get a kick out of it.

"Time for shots," Callie exclaims after we're all dressed and ready to go. The others should be here in about thirty minutes.

Callie and Ava head out of the workroom. Tad pulls me back when I start to follow.

"I'd kiss you right now if I wouldn't mess up your lips," he says.

I wrap my arms around him. "Lipstick can be reapplied."

"But then my sisters would yell at me."

"But you're going to have a mask on all night."

"But then you can take the mask off anytime you want after the costume contest."

Finally, somewhat satisfied with his response, I give him a quick peck, leaving a red lip mark on his cheek, then we head to the main room of the basement where Ava is behind the bar, shaking up a mixture in a silver cocktail shaker. Callie sets out four shot glasses, and Ava follows right behind, pouring a creamy mixture.

I've drank before, but I've never done a shot. I'm worried I'm not going to get it down right, messing up my makeup or dress in the process.

Tad holds out the narrow glass in front of me. Panic creeps across my face.

"You ever do a shot before?" he asks.

I shake my head.

"Just tilt your head back, open your throat, and let it slide down."

I do as he says, only my throat closes too soon and a trickle of the cinnamony, milky liquid runs down my chin. "I guess I need a bib."

Callie dabs my mouth with a small towel. "Just don't dribble it down your dress and you'll be good. Makeup can be redone. We'll touch up before we go and bring supplies with us."

Ava pours another round. "So, drink up." She holds up her shot glass. "Cheers."

Thirty minutes later, three shots have passed my lips and my mind has reached a state of euphoria. Tad has had double the amount of shots, and judging by the way his hands freely roam my midsection, he's on the same level of bliss as I am.

A buzzing sound comes from Tad's phone sitting on the countertop. "They just picked up Pepper. They'll be here in ten minutes."

I try to suppress a giggle, but it comes out sounding

like Mickey Mouse. "I'll go touch up the mess I created with my amateur shooting status."

Tad chuckles in response. "I'll go with you."

"Now, don't go messing up her dress, little bro," Callie calls out after us.

We make our way back to the workroom where I grab my makeup bag and turn on the Hollywood lights surrounding the full length mirror.

Tad comes up behind me, wrapping his arm around my waist, and plants kisses along my neck, his body armor of hard plastic pressing against me at every point. The points covering his hand touch my skin. An instant chill takes over as if the plastic is ice. His peacock blue eyes meet mine in the mirror and his smile is like a lazy Sunday afternoon, warming me.

I turn to meet his lips. The alcohol helps mask that Tad's kisses aren't to the same level of Hunter's, aiding me into letting go and being here in the moment. The moment goes on a little longer than usual, but not by much.

He pulls away, and his eyes dart to my makeup bag. "You better touch up your face. I need to go piss. I'll meet you back in the rec room."

The desire to be wanted boils over, and I tug at his retreating hand, pulling him back to me. I tease his lips with a kiss, pushing all the doubt away, then consume him with confidence. He gives me a bit more

then pulls away again with a wink and a grin as he exits the workroom.

What are you doing, Jade? Are you trying to make this a game? I feel like I'm over Hunter. I don't think I'm channeling feelings toward Tad because of Hunter no longer being available, but maybe I am.

I've been working on healing from my father's death, so I don't think I'm trying to fill this empty void with something that's just not there.

I know I can't snap my fingers and everything will be roses without thorns. But dammit, I want to feel normal. I want a real relationship. And Tad seems to want one too. Is he holding back or am I? Or is the hold up just a figment of my own imagination and I'm getting too antsy with wanting things to progress faster, with wanting to take the slow burn to a scorching inferno?

I touch up my makeup and join Ava and Callie in the rec room. It's nice to hang out with them—it's a dose of what it would've been like to have sisters. And I'm instantly hooked.

"You want another shot before we go?" Ava asks, shaking the cocktail mixer in front of my face.

I should say no. My head is swimming, but it's not drowning. This will be the last one. I'll sober up before the end of the night, just in case Janet is around when I get home. I respond, "Yes!"

My shot technique has greatly improved through-out the night. The liquid slides down my throat with

ease and I slam my glass down on the counter at the same time as Ava and Callie. Ava pours another round without even asking. This time, I beat them.

"Lookie who just graduated to a big girl shot," Callie says.

The giggle starts deep. I can't contain it. Pepper, Delani, Malachi, and Onyx walk in as I slip off the barstool in total hysterics and land on the floor. Yeah, maybe that last shot was a bad idea.

Ava runs over to Pepper and envelopes her into a gigantic hug, causing Ava's hoop skirt to flip up in the back. On a normal day, it wouldn't have been funny, but I can't stop laughing at the peek I get of the light blue and gold Cinderella-print leggings she has on underneath.

"Alright, who fed the princess alcohol?" Onyx hovers over me with a stern look on his face, holding his hand out. He looks funny with the Iron Man costume on without the mask. Did Tad look that silly? I glance over at Malachi and he looks funny, too, the laughter becomes even more uncontrollable.

After catching my breath, I realize I'm the only one laughing. I don't want to make a fool of myself in front of Tad's sisters having just met them. I center myself as best as I can with this liquid-filled head then grasp Onyx's awaiting hand, allowing him to pull me up without my assistance.

His arm, covered in the same hard plastic as Tad's, wraps around my waist. How is his armor touch warmer

than Tad's? Did he install tiny little heaters? His should be colder, seeing he just came in come from the chilly outside.

He whispers in my ear, "I've got you tonight, princess. You won't be leaving my sight."

A hard lump forms in my throat when his emerald and gold orbs probe me. I'm mad at myself for drinking now, knowing how Onyx isn't a fan.

He smooths out the yellow skirt of my Snow White dress. "You should've told me. I would've totally come as your prince charming."

Ava joins us and punches him on his shoulder, the plastic armor making a cracking sound. "Hey, you," she says with a glimmer in her eye.

The smile that crosses his face instantly makes a wave of destruction pass over me. "Hey, princess," he says to her.

The fact he called her a princess causes the wave to crash, thrashing me from the inside, taking me under in the ocean of liquor.

Tad's arm sneaks around my waist, easing the irritation a notch.

Why should I care if Onyx has a follower? He has so many followers at school. None of them ever bother me. And I never get upset when he and Pepper hang out.

Maybe that's because Pepper's told you they are nothing but friends.

Ava winks at him; he winks back.

Tad's mouth tickles my ear, reminding me of his presence. I spin around and wrap my arms around his neck, shutting off the view of whatever's going on between Ava and Onyx.

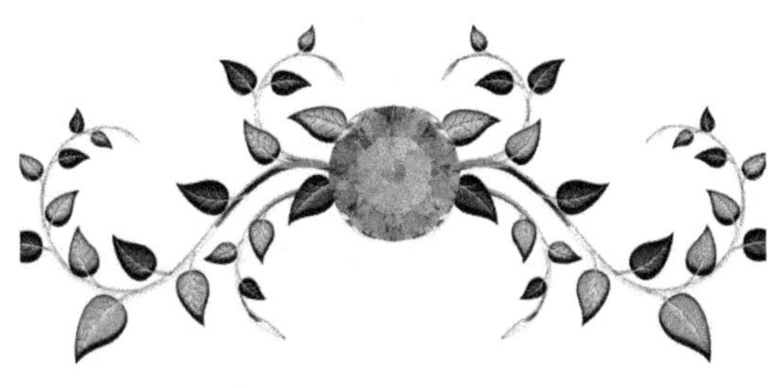

CHAPTER 23

ATCHING THE FLAMES lick the long branches helps the swirls still going on in my mind settle down.

We're in a football field-sized clearing in the center of the cornfield maze. In the center is a bonfire as big as a mini-van along with half the student population of Bradley and a ton of previous graduates. The party is an annual reunion of sorts for former and current students—a tradition that's gone on for ten years.

Onyx kept his promise. He hasn't let me out of his sight all night. Tad, Pepper, and Malachi have disappeared. Delani's hanging out with her volleyball friends near the big copper pot where the corn maze owner is boiling peanuts. Tad curled up his nose when Pepper mentioned heading over to get some. Of course, I had to try them since I seem to like most things that Tad thinks are disgusting. For once, he's right. They taste more like slimy worms than peanuts—at least what I imagine slimy worms taste like as I've never had one.

"Hey, Onyx," Ava yells from the other side of the bonfire. "Come join us for two truths and a lie."

Onyx flips his mask up and yells back, "I'll be over there in a minute."

"I need to pee," I say.

"Again? Is your bladder the size of a pea?" He rises from his perch on a log and holds out his hand for me.

"I can go byself." I take a step and stumble. Onyx grabs hold of my upper arm.

"No, you can barely walk."

"Onyx, hurry up," Ava yells. "You're on my team and we're starting."

I shake away his grasp on my bicep. "I can walk just fine. Just tell me how to get to the bathroom."

He glances at Ava again. "Third left, second right, then left, left, right."

"Second left, third right, then left, left right," I respond.

"No. Just let me take you."

I vehemently shake my head. Oh, I shouldn't have done that. I lean over and put my hands on my knees, closing my eyes and willing the violent tremors to subside.

Onyx bends down and lifts my head. "You okay?"

I straighten up. "Yeah, just really need to pee."

"Then, let's go."

"No, Ava's waiting. Just tell me how to get there."

He repeats the directions again.

"Got it," I say and head down the path that I hope takes me to the restrooms. Maybe I'll run into Tad again. He deserted me, saying he needed to take a piss, about thirty minutes ago.

When the small, wooden bath house comes into view, I let out a sigh of relief. I made it without any wrong turns. Take that, Onyx. I don't need you.

After washing my hands, I glance in the mirror. My lips are still a bright, cherry red. Tad hasn't kissed me again since we left his house. I need to go find him since the costume contest is over. Maybe he'll be ready to kiss me again.

He brought a tequila-filled flask with him and hasn't slowed down. If I'm feeling like I am—ready to pass out any minute but also slightly frisky—I can only imagine how he's doing with at least triple the amount of alcohol.

Grabbing one of the maps from the entrance to the maze, I head back in to search for Tad. He should be easy to find with his glowing eyes and chest. If I fail to find him, I should be able to find my way back to Onyx at least. All paths lead to the open field at some point.

Ten minutes pass and I'm far away from the center. I stop at one of the light posts and try to make sense of the map. But my eyes can't focus on it. Besides, I have no clue where I'm at. I haven't passed anyone lately. I

press against the side, looking for a bright orange glow over the stalks. Finally, I make out a slight brightness and turn right at the next path which takes me to a dark dead end. I'm disoriented for a moment, a combination of the darkness and the booze. I turn around to head back to the light post.

Two glowing eyes above a bright white light head in my direction. *Tad.* Remembering how he said his mask can easily be removed later for kisses, I run up to him, rip his mask off, and smother his lips, giving him everything my frisky self has.

He flinches back, but I refuse to give up, driven by so much disappointment and even more alcohol. My lips are hard and searching against his, demanding a response.

"Oh, fuck it," he says, covering my mouth hungrily with his, sending shivers racing through me.

It isn't the rough savageness he planted on me before. It's everything and more than Hunter ever gave me from a kiss. Desire burns and need aches deep within. A tiny thought of how he's held back on me all week, keeping me from having this level of purely passionate pleasure, enters my mind but quickly leaves when his tongue explores mine.

Blood pours through my heart and pounds in my brain, in a deeply satisfying way, making my knees tremble. This isn't a warning sign; the feeling's opposite of my heart bleed. It's a positive sign of so much

more. I want it to go on for eternity, to feel this level of consciousness as the flow, like a flame, grows more distinct than ever.

I gasp for air and my pounding brain begins to pulsate, making me woozy. The glow from his chest plate blinds me. I squeeze my eyes shut as a whirlwind hits my stomach. *Damn.*

"Jade," he draws out. His voice is heady and breathless and so wrong.

"Tad?" I ask, attempting to open my eyes but I'm blinded once again.

The light dims through my lids. When I open my eyes, I'm not greeted with an aqua storm. Instead, jade and gold swirl together in a lustful, molten desire.

I rush to the corner of the dark alcove and vomit.

"Good job, Onyx," he mumbles. "You finally kiss her and she pukes."

A moan escapes that I think comes from me. What have I done? I unknowingly cheated on Tad. And what's worse? It's with Onyx. What's this going to do to our friendship? I can't lose him. And I don't want to lose Tad over this.

"Come on, princess. Let's get you home."

"But Janet—"

"I'll worry about Janet. You worry about not puking on me."

My legs are swiped from beneath me and Onyx cradles me in his arms.

"Ow," I cry.

He pauses for a minute. "What's wrong?"

"That damn plastic armor hurts."

He stands me up, then rips off the top layer of his costume, leaving on the tight bodysuit. "Now, I'm going to carry you. Do you think you can carry this? Because if I don't return it to Tad, he's going to be even more pissed at me." He holds out the armor layer.

I nod and hug the pile of fabric and plastic to my chest with one arm. The other I wrap around his shoulder and he swoops me up again.

I hiccup then lean into his chest. "Thank you for taking care of me. I'm sorry for kissing you. I thought you were Tad."

A small sigh escapes him. "No sweat, princess."

In no time, we're out of the maze. He sets me down next to the passenger door of Janet's big Suburban that he borrowed for the evening. He opens the door and helps me in.

Are his lips still buzzing like mine are? Being so close to him right now, I want to pull him in and have him lull me back to euphoria. I kissed him, but he kissed me back. What does that mean? How will I be able to look at him the same? Or is it just the alcohol talking?

He doesn't seem to be affected. Maybe he's used to girls laying one on him. After turning on the vehicle and getting the heater going, he searches through the

armor layer of his costume then pulls out his phone and taps a few times before bringing it to his ear.

"What did you drive to the maze?" he asks whoever answers.

After a pause, he responds, "I had to leave. Jade's sick. Can you drive Pepper and Delani home? And make sure Malachi comes with you, no matter what he says. He's probably drunk, too."

Onyx nods his head a couple of times as the other person talks. I can't make out the voice on the other end.

"Oh, and tell Ava Becket I had to leave. She can get Sawyer to drive her, Callie, and Tad home."

Onyx hangs up and sets his phone in the cupholder.

"I'm sorry to take you away from Ava," I say. It was hard not to notice how he held her attention all night. Yes, it bothers me, but who am I to say who he can and can't date? "Look at you going after an older college chick."

He pulls out of the corn maze and hits the road that leads through town all the way home. "Ava only graduated last year. I'm actually older than her. And you didn't take me away from her. Nothing was going on."

"Oh, come on. Did you not notice the way she looked at you?"

"I can't help the way I look, not to mention my charming personality," he teases. "Besides, I've been there, done that, and threw away the fucking T-shirt. She's too much of a stuck-up party girl for me."

"Oh." I lean my head against the cool window and close my eyes to help slow my pulsing head.

"FUCK," ONYX YELLS. He slams on the breaks, jolting me awake as he puts his arm in front of me like he's trying to protect me from flying out the window. I stiffen at the impending impact, but it doesn't come.

"What was that?" I ask.

He drops his hand and picks up speed again. "A deer. Sorry. Didn't mean to scare you. It's the third one I've seen tonight. It's mating season, so you're not the only horny one out there."

"You better watch out. I might decide to puke on you." My stomach turns at the word—*puke*. "Can you pull over? Otherwise, I *will* puke on you."

Luckily, we're out of farm land and now on the outskirts of town. He pulls into a lit shopping center and parks the car. I hop out and run to the side of a building, letting it all out once again. Onyx holds back the hair that's fallen out of my red bow.

Behind us, a back door opens and a tatted-up guy with a long beard escorts a woman out. "Don't come back, Lily, until you can afford to pay your tab."

"Fuck," Onyx mutters. He lets go of my hair and turns his back away from them.

The lady stops beside me. "Oh, Mike. You've really done it now. This poor girl's having a rough night. I guess I need to call the sheriff to let him know you're serving the underaged. "

Mike crosses his arms, flexing his biceps. "And I'll tell him that you've propositioned every single one of my patrons this evening. Then, you can join your old man in jail. See how happy he'll be that you're out selling yourself for your next hit."

There's something familiar about her. Her long, wavy, brown hair lays in strings, framing her sunken face. She came to senior night, and Janet made her leave. She's the poster child of what meth does to someone. I can see it now. An image of a beautiful thirty-something next to this washed out chick with the title, *Meth-A-Morphosis*. Her glossed over hazel eyes stare down at me in my kneeled position.

"Oliver?" Mike says, adding, "Is that you, kid?"

Onyx turns around with a clinched jaw.

"Well, I'll be. I haven't seen you in ages. Perfect timing. You can take your white trash mom home." He pushes the lady toward Onyx.

Mom? Am I so drunk that I'm hearing things? The answer is yes. But I swear he said *mom*.

Mike turns around and walks through the back door, leaving the three of us alone.

"Ollie, baby." Lily wraps her arms around Onyx. He pushes her arms away and takes a step back. She pouts and says, "You have any money I can pay Mike to get him off my back?"

He hits his pocketless bodysuit then raises his arms. "I'm all tapped out from the last time you needed money."

"Can you at least give me a ride home? Looks like your date won't be much fun anyway." She picks up the bottom of my cape that's piled on the concrete path and slowly releases it.

"Leave her alone."

"Aw, does Ollie have a girlfriend?"

"I'll take you home under one condition."

"And what's that? You'll disown me again?"

"I've told you how you can earn me back. You just refuse to do it."

"Are you going to take me home or not?"

"I will but don't say another fucking word. One peep and you're out of the car."

He helps me stand and removes the cape from my neck, not meeting my eyes in the process. I lace my fingers with his and give his hand a squeeze as we walk back to the car.

Lily lets out a whistle and runs a hand along the hood of the Suburban. "Look at my boy, riding high."

As Onyx clicks to unlock the vehicle, Lily hops in the front seat.

"I'm fine in the back," I say.

"Thanks," he mumbles, opening the door. He lifts me up then buckles me in.

I reach out and touch his face to make him look at me. His hardened eyes stare back. It's not how his eyes are supposed to look.

"I hope you don't remember a single thing from tonight," he whispers.

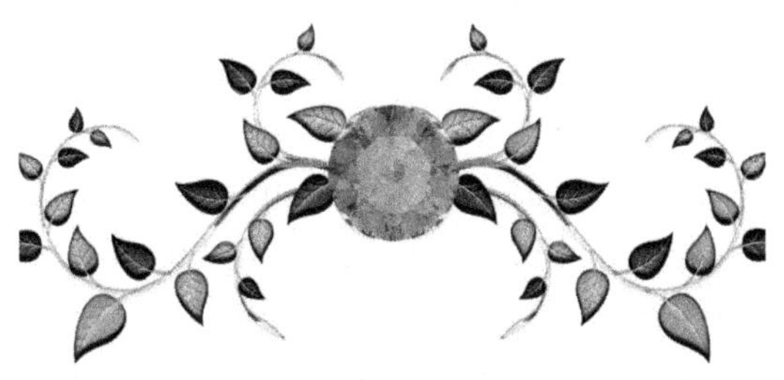

CHAPTER 24

SOMEONE'S DRIVING A drill bit into my forehead when I wake up. My entire body is stiff and sore. Light fills the room and I'm in an unfamiliar bed. I jolt up and take in my surroundings. *Onyx's room.*

A piece of notebook paper with Onyx's scribble sits beneath a bottle of water, two ibuprofens, and my charging phone on top of his night stand.

> Thanks for a "fun" night, princess. I hope you don't remember anything. I'm trying to forget EVERYTHING. Well, almost everything. There's one thing I'd like to keep in my memory bank. :)

I gladly swallow the painkillers and take a sip of water. My stomach revolts at the liquid, but luckily, there's nothing left to come up, not even my stomach juices.

I remember dropping his mother off at a dilapidated house with a broken chain link fence. I remember Onyx carrying me upstairs to his room. I remember puking again. I remember him helping unzip my dress in the back, then him freaking out and turning around when I went to take it the rest of the way off. I had on a bra and yoga pants underneath, but he muttered something about me kissing him and not needing to see me in a bra before tossing me a Metallica tee over his shoulder. I remember him making me take a shower. And that's all.

Did I even get out of the shower? Did he have to help me? Did he see me completely naked?

Why the hell did I kiss him?

And was that really his mom?

I'm never drinking again.

I pick up my phone and scroll through my text messages. Several from Tad wondering where the hell I went to, including a worried one from just a few minutes ago.

> **TAD:** Please message me when you get this. I don't know what happened to you last night.

I shoot off a quick message.

JADE: Hey you. I got sick and Onyx drove me home. Just woke up. I feel like hell. How are you doing?

TAD: About the same. Can I come over?

JADE: Of course.

Twenty minutes later, I'm rocking on the front porch, waiting for Tad. Onyx walks out of the house with a mug in his hand and a knowing smirk on his face. He hands me the cup of coffee.

"What do you remember from last night?" he asks.

I take a sip. It's just the way I like it—sweet with enough cream to make it a caramel color. "Not much," I admit. There are too many holes in the evening for me. Except for that kiss. I remember every single thing about it. The way his lips felt. The way his tongue danced with mine. The way my skin tingled all over when he held me tight.

He nods woodenly. "Good, let's keep it that way. I'll see you tonight. Nutmeg needs a good workout." His footsteps thunder down the porch stairs then he disappears into the Dogwood barn.

What does he not want me to remember? His mom? The kiss? Him potentially seeing me in the buff?

The drill headache has gone and been replaced with a hammer and nail. Every muscle still aches from the retching I did.

Tad's truck comes to a stop in front of the house. His face is downtrodden when he walks in my direction. Is this not going to end well?

I set the half-finished mug on the side table and walk toward him.

He glances up and gives me a soft smile. "Can we go for a walk?"

"Yeah, sure. Let's go down to the dock." I entwine my fingers with his, more out of wanting to know how this walk is going to go. He squeezes my hand then brings it up to his lips.

"Don't ever let me drink again." I say.

"Okay, because I don't want you disappearing on me again."

"But you disappeared on me first."

"I'm sorry. I lost track of time."

We make it to the dock and he hesitates on the semi-rotted wood. "Is this safe?"

"Yeah. Onyx and I have coffee here every morning."

His eyes narrow and he releases my hand. "I need to ask you something."

"Ask away."

"I've asked before but I need to ask again."

"Go ahead."

"Is there something going on between you and Onyx?"

I hope my cheeks don't redden at the thought of that kiss that I'm not supposed to remember or be thinking about. Although, I feel like I should come clean. "We're just friends." But are we?

He squints his eyes, studying me. Does he know something?

Might as well come clean. "I went looking for you last night and got lost in the maze. Then an Iron Man was heading toward me. I figured it was you. I ripped the mask off like you showed me and kissed the person. Only it wasn't you, it was Onyx. Then I puked and he made me come home because I could barely walk."

He lets out a sigh of relief. "My sister said she saw you kissing him. I've been sick about it this whole time. So, nothing is going on?"

I shake my head. "He's my best friend." I might have really enjoyed that kiss, but it was only because I thought it was Tad. Had I realized it was Onyx, it might not have knocked my socks off. And besides, Onyx seems to want me to forget it ever happened.

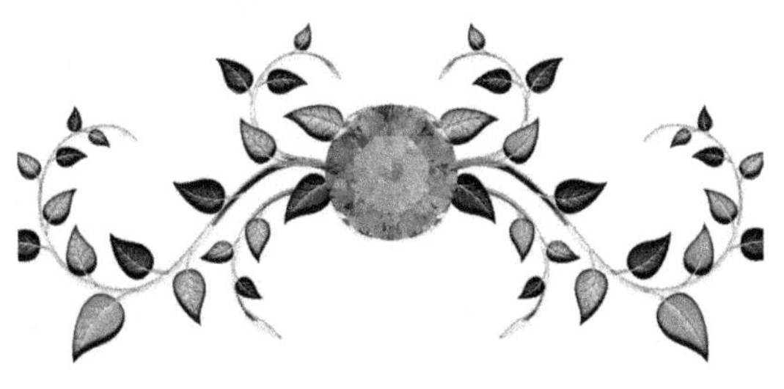

CHAPTER 25

TWO WEEKS FLY by to Friday night—the last football game of the season. The last football game for Tad, Onyx, and Malachi. Bittersweet, just like the past few weeks.

Things are going fine for Tad and me. It's still on that sweet level, but the passion is growing with each kiss. He asked me to hangout with him twice this past week, which we've never done before. We even have plans for after tonight's game, tomorrow night, and all day Sunday.

Onyx hasn't mentioned the kiss or the run-in with his mother. We still meet for coffee mornings and for hot chocolate nightcaps. He's definitely become my best friend—one that I can share almost everything with. Sometimes, I wish he'd share a bit more. I haven't asked him about his mom, but that doesn't mean I'm not curious about her. And I vaguely remember

something about an old man being in jail. Is Onyx's dad in jail? And why does everyone call him Oliver?

Malachi, on the other hand, has retreated from me once again. He's back to not speaking to anyone, and he's not eating with us during lunch anymore. The night after the Halloween party, once my hangover had finally subsided, I went to his room to chat. He gave me his, "Not in the mood, Jade." Later that week, I got a, "Just leave me alone." So, since then, I have.

I love him, and I'd do anything for him. But what can I do if he's not willing to let me help? Is it still about the guy that broke his heart? I feel his pain; I know how hard it is to recover from a broken heart.

I've thought about making the theme of my art project about heartbreak. After sketching out a couple of ideas on my iPad then painting one of the sketches on canvas, it doesn't feel right. I'm missing inspiration, as if my heartbreak wasn't strong enough. Art was never a struggle before, but every time I attempt to draw or paint, it feels like I'm climbing a rocky mountain in my bare feet.

The stadium erupts in cheers. A celebration occurs in our endzone. I guess we scored; I should pay attention considering my boyfriend is the quarterback.

Pepper pokes me in the side. "What's with you tonight? You're zoned out."

"Sorry. Thinking about my art project." The project that's going nowhere thanks to the lack of inspiration. "Who scored?"

"Pass to Malachi in the endzone."

Even though Malachi's been in one of his moods, he and Tad have been on point this entire game. It's the best I've seen them play together. The fourth quarter just started and it looks like it's now tied up. Well, it'll be tied up after Onyx makes the extra point.

"Let's go, Prince," someone yells as Onyx waits for the ball.

Instead of watching for the snap, Onyx turns his attention to a man wearing a black bandana standing along the fence close to the exit. The ball's snapped, the holder sets the ball, and Onyx just stands there, staring. The other team immediately tackles him.

What just happened?

Out of the corner of my eye, I see Janet run down the stairs in the next section and stop in front of another parent. She's animated, throwing up her arms, and talking fast. I can't make out anything she's saying.

"Hey, Pepper, who's my aunt talking to?" I nod my head in Janet's direction.

"That's Sheriff May," she responds.

I divert my attention back to the man in the black bandana. That's when I notice the lady standing next to him. *Onyx's mother.*

My eyes dart to the field, searching for Onyx. He's running across the field toward the parking lot. Without a second thought, I take off after him. My only advantage is that I'm closer to the lot than he is but not by much.

By the time I make it to the first row of cars, Onyx's already past the gym.

"Onyx," I scream.

He comes to a halt but doesn't turn around.

I rush toward him. When I finally reach him, my calves are tight and on fire, and I'm sucking in air and can't seem to fill my lungs enough. I lean over to catch my breath.

He removes his helmet, revealing his hard and distant eyes. "Can you take me home?"

"Yeah, my car is this way." I grab his hand and lead him to my car.

The drive home is quiet. With every glance I take his way, Onyx's face is frozen, and he stares off into nowhere. He walks zombie-like up the stairs and into his room where I help him remove all the football gear and strip him down to his boxer briefs. He crawls into bed and curls into a ball, facing the wall. My heart breaks for him and the level of pain I see. He's way too special to feel this way. To be this down.

I grab a Yoda T-shirt and a pair of shorts from his dresser and change out of my sweater and jeans in the bathroom. I then inch into bed and wrap my arms around him. His body shivers then relaxes.

"That was my father," Onyx whispers. "He's supposed to be in jail. He's the drunk driver who killed my grandparents."

With the exception of my father's death, every little heartbreak I've ever had seems so insignificant at this moment. He's been so in tune to my needs, helping me stitch my soul back together. A wave of apprehension washes over me. Have I been a bad friend in return? What can I do to help him?

He rolls over, with eyes full of tears. "My name's Oliver Prince."

I wipe a tear from his cheek. "You're Onyx Finch."

A soft smile graces his face but it's quickly masked by a melancholy frown. "Onyx Finch was my grandfather. I had my name legally changed when I turned eighteen."

"I bet he'd be proud for you to carry on his name."

He slightly shakes his head and glances away. "My parents are drug addicts."

I grasp his chin, forcing him to look at me. "It doesn't matter who your parents are. They don't define you. You do. And by my definition, you're an incredible human being because you think of everyone. You make people laugh. You can make someone who feels like there's absolutely no hope be optimistic. You proved to me that no matter what's thrown our way, that the sun always rises, making it a new day. And to make the most out of it. Don't ever forget that."

His face stills even more. "I'm the one who put my father in jail."

Pensively, I stare at him, taking in his hollow eyes, his flat-lined lips. Is he trying to tell me something here? I always thought Onyx let nothing bother him. That he's as strong as they come. His eyes always tell happy stories. His mouth is always curved in a mischievous grin. Is it all a mask?

"If your dad was driving drunk, then it was he who put himself in jail. Not you."

"He wasn't in jail for killing my grandparents." He rubs his hands over his eyes.

"I don't understand."

"No one knew it was him. There were no witnesses. According to the police report, it was a hit and run. My grandparents didn't mean enough to this town to pursue justice. You're either in or you're out. And the part of town I'm from, we're always out."

"How do you know he did it?"

"It's a hunch. His truck went missing after the accident."

Since Janet talked about the possibility of miss vain being involved in my dad's death, I haven't been able to get it out of my mind even though I'd tried to forget. I've combed through everything that happened before and after his death. Miss vain could've been involved if she knew she was getting everything in the Will. My hunch tells me she did have something to do with it. Miss vain is incredibly selfish, always

has been. But how can I prove that she was the mastermind in the shooting when all video evidence points to the robber?

"Did you ever bring your hunch up to anyone?" I ask.

He bows his head and murmurs, "No."

"Why not?"

"I'm the son of the town's drug dealer. And you saw my mom. Even though my grandparents were amazing to me, they weren't saints either. I don't ever talk to my father's family. They own the tattoo parlour in Maybee and are always in and out of trouble. I'm, by definition, local yokel, white trash. No one would've taken me seriously. And I can't prove it."

"How long ago was this?"

"Two years ago."

"What about now? Why wouldn't they take you seriously now?"

He rolls over and turns on his back, staring at the ceiling, weighing the question.

He has to know he's worth something, everything really. I blink away the tears welling in my eyes. I wish I could reach in and take away all his pain. "I don't know you as anything but Onyx Finch. And that's who you are and should be. Not some hillbilly hick who won the parent lottery. So, if you feel like you need to take him down, do it. I'll be here to support you." I curl up beside him and lay my head on his chest.

His silence is painful. I want him to talk. I want to know everything there is to know about the guy who's helped me feel again. I lift my head up to make sure he didn't fall asleep on me. His eyes read the ceiling as if it were a book.

He draws out a long breath then says, "I remember him coming home that night really late. He liked to take out his frustrations on me or mom. That night, he was beating the shit out of my mom, blaming her for ruining his life. She got pregnant with me when she was sixteen. For the first time, I fought back. But I had no chance. I missed school for a week. Broken rib, black eyes.

"When I caught wind of a big drug deal he was involved in, I called in an anonymous tip. He got thrown in jail. It was supposed to be a five-year sentence, but it's only been over a year and a half. He found out it was me that turned him in, and all my friends from that world turned on me." His face is marked with loathing.

"I stayed with my mom for as long as I could take it, but she was always strung out. I'd leave then she'd beg me to come home, telling me she'd clean up. I haven't been back in over a year. She just sees me as someone who can work to provide her with her next fix.

"I gave her an ultimatum last time. Either get clean and have a relationship with me or don't and never see me again. Since Janet has taken me in and made me

feel welcome, I don't know if I'd go back even if she did decide to come clean.

"It doesn't matter anyway. The minute I graduate, I'm on my bike and getting the hell out of this town. I'm not good enough for the elite, but I no longer fit in with the hillbilly hicks."

Every bit of my being aches for Onyx. I want to stitch him back together now that he's showing me how deeply shattered he is.

"Can we talk about something else?" he pleads.

"When are we going to the beach to go shrimping?" I say as a diversion. "I'm really craving shrimp and grits."

His laugh is triumphant. I love that he can turn on a dime, waving off the things that bother him so easily. "Spring break trip?"

"Sign me up."

He rubs his hand up and down my back. "I'm baking a cake for Reid tomorrow. His birthday's Sunday. You want to help?"

"Are you going to share your baking secrets with me?"

"Maybe."

"Then yes. How are you decorating it?"

"I don't know. Got any ideas?"

"Can we make it look like a stack of pancakes covered in mustard and ketchup?" I wrinkle my nose at the way Reid eats pancakes. The dude can be so weird.

"That would be perfect."

"So, Onyx Finch, are you the amazing photographer that signs his photos as *Prince* at school?"

"Oliver Prince took those photos."

I set my hands on his chest and rest my chin on top to see his face. "Well, I need a photographer and you're the best one ever. I need your help with my art exhibit."

"I don't take pictures anymore, unless they're on my phone."

"Why not?"

"That was Oliver Prince."

"Well, too bad. I'm not accepting no for an answer. Besides, the Princess needs her Prince to be her photographer."

A cold, congested expression settles on his face. "Please don't ever call me prince."

"I meant my prince charming."

His face transforms, spreading into a wide smile. "Now who's being funny?"

"I learned from the best."

"Thank you for being here."

"That's what best friends are for."

Within minutes, his hand stops rubbing my back and his body relaxes. I should go to the main house, but instead, I grab one of his extra pillows and curl up next to him.

I would've never guessed Onyx had such a dark past, and I'm sure it's worse than what he shared. I was blessed with a wonderful mother and father. I'm

sad that neither of them are with me today, but I have incredible memories to cherish forever.

Onyx doesn't.

The house and the store? They're just material. They mean a lot to me, but not having them doesn't mean I can't function like a normal person. It doesn't mean I can't fully pull together the pieces of my life that are shattered.

My thoughts take me back to my art exhibit as Onyx's chest moves up and down with sleep. Why not create an exhibit about the healing process? Start with pure chaos and bring everything together in a composed piece. It wouldn't be just for me, but for Onyx, too.

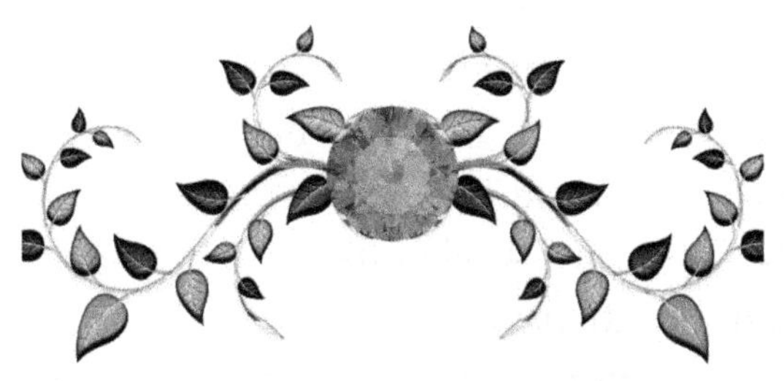

CHAPTER 26

"DAMMIT," TAD SAYS, throwing his controller on the ground.

"Give up already. This boss owns you." I grab his fingers to prevent him from picking up the game controller again.

He shakes his hand away. "I can't. I've got to beat this asshole."

I drag out a long breath. I would leave if I had my car. Spending four hours watching Tad play video games is not how I prefer to spend a Saturday night with my boyfriend.

Tapping my camera icon, I snap a picture then text it to Pepper.

> **JADE:** Please tell me all your dates with Tad were this riveting.

Pepper's parents went on a cruise, leaving her to fend for herself. She spent the entire past week with me. Most nights, we did more chatting than sleeping. She gave me her and Tad's entire dating history. It was pretty uneventful, kind of like how I've been feeling about our relationship.

They didn't have sex until they'd been together for a year and a half. And after that, everything went downhill. They were both virgins and had been dating for both freshman and sophomore years.

Is he going to make me wait that long? Because there's no way that's going to happen. Sometimes, I feel like he has no interest in taking it to another level. He hasn't even felt me up, and we've been dating for almost two months now. I know there's no set rules or guidelines when it comes to this shit. But I'd like to think that we're heading in some sort of direction.

Maybe Hunter ruined me. He felt me up on the first date. He showed me what it feels like to really be touched. Hunter used to be the best kisser I'd ever been with, but another unspeakable kiss takes the top there.

Jade, you're not supposed to even think about that kiss.

Even though Pepper was my guest for the past week, she encouraged me to hang out with Tad and not let her presence prevent me from doing so. But he only had me over one day. Granted, his house was full of relatives for Thanksgiving up until this morning.

I thought maybe he invited me over for a reason tonight since his parents and sisters are gone, even coming to the ranch to pick me up. But nope. I don't even remember him kissing me when he picked me up. He's been sitting here on the couch with a game controller glued to his hand—until he pitches a hissy and tosses it.

Why hasn't Pepper responded yet? She said she was going to hang out at home with her parents and to text her if I got bored. Well, I'm bored. *Answer me, Pepper!*

I shoot off a text to Onyx. He said he's hanging out with Malachi to play video games. I should've just told all of them to do it together.

> **JADE:** When are the photos supposed to be delivered?

> **ONYX:** They came in today.

> **JADE:** How did they turn out?

> **ONYX:** Breathtaking. What else do you expect when you have such an awesome photographer.

After five minutes, I give up on any response from Onyx and pull out my iPad to sketch design ideas for the remaining pieces I have to make for the exhibit. It's due in just over a week. I've decided to call my work *Shattered Life Healing*. It reflects a progression of overcoming, of putting the pieces back together.

The first one is a jumble of found objects, paint splatters, pieces of metal, with scratches and rips in the canvas. I'm going to take one of the photos Onyx took of me and tear it into tiny pieces and scatter them over the artwork. The remaining works come together in a similar look but show some parts coming together in a progression until the last piece when everything is whole.

My phone vibrates. *It's about damn time, Pepper!* I need her to end my boredom. The text is from a number not listed in my phone.

birthday. I just wanted to check on you to make sure you're okay, and if you ever need anything, don't hesitate to reach out to me or Diane. I sure miss you and your dad. The store isn't the same. I was shocked she even hired me back. When I came back, I realized why. It's in complete shambles, the books, the inventory. Everything. I don't know if I can turn it around. I'm no good at this text thing. But thought it'd be weird if I called you.

I drop my phone on the floor at the same time Tad drops the controller in another hissy fit.

He lays his head on my shoulder. "I can't do it. I can't beat this dude."

I don't have time for him to pay attention to me now. This text means everything. I lean down and pick up the controller, putting it back in his hand. "Yes, you can. You're almost there."

"Can you try to beat him for me?" he whines.

"No."

He pouts but focuses back on the large screen.

I quickly forward the text to Onyx.

JADE: Check this message out. This is my IN!

After the night Onyx opened up to me about his parents, we've left no stone unturned. He even, although begrudgingly, listens to me whine about Tad and his lack of wandering hands. Onyx always jokes about it, saying he can solve that problem and holds out his hands, wiggling his fingers as if he's testing the firmness of an avocado.

We've both determined that we're going to spend Christmas break formulating plans to figure out how to turn our hunches into something the cops can work with. He found out that his father went back to prison for another drug-related charge as well as breaking parole not even a week after the football game. He'd like him to stay there for good. Maybe that would help his mom eventually turn her life around.

ONYX: WHAT??? Did you message him back?

JADE: Not yet.

ONYX: DO IT!

I add Mr. Regal's number to my contacts and shoot him a response.

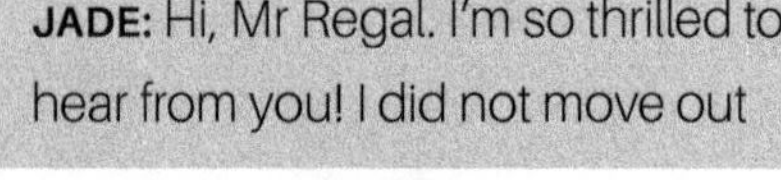

on my 18th. She kicked me out.
I'm now in Kentucky with my aunt.
I really am glad you reached out.
I need a huge favor. If you-know-
who ever leaves for more than a
day, can you let me know? I really
need to get into the store to look for
that ring Dad made for Mom before
she died. Dad had a few hiding
places that I'd like to check. She
has the house. She has the store.
But she can't have that ring!

MR. REGAL: I'm so sorry about
everything. I can't believe what has
happened to you. This is not how
your dad would've wanted things.
I will definitely let you know if she
ever goes out of town. Right now,
she's spending day in and day out
at the store. Well, Diane is telling
me it's bedtime. I hope to see you
soon.

I forward my message and Mr. Regal's response to Onyx.

> **ONYX:** We're going to find that ring for my pretty little princess's finger.

I laugh and send him a *Single Ladies* by Beyonce gif.

"What's funny?" Tad asks with his eyes still glued to the television. He may be boring, but the way his eyes sparkle with the glow from the television is sexy as hell.

I toss my phone on the coffee table then take the controller from Tad's hands, placing it next to my phone. A child-like fear takes over his face, but I ignore it. I crawl into his lap and straddle him, covering my mouth with his. His lips respond in that boring way I don't want them to, limp and lifeless. I attempt to lull him into the impossible kiss. The one where fireworks explode with a dreamlike intensity. No matter how hard I press, it doesn't happen.

A sigh releases from my mouth as his lips move to my throat, nibbling and sucking as they go. He takes it as a sign of enjoyment, and not the displeasure it was for, and flips me over, crushing me on the couch. It goes from sickly sweet and tender to too feral and clumsy. Pulling me up, he lifts my sweater over my head, revealing my black, lace bra.

Now we're going somewhere, but do I want to go there with him?

A gasp is followed by the sound of glass shattering from somewhere behind us. Tad jerks his head and looks up. He immediately climbs off of me and yells out, "Wait!" He runs after whoever just entered his basement through the sliding glass door.

I quickly put on my sweater and slip on my boots. By the time I make it to the front of the house, I see the taillights of Tad's truck flying down the road.

What the hell just happened?

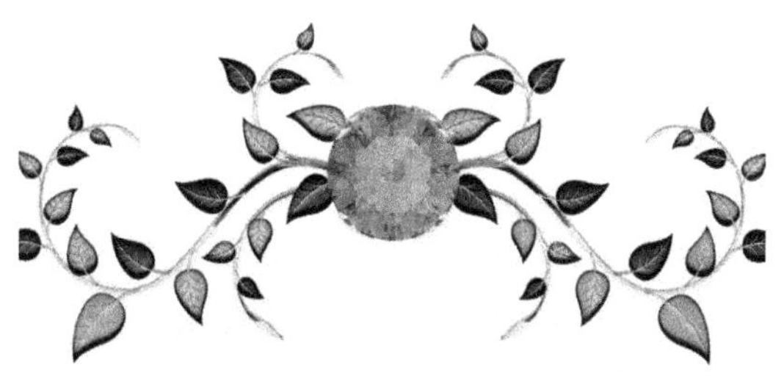

CHAPTER 27

AN HOUR HAS passed since Tad ran out. I tried calling him but he left his phone on the coffee table. I also tried snooping but his phone needs a fingerprint to access anything. I've cleaned up the shattered liquor bottle that whoever stopped by dropped.

Who the hell was he chasing? His absence tells me he caught up to whoever it was.

Pepper's not answering me. Was it her? Has she been lying to me this whole time, telling me they've been over for a long time only to try to steal him back when I least expect it? If she'd been honest from the start, I wouldn't have pursued him.

Stop it, Jade. That's too far-fetched. Pepper is my friend.

But it's the only thing I've got.

Maybe it's someone I don't even know.

Am I even surprised there's someone else?

I always feel like he's holding back. I've resolved to think that it's just the way he is. That getting all hot and heavy isn't his thing.

And if I'm being honest with myself, I've held back on my end, too. Maybe out of being hurt. Maybe because when I first met him, my heart bleed warned me. Afraid that I'd wind up right where I started when I moved here, brokenhearted.

So, why am I pissed? I feel like I've been played somehow. Like this was all a game. Some big joke and it's on me. My wounds opening up again. Am I just not enough to keep a guy interested?

No, Jade. That's not it. I just haven't found *that* guy yet. Soon, I'll go off to college and have many relationships. Some may hurt. One may last forever. It's called life and mine is just beginning.

One thing is for sure; I want to go home.

Onyx picks up on the first ring. "What's up, princess?"

"Can you come pick me up? You can drive my car. My keys are on my nightstand."

"Uh, duh. If you're letting me drive your car, I'd be happy to come pick you up. Are you at Pepper's or Tad's?"

"Tad's."

He blows a heavy breath into the phone. "Is he too drunk to bring you home?"

"No. He hasn't been drinking tonight. He just disappeared."

"What do you mean disappeared? Like poofed? Vanished into thin air?"

"No, like ran out of here as if he was on fire."

"Were you trying to set him on fire?"

"Onyx, please, just come get me. I want to come home."

"Okay, princess. I'll be there in fifteen."

I head outside and sit on the front porch to wait despite the freezing cold. It feels strange and uncomfortable being in Tad's house all by myself.

When Onyx pulls in, I hop in the passenger side. My heated seat is already on and the heater is on full blast. Onyx knows I don't like to be cold.

He keeps the car in park and stares at me.

"What?" I ask.

"What's going on?"

"I don't know."

"Care to elaborate?"

Fatigue hits me like a ton of bricks, making my nerves throb. I roll my neck and sigh. "Just drive."

"Fine." He pulls out of the driveway and heads toward the main road.

"Wait." It's killing me. I have to know. I have to rule it out. "Can you drive by Pepper's?"

"Why?"

Irritation builds. "Because I asked you to."

A shadow of annoyance crosses his face. "Geez. Did you have a pea under your mattress last night?"

This isn't Onyx's fault. He did come to my beck and call. I don't need to take it out on him. "I'm sorry. I just really don't know what happened tonight. One minute we're making out and the next he's out the door."

"So, why Pepper's?"

"I need to rule out that he isn't there."

"Why don't you call her?"

"I've been texting her all night and she hasn't responded. I know I'm being paranoid. I just need to confirm that she's a true friend and not playing some big game with me."

"Pepper wouldn't do that."

"I don't think she would either, but I've got nothing else."

When we drive by Pepper's house, her car is there, her parent's two cars are there, and another I wasn't expecting. One of the ranch's work trucks. But Tad's truck isn't.

Relief but also frustration wrecks me.

"Happy?" Onyx asks.

"Yeah, but is Malachi here?"

"He has his own car. He wouldn't drive one of the work trucks."

I already know this, but who else would be there from the ranch? "Then who's here?"

Onyx bites the side of his cheek.

"You know something," I say.

"I'm not supposed to say anything."

"Okay, then stop. I need to go see who's here." I grab onto the door handle, waiting for a chance to exit.

"Ms. Nosy."

"Stop, please."

"Will you drop it if I tell you?"

"Yes."

His eyebrows raise. "Like never mention it again?"

"Yes."

"Mica."

Mica? What the hell is Mica doing at Pepper's house. "What?"

"I told you, now drop it."

My mouth drops open, finally fully registering what it means. "How long?"

"Drop it."

"Just tell me how long," I beg.

"About as long as you and Tad."

"Huh. Well, let's hope they last longer than Tad and me."

He gives me the side eye. "So it's over with Tad?"

"Most definitely."

Onyx tries to ask me more questions on the drive home, but I zone him out.

Pepper and Mica? How could she not tell me? I mean, knowing her now and not as the girl I first met, I can actually see it. So, why is she hiding it? Is it because

Mica's younger than her? Is that why she snuck out of my room a couple of times when she stayed with us? Is that why she encouraged me to go hang out with Tad?

Wow. How did I not notice this? Onyx and I went horseback riding with them about a month ago. Looking back, a lot of smiling, laughter, and flirting occurred.

I was hungry and made Onyx come back with me so I wouldn't turn hangry. They stayed out, not showing back up to the house for two hours. How did I not register it?

I'm blind, obviously.

More concern for another day. It's cool, though. I need to tell her that I know and that I'm happy for her. And she needs to give me all the juicy details, not that I want juicy details about my normally silent cousin. If anyone can get Mica to talk, it's her.

Onyx parks and shuts off the car. "Look, honey. We're home."

I grit my teeth. I'm not in the mood to laugh.

His glare burns me. "Welp, you're welcome."

I flinch at the irritation in his voice. "I'm sorry. It sucks to be cheated on. I don't know how to process it."

"You think Tad's cheating on you?"

"Someone walked in on us. That's why he ran out."

"You didn't mention that."

"I don't know who it was. I heard a noise and whoever it was dropped a glass bottle. Then Tad bolts."

Onyx purses his lips and nods.

"You know something?"

He quickly shakes his head. His Adam's apple bobs as he swallows hard.

"You know something."

"No, I don't."

"Yes, you do. I can see it all over your face. Just tell me who it is."

His expression is taut and derisive when he says, "I don't know who it is."

"Fine. Don't tell me."

He closes his eyes and massages his temple. "Jade."

"It's okay, Onyx. Just. Whatever."

"You're blind."

"Obviously."

His face stills and grows serious. Icy contempt flashes in his eyes. A black silence surrounds us. Finally, he says, "You're blind, Jade. You need to see what's right in front of you."

"What's that supposed to mean?"

His eyes drop from my hardened gaze. "Just forget it. Here's your keys." He drops them in my lap then opens the door and walks away.

My pulse beats erratically as my mind is consumed by anxiety. I run to my room and lock the door. Curling up in bed, I let my tortured thoughts take over. Pepper doesn't trust our friendship enough to share her love life with me. My boyfriend is cheating on me. My best friend knows something about the cheating, but he's not telling me. What the hell am I missing?

Not even thinking about Mr. Regal contacting me today can pull me out of this dark place.

I've back-tracked to the first piece in my art exhibit. Broken chaos.

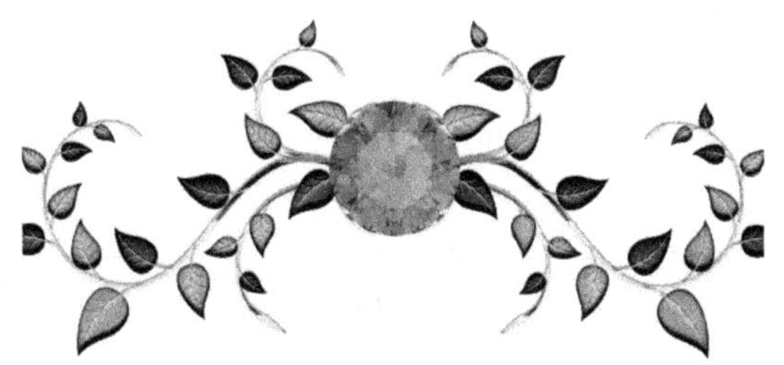

CHAPTER 28

ONYX DIDN'T MEET me for the sunrise Sunday morning. He wasn't around when Janet made breakfast. I took a walk through the stables and around the property but never saw him. His bike was there. All the work trucks were there. He was there. I guess he's just too pissed to talk to me.

My thoughts keep bouncing around in my head. What the hell am I missing?

By two in the afternoon, I've sent three text messages to Tad, but my phone hasn't buzzed. And Onyx has yet to surface. I don't know who I'm more pissed at for ignoring me: Onyx or Tad.

I'll let Onyx cool off until tonight. If he doesn't show up to the cupola at bedtime, I'll go seek him out.

But Tad? I'm doing something about it now. I grab his letterman's jacket off my desk chair and head to his house. His truck is in the driveway. His parents are due back home sometime today, but they don't appear to be back just yet.

I knock on the front door and wait. After five minutes, I walk around to the basement. The sliding glass door is unlocked, so I slip in.

A light murmur of the TV comes from the recreation room, along with voices and laughter. I can't make out another distinctive voice, but he's definitely not here alone. Part of me wants to turn around and wait to face him at school tomorrow. But I really don't want another restless night. We've reached the point where our relationship needs to be resolved—it has to end.

I slink closer and closer to the sounds as my heart pounds out of my chest.

"Thank you for not giving up on me," Tad says. I still can't see him.

"I almost did this time," says another voice, only it's not a girl's voice.

It's familiar and it vibrates off my eardrums. Then, everything clicks in my mind. I finally realize what I've been missing and hurtle back to Earth as reality strikes. It's an awakening experience that should leave me reeling, but it doesn't. It leaves me mad at myself and even more mad at Onyx for not telling me.

He knew this was going on and he left me hanging, causing me to hurt everyone, including myself.

I walk around the couch, not surprised at what I see. Malachi and Tad cuddled up together on a pile

of pillows and blankets. Malachi's head rests in Tad's lap. His mouth curved in tenderness as Tad weaves his fingers through his hair.

My voice is resigned when I say, "I finally get it."

Tad jumps up, dropping Malachi's head onto a pillow and revealing he's in nothing but boxer briefs, and stands in a catatonic pose.

My body trembles as my gaze clouds with tears. I'm not sad. I'm not upset. I'm relieved. Utterly relieved. It's like I've been on this raging river, thrashing about on the roaring rapids, only to now come to the calm parts. I can stop unintentionally hurting Malachi. And maybe we can go back to what we've always been: best friends.

Malachi's stormy, gray eyes catch and hold mine. "Jade," he whispers.

I gulp hard and the hot tears slip down my cheeks.

He stands and walks toward my frozen body, inhaling a deep breath as his hands rest on my shoulders. "I'm so sorry."

A smile trembles on my lips. "No, no, no. Don't be sorry. I'm the one who's sorry. I should've known. If we'd been honest with each other, we could've saved all this pain." A cry of relief breaks as I gather him into an embrace.

The door from upstairs opens and Tad's mom calls out, "Junior, we're home."

That breaks Tad out of his rigid stance. "Okay, Mom. I'll be up in a minute." He rushes around, finding shirts

and jeans, and tosses them to Malachi. "Please leave." His voice breaks in a strangled apology.

Malachi gets dressed then puts his hand to Tad's waist, drawing him in. "I'm leaving with Jade, but you're not doing this to me again."

Tad bends his head to study Malachi's chest, but Malachi leans into him, tilting Tad's face toward his own. Unspoken pain is alive and glowing in Tad's eyes.

Malachi presses his lips to Tad's. Even though Tad is taller and wider, he crumbles under Malachi's urgent and exploratory kiss. He gives Malachi everything and more than I ever wanted from him. I watch in somber curiosity, finally putting all the pieces together.

Tad breaks away breathless and touches his forehead to Mal's. "I love you," he says in a hushed tone, "now please go because I can't face this tonight."

Malachi nods and gives him a quick peck. He lifts his chin to me then in the direction of the door I just walked through. I follow him, stopping in front of Tad, holding his letterman's jacket out. He takes it but doesn't meet my eyes. Should I feel guilty for the relief I'm feeling?

Malachi and I slip out the back and leave in my car in silence. When we turn off of Tad's street, Malachi releases a long breath; it's like he's releasing all the tension that's been built up between us the past few months.

"How long has this been going on?" I ask.

"Off and on for about a year and a half, ever since we broke up with Pepper and Delani."

I can't hold the shock back. "A year and a half? Mal, why didn't you tell me?."

"He had called it off after the summer, saying he just wasn't into it. That he wanted to be normal. But he kept on coming back and I kept on letting him toy with me. He told me to hang on until next fall. We would go off to a faraway college and be together. Then you came along and I finally resolved that it was over with him. On Halloween, he kissed me and told me how much he missed me. And it's been a push and pull ever since. He kept telling me that he'd end it with you. I wanted to tell you, but I didn't want to hurt you. You've already gone through too much."

I reach over and take his hand in mine. "I would've been okay."

"Life had finally come back to your eyes, Jade. I couldn't do it."

"Tad isn't the reason for it." If I'm being honest, part of that reason is Onyx and the other part is myself. It's been a gradual building process of healing.

"I'm sorry," he says, gathering my hand into his.

I squeeze his in response. "Me too."

The floodgates have been opened and Malachi tells me all about the back and forth relationship they've had over the past year and a half. Malachi swears that Onyx didn't know. If he did, he figured it out on his own.

They've been very discreet, at first afraid of anyone knowing, but the last holdout was Tad being afraid of his dad. Malachi's been ready to come out for a year now, but he's waited on Tad.

It upsets me that Tad isn't capable of facing it, that he's willing to live a lie just to save face with his father.

I follow Malachi to the Dogwood apartment and hang out with him for the rest of the evening. When I leave his room and head to my own to go to bed, Onyx comes up the stairs to their apartment, not paying attention, and reaches a halt right before he's about to run into me.

He jumps down a step and grabs hold of the handrail. "Shit, Jade. I didn't see you."

Unapologetically, I erect my defensive wall. "I know about Tad and Malachi. If you would've only told me, I could've resolved this a long time ago. You don't have to worry about me anymore. I see perfectly clear now. I'm no longer *blind*." I push past him to head down the stairs.

He grabs hold of my wrist as I pass. "But you're still blind." Dark snappy eyes cast a disapproving glare that startles me. I jerk my arm from his grasp and walk away.

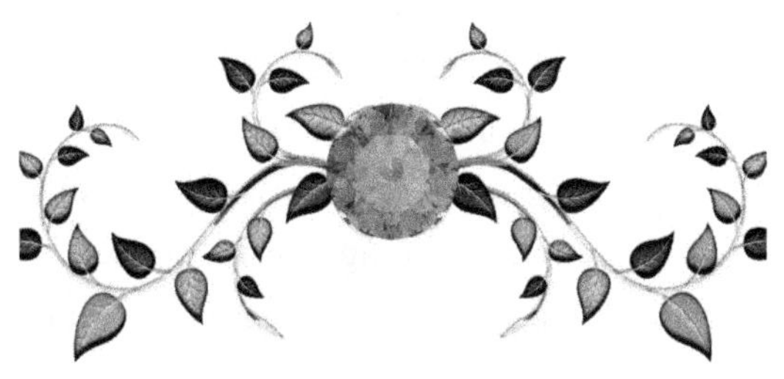

CHAPTER 29

O VER THE NEXT week, Onyx and I don't meet for morning coffee, nor do we meet in the cupola in the evenings. The only words he's said to me since we met on the stairs were *please pass the salt* in cooking class.

I keep busy all week, preparing for the upcoming finals and putting the last minute touches on my five pieces for the art exhibit. I skip lunch just to stay in the art dungeon. I've discovered throwing pottery on the wheel is quite therapeutic, taking a lump of wet clay and sculpting it into some sort of balanced shape makes me feel like I'm sculpting myself. It makes me feel like I have control over something because I sure don't have control over my thoughts.

Pepper confessed that her and Mica were a thing, but she's trying to keep it on the downlow. I asked her why, she said she's scared of the backlash she might get for dating someone who's two grades below her. I told her who the fuck cares. That's what I want to say to Tad who won't look at me or talk to me.

His silent treatment is one of the reasons I slipped into the pottery barn during art on Monday. When Mrs. Hennigan came in to check on me, she said I should throw the piece in the kiln, and once it's dried out, shatter it and add the broken bits to my canvases. I was worried that it would clutter the piece, but she assured me the more chaos, especially on the first piece, the better.

She was right.

It's now Friday and I'm ignoring Tad again by hanging out in the pottery barn, attaching the broken clay pieces to my canvases. As the exhibit progresses, I'm creating faux stitching using thin strips of black fabric on some of the broken clay as more symbolism of coming back together. Each canvas represents a point on the journey of healing.

I stand back and take in the five canvases that lean against the wall. It's a voyage from dark and twisted to light and calm, but there's something missing on the last canvas. The one that represents who I want to be.

"Woah," a voice says behind me. I turn around to see Tad, staring at my artwork. "These are wicked."

I take that as a compliment. "Thanks."

"Seriously, Jade. You know I don't care much about

other types of art, but these are really cool. What're you going to do with them after the exhibit?"

I want to say, *oh, now you're talking to me,* but I bite my tongue. "I don't know."

"Can I have one?"

"What?"

"I'd love to have this one." He points to the first canvas that represents pure chaos, offering no shape or form, just movement. "I've never seen anything that represents the way I feel inside better."

I study him. His eyes are moving aimlessly from one end of the canvas to the other, the way I intended it to be viewed. "It's yours."

"Seriously?"

"Yeah."

"Thanks."

"You're welcome."

He stands in front of the fifth piece. "This one's missing something."

The canvas is covered in painted vines weaving through bright, happy flowers. The shape of a butterfly made out of the broken bits of clay, pieces of found objects, and various scraps of metal I acquired after a trip to shop class—another idea of Mrs. Hennigan's—come together in the center of the canvas. I then cut myself out of one of the photos Onyx took and adhered it on top.

"I know but I don't know what," I admit. It's plagued me since I finished it.

"I think you need to put something in your hands." He touches the photo of me looking down at my open hands.

He turns to leave then pauses. "Jade?"

"Yeah."

"Can I tell you something?"

"Of course."

"I like you."

An unexpected warmth surges through me at what's meant to be his apology. My face breaks into an open, friendly smile. "But you love Malachi."

He glances down at his feet and nods. The bell rings and he leaves me. He's got a lot to process and deal with. I'll be here to help him as a friend and to call him out if he's being unfair to Malachi.

After fifteen minutes of staring at the fifth and final piece then going through my box of objects, I'm drawing a blank as to what to put in my hands. It will have to be the way it is.

I gather up my canvases and take them to the theater where everyone but me has already set up their exhibits. I place my canvases on their easels then set my framed description on the small table beside the first piece.

With twenty minutes before the bell rings, signaling the end of my lunch period, I walk around, checking out the other works.

I come across Tad's. The first four of his pieces are exactly what I expect. Fierce but cute cartoon illustrations of various animals. But the last one makes my jaw drop to the floor. It's still cartoon-like but it's the back view of two guys in football uniforms walking hand in hand with the caption *Love is Weird*. There's nothing distinguishing about the guys. No jersey numbers. But the fact that he put himself out there like this, whether someone gets it or not, is satisfying.

One last exhibit lies hidden in an alcove of the stage. One could easily miss it, and I almost did after the impact Tad's last piece made. The description on the small table says only two words, *See Me*.

As I take in the first picture, the hair on my arms stands at attention as the chillbumps spread. The image is in a gold, ornate frame and it's of me, standing in my room, with a smile on my face. I look a little pale, dark circles on my eyes, but the smile is bright. It's the picture that Onyx snapped of me on the day he claimed the make-Jade-smile victory. The other photos are mounted in the same gold frame as the first. Every photo is of me. One is my bare feet sitting on the dock at the ranch. The third is just of my arm, showing off my tattoo. The fourth is me asleep in Onyx's bed. The last photo is the same one that's on my fifth canvas. The only difference is I'm not cut out and I'm holding something in my hands: a tiny black rock, a piece of onyx.

My calves burn as I run back to the art dungeon. "Mrs. Hennigan," I yell when I enter.

She jumps a mile high as her fork clatters to the floor. "Jeez, Louise, Jade. Don't scare me like that."

"I'm sorry. I finally realized what I need on my fifth piece. Do you have any small rocks or gemstones?"

She picks up her fork, dropping it in the sink, then walks over to one of the supply cabinets and pulls out a bin. "Look in here."

I run my fingers through the collection of smooth rocks, searching for the perfect one. A black one with a shape that somewhat resembles a heart catches my eye. I grab it and shove the bin back in the supply cabinet and grab a tub of E6000. "Thanks, Mrs. Hennigan," I yell as I leave the classroom.

My lungs seize when I make it back to the theater. I quickly adhere the stone in my open hands of the photo and count to sixty, begging the glue to adhere quickly. Once it's stuck, I race off. The bell will ring any minute now.

I pause in front of the large, glass window before the double doors that lead into the cafeteria. I'm taken aback by him, just on the other side of the glass. His gold and jade eyes stare back at me, filled with a curious, deep longing. It's the same way he always looks at me. Only now do I truly realize why.

The bell rings and movement flutters around us.

294

I point to my heart and say, *I,* then point to my eyes and say, *see.* Lastly, I point to him through the glass and say, *you.* I then take my hand and place it against the window. He repeats the same thing then places his hand on the glass against mine. It's like I can feel it.

"There you are," Pepper says. She drags me away to our next class. I only break eye contact with Onyx once we're around the corner.

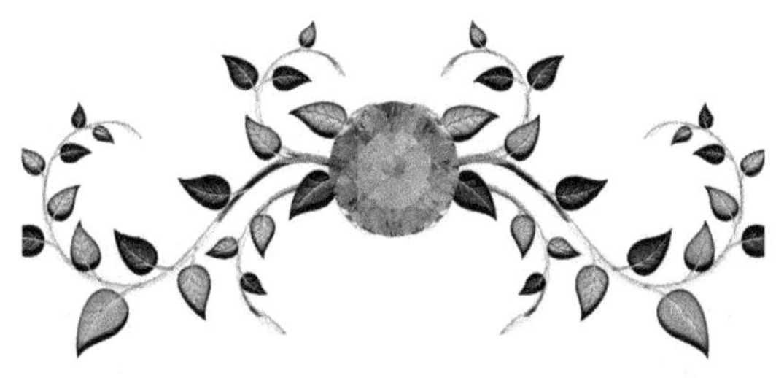

CHAPTER 30

"OW, THAT HURTS," Pepper whines as I French braid her hair. "Why are you being so rough?"

"Sorry," I say. "Just trying to get you ready and on your way."

She teasingly winks at me. "Do you have somewhere to be?"

I roll my eyes and flip her a bird.

I regret telling her about Onyx. I also regret telling her earlier this morning that I'd help her get ready for her afternoon horseback ride with Mica. Once she told me that they planned on telling Janet tonight that they were dating, I couldn't back out on her.

She's afraid Janet may not like Mica dating a cougar—her words. Me helping her get ready is more of a way of hyping her up than actually beautifying her. She doesn't need any help with that.

Onyx would have to wait. He's already been waiting for two and a half months now. He can wait another

thirty minutes. Although I'm not sure I can. I want to feel his lips again. As much as I've tried not to think about that kiss on Halloween, it's haunted me day in and day out since.

I wrap the ponytail holder around her hair and run my fingers through the braid, evening out the weave. "Okay, you're all done. I need to go see Onyx now."

She wiggles her eyebrows and blows me kisses as I head out the door. "Maybe I'll see you tonight, maybe I won't. Go get your man."

My man. And he is my man, or will be in just a matter of minutes. I'm sure of it. The minute I saw that picture of me holding the onyx stone everything clicked. My eyes opened wide and I suddenly felt whole again. Like I'm that butterfly who just burst from the cocoon. Everything made sense for once.

Every sign I've ignored the past several months came back. Onyx has been trying to tell me how he feels, how he sees me, ever since I got here. He's even came out and said it, but I always thought he was joking. He is right; I'm so blind.

I speed down the two-lane, hoping for no speed traps, then roll under the familiar Diamond Ranch sign, *my home.* I park just outside the Dogwood stable and run up the steps to the apartment. I pause to catch my breath and slow my racing heart just outside his door.

Closing my eyes, I knock on the door.

His voice is pained when he says, "Come in." He

sits on his bed in a T-shirt and gym shorts, his body rigid and his lips turned downward.

I'm suddenly frozen and speechless. I've done nothing but hurt people since I got here. Taking away Malchi's love. Trying to give a reason to that person to not be gay. And worst of all, tearing down the brightest person around. The same person who helped me see the light.

All I can manage to say is, "Hey."

"Hey back," he says. A hardness blazes in his eyes that creates a deep, unaccustomed pain in my chest. "What did you mean when you said you see me?"

I take a step closer, reducing the distance between us by half. "I meant I see you how you see me."

He shakes his head as he rubs the back of his neck. "No, Jade. You don't see me how I see you."

I take another step. "Yes, I do."

"You can't," he says, his voice low, "because I'm in love with you."

I close the distance between us, putting my body between his legs and wrapping my arms around his neck. The emotions hit me as if I'm riding a roller coaster, taking my breath away and knocking me down to my core. I crush my lips to his, claiming them as my own. His response is immediate, his kiss sending spirals of ecstasy through me.

He pauses, resting his forehead against mine. "Damn, woman. It's about time you got your fucking eyes checked."

My laughter comes out with sheer joy. "Yeah, baby," I mumble against his lips. "I'm seeing for miles, a perfect twenty twenty. What are you going to do about that?"

He nibbles on my bottom lip. "Oh, I'm going to do everything about that."

With every kiss, with every touch, with every gaze that looks deep within my soul, he stops my bleeding heart.

interlude 3

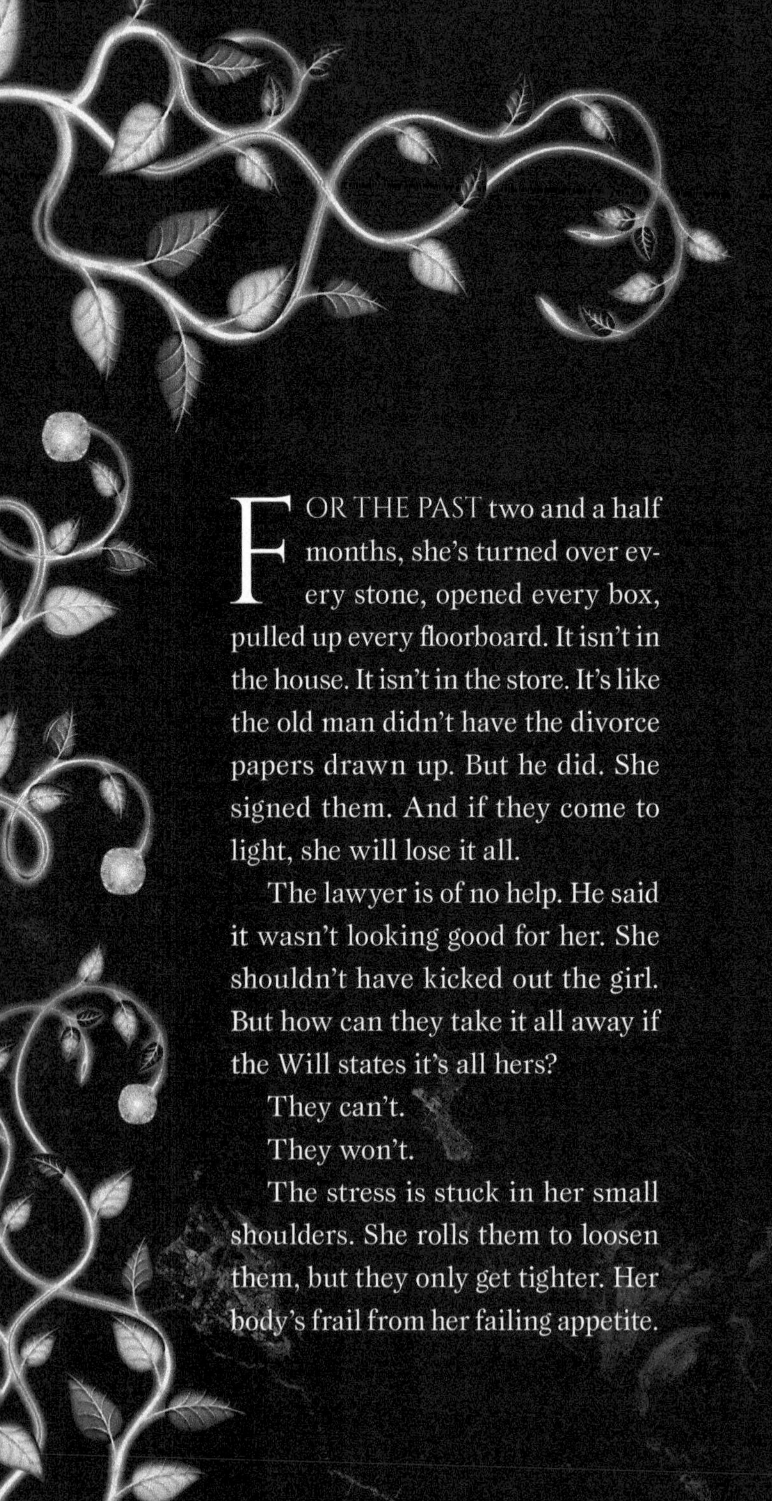

F OR THE PAST two and a half months, she's turned over every stone, opened every box, pulled up every floorboard. It isn't in the house. It isn't in the store. It's like the old man didn't have the divorce papers drawn up. But he did. She signed them. And if they come to light, she will lose it all.

The lawyer is of no help. He said it wasn't looking good for her. She shouldn't have kicked out the girl. But how can they take it all away if the Will states it's all hers?

They can't.

They won't.

The stress is stuck in her small shoulders. She rolls them to loosen them, but they only get tighter. Her body's frail from her failing appetite.

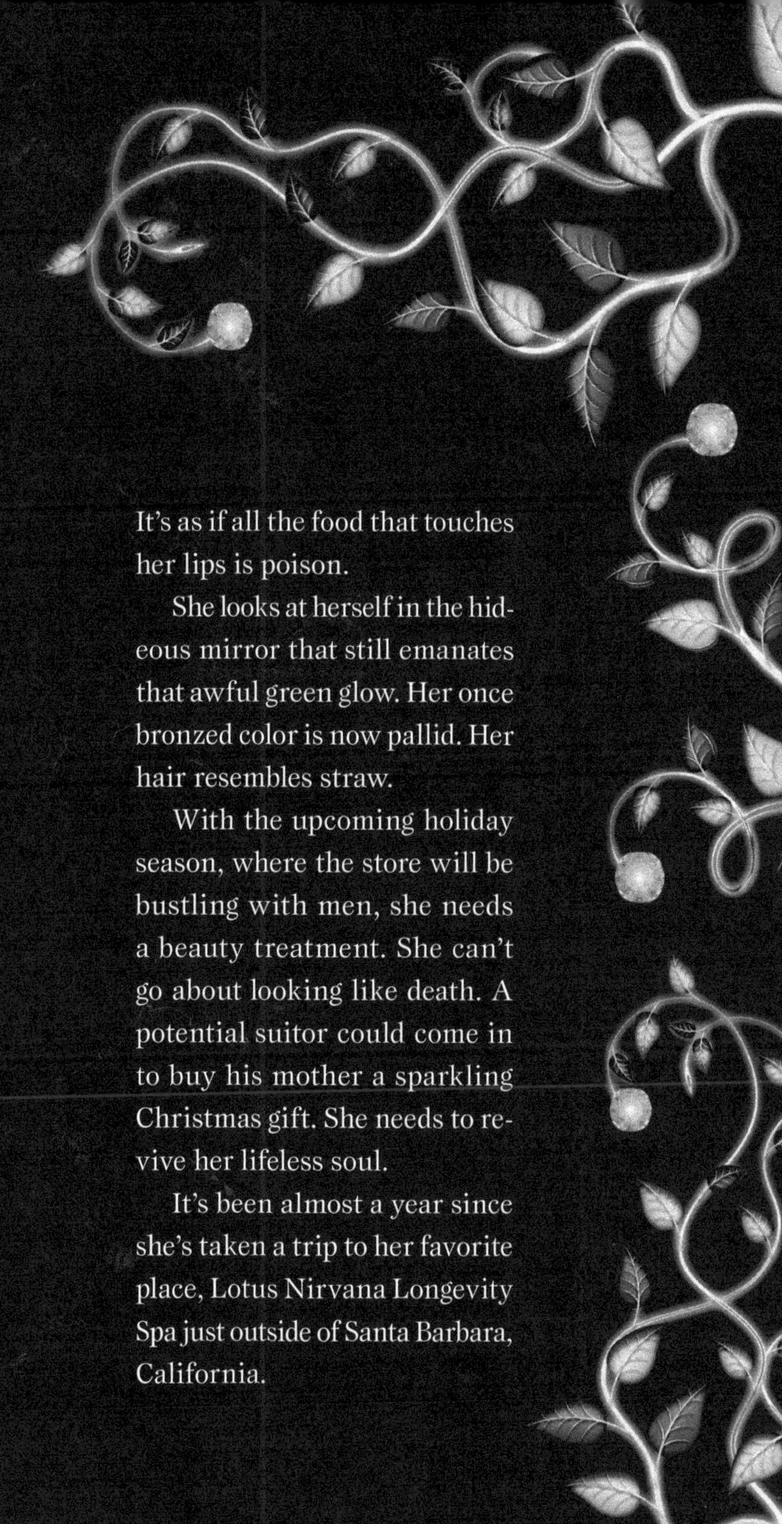

It's as if all the food that touches her lips is poison.

She looks at herself in the hideous mirror that still emanates that awful green glow. Her once bronzed color is now pallid. Her hair resembles straw.

With the upcoming holiday season, where the store will be bustling with men, she needs a beauty treatment. She can't go about looking like death. A potential suitor could come in to buy his mother a sparkling Christmas gift. She needs to revive her lifeless soul.

It's been almost a year since she's taken a trip to her favorite place, Lotus Nirvana Longevity Spa just outside of Santa Barbara, California.

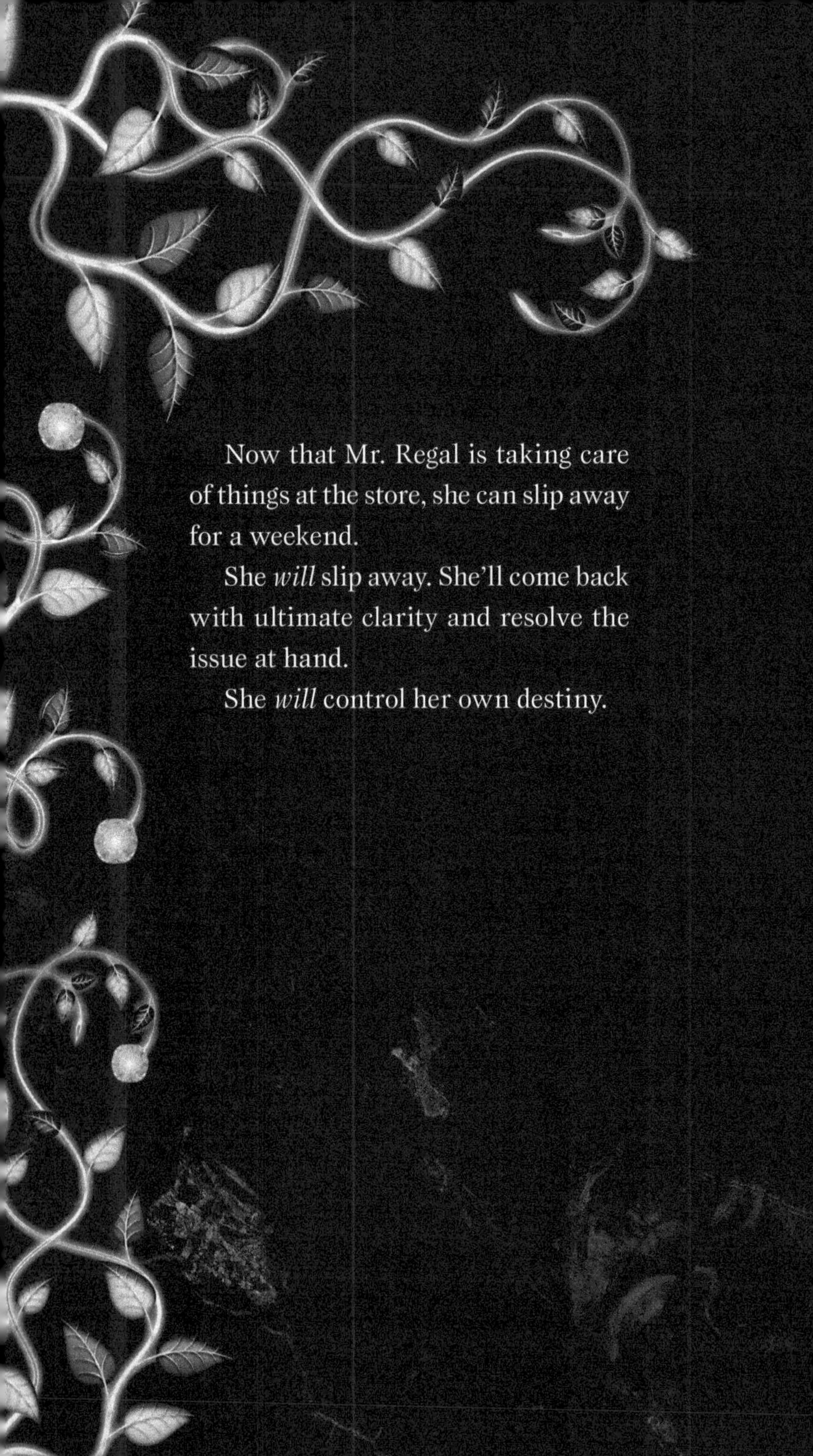

Now that Mr. Regal is taking care of things at the store, she can slip away for a weekend.

She *will* slip away. She'll come back with ultimate clarity and resolve the issue at hand.

She *will* control her own destiny.

Onyx

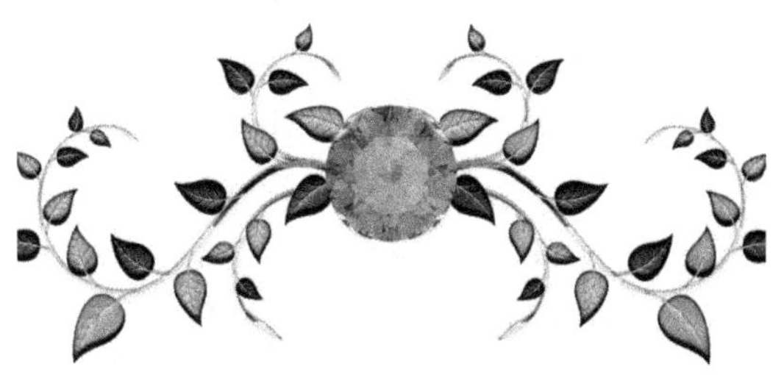

CHAPTER 31

THE SUNLIGHT PEEKS through the tiny window of my clos-room when I wake up. A warmth runs up my left side, with a tiny heater resting on my chest.

Please let this be real.

I pinch myself hard on the forearm, needing to make sure. I flinch at the pain that surges through to my fingertips.

This is fucking real.

I roll on my side, taking her hand in mine. Her rosy red lips are slightly parted in sleep. Her jet black hair lays out in waves against my white pillow. I want to wake her, to stare in her cobalt blue eyes, but I can't take away the peace that's on her face. I'd like to credit myself for that peace. Even she'd say it was because of me. But I know the truth. That peace is because she found it herself.

A buzz comes from my nightstand. Jade's phone flashes a message on her home screen. Jealousy and curiosity causes me to pick it up and read the name. *Mr. Regal.*

"Princess." I gently shake her, knowing this message might give her an even higher level of peace.

She stretches like a baby then rolls over with her back to me. I wrap an arm around her waist and pull her body against mine, spooning her. I nuzzle her neck, trying to control myself. "Princess," I say again.

She mumbles.

"You might want to read this text." I hold the phone in front of her face.

She turns over, her face lit, and reads the text to me in the cutest sleepy voice. "I took her to the airport this morning. She said she won't be back until midweek. This is your chance. Message me when you get this."

Her tiny fingers dance over her screen. Her wide-eyed innocence captures me. "You up for a road trip today?" she asks.

"Ready when you are."

She curls into my chest. "If it wasn't so important, I'd stay right here."

I kiss her nose. "We have all the time in the world to stay right here. Let's go get my princess's ring."

"'Kay. I'm going to take a shower. Meet me at my car in thirty."

She leaves me and I pinch myself again, leaving a red mark on my calf.

I don't deserve her but I'm going to try my damndest to keep her. My life never made sense until she came along. The minute she stepped into my world, I stopped counting down the days until graduation. I stopped thinking about hopping on my bike and heading to parts unknown, to never return to Maybee. But now, I'm tied here because of her. I'm tied to wherever she goes. If she decides to stay here forever, then I will too. If she decides to go to Antarctica to live with the penguins, then I'll be freezing my fucking ass off for her.

My home is her.

After taking a quick shower and getting dressed, I make my way to the porch of the main house where Janet's rocking and drinking a cup of that herbal tea crap.

She narrows her eyes and presents that signature smirk. "Is there a reason why I saw my niece make the walk of shame this morning in the same clothes she had on yesterday?"

I respond with my own smirk. "To make the walk of shame, she'd have to be ashamed of something she did. And to my knowledge, she didn't do anything she needed to be ashamed of."

She nods her head but doesn't drop the smirk. I've known this lady since before I can remember. In the past few years, she's become so much more than one of my friend's moms. She's become my adopted mom. This look means she's not satisfied with my answer. She's brutal and honest but also loving and compassionate.

I wouldn't be where I'm at today if she hadn't taken me in almost a year and a half ago.

I sit down beside her and mimic her rock. "The truth is, Janet, I'm in love with your niece. And one day, she may do that walk of shame, but I'll make sure it's not on your grounds. I respect you too much to take advantage of the hospitality you've given me."

She scratches her chin as if she has a beard. "It seems Cupid's been playing weird tricks lately. Mica informed me last night that he's crazy about Pepper. Kind of shocked about that one. Who knew the strong, silent type like his daddy would go for the girl that talks more than you do."

"No weird trick there. Like father, like son."

Her whole face spreads into a smile. "I'll give you that. I do love to talk, but that girl talks more than me."

"I disagree," I tease.

"And I think Malachi is finally ready to tell us something that we already know."

"How long have you known?"

She holds her hand against her heart and pats. "Probably before he did. You?"

"I was suspicious, but it was confirmed for me yesterday."

"I'm a pretty happy mamma right now."

"It's because you're the best mamma."

Jade joins us on the porch, and my eyes squint because of that big cheesy ass grin that always comes

to my face when she walks into a room. Her eyes flit between me and Janet as she puts her hands in the back pockets of her yellow jeans. "We're driving to Merryville today to look for the ring. The witch is out of town."

Janet stops rocking and leans forward, placing her elbows on her knees. "Are you sure she's gone?"

"Mr. Regal said he dropped her off at the airport."

"Please be careful. Any sign of her, disappear. Do not let her catch you snooping around. And stay away from the house."

Jade nods and motions for me to stand. "Wish us luck," she says and heads to her car.

I catch up with her, and she squeals when I pick her up. She tries to pull away when my lips brush against hers. "I already told her," I say.

She wraps an arm around my neck and snuggles against my chest. "What did she say?"

"That she's a happy mamma. And why are you dressed like Snow White?" Her yellow jeans are topped off by a royal blue sweater. Her black hair is held back by a red headband.

"Just thought now that I have my," she pauses for a few seconds then starts again, "charming, I felt like I need to dress for the role."

"I hate to break it to you, but your *Prince* charming is a dwarf in disguise."

She giggles. "A very tall dwarf."

T HE LAST TEN minutes of the drive, as we head through the streets of Merryville, I won't let Jade's fidgeting hands go. I'm glad I insisted on driving her car. She directs me to the store's parking lot and drags out a breath that would easily blow my old house down.

The door to the two-story brick building is locked and a sign that says, *out for lunch, will return at 1 p.m.,* hangs from the glass door. She peeks through the darkened glass then knocks.

A slender gentleman with a bald spot on the top of his head unlocks the door and ushers us in quickly, waving a path with a flashlight. "I shut down the breaker to reboot the security system. We've got about fifteen minutes before it comes back online." He hands her a blonde wig and a pair of black-framed glasses. "Put this on so she won't recognize you, in case the system comes back online before we're done. If she asks, I'll tell her the power stayed on so I didn't realize the security system shut down."

Jade puts on the wig and glasses and hugs the man. "Thank you, Mr. Regal. You have no idea how much I appreciate this. This is my boyfriend, Onyx."

Boyfriend. I definitely like hearing her use that word. I shake his hand. "It's nice to meet you sir."

"You too." He pulls Jade's hand toward the back of the dark store. "I'm sorry to rush you, but if we can get that old safe open before the security system comes back on, we can head across the street to have lunch and chat. If not, just pretend to be shopping for jewelry."

He sets the flashlight down on a glass display counter and turns on several camping lanterns that illuminate a large mirror framed by a rose vine. It's just like her tattoo. Jade twists one of the roses then pops it out, revealing a split in the exterior of the mirror. The inner mirror opens wide to a vintage wall safe.

She closes her eyes and places her forehead against the safe. "Please cooperate with me today," she whispers, then quickly dials through the numbers. A loud click sounds and the door creaks open. The safe is jam packed with jewelry boxes and stacks of paper and envelopes.

Jade hones in on a box made out of her namesake and tugs the top off. Her eyes light up with tears as she pulls the ring out of the velvet holder and places it on her finger. She holds her hand up to me, channeling her inner Beyonce, and smiles brightly. She looks so wrong with the blonde wig, but that smile is the true Jade.

Mr. Regal moves the rest of the contents out of the safe and into a box then closes the safe and pushes the mirror back in place. He looks at his watch. "And we have ten minutes to spare. Let's head to Hattie's."

He hands me the box, locks up, and we walk across the street to a little cafe that smells like cinnamon rolls. After ordering, Jade pulls out each jewelry box from the stash and gives us a story behind the ancestral trinkets. Club sandwiches and fries arrive and we chow down. Jade stops to admire the ring after every bite. The memories bringing the brightest smile to her face.

Mr. Regal wipes his mouth then drops the paper napkin onto his plate. "Let's have a looksy at the papers that were in the safe."

Jade pulls out the stack and starts flipping through the papers. "Mainly just a bunch of old jewelry certificates." She opens up a manilla envelope that's falling apart at the seams. "More certificates." Lastly, she opens another envelope that's fresh and crisp. Writing in black marker covers the front of the envelope. *Delivery to Jeremiah Jackson Diamond.* She dumps the contents of the envelope out on the table and quickly flips through the documents.

An intense astonishment touches her pale face as she drops the documents onto the table. "I knew you wouldn't desert me, Daddy," she cries out, brushing away the tears so she can take in the documents again.

I look at the two bundles of papers. One says divorce decree and the other says Last Will and Testament.

Mr. Regal glances through them. "She even signed the divorce decree." He stands and gathers her into a hug. "I knew he didn't desert you either, sweetheart."

Suddenly, I feel out of place. This was Jade's life, and it appears she'll get it all back. She'll probably move back to Merryville over Christmas break and finish out her senior year here.

I don't fit into her bougie life. This isn't about Snow White and the dwarf. It's about the Princess and the pauper, only the pauper doesn't get his happily ever after.

Who knows? Maybe she'll try to get back with that douche bag Hunter. He's more of a prince than I'll ever be.

As much as I've tried to get her attention since the day I met her, I can no longer deny the truth. We just don't fit together, no matter how perfect it feels.

The air chokes me. I stand, ready to hightail it out of here. I'll hitchhike my way back to Maybee. She tugs on my arm then buries her face in my stiff chest.

She feels like heaven.

Way. Too. Good.

I fight the urge to hug her back, to kiss her. If I did, her happiness would come through in that kiss and win me back over, only for it to hurt worse the day she leaves.

She will leave.

Everyone leaves.

"Um." I clear my throat. "How about I go outside and you and Mr. Regal talk through all of this."

Panic snakes across her face. She vehemently shakes her head. "I want you here."

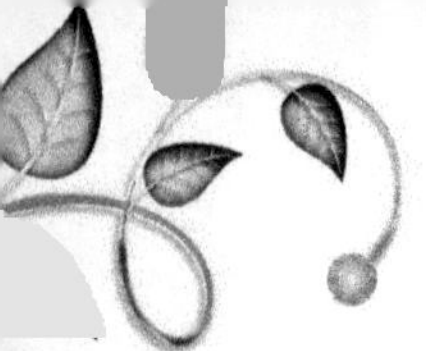

I feel like a volcano about to blow. I can't hold on to good things. It's not the way my life goes. "This is so personal, Jade. This is your life for you to figure out. You suddenly have everything you've wanted."

"And that includes you. I *need* you to stay. You're my best friend. You're my rock. You're my dwarf. You're my Onyx Finch Charming. I can't do this without you. I don't want to do this without you. I'm not letting you leave me."

Her blue-eyed gaze meets mine, turning my heart over in response.

I'm putty in her hands.

Always.

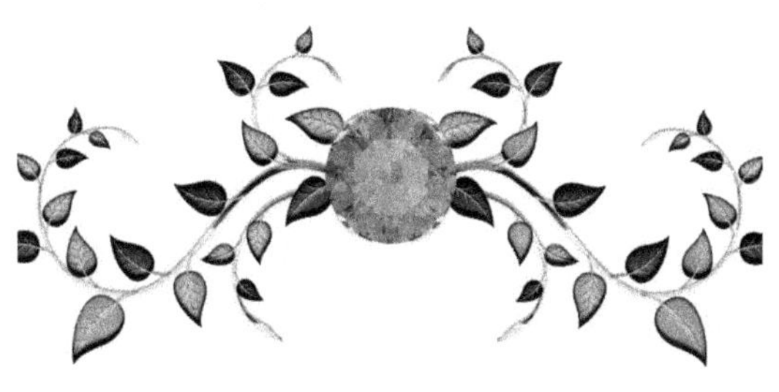

CHAPTER 32

AFTER SPENDING AN hour at the cafe going over the documents her father left with a fine tooth comb and talking to two attorneys over the phone, Tad's dad being one of them, we head back to Maybee with a plan.

Everything needs to stay the way it is until they can get the new Will probated. In other words, Jade needs to stay away from the house and store. They're doing everything in their power to speed up the process. They're also filing a restraining order against the witch to ensure she also stays away from the house and the store. It will be delivered to her the moment she steps off the plane.

I kept waiting for Jade to say when she'd be moving back to live in Merryville, but she didn't. In fact, she told Mr. Regal that she wants him to manage the store until she graduates from college. That she planned on finishing high school in Maybee and possibly heading to Savannah, Georgia to go to school. She squeezed my hand after that. I finally released the thoughts I'd been harboring, now accepting that I'll be getting out of Maybee after graduation and heading down south.

She wants me. And she deserves to have what she wants.

She passes out on the drive home but doesn't release the tight grip she has on my hand. I lost feeling in my arm over an hour ago, but I don't dare move it. Now, we're driving under the Diamond Ranch sign.

I gently shake her. "Princess?"

She does her cute little baby stretch but then sits up, taking in the bridge over the creek as we head down the drive.

After parking her car, we walk hand-in-hand to the porch, happily staring into each other's eyes.

"Welcome back," Janet says from her rocking chair. "Glad you had a successful trip."

But she's not alone. Sitting next to her, in the rocking chair I sat in just this morning, is my mother looking like a wilted flower.

"Hey, Ollie," she says, giving me a soft smile. For once, she's not high or drunk.

"Onyx," I demand her to say.

Janet stands and extends her hand. "Jade, why don't we go inside and let these two chat.

I tighten my grip on Jade's hand. "No one needs to leave. I have nothing to say to her."

"Onyx," Janet says in her pleading mother voice. That voice makes me do anything. "You need to hear her out."

"Fine, but Jade's not leaving my side. I *need* her."

Jade squeezes my hand, making my spirits soar. I sit in the chair Janet left and pull Jade into my lap.

"Hi," my mom says, "you must be Jade. Janet has been telling me all about you. I'm Lily, Ol—Onyx's mother."

"Enough of the small talk, Mom." She flinches back from my tone. "What do you want?"

"I have a favor I need to ask of you."

"Can't someone else do it? One of your many suppliers or special clients?"

"It needs to be you, Onyx. Please."

"What is it?"

She holds out a manila envelope similar to the one that held the paperwork that changed Jade's future, and hopefully mine if I can manage to keep her.

Don't give up, Onyx. Remember what your grandfather always said—in the words of Yoda, *Do or Do Not, There is No Try.* I won't try to keep her. Keep her I *will.*

"What's this?" I ask, eyeing the envelope.

"Divorce papers. I need you to deliver them to your father in prison."

"Why can't you do it?

"I'm checking myself into rehab first thing in the morning. No one else can do it. It has to be you. He needs to know I'm serious about taking back control."

She's made similar attempts in the past, but the fire burning in her hazel eyes is using a different fuel. It's burning harder and brighter than ever before.

"I know it's probably way too late to win you back. But I'm not doing this for you. I'm doing it for me."

"Fine." I take the envelope from her hands. "Is that all you need?"

She stands and nods. "Thank you, son. I know I don't deserve it, but when I'm out, I'm hoping you'll give me another chance, even if it's just an occasional dinner here and there. And I'm happy you've finally got a girl who truly cares."

After kissing me on the forehead and patting Jade's hand, she heads to her old beater and leaves.

Please let this be the time that sticks.

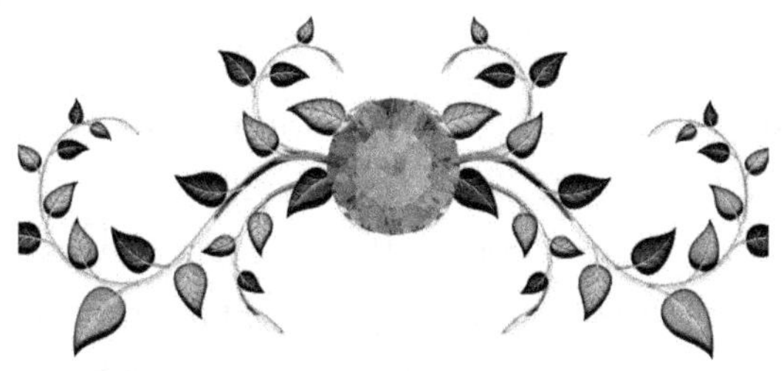

EPILOGUE

I STARE AT THE beautiful victorian-style house just off the main street of Merryville as twilight steps in. The house stands three-stories tall, although Jade says the third floor windows are in the attic. It's a lavender color with white trim of ornate woodwork. The porch wraps around halfway and a tower stands on the left side. Jade said the part of the tower on the second floor used to be her room.

I can't believe this small castle is my girlfriend's house. I can't believe that I get to stay in this house tonight, on Valentine's Day, alone with Jade. Well, I guess I should believe it. My girlfriend is a princess after all, and princesses live in castles.

The warmth of Jade's smile sends shivers down my spine. Over two months of officially being a couple and I still get shivers from her. She grabs my hand and pulls me up the porch steps. Slipping the key in the door, she jumps up and down, not able to contain the excitement. This is the first time she's been to the house since the ugly stepmother kicked her out almost five months ago.

It's all hers now. The store shares the same fate. The minute the witch stepped off the plane, she was served the papers. She immediately booked another flight to who-knows-where, never to be seen in Merryville again. She's lucky she disappeared. Just last week, they issued a warrant for her arrest for contract killing, a form of murder.

Jade hasn't paid much attention to the case, wanting to forget everything about the lady. Janet and I have had many nightly conversations about it, vowing to each other we'd always protect Jade no matter what.

We've also chatted about my mother. She's still in rehab, refusing to leave until she feels she can control her addiction which started when she was fifteen, after she met my father. Jade's made me go visit her a couple of times. I went begrudgingly, mainly out of guilt after Jade said that she'd give anything to have a relationship with her mother. I delivered the divorce papers to my father like my mom asked. He signed them without a word or a glance at me. I'll be happy if that was the last time I ever see him again.

As Jade turns the key to her old home, her mother's ring catches the light of the porch and sparkles. She hasn't taken it off since she got it back. Before she can open the door, I wrap her in my arms and smother her lips with my own. She quivers at my touch, letting out

her low moan that always does things to me when I'm trying to be good, trying to respect Janet.

But tonight, there is no Janet, therefore no being good.

I kiss the tip of her nose to cool us off, not wanting to cause a scene right there on this porch.

She pushes open the door, revealing an immaculate, though covered in a thin layer of dust, modern home, completely mismatched from the exterior. She gives me a quick tour of the downstairs then drags me upstairs.

I know this room pains her, the master bedroom. One day, she plans on converting it back to the three bedrooms it once was.

Jade has decided that she is going to follow in her mother's footsteps and attend SCAD for jewelry design, only under one condition. She wants me to go to Savannah with her. It wasn't even a decision I needed to make. I didn't even have to think about it.

I want to be wherever she is. I just might decide to enroll and study photography while working as a line cook. Savannah seems like a cool place to spend the next several years. Tad and Malachi have also decided to go to college not too far from there.

But for now, this room will stay in it's currently enlarged state, and I plan on getting as much use as possible out of the king-sized bed, oversized clawfoot tub, and shower large enough to house the offensive line of Bradley County.

I've kept my promise to Janet. It's been the hardest thing I've ever had to do, especially when Jade tries everything in her power to make me break it.

"Hey, Siri," Jade says as she forces me to sit on the edge of the bed, "play Bloodstream by Stateless on repeat." She takes a couple of steps back and stares me down with her sapphire eyes.

Raw, wild need passes through me when she removes her red sweater. My eyes follow the creamy expanse of her skin to her black lacy bra.

"Are you trying to seduce me?" I manage to ask, my voice breaking with huskiness.

She bites her lip and nods. Her innocence scares me and excites me at once. The truth is, I've never been with a virgin, and I've never had sex with anyone I've cared about. So in a way, even though I lived a promiscuous life in my younger days, by the words of Madona, I feel *Like a Virgin.*

Taking a step closer, she slips out of her jeans. "Is it finally working?" Her tongue sweeps over her upper lip.

I reach for her, tugging her gently by her black, lacy thong, and bring her to my lap. Nibbling on her hot skin, I say, "You tell me."

A victorious smile passes over her lips. She cradles my head in her hands. "I love you."

My heart captures her words, but my brain teases her. "I know." It's the first time she's said it aloud, and it feels so fucking good to hear it.

She lets out her cute little giggle.

I kiss my way up her throat, feeling the blood throb in her veins. "I knew you loved me before you did."

"When did you know you loved me?" she asks.

"When I saw you naked."

Pink tones overtake her light skin. "So, you did have to pull me out of the shower that night."

"One of the best nights of my life," I admit. I told myself not to look, but my lips were still buzzing after that punishing kiss.

I admit it. I took a quick peek.

Luckily, after wrapping her up in a towel, she came to enough to dress herself, or unluckily as I would've had an even longer vision to overtake my dreams.

Needless to say, the quick peek vision haunted me on a nightly basis.

Her kiss starts out slow then tears through me, tingling my bones. Breathless, she whispers, "You helped my heart heal. You stopped it from bleeding out."

I lift her up, gripping her thighs, and lay her gently on the bed. She tugs the zipper of my jeans and wrestles with them, until they're down around my ankles.

"You got my heart beating again," I say, adding, "I love you, princess."

She tugs at my boxer briefs, running a finger along the black lines of my tattoo peeking out. "You're finally letting me see this?"

An idea flashes in my mind at how I can prolong this, to drive her a little bit more crazy. I raise my boxers back above my hip bone and step away. She releases an anguished cry.

I reach into her bag and pull out her iPad still playing *Bloodstream* on repeat. Tapping to the drawing app, I put today's date and draw the wonkified vine around the edge.

Even after Jade's attempt at giving me drawing lessons, it still looks like it's drawn by a kindergartener. I hand her the device and wait with my knowing smile. Originally, I was happy with one of the entries always being about me. But now, if I don't get at least two of those spots, I pout.

Sometimes, the pout is on purpose because she always gives me a kiss when I sulk.

She writes in her beautiful, script handwriting:

> 1) I told Onyx that I loved him for the first time. Even though he said, "I know," his eyes told me he was happy to hear it.

> 2) In just a few minutes, I will finally get to see his tattoo. My guess? It's Yoda with his favorite saying, Do or Do Not, There is No Try. And "do" we will.

> 3) And the tall dwarf lives happily ever after with his Snow White.

THE END

I hope you enjoyed my modern take on the fairytale *Snow White*. I would love to have your reviews on Amazon, Goodreads, and/or Bookbub.

If you would like to stay in touch, please join my readers group on Facebook, Vivid Voices With Victoria. Want a free book? Join my newsletter list. Links to my group, newsletter, and other social media links can be found here:

linktr.ee/victoriaanders

Thank you so much for your time. I appreciate you!

ABOUT THE AUTHOR

Book designer by day and writer by night, Victoria Anders lives in the world of books. And she feels extremely blessed with that! Originally from Atlanta, this Georgia peach now lives in the land of sunshine and barely a winter just north of Tampa, Florida with her husband and two Great Bernese pups: a 130-lber total ham named Zeus and 85-lber sweet lovegood named Luna.

Thanks to her daughter's escapades in high school (and maybe her own), Victoria loves bringing you tales on the inner workings of the teenage mind. No fantasy or science fiction here. She brings you nothing but contemporary, realistic stories about kids growing up and discovering who they are. Oh, and yeah, there's always a little bit of love thrown in from every angle.

Red Hots, Lemonheads, Diet Dr. Pepper, and japaleno margaritas were consumed in mass quantities during the writing of this book.

He's the musician with the total bad boy vibes…
…she's the poor girl who can't date.
Will she break the rules for a rockstar?

My Life as Kelsey is a roller coaster ride of
discovery about love: letting it in, handing
it out, and releasing it to the wind.

CHAPTER 1

Welcome to the Working Week

Watching paint dry is more exciting than what my summer has been. I thought that working at Adventures, an amusement park in my hometown of Oak Hills, NC, would add that spark I so crave to my dull life. It's done nothing but give me a farmer's tan and a mother who nags me even more about good grades, no boys, and college, college, college. Granted, real money in an actual bank account—not just pennies in my piggy bank—is nice.

In less than two years, I will finally escape this town and the clutches of my over-bearing mother.

Bertha the coaster grinds to a halt, pulling me from my personal pity party. The smell of smoking rubber fills my nose. "Lift your arms and wait for the bar to raise," my voice automatically says. "Exit to your left."

The human sheep exit the train, and a child's scream pulls me from the monotonous work.

"Dad, I'm stuck," the sweet little lamb cries out.

I rush over and squat down, looking in her tear-filled eyes. "It's okay, sweetheart. You're so special that Bertha wants you to stay with her." Her eyes grow larger, and her cheeks look like two ripe tomatoes. "But, the good news is, I have a special key so she can't keep you."

I jingle the key in front of her face before inserting it in the release slot. *Click.* The stuck safety bar pops open, and she jumps out of her seat with relief.

"And now you get a special treat. Do you like ice cream?"

The gentle lamb nods.

"When you exit, go to the right and present this card to Micah at the ice cream stand. He'll give you a free cone."

She grabs the coupon with her tiny little hand, crumpling it in the process. Her cuteness causes me to giggle as I pat her blonde curly head.

With a smile from ear to ear, she skips to her dad on the exit platform. "What do you say, Zoe?"

"Thank you," whispers the girl in a sugary voice.

The gate opens, allowing the next sets of sheep to file in, and my auto-play continues. "Pull the bar down until it clicks."

The sweat rolls down my cheek as I meander to the

last cart in the back of the roller-coaster. My chafed thighs burn with each step. When are they going to fix my fans? It's ninety-seven degrees today with no hint of an afternoon thunderstorm; the thick air feels heavy in my lungs.

I walk the length of the train, tugging on each unmoving bar. Safety check complete. My hand raises, not caring about any potential sweat stains. The extra deodorant applied during my lunch break feels long gone.

A new train with its cheering occupants replaces the outgoing one that is now clicking up Bertha's wooden hill. And it all begins again. Monotonous. That's my job.

"Sir, take your sunglasses off, please," I say, pulling on the safety bar as I see my flushed face in the mirrored frames.

"What do you want me to do with them?" the teen sheep barks. His pinched face makes me want to punch him. I'm usually not a violent person. I blame it on the heat. My grandma always tells me I'm sweet as peaches as she squeezes my cheeks, because I put spiders outside instead of squishing them to oblivion.

My customer service attitude toward hostile teens disappeared once it hit a sweltering ninety-five degrees. "You're supposed to put them in a locker before getting in line." *But since you can't read,* "I'll take them and put them on those shelves right over there." My middle finger points to the shelves at the exit with the sign "WE ARE NOT RESPONSIBLE FOR ITEMS LEFT

IN CUBBIES" hovering over. "You can get them on your way out."

He removes the glasses, revealing sapphire eyes that lighten in the afternoon sun as it peeks into the station. My unchanging brown eyes scream jealousy. "Can you hold onto them for me? They're kind of expensive." His friend guffaws and punches him on the shoulder.

I huff and paste a glower on my face, but hang the sunglasses on my collar by the temple. I'm a sucker for blue eyes.

He grabs my hand, forcing me to look even deeper, causing my knees to go weak as a surge of energy courses through my body. "Thanks, Ma'am." His tone holds condescension, and all five guys he's with snicker.

I'm not willing to let this guy have any effect on me. My arm jerks from his grip, then I continue to check the remaining safety bars.

I hate rich kids. And this guy—although his strategically tattered t-shirt and khaki shorts are nondescript—has rich and entitled written all over him. He looks like one of those rock band singers who graces the covers of teeny-bopper magazines. His friends look like they belong in a gym advertisement.

I could accidentally drop and step on the sunglasses, or better yet, I should tell him I lost them then sell them on eBay. The profit would be more than my next paycheck. But that's not me. The dollar signs dissolve as I shake the mean idea away.

Rich rocker guy's train returns to the station. He stands, struts over, and tries to grab the sunglasses from my shirt. "Thanks, sweetheart."

My hand wraps around his wrist with a firm grip causing my knuckles to go white. "Don't call me sweetheart." I release him then remove the sunglasses from my shirt and drop them in his awaiting hand.

"Thanks, Ma'am." He puts on the sunglasses, covering the sparkling beauties, which makes it easier for me to be meaner.

"I'm not an old lady; I'm your age. Don't call me Ma'am," I snap and start to stomp off.

"Thank you, Kelsey." His tone is musical, halting me; his sweet voice won't sweet talk me. Its cadence is not glazed in creamy milk chocolate and covered in rainbow sprinkles like my favorite donut. *Liar.*

I cast a sneer in his direction. "How do you know my name?"

His mocking smile causes the hair on my neck to rise. "Nametag."

Turning on my heels, my ponytail smacks my face as if trying to slap the unusual nastiness away. The laughter of teenage boys echoes behind me as they head out. The tallest one winks at my mean girl co-worker, Willow, as he brings his hang-ten hand up to his ear. Her blinding teeth show as she acknowledges him with a thumbs up. She collects more phone numbers than Bertha's wishing well—disguised as a feeding trough—collects pennies.

Put your game face back on, Kels. I run to check the safety bars on the next herd of seated guests, smiling at each of them, giving special attention to a boy crying to his older brother. Patting his head with reassurance, I say with a voice as sweet as my favorite donut, "Don't be scared. You're going to love Bertha." He stops pouting and smiles at me.

Ten minutes later, rich rocker guy is back at the front of the line with his sunglasses on, and my bad attitude returns. Wednesdays at the amusement park equal short lines for repeat customers. As he sits down in the cart, he hands me his glasses again.

I slip them in my collar with a roll of my eyes and a snarl to my lips, knowing he *forgot* about the lockers on purpose. He's not surrounded by his male chauvinistic entourage.

"Did your winning personality run your friends off?" I ask.

He sneers. "Well, aren't you funny? They had somewhere to be."

I turn to the short queue and yell out, "Need a single rider." Two people raise their hand, the closest being a rotund male. *Perfect.* I walk over to release the gate and let him through.

Rich rocker guy narrows his eyes and presses close to the opposite side of his seat as the large man squeezes in the cart. Rich rocker guy mimics my sinfully sweet smile as I check his safety bar, ignoring his hard but beautiful eyes and the way those eyes seem to look deep down into my soul. *Payback.*

Through the intercom, Jett, the lead foreman, says over the clicking sound of rich rocker guy's retreating cart, "Kels, it's five. You can go."

A real smile crosses my face when my fist pumps to victory. I don't know why I'm excited to leave other than getting out of this blazing heat. I usually stay and work a double when my mom can't pick me up until ten. Today, it's just too darn hot to offer myself up for overtime. The cool cafeteria is calling my name, and so is the last book on my summer reading list. Two weeks should be plenty of time to read *Jane Eyre* before eleventh-grade starts.

A burst of cool air hits my face when I open the door to the control room. "Thanks, Jett. Tell Sophia I said hello, and I hope she gets to feeling better." I walk over to the panel board and give him a departing fist bump.

I grab my see-through purse from the cabinet, standing for a minute as the icy air blasts me, momentarily relieved. I wipe my sweaty palms on my uniform shorts then hold them up to the vent. Maybe next year, I'll be tenured enough to work in this luxury. Departing the igloo in revolt, my feet take me down the stairs to the exit, and my eyes squint when I'm blinded by the afternoon sunlight.

"Kelsey!"

Rich rocker guy runs down the stairs toward me, his jet-black hair spiked in all directions and not even flopping. What does he want now?

The sunglasses still dangling from my collar reflect the bright sunlight into my eyes causing them to burn. *Shoot.* I hand them to him. "Sorry. I forgot I had them. That's why we recommend the lockers and not the workers."

I make a one-eighty as the sweat starts to roll down my neck. Cafeteria, here I come. I'm so ready for this scorching work day to end. Only for it to begin again tomorrow, precisely the same. Monotonous. That's my life. Work. Rinse. Repeat. At least for one more week.

The musical voice draws my attention, and I make an about-face as he steps right in front of me, invading my personal space. "Hey, since you're off, you want to walk around with me? Ride some rides?"

Is this some lame ass joke? Am I being punk'd? I scoff and elude him, stepping toward the employee gate. What should come out of my mouth is, *I live in a trailer down a dirt road. And not a double-wide. A single-wide two-bedroom with my mom and grandma. I share a room with my mom. Why would a rich boy like you want to walk around with a poor girl like me?* That would shut him up instantly.

Boys don't fit in the monotony of my life.

Read *My Life as Kelsey* today!

It's available as an eBook, paperback,
and in Kindle Unlimited

ALTERED MAGIC

FATED TO THE WOLF – BOOK TWO

HEATHER RENEE

ISBN: 979-8821925435

Development Editing: Amy McNulty

Line Editing and Proofing: Jamie from Holmes Edits

Cover: Covers by Juan

Character Art Images: Samaiya Art

CONTENTS

eatrix's Coven
ll House
s Angeles
Holden's Pack
arlock
Vampire House
FATED TO THE WOLF

1

ANDIE

If someone had told me a few months ago that I'd be sitting on a balcony trying to create magic with my hands while watching a pack of wolves shift from human to animal, I'd have told them they were out of their minds. Yet, there I was under the new moon at Holden's pack, trying to tap into the energy from my Aunt Junie.

Only, the power I was given wasn't doing what I, or even Beatrix, had expected.

It had been just over four weeks since Moira had attacked Spell House. Thanks to those events, I'd missed the first new moon during which Foster had run with Holden's pack, and I was thankful not to be missing another.

For the first week after our night in the cabin, I'd attempted to keep Foster at a distance and slow things down a little, but once I realized I was only causing myself misery, we'd spent nearly every moment together. Other than when I was working on connecting with Aunt Junie's magic and when he was helping at the pack.

Foster had fought his connection to these wolves, but I watched him from the balcony, gearing up for the monthly run, and it warmed a piece of my heart I hadn't known existed. I locked gazes with him as he prepared to transform into his wolf alongside the other. His eyes glowed a deep blue, sending shivers down my spine.

"Intense, isn't it?" Gemma asked. She was a shifter in Holden's pack who'd stayed behind, thanks to her protruding stomach and maybe a little out of guilt that I couldn't join the pack for the run.

I nodded in response, unable to take my eyes off Foster. He stood there, staring at me while I watched him. I thought I'd feel awkward. Instead, my core tightened, my heartbeat increased, and I leaned forward.

His blue eyes brightened as he prepared to shift, and he ran a hand through his shoulder-length dark russet hair. I watched his broad chest expand and tattooed arms ripple while the transformation magic slowly seeped from his skin.

A shimmer of light covered his body, and he lowered his head, breaking our stare. A second later, he no longer stood on two feet. His wolf appeared. Tall, wide, covered in ebony fur, and with vibrant eyes.

He howled, and the sound pierced my heart. The bond I hadn't thought I could feel was finally alive, and it didn't care that there wasn't a wolf inside me. Foster's wolf had claimed me, and the way he watched me had my heart swelling.

Gemma fanned herself and chuckled. "Girl, you've fallen so hard. I love it."

I finally turned toward her, giving her my full attention

once Foster's wolf trotted to join the pack. Her light-brown eyes were focused on me while she played with the end of her blonde braid. Her green sweater hugged her expanding belly, and her hands rubbed over the top.

She gasped, then groaned. "Easy, boy. Momma isn't ready to get up again."

I laughed. "The baby wants you to move around?"

She wiggled in her seat. "No idea, but his super kicks make me want to pee every five minutes. I'm ready for this pup to be on the outside."

I'd never been around pregnant people before, so I had no clue how she could be feeling. Though, staring at her stomach and hearing her moans, I felt sympathy for her growing inside me.

"I didn't stay to talk about me, though. How are you handling everything? The pack has of course talked about you, but I'd rather hear details about *you* from you." Her thin lips offered me a smile, but there was a tugging sensation inside me that had me turning away from her before I could answer.

My eyes once again landed on the pack down below. Holden was the only member who hadn't shifted. His auburn hair was highlighted under the sliver of moonlight that peeked out, and his normally light-green eyes were brighter than normal. I assumed the new moon was making the pack extra charged with energy.

The alpha's hands were moving, and he faced the wolves, so I assumed he was giving a speech. When he stopped moving, every shifter howled in unison, then Holden finally shifted into his light-grey wolf.

Foster's wolf looked back at me again. I gripped the

sides of my chair, and my body trembled when he bowed his head toward me and took off to follow the rest of the pack into the trees.

"Not much of a talker, are ya?" Gemma asked, swinging her legs off the lounge chair. "I can leave you alone if you'd rather."

I frowned and turned toward her again. "I'm sorry. This bond is new. I've only known Foster a month, but ever since the attack, each day, the connection to him grows stronger. I didn't think it was possible to feel so much so quickly, but he makes it hard to even consider fighting my feelings."

With a groan, she settled herself back onto the cushions. "You know the best way to take the edge off the bond is to accept it *fully*, right?" Her tone was filled with glee, and she waggled her brows.

Charlie had told me the same thing, but even though I no longer had any doubts about the bond with Foster, there was still something missing—a part of me that was not quite right.

Still, I returned her smile. "Oh, I'm well aware. Things are just complicated."

I wasn't sure I could accept Foster without knowing who *I* was. I needed to know more for myself before we took things further.

Physically, I was more than ready. Foster tempted me with every light touch and darkening look he gave me, but he deserved more than my physical attraction and still-slightly-muddled heart after all he'd been through. When we finally bonded, I didn't want there to be any lingering doubts inside me. Not even ones that had nothing to do with the man eager to claim me.

"Like I mentioned before," Gemma said, "the pack has been talking about the two of you. A witch bonded to a wolf isn't common, but we're all hoping you two can work things out. I know you have your coven, but there are things they might not understand about your connection to Foster. I hope you know you can count on the pack as well, including me." She reached a hand for me, and I easily accepted her gesture.

Her words loosened a knot in my chest. My time at the pack was special. I'd thought after the attack that I was going to lose that, but Beatrix had been making great strides in becoming more reasonable. Without telling me, she and a dozen coven members had come to the pack and created a shield over the main areas that would keep me and the wolves nearly as safe as if I were with the witches.

Gemma and I sat in comfortable silence until she sneezed and squealed, wrapping her hands around her stomach. "Uh-oh."

My eyes widened. "Please, don't tell me your water just broke."

She blushed. "No, but I do need a change of clothes. Hazards of being nine months pregnant."

I closed my eyes and sent up a silent thanks that I wasn't going to be left trying to deliver a wolf baby on my own. That wasn't anywhere near the list of things I wanted to do in my lifetime. My stomach and gore of any kind were not friends.

Gemma struggled to stand, so I moved and wrapped

my arm around her waist. Her hands gripped my shoulder, and together, we got her on two feet.

"Let's get you to your house," I said when I saw the wet spot on the blue chair cushions. I hadn't thought much about one day having my own babies, and this was pushing those potential thoughts further into the recesses of my mind.

My light-pink hair tickled her face, and she fought a giggle. "I'm loving this color and your fair skin. It's not fair that you're so pretty and fit and...sigh. Being nine months pregnant sucks some days."

I openly appraised her. "Um, do you see your sun-kissed skin and how it shines over my paleness? Or how you look maybe twenty-five, but you're actually in your forties? Plus, your hair glows like the stars above. Probably thanks to all those extra vitamins you're taking because you're pregnant."

Gemma blushed and grinned widely. "You're a sweetheart, and not only for your words, but for helping me." She paused, then laughed. "And for not making me feel like a child for peeing my pants."

I squeezed her hand. "You're creating life. If anyone shames you for the hazards that come with that, tell me and I'll send Foster's wolf after them."

She groaned while laughing. "Oh, please don't make jokes. I don't think I can handle two accidents in the same night."

I grinned. "I mean, it wasn't really a joke, but you got it."

We made our way back into the house, and the scent of pine filled my senses. The sense of calm the smell provided almost seemed like magic taking away my worries.

"I have an ATV outside," she said. "If you're comfortable driving that, then getting me home will be a whole lot easier. You can bring it back here to wait for Foster, and then Joey can use it when they're back."

I grimaced. "I'm sorry. I'm horrible at conversation, and I feel like I should know this already, but is Joey your husband?"

Her smile widened. "He's my mate."

I gave my head a shake. "Right. Mate. Some of the human terms are hard to let go."

She nudged me softly while we carefully made our way down the stairs. "Understandable. You've only been here a month and you seem to be handling everything well, considering."

"That's in large part due to Beatrix using magic that allowed me to remember my early childhood with unreal clarity. Plus, the bond with Foster helps keep me calm. I've always been one to trust my instincts, and when something gives me the warm and fuzzies, I don't tend to run away."

Gemma winked at me. "Is that what the kids are calling it now? 'The warm and fuzzies'?" I choked on nothing, and she patted my back. "I'm kidding, Andie. Seems like neither of us is very good at conversation."

The fact that she didn't stop grinning prevented me from being utterly embarrassed, but still, I wasn't used to having these talks with people. Though, I had a feeling Charlie was going to stop taking things easy on me soon enough.

Gemma looked over at me while I got the front door opened. "You know, after over four decades on this Earth, I've lost a lot of my filter. The more years that pass, the more I realize that if I can't share what's on my mind with a person without feeling bad, then they're not good company to keep. I hope I get to chat with you again."

My gaze fixed on Gemma and my shoulders relaxed. "Thanks, Gemma. That means a lot, and I hope so, too."

"Now, come on. Let's get back to my house and I'll share my brownies with you," she replied excitedly.

A pregnant woman sharing her sweets with a new friend? I was suddenly feeling pretty damned special.

I DIDN'T HEAD BACK TO THE PACK HOUSE FOR ANOTHER HOUR. Gemma assured me that the run would last closer to two hours, but I didn't want Foster to return and not know where I'd gone.

Driving the ATV through the trees was interesting. There were little dirt roads and wooden signs nailed to the trees that I was thankful for at least twice when I realized I had taken a wrong turn.

By the time I got back, the two hours were almost up, so instead of waiting inside the house, I headed toward the yard where they'd taken off from. The stars burned brightly above me, and the sudden urge to lay on the grass and stare up at the sky came over me.

Once I was settled, my eyes focused on the moon. It reminded me of a partial eclipse. Most of the surface was dark, but there was the thinnest sliver of light that still stood out amongst the surrounding darkness.

I closed my eyes and crossed my hands over my stomach, soaking in the peace and energy of the Earth. Shivers traveled over my body, and I took a deep inhale, then slowly exhaled. Warmth filled me, reviving my energy, and a sense of peace settled in my core.

Minutes ticked by while I listened to the sounds of the night. Even the howls I could hear in the distance further relaxed me, and I was nearly asleep when a snarl jerked me out of my tranquility.

My hands began glowing such a dark pink that, for a moment, they almost appeared purple instead. I got to my feet, searching for whatever had made the noise. When I heard it a second time, the growl echoed from behind me.

Slowly, I turned around with my arms out. There was a russet wolf pacing and snapping his jaws in my direction. He was smaller than Foster's wolf, but no less intimidating with dark eyes and saliva dripping from his jowls.

"Did something happen?" I asked, hoping whoever it was would shift back to human.

The eyes on the animal turned black, and his snarl deepened while he took several paces forward.

I began to walk backward but tripped over my untied shoe. "Mother shitter."

Come on, magic. Don't fail me now, I thought while I scrambled to get up and put my full concentration into creating an orb I'd only managed to manifest a few times in the last several weeks.

More wolves sounded off from the trees, closer this time than before. Still, I didn't think they were close enough to make me feel safe. Especially when I considered the possibility that they might not be coming to help *me*.

Back on two feet, my palms pushed together, and I imagined the orb I wanted to create. One that would stun or knock out the beast getting nearer.

With bated breath, I pulled my hands apart. There was a two-inch ball of light purple magic swirling between my fingers and heating my skin. It wasn't as big as I'd been hoping for, but this was better than nothing.

The wolf stepped forward and I raised my hand. "I don't know why you're angry, but I highly recommend not coming any closer."

My chest was pounding, my knees shaking, and my spine was rigid, but if this wolf wanted to attack me, then I wasn't going down without a fight.

The shifter leapt into the air, and I shoved my hands up. I pushed the ball of magic I'd managed to create against the wolf's chest, and he let out a sharp yelp before crumpling to the ground.

The claws on his back legs scraped my arm on his way down. When I glanced over, I expected there to be deep gouges based on how badly my forearm was burning, but I only saw surface scratches on my skin. I blinked, trying to understand where the pain was coming from. When I refocused on the marks, black ooze was seeping from the wound.

"What the hell?" I muttered, slowly lowering myself to the ground and battling a wave of nausea.

The wolf was twitching beside me on the grass. At least my little ball of energy had packed a punch.

I leaned forward until I was resting on my hands and

knees. With my palms pressed against the earth, I could feel a vibration on the surface, but I couldn't find it within myself to look over and see who was coming.

I took steady breaths in and out while trying to call my magic forward again. My arm was numb, and the ooze was dripping toward my hand. Everywhere it touched left scorching trails of red on my skin.

"Andie." Foster's voice boomed one second, and, in the next, he grabbed the still-incapacitated wolf who'd attacked me by the legs and threw him a good twenty feet away.

I groaned and started to fall over, but Foster caught me. "What happened?" he asked, his voice only slightly calmer than before.

"I don't know. My arm burns, though. I think that wolf had poison on his claws." I winced, trying to pull my arm up so he could see.

Foster gently looked me over, and then a rumble from his chest echoed around us. "I'm going to kill him."

He stood and took a step back, but Holden was already dragging the wolf by his neck toward the pack house.

"Give him to me, Holden," Foster demanded.

Holden stopped and sighed. "No. Whatever happened, this wolf wasn't in control of himself. Something, or someone, managed to disconnect him from my pack and I'm going to find out how that happened. If you can't accept that, then you're not welcome here any longer."

Foster's shoulders went rigid, and his hands balled into fists at his sides. "He tried to kill Andie."

"I know that, but this wolf right here? He's only

thirteen. Whatever happened, I assure you that he didn't willingly want to hurt your mate."

"Fuck." Foster kicked the ground, sending a chunk of grass flying past the alpha.

Holden resumed heading back into the house, but before he got too far away, he turned back and looked at me. "I'm sorry, Andie. This never should have happened. Not on my land."

I glanced up at him and back down at the wolf still twitching in his hold. "It's okay. I'm sure whatever this is, Beatrix can fix it."

Holden nodded stiffly before continuing toward the back door.

Foster returned to my side. "This is far from okay. You're supposed to be safe here."

I swayed, and my head almost hit the ground before Foster gathered me into his arms. "I'm taking you to the coven."

There was so much I wanted to say, but the intensity of the burning sensation was growing. All I could do was nod in reply.

The farther Foster ran from the pack house with me, the more familiar my pain seemed. The heaviness of the energy, the way my soul was rapidly tiring, and the darkening thoughts racing through my mind…

This wasn't poison. This was something I'd experienced before.

"Moira did this," I murmured.

"What?" Foster asked as he leaned his head down.

"Dark magic, not poison." My words were so low, I

wasn't sure he would hear them, but I knew the moment they registered with Foster.

His grip on me tightened, and his body heated up while his speed increased tenfold.

Moira was already making moves again while we hadn't even *talked* about retaliation for what her witches had done to Spell House. If Beatrix didn't take this current attack more seriously, I wasn't sure how I was going to keep Foster from putting his own plans into motion.

Plans that just might get him killed.

2

FOSTER

eat smacked me in the face as soon as we crossed the barrier into the witch coven. Beatrix appeared out of nowhere, and energy was pulsing off her.

"I gave those dogs a shield to keep Andie safe. Not so she can nearly get killed again," she spat.

I wanted to snap back at her and remind her that the wolves were nothing like human house pets, but I agreed with her rage. I had no idea how one of the pack members had been compromised—especially a child—but Holden had better find out quickly. Otherwise, I wasn't going to walk away next time I saw the wolf responsible. Teenager or not, I wanted answers.

Andie groaned in my arms while I followed Beatrix toward the coven infirmary, a place I'd been all too familiar with lately. Andie, who obviously didn't want to let Beatrix off the hook so easily, said softly, "Wasn't their fault. Moira got to a kid."

"You've been putting off talking about what we're

going to do. I understood because Andie needs time to accept Junie's power, but we can't wait any longer," I said, my tone low but demanding.

Beatrix's long, silver hair floated behind her, and wrinkles scrunched around her emerald eyes that darkened with a bit of disdain. "I'm well aware of what we can and can't do, Foster."

At least she hadn't called me "Wolf."

It helps when you're not trying to rip her head off every five minutes, my wolf said.

I grunted. *She deserved every time I attacked her.*

Maybe, but two wrongs don't make any situation right.

I didn't have time to argue with my inner beast. Andie's eyes were rolling around, and the ooze on her arm wasn't only burning *her* skin. It was dripping onto mine, and we needed to get this shit out of her.

The infirmary was in the middle of the coven, past the main cobblestone streets that half the witches lived on but before the more spacious cabins started popping up. I began to run with Andie, doing my best to keep my stride even and not further jostle her.

I passed Beatrix. She huffed, but I didn't bother to look back. I knew where I was going. Only, when I arrived in front of the light-tan metal building, Beatrix was already waiting at the door.

"If you'd told me you wanted to get there quicker, I could have helped." She smirked at me before opening the double doors and waltzing inside.

I slipped in the stark, white building before the doors closed. There were six beds on each side. Only one of them had the curtain pulled shut to give the patient privacy. I headed to the bed right next to him, because I knew that was what Andie would have preferred.

Camille and Ava rushed out of the back room. I was glad to see the former, because she'd been the one to heal Andie last time she'd been scorched by dark magic. Ava, on the other hand, had better be in a good mood, because I wasn't in a mindset to tolerate any of the attitude she liked to throw around when she was stressed.

"What happened?" Camille asked as she gently picked up Andie's arm. The healer's dark eyes inspected the injury before she looked back up and pushed brunette strands behind her ears.

A rumble built in my chest as I settled Andie onto the bed. "I wasn't there. I was with the wolf pack for the new moon run, but from what I could tell, Andie was waiting for us to get back when one of the younger wolves attacked her. She did something to him that caused him to convulse on the ground before he reached her, but he scratched her before he went down. Before Andie went unconscious, she mentioned whatever that is"—I pointed to the black ooze—"was caused by Moira's dark magic."

Beatrix moved to stand much closer to me than I was comfortable with, peering at me with narrowed eyes. "Where is that wolf now?"

"Holden is handling him," I answered, holding Andie's hand on the uninjured side.

The old witch made an odd noise from the back of her throat. "I'll be back."

I paid her no attention when Ava's black bob of hair caught my attention. She was bringing over a cart full of bottles and containers. Her light-grey eyes focused on Camille. "Use this first. I made it after the last attack."

Camille opened the offered jar and smelled the pink lotion-looking stuff. "Genius."

Ava grinned, and I had no idea what they were talking about, but as long as that shit helped Andie, I didn't really care.

Camille grabbed a wooden spoon from the top tray and scooped out some of the goop. She dribbled a bit over the scratches on Andie's arm, and a wave of energy pulsed off my mate, sending all three of us onto our asses.

"What the fuck was that?" I roared, getting up off the floor and taking a step toward the two witches doing the same.

Only Ava and Camille were both smiling, and I was ready to tear their heads off until Ava answered. "Andie's magic. Look at her."

I whipped my head around to check on my mate. I blinked and tilted my head. She was glowing a faint purple color. "Why isn't she pink?"

Andie's hands had glowed pink before. I assumed that was the color of her magic, something that wasn't supposed to change over a witch's lifetime unless they began tampering with power they had no business getting involved with.

"Her body is finally merging with Junie's energy," Ava said.

The three of us moved closer to the hospital bed again.

The magic surrounding Andie was thrumming and shimmering around her. I glanced at her arm, and the black ooze was drying up by the second.

Camille approached my side. "Let me help you while Andie heals herself."

I couldn't tear my eyes from my mate. "Is that what she's doing?"

"Not in the conventional way, but yes. Her magic is removing that which doesn't belong in Andie's body." Camille grabbed my arm without waiting for my permission. Cool liquid poured over my skin, and my jaw tightened until whatever Camille was doing began to warm.

I wanted to watch what the witch was doing to me, but seeing Andie's cheeks take on the rosy shade I loved so damned much and making sure her chest continued to rise and fall at a normal pace was more important to me than anything else.

"This is exactly what we needed," Ava said, standing across from me.

I finally looked away from Andie. "What do you mean?"

Ava gestured toward the energy around Andie. "Beatrix wouldn't retaliate until we knew what Andie was capable of. Andie's ability to take control of the magic inside her determines just how worried we need to be about the necklace in Moira's hands. Andie successfully bonding with Junie's power proves the spell on the moonstone is unbreakable."

I glanced back at my mate. "How so?"

"If Andie wasn't strong enough to receive ancestral magic, then it would have told us that she wasn't the witch her family hoped. Not that it would have been terrible, but it would have changed our tactics. Now, we should be able to test the merged energy, confirm what we've been hoping for, and finalize our plans."

"How long until we get to go after Moira, then?" I asked with a growl filtering through my words. I had no doubts Andie would be the powerful witch they'd been suspecting her to be.

Before Ava could answer, Andie's back arched, and the shield around her shattered into glowing pieces of magic that dissipated within seconds. She sucked in gulps of air and began to cough.

I stepped forward and helped my mate onto her side. My hands rubbed over her back, and I bent down so I could get level with her face. "Andie?"

She smiled at the sound of my voice, and the connection between us ignited—no, *exploded*. I was nearly on my ass again, but Andie reached for me. "Foster."

Fuck.

Heat enveloped me, and my wolf howled inside my head. I locked gazes with Andie, doing my best to maintain my composure, but the tingling in my chest, the clenching in my stomach, and my shortness of breath were making every normal action seem unbearable.

I dropped to my knees and moved one hand until my fingers stroked her cheeks. "Do you…" I wasn't even sure what I wanted to ask. The bond was too damn powerful to allow me to think straight.

"I thought I felt the connection before, but this is… It's everything," she replied, tears brimming in her eyes.

I leaned forward and pressed my lips to hers. Her tongue darted out, and I opened fully for her until a throat cleared, reminding the two of us that we weren't alone.

"We should double-check the dark energy is gone before the two of you continue," Ava said, trying and failing to maintain a straight face.

Camille was bright red and still standing near me. I'd forgotten she was trying to wrap my arm when Andie had begun to move again.

I glanced down at my forearm, and there was white gauze mostly secured to me. I finished pulling the fabric taut and stood, but I didn't back away from my mate.

"How can you be sure Andie is free from whatever caused the black ooze?" I asked.

Ava rubbed her hands together, and pale-green swirls grew between her palms as she pulled them apart and held them over Andie's feet. "I'll scan her body, and then she'll be free to go if everything is clear."

I helped Andie roll onto her back again. Her eyes wouldn't leave me, and her hand held tightly to me. This was the moment I had been hoping for when I'd first arrived at the coven. This was the bond I hadn't known I'd crave more than my next breath.

Our mate, my wolf whispered.

All ours.

He'd already accepted Andie, but until the bond had been complete, there'd been a sense of despair from him I couldn't ignore. Now? Now, I couldn't wait to get Andie alone and show her just how much she meant to me.

Ava finished her scan and smiled at my mate. "Congratulations. You have active magic inside you, Andie."

"Thanks, Ava," she replied with a grin.

Ava nodded and stepped back. "We'll leave the two of

you alone. Just don't forget you're not the only one in here."

Andie's cheeks brightened while I watched Ava and Camille leave, shutting the door behind them. When I glanced back at my mate, she was trying to sit up.

I wrapped an arm around her and lifted her into my arms. "To your house?"

She glanced at the curtain next to us. "Maybe we can check on him really quick since we're already here?"

I smiled. "Of course."

Andie wiggled out of my hold, and I followed her to the next bed. She pulled the curtain back to reveal the boy I hoped would be awake.

Benjamin was laying silent on the bed, eyes closed and hands folded over his stomach. His chest still rose and fell on its own, but black veins pulsed beneath his fair and freckled skin, not allowing for much hope.

Andie reached for him, grabbing his hand just as she did twice a day, every day since we'd brought him back to the coven.

Ava had managed to shield his heart before the dark magic could penetrate the vital organ while we'd been at Spell House, holding off what I was certain to be his imminent death. When we'd gotten him back here, a half-dozen witches had worked on Benjamin until he'd been as healed as they could get him to be.

The rest was up to fate and Benjamin. He had to be stronger than the foreign energy inside him. Fate got to decide if that was enough. All the rest of us could do was wait and see what happened. Though, what I worried about most was Andie losing him a second time.

She hardly knew Benjamin, but I couldn't deny that they shared some sort of connection. I wasn't sure if that was because of what had happened in the attic that day or something else, but whatever the cause was, I wasn't threatened by the pull she felt toward him.

Andie's thumb stroked over his frail skin, a small smile tugging at her lips. "Hey, Benjamin. I hope I didn't disturb you when we came in. I wasn't expecting tonight's visit to include me being a patient, but good news. The magic from Junie is finally cooperating with me."

She held her hand out in front of her, and within the blink of an eye, a four-inch orb pulsed over her palm.

The pride she was exuding soaked into me like it was my own. I could taste her excitement as I watched her grin grow and the orb bouncing between her hands.

Gratitude filled me, lightening the tension I'd been holding on to and allowing me to breathe easier. All I wanted was for Andie to be mine and to be happy. Knowing she had access to Junie's magic brought us another step closer to both of those things.

Andie closed her hand, and the orb shattered into tiny flickers that flew in the air before falling onto Benjamin, settling over his arms and face.

I waited for them to disappear like the shield around her had before, but instead, they embedded into Benjamin's skin, growing brighter by the second.

Andie's eyes fluttered shut, and she reached to hold both of his hands. I took a step closer and tried to ask what was happening, but Andie began to glow again, the energy warning me to stay back.

The door to the infirmary opened, and Beatrix strode

toward us, but I didn't pay much attention to her. Not when Benjamin began to cough and Andie groaned, seeming unable to move.

"What the hell is going on here?" Beatrix demanded.

She approached the bed, standing at the end, and then began to cackle. "Oh, Junie. You sneaky, sneaky witch."

3

———

ANDIE

At first, I didn't understand what was happening to me. Heat scorched my insides, magic ignited around me, the pull I felt to Benjamin became heavy, and I had to hold on tightly to him while everything else became dark for a few moments.

Though, between all of that, there was a layer of peace settling inside me. One that told me no matter what was about to happen, everything would be okay. Once I accepted that as truth, I let the newly expanding magic within me move freely, forcibly sharing the power with the boy too young to die.

Benjamin was still filled with the dark magic he'd willingly taken to save me from the fate he seemed to be stuck in. While I hadn't voiced the thought out loud, a part of me wondered if he had to willingly give the energy up before he could come back to us.

Except if my theory was true, then it was a lose-lose situation. If Benjamin couldn't wake up, thanks to the dark magic, how was he supposed to consciously reject the energy?

With Junie's power ebbing and flowing inside me, I finally had the answer.

Benjamin needed more magic inside him. Not the kind to heal him, but the kind to force him back to life—and not in the gentlest way, either.

The sparks from my orb that had burrowed into his skin were glowing a light purple. I called more of my newly inherited power forward and pressed my hands over his chest, sending energy toward each of the bright spots.

Benjamin's white shirt began to smoke, but I ignored the burning and continued to pulse power into him.

I could hear Beatrix and Foster arguing, but that was nothing new, and there wasn't anything I was going to let distract me until I woke Benjamin up.

He had been lying in this bed for over four weeks because of me. I had to help him, just like he had helped me.

Warmth traveled up my spine, extending into my arms before spilling out through my palms. The harder I drew on the magic, the darker it became until the light purple was almost midnight in color.

Benjamin's veins throbbed with such intensity that I worried they might burst and I'd end up killing him instead of saving him, but my instincts were guiding me forward, and I listened.

Something pressed down on my shoulders, and I closed my eyes, squeezing tightly. My chest expanded, and goosebumps traveled along my body. Yes, this was right. Benjamin was going to be okay.

I leaned forward, pressing all my weight onto Benjamin's chest. When I did that, sharp pains pierced my hands, and I winced but didn't let up.

"Andie, stop!" Foster shouted, but I couldn't listen to him.

It didn't matter that the bond had taken my breath away when I'd woken up and that I had no desire to cause my soulmate pain. I had to do this. I couldn't give Foster all of me without saving Benjamin.

There was something about him that I felt connected to. Not romantically, but maybe the kid was more important than any of us knew. Whatever the reason was, he had to live. I knew that deep in my soul. Even if it meant I had to take on the dark energy plaguing him without knowing what those consequences might mean for myself.

Benjamin groaned, then began to flail. I almost lost hold of him, but I dug my nails into his skin and pressed harder.

Pain roared up my arms and struck my chest. I threw my head back and screamed until the hands on my shoulders slid to my spine. At the contact, the burning inside me lessened to a dull throbbing.

"I've got you, Andie. Just keep at whatever you're doing." Beatrix's calming voice soothed through my thoughts.

A rumble I knew came from Foster vibrated around me, and I smiled. Foster might not have magic to aid in whatever was happening, but his presence was more than enough to help me. It was encouragement to make sure I didn't screw anything up.

I finally reopened my eyes and was shocked to find Benjamin completely encased in a purple cocoon of sorts. Dark swirls of energy whipped through the shell, bouncing off the shimmering barrier and leaving lacerations on my forearms when they got too close to me.

Benjamin's eyes blinked rapidly, then widened before landing on me.

"Just stay still," I said through gritted teeth.

He did as I requested, and when his veins stopped pulsing with black, I turned back to Beatrix. "What do I do with the energy I didn't absorb?"

"You're not in pain right now?" she asked, and I shook my head. "I'll take care of the rest."

Beatrix removed her hands from my back. The moment she did, I wanted to cry out, but I stuffed my agony aside. The quicker she helped Benjamin, the quicker I could get this shit out of me.

Foster stepped closer, but I shook my head. "Almost done." I didn't want him to accidentally absorb any of what I'd taken from Benjamin.

Foster glowered at me, and I hated how hard this was for him, but the fact that he stayed put and let me finish on my own wasn't missed, either.

Beatrix shoved her hands into the cocoon and began rolling them in quick succession. The faster she went, the smaller the shield around Benjamin became.

"Foster, grab the biggest glass jar on that cart that you can find," Beatrix said with forced effort.

My hands lifted from Benjamin's chest, and when I

flipped them over, black scorch marks covered my palms. Damn, dark energy had an uncanny resemblance to fire.

Foster held a gallon-sized jug next to Beatrix. She had a pulsing, midnight-colored orb intertwining with her hands. Skin bunched around her eyes and muscles throbbed along her neck, but she didn't make a sound while she twisted at the waist and shoved the energy into the waiting jar.

Once everything was inside, Foster tightened a lid on the glass and Beatrix took it from him. "I'm going to light this on fire with a spell that will dispose of the dark magic before anyone else can get their hands on it. You should join me. And then I'll take care of what's inside you. It's doubtful you'll be able to do it on your own after that," she said to me.

I took a deep breath that burned through my chest. She wasn't wrong. I might have saved Benjamin, but I wasn't suddenly a master witch. I'd followed my instincts and allowed the adrenaline rush of saving Benjamin to help keep me calm, but I wouldn't chance hurting myself by trying to do too much on my own.

"We'll be right behind you," Foster said. Then he looked at Benjamin, who was trying to sit up.

Beatrix nodded. "I'll call for his mother."

I gave the kid my full attention. "How are you feeling?"

His eyes were glossy. "You saved me."

I chuckled. "You saved me first."

He glanced at Foster. "Did you kill that witch?"

Foster snarled. "I shoved her into a wall, and she no

longer walks this Earth, but I'm not sure I'm the one who ended her life."

Benjamin shuddered and swung his legs off the bed before anyone could object. I moved to help and wrapped an arm around his waist, but Foster gently nudged me aside, which was good. Benjamin began to teeter, and I wasn't sure I would have had the strength to keep both of us up.

Benjamin's eyes met mine again once he was steady. "Thank you, Andie. I couldn't break through whatever was keeping me unconscious. I don't think I would have woken without you."

I smiled and reached a hand for his arm. "I wasn't going to let you die on my watch."

He winced, then jerked away from my touch. "Your skin is really hot."

Foster snarled and leaned Benjamin against the bed. "We need to go meet with Beatrix."

Benjamin nodded. "I'll be fine here until my mom arrives."

Foster picked me up, and his long strides ate up the distance toward the door in seconds. When he reached to open it, the handle was already turning.

A woman with dark-brown hair and light-green eyes looked at Foster first, then her eyes fell on me. They softened and she let out a quiet gasp. "Andie."

My brows creased and my heart rate picked up. "Uh, hi."

She looked familiar, but I had no idea who the woman was.

"I'm Benjamin's mother—" she said, and it sounded

like she wanted to say more, but Foster cut her off.

"He's on the right. Last bed in the row." He didn't wait for the woman to respond before pushing past her and out the door.

I looked up at his tense jaw. "That was a little rude."

He tightened his hold on me and ran faster toward the tree line behind the small cottages. "Andie, the fact that you don't realize how hot your skin is right now concerns the hell out of me. Slighting a woman I've never met before is the least of my worries."

"Oh," was all I could say, because I didn't think there was anything wrong with me other than my energy feeling zapped. When I gave myself a onceover as best I could in Foster's arms, I swore I could see dark magic moving under my skin, but every time I thought I saw it, the inky color disappeared.

Foster slowed his pace when we arrived at a fire pit surrounded by three tall rock pillars. Beatrix was standing near the silver flames emitting from the stone circle in the ground, and she still had the jar in her hands.

"Did you see Ava or Evelyn on your way over?" she asked Foster.

"No, but Andie needs help now," he said. His tone was so deep, it vibrated my skin.

Beatrix came closer, then muttered something under her breath before shouting, "Ava, Evelyn!"

The two witches appeared out of thin air, breathing hard. "Sorry, we couldn't find the vampire blood. I think we used all that we had left after the Spell House attack," Evelyn said with a final huff.

Beatrix shoved the jar at her. "We'll deal with that later.

Don't let that out of your sight." The coven leader turned to Ava. "Come help me."

Foster loosened his hold on me, and when I was back on two feet, red welts covered his arms. "Did I do that?" I asked hesitantly.

"It's nothing that won't heal soon," he said, brushing pink strands of hair out of my eyes.

Just when I thought I'd made strides in figuring this magic thing out, I was struck with the realization that I still didn't have a clue what I was doing.

Two hands roughly pulled me away from Foster and he stayed put, his jaw tense and unmoving.

"Damn, child. You're lucky you haven't turned to ash," Beatrix muttered, then she let me go.

The sudden lack of assistance had me falling to the ground, but Ava caught my shoulders before I smacked my head on anything.

"Be careful with her, Beatrix," Foster warned.

She sighed but didn't respond. Instead, she appeared in my line of sight with glowing, silver hands. "This might hurt a little."

Her palm slammed onto my breastbone, and my back arched. Ava settled my head onto the grass, smoke rising around me. Someone grabbed my feet, and I let out a high-pitched screech.

"What the fu—" My words were cut off when water poured over my face, and I was certain I'd drown until the flow began moving down my body.

"There. All better," Beatrix deadpanned.

By the time I'd wiped the water from my face and could see again, Ava was holding a medium-sized orb of swirling dark energy between her hands, and Evelyn was coming closer with the jar. I hadn't realized before that the dark magic didn't just dissolve into the air, that it had to be destroyed.

Foster leaned down and lifted me up, but then took his shirt off. "Wear this." He slipped his black tee over my head before I could see what was wrong with my own clothes.

"We can't burn the dark energy without the vampire blood, so this is on pause for now. Do you want to be here when we do?" Beatrix asked us.

I nodded. "We also need to talk about what I was just able to do and what happened at the pack."

Beatrix grimaced. "Yes, we do. I suspect Holden will be here in the morning. Take tonight to rest, and we'll meet first thing in the morning."

Foster grabbed my hand, but he looked right at Beatrix. "First thing. We can't procrastinate on this any longer."

Beatrix waved her hand. "Yeah, I know that, but you need to remember, I also know what I'm doing."

Foster growled. "You can't be the only one, Beatrix. Not anymore."

Creases formed around Beatrix's aging face, and she nodded once before turning away.

I pulled on Foster's hand, tugging him toward the house. "She's trying to be better."

He grunted. "No, she's trying to take everything on herself and she's going to get someone killed because of it. I won't allow that someone to be you, Andie."

I leaned my head against his arm and took a steadying breath while my strength slowly returned.

"Everything is going to work out just the way it's supposed to."

Foster said nothing to my words, and we walked in silence toward my old, yet new house. Beatrix had given me the home I'd lived in with my parents, but it hadn't sat untouched for all the years we'd been gone.

Another family had lived there. They'd changed the exterior color from green to blue and painted the cupboards white, covering the old oak wood I remembered. The flooring had also been removed and changed from carpet to mahogany hardwood, and the walls were all painted a light tan.

The life I remembered pulsing inside was no longer present, but I hoped, with time, I could bring that energy back and consider the place home once again.

Charlie was storming up my walkway when we turned around the corner. She pounded on the door and yelled my name before twisting the handle.

"We're behind you," I called out as she took a step inside my house.

She whipped around, her golden hair floating behind her and amber eyes glaring down at me. Creases formed between her perfectly arched brows, and a shimmer of magic pulsed from her light skin.

Charlie pointed a finger at me once she was closer. "Why the hell did I have to hear from my mother that you were attacked?"

I glanced up at Foster, looking for some sort of help, but he only shrugged.

Charlie was suddenly in front of us, and her arms

wrapped around me. "Are you okay? Why are you wet? What happened and who do I need to kill because of it?"

I grinned and pulled back from her embrace. "How about we chat inside?"

"Yes, why don't we?" Instead of waiting for us, she strode off and walked into my house as if it were her own.

I took a step forward, but Foster snagged my arm. When I met his stare, the bond between us nearly put me on my ass and he had to grab my waist.

The growing smirk and lightening of his eyes calmed my remaining frayed nerves. "I just had to be sure I didn't imagine what happened earlier," he whispered against my cheek.

How could I have momentarily forgotten I'd been ready to jump him in the infirmary before being reminded we hadn't been alone?

My core tightened, and I regretted inviting Charlie into the house.

Foster kissed me softly and much too quickly. "Don't worry. I won't let you forget again."

My body shuddered, and I closed my eyes until he started pulling us inside.

4

FOSTER

Charlie showing up wasn't ideal, but maybe it was for the best. While time meant nothing to me, I knew it still meant something to Andie. She'd accepted the idea of the bond—I had no doubts about that—but completing our connection was something else entirely. I wasn't sure she truly understood that, and if she did, was she ready? Probably not so soon after having been raised human for so many years.

She needed more time, which I'd give her, but I couldn't deny there was a small amount of disappointment flowing through me when we walked into the house together.

Charlie was lounging on the light-grey couch, but Andie skipped past the living room and went straight to the kitchen.

She shivered, her hair still wet from having a bucket of spelled water poured over her. "I need something warm."

I pressed my hand to her lower back. "Why don't you get cleaned up and I'll make you some tea?"

She glanced down at herself and frowned. "What happened to my clothes?"

They were singed in several spots, and pieces of her pants were barely staying on her legs. The only article of clothing fully intact was my shirt that she was still wearing.

"I think you burned them. I wasn't kidding when I told you how hot your skin was."

Her eyes moved to my arms, but the burns I'd received while holding her were nearly gone, thanks to my wolf healing.

"Are you sure that you're okay?" she asked with a frown.

My hands grabbed her biceps, and I brought her closer to me, giving her another kiss. "I promise, I'm fine. Go take a minute, and we'll be here waiting for you."

Andie moved hesitantly out of the kitchen and down the hallway. I opened the cupboard above the instant coffeemaker and pulled down Andie's favorite cup, which her mother had given her.

Just as I set it under the machine and pressed the button for hot water, Charlie made herself comfortable by jumping on the counter and dangling her legs above the ground.

"So, what happened?" she asked.

I ignored her until the cup was full and I had a tea bag inside. "A wolf was possessed and attacked Andie. She used her magic to protect herself. We came to the coven. She gained control over Junie's energy, and she woke up Benjamin with it. Then she almost turned to ash when her body overheated. Beatrix helped her, and we came back here."

Charlie's eyes were nearly popping out of their sockets, and she huffed loudly. "How can you say that all nonchalant-like? As if most of that isn't the biggest freaking deal ever?"

I shrugged. "It's been a long night. I'm tired and not in the mood for storytelling."

She hopped off the counter and took a step toward the hallway.

"If you go and make her relive all of that right now, we're going to have problems," I added.

Charlie turned back to me, murder in her eyes. "I'll do whatever I damn well please. She's my best friend."

"Charlie," I warned, my tone low.

Our staring contest lasted nearly a minute before she gave up and threw her hands in the air. "This is bullshit," she muttered, but the words lacked her earlier conviction.

I put Andie's cup in the microwave to help it stay warm. "I agree, but Andie's okay and that's what matters."

Charlie's eyes roamed over me. "How are you *okay* right now? Where's the possessive Foster when I need him?"

I smirked and ignored her questions. She wouldn't understand. She couldn't. She wasn't a wolf shifter.

Her hands flew into the air. "Damn wolves."

I watched as she ventured back into the living room, then peeked down the hallway. I could hear the shower running and was glad that Andie was taking care of herself.

I'll be at the coven in the morning. Beatrix crossed a line tonight that can't be touched again if we're going to make this work. Holden's voice sounded in my mind.

What did she do?

Holden scoffed. *She injured several wolves and threatened to take the shield down in front of half the pack.* Then, *offered to help us heal James.*

Shit. I hadn't thought she'd go to Holden when she'd disappeared earlier. *I'm sorry.*

It wasn't your fault, but better boundaries need to be set and soon.

Holden's presence disappeared. I agreed with him. I'd acted on emotion when I'd first arrived, and Beatrix had taken advantage of my weakness by making things worse. Someone needed to remind her—like Holden had done for me—that acting out wasn't going to make any part of our fucked situation better.

The water in the shower turned off, and Charlie got back up. "I'll be back tomorrow. Andie needs rest more than she needs to answer a million questions. Remind her that we're having lunch with my parents, though?"

I nodded, thankful for Charlie's understanding.

She saw herself out, and I resumed waiting in the kitchen.

When Andie came back, her light-pink hair was piled on top of her head in a loose twist, and she was still wearing my shirt with tight but thick, black pants beneath. She glanced around. "Where's Charlie?"

I took a step forward, reaching for her. "She went home. We'll see her in the morning."

Andie looked up at me and grinned. "Did you scare her away?"

I raised a brow. "Do you really think I could do that?"

Andie laughed. "No, probably not with Charlie."

My arms tightened around her before grabbing her hand and leading her into the kitchen. She leaned against the counter, and I grabbed the still-hot mug from the microwave.

She accepted it, dunking the tea bag a few times before taking a sip. "Thank you."

"Of course. Are you feeling better?" I asked.

You already know the answer to that question, my wolf said.

I know that, but I'd rather have her tell me herself.

Between my wolf senses and the bond only getting stronger between Andie and me, sensing her emotions was becoming second nature. It was how I'd returned to the pack house before the other wolves. I'd felt her panic, and there was nothing to stop me from racing back to her.

"I am. I don't understand what happened, but I'm glad Benjamin is okay and my skin isn't trying to melt off anymore," she said, then she took a big gulp of the tea and yawned. "I didn't realize how tired I was until I got out of the shower."

"We had a long day with the pack and, thanks to everything afterward, it's almost midnight now." I stepped closer to her, set the mug on the counter, and picked her up before grabbing the tea again and letting her hold it while I walked. "Let's go lay in bed."

Her head nestled against my chest, and her eyes fluttered closed. I wanted to explore the changes in our bond, but that wasn't happening tonight. A wave of frustration rolled through me at the thought that we couldn't have a normal bonding, but I ignored the feeling, because, more than that, I was grateful to have my mate in my arms. Everything else would happen when it was meant to. Andie had taught me that over the last month.

She looked up at me, her lips pressed into a tight grimace, and she gave her head a slight shake.

"I don't feel like I did a moment ago, and I don't know why," she admitted.

She's feeling you already, my wolf said.

His words made my steps falter, and I took a steadying breath. I didn't know why I would have thought differently. Witches' heightened senses might have been different from wolves', but they were still enhanced abilities.

I forced a wall up within my mind, hiding my emotions. Andie shuddered within my hold. "What was that?"

I pushed open her bedroom door and set her on the bed. "You don't feel better now?"

She frowned, still holding tight to her warm drink. "I feel empty."

Shit. That wasn't what was supposed to happen. "I'm sorry. I was trying to make you feel better."

Andie reached for me, tugging my hand until I sat with her on the bed. "You have nothing to be sorry for, but an explanation would be nice."

I took a seat next to her and pulled her into my lap. The cup of hot tea almost spilled from the movement. Andie took another long drink before setting it down on the nightstand and turning to look up at me.

"What is it?" she asked, placing her hands over my fidgeting arms.

"Do you remember me telling you about how the bond for us would likely be different?" I asked, and she nodded. "Well, normally, we shouldn't be able to feel each other's emotions until we've, um, consummated the bond, except I knew tonight when you were scared, and you knew just now when I closed off the connection."

Andie bit the inside of her cheek and stared at the wall for a moment before looking back up at me. "But before you closed the connection, there was something else. Frustration or disappointment, maybe?"

Damn her for being so intuitive when she'd already been through so much.

"That was nothing other than being stressed about what happened tonight," I lied, because there was no way in hell that I would pressure Andie into taking our bond to the next level. We'd know when the time was right. Just because she had magic now didn't mean we had to rush.

"Are you sure?" She raised a brow.

I nodded. "Absolutely. There's nothing to worry about."

She fought off another yawn as her palm pressed over my chest. "What about the changes in our bond? The connection we shared tonight—not once, but twice. That means something."

I placed my hand over hers. "It does, but we have time for that, Andie. I won't rush anything between us, not for any reason. You've had one hell of an evening, and what I want more than anything is to make sure you get all the rest you need before tomorrow morning. Something tells me it's going to be eventful. Plus, Charlie mentioned you have lunch with her parents tomorrow."

Charlie's parents, who I'd learned were named William and Marlene, had gone to the Supernatural Council right after the Spell House attack. I hadn't been able to meet them myself, and when Andie had been stuck in bed for several days, I'd hoped they'd visit before learning they'd had to leave.

Her lips lifted into a smile. "Hopefully. I can't believe their trip took so long. It worries me that something might have gone wrong. Beatrix told me I had no reason to be concerned, but that didn't help."

I pressed my lips to her forehead. "I'll make sure your lunch with them happens, no matter what. And Beatrix is right. If there's something else to be concerned with, we'll know. Until then, just try to relax and rest."

I'd been trying to give Beatrix the benefit of the doubt for Andie's sake, but that was getting harder with every passing day.

"Thank you." She nestled closer to me and hummed. "Can you open the connection again? I don't think I'll be able to sleep without feeling you now that I know what it's like."

I stood up from the bed with her still in my arms, then laid her head against her pillow. "Of course."

She grabbed my hand before I could walk to the other side. "Promise me that no matter what you're feeling or what happens, you won't hide from me like that again. If we're supposed to be bonded, then that means we need to work through things together. Even the hard and uncomfortable things."

Fuck, it was like she knew I'd lied to her. I was tempted to tell her the truth of my earlier feelings, but she yawned, and I smiled instead. "I promise, from here on, I won't shut you out again unless you ask me to."

My words were a promise I intended to keep until my last breath.

5

ANDIE

Everything ached when I rolled over to see the sun peeking into my bedroom. My arms, legs, head—hell, even my toes—protested when I stretched across the bed.

Foster's warm body was still pressed against me. He was a stomach sleeper. For the first few nights we'd stayed together, I'd worried he would suffocate, but he assured me several times over that he hadn't died yet from sleeping and likely wouldn't anytime in the future. Even so, some mornings, when he was really still, I'd stick my finger under his nose until I confirmed he was breathing.

Freaking weird stomach sleepers.

I slipped out of bed, trying my best to be quiet, but instead, I tripped over the jeans I'd tossed on the ground the night before and nearly face-planted into the hardwood floor. My ass was up in the air—thankfully covered by the yoga pants I'd never changed out of—but Foster's shirt was several sizes too big and quickly slipped forward, putting my boobs on display.

When I got back up and peeked at Foster, he was on his knees and leaning over the bed, grinning while his body shook.

I raised a brow at him while I fixed the shirt. "Not even going to ask if I'm okay?"

His silent laughter turned into audible chuckles. "You're not cursing the ground or crying, so I figured I already had my answer."

I huffed. "Right. Well, good morning."

Foster reached out and snagged my hand when I tried to walk toward the attached bathroom. Before I could even protest, I was lying on the bed with my feet dangling over the edge and Foster leaning over me. All irritation from my fall was gone in an instant as he stared so intently at me that I swore he could see inside my soul.

His blue eyes darkened, and he licked his lips before dipping his head closer, but at much too slow of a pace.

I grabbed on to his arms and pulled myself up, kissing him first, nipping at his bottom lip. Half his weight settled onto me, pressing me down onto the mattress, and his tongue snaked into my mouth, owning every inch.

My back arched, and one of my hands slid around his head, grabbing a fistful of hair. His chest rumbled in response.

"We should get ready to meet Beatrix and the others," he murmured between kisses.

"That's what I was trying to do before you forced me back into bed."

He smirked. "*Forced*, huh?"

I nodded and shoved at him. "Yep. Now, excuse me while I go use all the hot water."

Foster growled from the bed, and I ran into the bathroom, shutting and locking the door behind me while I laughed.

What I assumed to be a pillow thudded against the door, and I could hear Foster's footfalls leaving the room. "I'll just use the guest bathroom. Better hope you get the hot water before I do."

Damn him. I rushed to the shower, then remembered I had more access to my magic now. Maybe I didn't need to worry about not having hot water anymore. Maybe I could make my own…

I turned the water on lukewarm just in case my plan didn't work, then got undressed before stepping into the charcoal-tiled shower. Shutting the glass door behind me, I shivered and pressed my hands together.

Until yesterday, my use of magic had been rather lackluster. Nobody had shown or told me much about spells. Regardless, I acted on instinct and thought hard about what I wanted.

But I must have thought too hard because I yelped and slammed my back onto the freezing tile. Maybe hot water wasn't the right thing to think.

A light-purple hue grew around my fingers, extending up my arm. I reached my hand toward the showerhead and closed my eyes. Sparks of energy tingled over my skin, and I took a step under the water. It wasn't scalding any longer, just steamy enough to relax my tense muscles.

My shoulders shuddered, and I began to clean myself up. Just as I was finishing, Foster banged on the bathroom door that was still locked.

I turned off the water and opened the glass door to

grab my towel when I heard the door pop open with a loud crack.

Foster strode in, his own towel wrapped around his waist, catching the beads of the water that fell from his long, wet hair and down his chiseled chest.

I raised a brow at him. "Can I help you?"

He wasn't staring at my face. Instead, he was taking in my still-wet and very naked body. A rumble built in his chest that was heaving up and down while his fingers were stretched out at his sides, nearly turning to claws.

I'd never seen him so out of control. Not even when I'd almost died.

"Foster? What happened?" I asked softly, wrapping my towel around me and stepping forward with extra care so I didn't slip on the hardwood floor.

He finally looked up, and his eyes were nearly black, just like the wolf that had attacked me the night before.

My steps faltered and I shuffled back. "Foster, talk to me."

"Are...you...okay?" he asked, but the words were clipped and overly growly.

I nodded. "Are you?"

Foster closed the distance between us. His hands were like lava over my skin as they hovered over my arms, moving up and down slowly. He took several deep breaths before speaking more normally.

"My wolf heard you yelp. I told him you were fine, reminding him that we couldn't sense any panic coming from you, but he started to recall last night and how it could have been so much worse. Then his thoughts made mine return to the night I lost my family and pack… I can't lose you, Andie."

I wrapped my arms around him and held on as tightly as I could while tears pricked at my eyes. "I'm so sorry, Foster. I'm really okay. I was just playing with magic when I shouldn't have been. Everything is fine."

His hands cupped around my ribs, and he picked me up with ease until our faces were level. "I'm sorry I overreacted."

My palms cupped his cheeks. "You never have to apologize for your feelings. Not ever with me. What you've been through, that doesn't just go away once you start living again. You'll have moments of grief that sweep your feet right out from under you, that take all the air from your lungs and make you believe that nothing will ever be okay again. But I promise it will be. We're going to find a way to make sure that happens. Together."

Foster closed the remaining distance between our lips, and I wrapped my legs around his waist while his tongue demanded entry into my mouth. It was only when I locked my ankles around his back that I realized I was butt-ass naked in his arms.

Sure, we'd done plenty of sexual things over the last month, but this was more intimate than anything else with our emotions flying high.

Foster moved a hand down my back and cupped my ass, seeming to realize the same thing I had, just a moment later. He pulled back and pressed his forehead to mine. "Thank you for not pushing me away when I lose control like this. I'm trying to be better."

My fingers gripped his hair, and I tugged until he

looked directly at me. There was so much pain within his cobalt eyes. The heavy emotions had my chest constricting for this man. I was beginning to love him so deeply that the feeling caused me physical pain. Only, it wasn't the kind I wanted to run away from. It was the kind that I wanted to jump right into the flames for.

"You *are* better. There's nothing wrong with the man you are, Foster Kline." I pressed my lips to his again, then loosened my hold. "But we really should finish getting ready or we're going to be late."

He finally smirked. "You're naked."

I feigned a gasp. "Am I? I had no idea."

His hand smacked against my wet ass, then he lowered me to the ground. "I can't wait to make you mine in every way." His voice was deep as he whispered against my ear.

I had to grab on to his arm to prevent myself from falling over, thanks to the impact his words had. The bond between us had me fully invested, and I was more than ready to complete this connection with him now that I had magic pulsing inside me.

Except, not like this. Not when we had somewhere to be. Not when people would come looking for us if we didn't show up. When we claimed each other, I wanted no chance in hell that we'd be interrupted.

Once I had my wits about me again, Foster picked up my towel from the floor and wrapped it around me, tucking the fabric tight under my armpit. "I'd say I was sorry for that, but..."

"You wouldn't actually mean it," I finished for him, then shook my head as a grin spread on my face.

He winked. "Look at us. Already finishing each other's sentences."

The darkness was gone from his eyes, and I was glad. We both needed to be fully focused on the meeting we were about to have. Beatrix had kept us mostly out of her research. I was okay with that, knowing I wasn't capable of properly defending myself, but with this new energy pulsing inside me, there were no other reasons for us to wait.

Whatever I'd inherited from Aunt Junie was more powerful than I'd expected, and with every passing moment, I felt like the magic was only growing stronger.

Foster left the bathroom, and I dried myself off before getting ready. Within five minutes, I was dressed and had magically dried hair. This whole you're-a-witch thing wasn't so bad now that I could use my power.

When I entered the room, Foster's hair was still dripping at the ends and leaving dark spots on his grey shirt. I placed one hand on the back of his head and smiled.

He looked down at me, then felt his hair. "New trick?"

I nodded. "I'm sure I'll have several of them as soon as I get back to practicing with Charlie."

Foster looped his arm around my waist and brought me flush against his chest. "As long as you don't try to turn me into a toad, I'm happy to be your test subject anytime you need one."

I patted his pecs with both hands. "Good to know. Now come on before—"

"I hope nobody's naked because I'm coming in," Charlie's voice shouted from the doorway.

Foster growled. "We're going to need to set some better boundaries."

"Or we can spend our nights at the pack," I said with a smirk.

A rumble vibrated beneath my hands on his chest. "Yes."

Charlie knocked on the hallway wall as she continued closer. "Seriously, don't be naked, please."

"We're not naked, but you're going to lose door access privileges if you barge in whenever you want," I said when I turned toward our bedroom door.

Charlie scoffed when she leaned against the frame. "As if I want to see you two going at it like rabbits. I'll knock next time. Unless it's urgent. Then, maybe not. Anyway, you two lovebirds ready?"

Foster sighed and grabbed my hand. Charlie moved out of the way, and we followed her down the hallway.

She headed toward the door, and I went to the kitchen. I needed breakfast before the meeting or I was bound to get hangry at some point.

I grabbed a cinnamon roll. Foster stuffed a few granola bars into his pocket and grabbed two bottles of water.

Once we were outside, Charlie looped her arm through mine. "So, how are you feeling now?"

"Better than I have in years if I'm being honest," I said between bites.

Charlie grinned. "Great. We'll resume practice tomorrow since we have lunch with my parents today. You didn't forget, right?"

"Of course not," I said with a mouth full of gooey deliciousness.

She pinched off a piece of my cinnamon roll and popped it into her mouth while ignoring my glare. "Good. Mom and Dad are really looking forward to it." Charlie glanced behind us. "You're coming too, Foster."

He stepped beside me and glanced down. "Are you okay with that? You've been talking about seeing them for weeks. I don't want to intrude."

Charlie leaned forward, answering Foster before I could. "Andie doesn't get a choice. Mom said you had to be there. No idea why. She just said to make sure you knew your attendance wasn't optional."

Foster still stared at me, waiting for my approval. "William and Marlene are like family. Of *course* I want you there when I see them again."

"Then I'll be there," Foster said with a wink. I let out a sigh of relief.

I knew family was a sore subject for him, and I didn't want to pressure him into these types of situations, but I also didn't want him to doubt how I felt about our bond. Having Foster be part of today was important to me.

A few minutes later, we arrived at the meeting hall. I immediately recalled my first time here when Foster had pinned Beatrix to the wall for hurting me when I'd stepped in front of her spell. I hadn't been back since, and the tension in the room was just as thick as it had been before.

With a heavy sigh, I followed Charlie toward the row of chairs and took a seat, hoping like hell that all the alphas in this room could keep their cool long enough for us to actually get something accomplished.

6

FOSTER

Walking into the meeting room felt like running straight into a wall. The air was thick, and nobody was smiling, least of all Holden.

I leaned over and gave Andie a soft kiss on the side of her head. "I'll be back to sit with you before things start."

She nodded and offered me a small smile before glancing toward my alpha. Her shoulders drooped as I strode toward the corner that he and Mack were currently glowering in.

I reached my hand toward Holden first and he accepted the gesture. His grip was firmer than normal, and his frown didn't lessen.

Mack at least offered me a quick grin and fist bump. "How's Andie?"

"She's doing—"

Holden cut me off, his eyes examining my mate from across the room. "Seems what happened to her was just what she needed."

I sighed. "Yes, Andie was able to fully bond with her aunt's magic last night."

"So, there was no reason for Beatrix to show up at my pack, waving her magic around, and yelling at any wolf she crossed paths with," he pressed.

"No, but is there ever a reason for what that witch does?" I countered.

Holden straightened his shoulders. "There better be when she steps foot on my land. What the witches do here or elsewhere isn't something I've let bother me before, but my territory isn't a place for her to do as she pleases. Not without just cause. I'm not happy Andie was hurt or that one of my wolves was compromised, but acting without thinking isn't acceptable and Beatrix is going to understand that. Today."

Holden made some good points, and I didn't blame him for still being furious. If this had happened at my original pack, I'd have been at the witches' coven, ready for war, but him being willing to come here and talk things through showed me again why I'd made the right choice in joining Holden's pack.

He's a good alpha. He'll take care of us as long as Beatrix keeps herself in check, my wolf said.

I know he will, but I'm not so sure about the witch.

My wolf rumbled in agreement.

Evelyn rang a bell to presumably get the meeting started, and I turned to find Andie, but she was already coming toward me. I didn't have to leave the members of my pack to go sit with her. That was an action that hit me harder than I'd expected it to.

My chest warmed when I took Andie's hand and led

her to the nearest seat, with Holden and Mack right behind us.

Charlie came over as well, sitting on the opposite side of Andie. She leaned forward and raised a brow at Holden and Mack, then whispered not-so-quietly to Andie while fanning herself, "Dude. Wolf shifters. Yum."

Mack nearly choked, and Holden's lips at least flinched at her comment, but before anyone else could say something, Beatrix moved to stand before the room of a dozen witches and warlocks, plus three shifters.

"For the last five decades, it has been my responsibility to keep this coven safe. While my methods haven't always been conventional, I'd say I've accomplished what I set out to do all those years ago. Though, I'm not senile, regardless of my age. I know things are changing, and last night reminded me of that."

Beatrix turned toward Holden and nodded. "First, I'd like to formally apologize to Alpha Holden Carson for storming into his pack the way I did. That was irresponsible of me, and I shouldn't have let my emotions control my actions. I hope you can forgive my misbehavior and rest assured that it will not happen again under the same circumstances."

Holy shit. Beatrix was apologizing to a wolf shifter in front of the most important members of her coven. I didn't know her well, but I knew enough to understand what a huge fucking deal this was.

Holden stood and met Beatrix's gaze before giving those in attendance a quick glance. "Your apology is appreciated and noted. My wolves were ready to tear the coven down after receiving such disrespect last night, but I know they will appreciate your words when I share them. Just know that words only go so far."

The alpha's brow raised pointedly at Beatrix who nodded respectfully.

He continued, "Our pack is not opposed to continue our work alongside the witches, but we won't be treated as though there's no trust between our lands while doing so. We expect to be considered equals for however long this partnership lasts, and that includes being privy to information learned about this witch who dared to touch one of my wolves."

Holden sat back down, and Beatrix straightened her shoulders, addressing the room as a whole again. "Before we move forward with the rest of the meeting, does anyone here object to a secrecy spell?"

Voices murmured through the room, but nobody stood to disagree with their coven leader. I had a feeling if they did, she'd be sending them right out the door.

Beatrix went to Holden and whispered into his ear, low enough that the rest of the room shouldn't have heard, but my wolf ears had no problem picking up her words.

"You and your wolves won't be included in this, but you will feel the magic. Do I have your permission to proceed?"

Holden gave her a curt nod and kept his face neutral. Beatrix really was shocking the hell out of me at every turn. Andie getting injured for what felt like the hundredth time must have shaken her more than any of us had realized.

Do you understand what's happening? Holden asked me through our pack connection.

I do. Seems the old witch has learned a few lessons.

We all have. That's part of being a good leader, as you well know.

I most certainly did, but this wasn't about me. This was about keeping Andie safe and stopping a crazy-ass witch from stealing more power that didn't belong to her.

Ava and Evelyn joined Beatrix, and they each placed a hand on one of Beatrix's shoulders before closing their eyes and lowering their heads. Beatrix pressed her palms together, and they glowed the light-silver color I was becoming used to from her.

"*Ligamintus sacrutim historius.*" She only said the words once, then clapped her hands, and a wave of magic washed over me. My skin tingled and warmed from the energy, but I was more concerned with how Andie stiffened in her chair.

Her eyes were closed, and she let out a slow breath before reopening them and turning toward me. "I'm okay."

I doubted she'd tell me if she wasn't okay in front of all these people, but when she also offered me a soft smile, I didn't let my worry linger.

"Now, if you try to speak of things that you shouldn't, I will know and so will you. Painfully so." Beatrix paused, a smirk growing on her face.

Well, she hadn't changed all that much overnight.

She cleared her throat and scanned the gathered group. "Let's start with something we haven't talked about. Some of you are aware that William and Marlene have just returned from their quarterly meeting with the Supernatural Council. They will be privy to some of the things we're discussing here today, but we thought it best to keep them out of the finer details in case they need to leave again."

Evelyn and Ava shifted on their feet, standing several feet to Beatrix's left. It made me believe the three of them knew there was something going on and had failed to tell us. Again.

The warlock I knew as Chase shoved out of his chair from the row behind us. His hand rubbed over his shaved-down, dark hair before gripping his neck.

"Yes?" Beatrix asked.

He took a calming breath. "What happened with the council? Why were they gone for so long?"

Beatrix shared a glance with me and Andie before answering. There was a hint of something maybe like regret peeking through her green eyes, but it was gone just as soon as she began speaking.

"Their trip didn't quite go as planned. The council kept them longer for questioning in regard to the bonding of Foster and Andie. Apparently, other covens and packs have found out about the pairing and aren't happy. While there have been cross-species bonds in the past, there has not been one for many decades. With the human-born shifter coming to light last year, the council being compromised, and other things they would not reveal, the council members believe there is valid reason for concern in regard to the bonding of Foster and Andie."

My wolf roared inside my mind. *This council will die before they keep us from our mate.*

My chest rumbled. *Agreed, but let Beatrix finish before we say our piece.*

Andie squeezed my hand and leaned closer to me, helping to calm myself and my wolf.

"Shouldn't they be more concerned with Moira trying to take a founding family's magic and using it alongside dark energy?" a stout woman I didn't recognize asked.

Beatrix grimaced. "Until Moira causes problems outside of the covens, she is not their concern."

"Even though Andie and Foster haven't caused problems within or outside of the coven, they're considering them their concern? That makes no fu—*freaking* sense." A pinched expression graced Charlie's face, and she crossed her arms with a huff.

Andie frowned, and her mood dropped drastically. "What does their curiosity in us mean?"

Beatrix's eyes landed on my mate. "It means that we'll need to be careful when it comes to the information we share outside of this room and, when the two of you are in public, do your best not to draw attention. Outside of that, until we hear just what the council intends to do about these other 'complaints and concerns' they've received from outside sources, we do nothing."

Beatrix paused, but nobody else piped up. I wanted to say something, but the old witch was in a mood unlike I'd ever seen before. One that made it seem like there was more forthcoming, and I wasn't about to be the person to shut her up.

"I know some of you believe I haven't been doing enough when it comes to Moira." Beatrix paused, and her eyes briefly landed on me. "I understand why you'd think that, and I'm ready for full transparency."

Andie squeezed my hand tighter as we waited for Beatrix to continue.

"I know the interest from the Supernatural Council seems daunting, but that is going to be the least of our worries for now. They've been through their own ordeals over the last year, and we need to only concern ourselves with the more immediate problems."

Beatrix met my gaze, and I raised a brow. "What if the council becomes an immediate problem and we wasted needed time pretending there was nothing to worry about?" I asked.

The old witch smirked. "I didn't say there was nothing to be cautious of, but Moira is the more prominent threat. If the wolves would like to send their own representatives to the council and request that they keep their cloaked heads out of our asses, then you're more than welcome to do so."

Mack snorted next to me, and I just shook my head. Beatrix might be acting more respectfully, but she was still the snarky witch we all knew.

I'll speak with the wolf council before we take this any further. Don't worry. We won't let this get out of hand, Holden said to me privately.

Thank you.

Beatrix continued. "Moira is the biggest issue and where our focus shall remain. She has been able to infiltrate our Spell House and get to one of the wolves. Holden, have you uncovered when or where the pup was compromised?"

The alpha stood, facing the rest of the group. "From what he remembers, he was still within our territory, but outside of the barrier your coven created. He recalled tiring quickly and possibly sleeping in the forest, but nothing more than that. We've pulled as many of the pack members we could to stay within the barrier, but not all of them were willing to leave their homes."

I'd expected nothing less. It wasn't often wolves cowered from a threat, even from a powerful witch.

"My team and I will come back and extend the barrier as far as we can without compromising its integrity. Does this work for you?" Beatrix asked Holden.

Andie's brows furrowed and she glanced over at me, nibbling on her lower lip. She leaned closer. "I'm worried about her."

"She'll be fine," I whispered, draping my arm over Andie's shoulders.

While this wasn't even close to normal behavior for Beatrix, I wasn't considering the change a bad thing. At least, not yet.

Holden had already retaken his seat and nodded in confirmation to Beatrix's suggestion about expanding the shield around the pack.

The witch then addressed the group as a whole again.

"Our partnership with the wolves isn't only important because of the bond that Andie and Foster share. I bought this land with a purpose. I knew there would one day come a time when we needed to work with other supernaturals in order to keep the coven safe. We have an alliance with the wolves that's been made stronger as of late, and we also have an agreement with a group of vampires who are trying to change things for their race."

Beatrix shifted her feet and checked the time on her

watch. "In fact, a group of them will be coming by later today. I normally keep such meetings confined to Spell House, but given that it was compromised, I've agreed to let these vampires come here as a show of good faith."

A woman I didn't recognize shot out of her seat. Her stout form teetered before she grabbed onto the chair in front of her. "First wolves and now bloodsuckers? How far are you going to take this, Beatrix?"

She narrowed her dark eyes on the grey-haired witch. "As far as I need to, Sheila. If you have a problem with that, I will gladly take back the knowledge I have shared with you and release you from this coven right now."

Sheila's shoulders hunched, and her voice lost some of its previous bravado. "Why do you suddenly feel it's right to involve outsiders in our business?"

Beatrix sighed. "Because our communities will never thrive until we learn to work together. We all have something to offer, and it's taken a long time for me to see that. I won't be rushing to invite the world into our coven, but those who have proven themselves will be trusted to an extent. I assure you that nothing I decide is done so lightly. I have kept quiet over the last month because I didn't want to disclose the direction my instincts were taking me until I was certain they were right."

Sheila quietly took a seat, but another witch I couldn't see spoke up. "And what direction would that be?"

"One that won't be easy, but it will strengthen us for centuries to come. One where, in the end, barriers will come down, and those who live in fear will no longer have to do so. We might believe that Andie and Foster's bond is rare, but how do we really know that when we spend our years avoiding the other supernaturals we could be working alongside?"

Holden leaned forward in his chair. "Are you suggesting the possibility of a future where the races no longer live separately?"

Beatrix grinned, and her eyes sparked with interest. "I am. Even more so, I'm saying that Andie and Foster will be the first of many bonded mates to prove why this is exactly what our world needs to thrive."

My grip tightened on Andie's shoulder. "How are we going to prove anything? More importantly, *why* would we?"

Being in the spotlight wasn't something I was fond of. That brought unwanted attention that typically caused more trouble than it would ever be worth.

"Because when the two of you finally"—Beatrix raised her thick brows—"*consummate* this bond, the power you share is going to be what helps us win against the most powerful dark witch who has ever existed. All without sacrificing what we should be standing for."

"And what's that?" Andie asked, leaning closer to me.

"Peace, light, and community."

7

ANDIE

Hearing words like peace and light come from Beatrix surprised me nearly as much as her heartfelt and public apology to Holden had.

With every scare, she was showing me that she could be someone I considered family again. I didn't have that anymore and wished for it dearly. Though, I hadn't missed some of her snarky comments about the council and the "consummating" of my bond with Foster. Those ones had at least made me want to chuckle.

"While peace, light, and community sound grand, I don't understand how that's going to help us stop Moira from getting access to Andie's magic and becoming unstoppable," Holden said, and murmurs of agreement echoed through the small room.

Beatrix held her hand out, and Evelyn deposited the jar of dark magic into Beatrix's waiting palm. "Last night, I did a lot of thinking while staring at this energy. This is tainted original magic. Moira used to be just like the rest of us, and then something changed. Maybe someone wronged her. Maybe she bargained for the wrong power, and it corrupted her. Whatever the reason, I want to know what happened. I want to know why the two other remaining members of her original line are hidden away. When we have those answers, we're going to know how to beat Moira."

Foster's grip tightened on my shoulder. "What happened to the contingency plans you mentioned before? How do you intend to keep Andie, the coven, and the pack safe while we find the answers to these questions?"

My eyes stayed on Beatrix. Keeping the pack safe shouldn't have been something she had to worry about, but if I wanted to visit them with Foster, then that made it just another thing to add to her list. I didn't like feeling responsible for adding more onto Beatrix's plate when my magic was the cause for most of the coven's current problems.

"I won't be going back to the pack until this is resolved," I said. "Beatrix doesn't need to worry about protecting them any more than she normally would if there were a mutual threat."

Foster's darkened emotions hit me in the chest. They were sudden and sharp and had me fighting for air.

His chest rumbled, but it was Mack who spoke first. "Andie is partially right. Beatrix doesn't need to worry about our pack. We will take care of our own, so long as we're privy to new information and lines don't get crossed." He leaned forward and turned to me. "You will come back to our land whenever *you* want."

Foster calmed, and the thunderstorm of his emotions

that I was feeling faded away. I smiled at Mack. "Thank you."

He winked before facing forward again.

Beatrix cleared her throat. "Yes, everyone in this room will be included in all new information. The plan moving forward is to continue searching through ancestral information for anything that will be helpful in learning why Moira has been led down this path and to prepare for what we can do to combat her dark energy."

Beatrix lifted the jar of dark magic again. "Leaving this type of power around isn't something I normally like to do, but we're expecting a visit from the vampires tonight and I intend to do some experiments with this. Who would like to volunteer to help with this?"

Several hands shot up. One of them being Sheila's, who hadn't seemed on board with all of this earlier.

"Chase, Merrit, and…Sheila. All three of you, meet me at my house after lunch. Between now and then, I'll be emailing the rest of you a list of tasks to begin." Beatrix raised a brow at Holden. "Would you like me to include you on that as well?"

He grinned. "I'm happy to take some suggestions."

She nodded, fighting her own smirk. "I assumed that would be the case. Does anyone have any questions?"

No hands went up. I still had a few of my own, but they weren't anything that couldn't wait until I saw what Beatrix assigned Foster and me to do. I was ready to deep dive into Moira because Beatrix made a valid point.

If we didn't understand what the monster wanted, then there was zero possibility of stopping her.

A couple of hours later, I was walking with Foster and Charlie to her parents' house. My clumsy was out in full force, and my hands were extra jittery.

Foster wrapped his arm around my waist, keeping me from falling face-first into the cobblestone path when I failed to pick up my feet properly—and not for the first time.

"If you trip again, I'm going to carry you over my shoulder," he whisper-growled in my ear, pressing me tightly against his side.

Charlie laughed. "Please do. I need a picture of that in my life."

I glanced up at Foster. "Please don't give her that kind of happiness."

He didn't respond, and I knew he was seriously considering her request. Instead of trying to convince him otherwise, I focused my eyes on the ground and made sure I didn't let my nerves continue to make me more prone to injury.

Charlie jogged ahead and then turned around to walk backward while smirking at me. "All you have to do is trust your instincts, Andie. Don't overthink your movements, and nature will take care of the rest."

I barked out a laugh, leaning my head against Foster. "I'll trust Foster's iron grip over the nature of my feet any day."

Charlie did this weird shuffle with her feet and then spun around before we had to turn the corner to the street her parents lived on. "One day, you'll see."

She ran ahead, and Foster pressed his lips to my head. "I think she's right."

My eyes widened and I glanced up. "About nature keeping me safe?"

He chuckled. "No. Well, sort of. I'm going to guess that you weren't accident prone when you were a child."

I thought back, even in the early days of living alone with my mother. "Not particularly."

Most of the incidents had started a few months before I'd gotten my period at the ripe age of nine. Like, screw you, Mother Nature. That wasn't freaking cool. More like frightening when I'd thought I'd been dying in the middle of the night and screaming for my mommy like a toddler.

Though Foster didn't need to know that, so I kept those thoughts to myself.

"If my theory is correct, you started feeling off-kilter with your body around the age of ten?" he suggested, and I nodded since he was close enough to correct. "I think it took some time for your body to realize the energy you were born with had been taken away. Once it did, everything else was thrown off. When you get your power back, you'll be whole for the first time in over a decade."

Shit. Maybe my clumsiness hadn't had anything to do with puberty. His reasoning made a truckload more sense and wasn't nearly as embarrassing, so I shrugged.

"You might be on to something, Mr. Kline. I knew there was a reason I've been keeping you around," I joked.

He growled in my ear, sending shivers down my spine. "Do I need to remind you of the many other reasons you've 'kept me around,' Ms. Bishop?"

I was oh-so-tempted to say "yes," but Charlie

reappeared in front of us. "What's the holdup? You know how hard it is to keep my parents from rushing outside to greet you like fangirls?"

I grimaced. "Sorry."

She shushed me and grabbed my hand, yanking me out of Foster's tight hold. "Come on."

Foster lengthened his stride and kept pace with Charlie's quick movements while I somehow managed to stay on my feet, despite the butterflies swarming inside me.

Charlie's parents had always been kind, but I only remembered them from a five-year-old's perspective. I had this idea of who they were. The more I thought about seeing them again, the more I worried the reunion wouldn't be what I imagined. The possibility of that scared the hell out of me for some reason.

Their yard was just as I remembered with two oval-shaped strips of grass surrounded by white rocks and a stone pathway leading to a light-blue door. Charlie barged through the entrance and positioned me in front of her.

After making sure I was steady on my feet, I looked up into familiar hazel and green eyes, seeing William and Marlene for the first time in much too long.

William's previously dark hair had lightened several shades, not quite grey, but not vibrant, either. Marlene still had her golden-blonde locks that matched her daughter's, and she was the first to step forward.

"Oh, Andie. Look at you." Tears welled in her eyes, and her arms wrapped around me. I melted into her embrace, fighting back my own emotions, and held on to her waist like I was still a child, even though we were nearly the same height now.

Warmth, home, love, and so many other versions of happiness filled me until I heard William greet Foster.

"I've been eager to meet the man who possibly saved my Marlene's life," he said.

I pulled out of the hug with Marlene and whipped my head around. "What?"

Foster met my confused gaze. "I didn't know until we walked in the door. Back at Spell House, when I was helping outside, I left the door I was guarding to help one of the witches. I'd been furious with myself because I'd assumed my choice had allowed the one who hurt you and Benjamin to sneak in, but maybe there was a reason I was out there."

William clasped his shoulder. "There's always a reason for everything, young man. Even if we never find that reason out. Believing there's a purpose for everything we do in this life is the only way I've survived living in our twisted world."

Marlene scoffed. "I'm sure you mean that's *one* of the ways. Right, dear?"

William's eyes softened for the woman next to me. "Of course, my love." Then he took a few steps forward and pulled me into a hug.

His embrace seared parts of my heart I hadn't known I could feel. His earthy aftershave sparked a memory of my father, and I hiccupped from trying to fight back my tears.

William pulled back, his lips turned down. "Andie?"

I swiped at my face and glanced over his shoulder at

Foster, speaking to him first, then William. "I'm fine. It's just a lot. Your cologne reminds me of my dad."

William gathered me back up, then quickly let go. "I didn't even think about that. Let me go change."

I snagged his hand before he could get more than a step away. "No, these are happy tears. Unexpected, but happy. I promise."

He smiled softly. "If you're sure."

I nodded. "Absolutely."

Marlene came around and ushered us out of the entryway. "Well, then. How about we go out back and have some lunch while we catch up?"

William went ahead, and I turned back to Foster. The crease between his brows couldn't be missed, and even Charlie gave us some privacy.

I'd known this was going to be hard. I just hadn't understood why until the moment Marlene and William had embraced me. There was something about a parent's love that couldn't be replaced. My mom and dad had loved me with their whole hearts. For so long, I couldn't remember the safety of my father's hugs. Or the way I'd giggle when he hadn't shaved and tickled my face with his kisses and love.

And as I'd gotten older, it had been the look in my mother's eyes that told me she'd understood me better than I'd yet to comprehend, especially when I'd been a teenager. She had always been kind and patient with me. Always supportive with her words and actions.

Losing all of that—having them both ripped away from me so early in life—wasn't okay.

Foster's arms curled around me, and I took a

shuddering breath. He kissed the side of my head. "You're hurting."

I nodded. "I miss my parents. Remembering how close our families were before I left here… It's bringing back emotions I spent a long time burying while I was on my own."

Foster pulled back and cupped my cheek. "You're not alone anymore, but that doesn't mean you have to face this head on, right this very minute."

I leaned into his touch. "I know, but I've missed William and Marlene since the moment I could remember them again. I just wasn't in a hurry to rip old wounds open. Now that they are right here, I don't want to hide anymore. That's not how I'm going to move forward."

He pressed his lips to mine and grabbed my hand. "Then let's go enjoy some peanut butter and jelly sandwiches cut into stars, macaroni and cheese, and chocolate-dipped fruits."

My head tilted to the side. "What?"

Foster pointed to his ears. "Wolf perks. I heard Charlie complaining about the menu."

I smiled brightly. "Those were our favorite foods as kids."

Charlie's parents hadn't changed much at all.

With one last shuddering breath, I squeezed Foster's hand and we ventured through the living room we'd been standing next to and around the dining area, where there were sliding glass doors leading out onto the covered concrete patio.

A light-pink tablecloth with teacups all over it was on

the table. I laughed and cried a little more at the same time. "You still have that thing?"

Marlene's smile glowed. "Of course. Tea-Party Tuesdays with my two favorite girls were my favorite day of the week."

She was already sitting, but I went to her anyway, wrapping my arms around her from behind and giving her a tight squeeze. "Thank you, Momma M."

She let out a small sob, and her fingers dug into my forearms for another second before she cleared her throat. "Today wasn't supposed to be a sob fest. We can save that for another time. Come have a seat and tell us all about the woman you've become."

I took the chair between her and Charlie, who reached under the table and gave my hand a squeeze. I met her gaze, which was also filled with tears. I might not have any blood relatives left in this world, but these people right here were still my family, and I would cherish them for as many years as I could.

8

———

FOSTER

Knowing Andie was nervous about seeing Charlie's parents and watching her come undone were two different things. I'd known there were deep scars that she carried from her past, but I hadn't realized how fresh they still were.

Though, as much as I hated to see my mate hurt, I knew that facing the harder emotions was the right thing for her to do. While her parents couldn't be part of her life anymore, remembering the happier times and finding a way to accept that she still had plenty of people who cared about her would only help strengthen Andie.

We stayed at William and Marlene's for several hours before going back to Andie's to wait for the vampires to arrive. I leaned my back against the arm of the couch with Andie sitting between my legs.

She hummed while I ran my fingers lightly over the tattoo on her bicep, following the feather up, and passing around the birds before I made my way to her neck. I used my thumbs to work on the knots I could feel under her skin.

Her head lolled forward, and she sighed. "Can we just stay here for the rest of the day?"

She moaned loudly when I pressed harder on her shoulder blade. I tried not to let my mind wander, but my dick had other ideas.

I shifted beneath her before answering. "We could, but then you'd miss meeting some important people. Beatrix wouldn't let just anyone into the coven. I think you'd regret that later on."

She groaned and half-moaned. "Probably, but I'm also going to regret letting you up."

I laughed. "I promise to resume my services later tonight when we're sure not to be interrupted."

Andie's phone vibrated with a text on the coffee table. She burrowed deeper between my legs, but I reached over and grabbed it. As much as I enjoyed having Andie to myself, I was intrigued with what Beatrix had said that morning.

A future in which supernaturals didn't feel the need to live separately wasn't one I'd ever pictured, but it would be the start to maybe not remaining in hiding from the humans for centuries to come. Before meeting Andie, I wouldn't have given two shits about that kind of unity, but knowing my mate had been raised human had given me a different perspective on things.

She saw things in humanity that most supernaturals never could. I didn't want to take that part of her life away.

Andie took her phone from me when I waved it in front of her and tapped the screen.

Beatrix: Come to the rock pillars.

Andie sighed. "She might have shown us a side of her we'd yet to see this morning, but she still isn't polite with her words."

I let out a small laugh. "Would she really be Beatrix if she used words like 'please' and 'thank you'?"

"No, probably not, but we might want to strangle her less if she did." Andie groaned, then sat up and looked back at me. "Your fingers are too powerful for their own good."

Her words were not helping me keep the desire to take her into the bedroom in check, but I wouldn't deny that I enjoyed when she shared her thoughts in any form with me. It was something she did more and more every day.

I swung my feet off the couch and pressed Andie back into the cushions before she could get up. I blocked her in with my arms and legs and captured her lips with my own.

She opened for me without hesitation, and my tongue tasted every corner of her mouth until her chest was heaving between us. Then I stood up.

Andie huffed and glared at me. "What the shit was that?"

"That was payback for the moans you took pleasure in while I rubbed your neck. Come on. We're going to be late." I turned my back before she could see the grin growing on my face.

Except I wasn't getting away with that so easily.

I walked behind the couch toward the door, and Andie

launched herself at me. I caught her with ease. Her legs wrapped around my waist while her hands gripped my shirt.

"That was rude."

I winked. "I'll make it up to you tonight."

She glanced behind us as I opened the door. "The stars are already out. It's nighttime."

I shook my head, smiling. "You're killing me, Andie."

She slid down when I paused to shut and lock the door, then she patted my chest. "Good. This wouldn't be a proper relationship if we didn't torture each other."

My chest loosened and tightened all at once with conflicting emotions. I never thought I'd care for another after losing my pack that had included my own blood family. I'd never wanted to risk the pain I'd experienced because I couldn't keep another safe.

But seeing Andie walk ahead of me, her head up and shoulders strong, I knew that any life I might have lived without her would have been like living in hell.

She was the light I was happy to follow. To guard and make sure no one ever stole the goodness from inside her.

Andie stopped in her tracks, and I closed the distance between us in two strides. "What's wrong?"

She tapped her foot and looked around. "I have magic now."

I nodded. "You do. Does something not feel right?"

"Everything is fine, but shouldn't I start to *use* the magic? I mean, if I'm going to try to get my necklace back from Moira, then I need to be comfortable with the energy inside me."

She was talking fast and still looking around.

I placed my hand on her lower back. "Yes, that would be good, but we still have time. Moira hasn't made any other appearances."

Andie's eyes fell on mine, wide and bright. "But she could. At any moment. We don't really have time. We just have the false sense of peace that could be ripped away tomorrow."

Before I could respond, she took one step forward and rubbed her hands together. When light-purple sparks flickered from her fingertips, I stayed where I was and let Andie do what she needed to do to calm the sudden nerves she was displaying.

Though, when she disappeared a moment later, I thoroughly regretted that decision.

A snarl ripped from my chest, and I gripped the back of my neck as I looked around for her. When I couldn't see my mate anywhere, I closed my eyes and searched for her scent.

She's still within the coven, my wolf said coolly.

Where? I demanded.

If you'd calm down, you'd know where.

I wanted to be furious with his pretentious tone, but he wasn't wrong. I still had work to do myself before we faced Moira. If I panicked every time I couldn't see Andie, then I wasn't going to be any real help to her.

Just when I considered shifting and running toward the ritual rocks, Andie's form flickered back into appearance, and she was grinning widely.

"I did it," she exclaimed.

I forced a smile to my face. "Yes, you did."

She reached her hand out and grabbed mine.

"Come on."

Before I could object, the world caved in around me and darkness surrounded us. The sensation only lasted a half-second, but as a shifter, teleporting wasn't something we did. Ever. My stomach churned, and my wolf's growls echoed inside my mind.

We're going to have to get used to that, I reminded him.

He groaned and didn't respond with words.

Andie let out a relieved sigh. "Oh, good. I didn't lose you."

I glanced behind her shoulder at Beatrix who looked amused on my behalf. "Can that happen?" I asked.

The old witch shrugged. "People have been left behind but never lost in the ether. But that doesn't mean it won't *ever* happen."

Her lips twitched, and I fought a shudder. Andie grabbed my wrist. "I promise you won't be the first."

I pulled her toward me and kissed the top of her light-pink hair. "I trust you."

She didn't need my doubts. She needed me to stand beside her, believing in her abilities every step of the way, even when I had to be her test subject for certain tasks.

I didn't sign up for this when I agreed to find our mate, my wolf grumbled.

One day, you'll appreciate Andie's magic even more than I do.

At least, I hoped he would.

A man about my height with burgundy eyes and dark coffee-colored hair stepped forward with his hand out. "Foster. I'm Maciah. This is my better half Amersyn and my second-in-command Zeke."

Amersyn nudged Maciah out of the way and flicked her long ebony hair back, revealing a tribal tattoo inking up her toned arm and a glint in her muddy red eyes. "The better *and* more capable half of our relationship." She smirked, then pointed at me. "I remember you." The vampire glanced at Beatrix next. "He's the rogue wolf from Warlock, right?"

She nodded. "Good memory. Yes, I was trying to help him connect with a pack so that he didn't cause problems in my area, and I ended up with him in my coven. Go figure."

Zeke stepped forward and shook my hand, grinning widely. His white and pointed teeth stood out against his dark skin. "Nice to meet you, Foster. Have you met the East Texas Pack yet? They're a solid pack you can trust as well. Beatrix knows."

I shook my head. "I don't get out much, but I'll remember that."

Andie's nervousness before she'd teleported had been justified. At any point, Moira could show up and we just might need all the help we can get in defeating her.

"So, is there anything besides blood that you need from us, Beatrix?" Amersyn asked, shifting on her feet and looking around.

Beatrix sighed. "Nobody is going to come out of the shadows who isn't supposed to. You can put your fangs away."

Amersyn scoffed. "Right. You don't know what we've been up to lately. If you did, you might think otherwise."

Andie moved a little closer to my side. "I'd like to know."

The female vampire smirked and opened her mouth to likely answer, but Maciah cut her off. "We search for vampires who don't respect human life and make sure they can't hurt anyone else."

Amersyn crossed her arms and glared up at him. "I was going to say the same thing."

He tugged her against his side. "Of course you were, but with just a few more details."

She shrugged and winked at Andie. "Details never hurt anyone."

"I won't lie. I'm good without the details," Andie said with a short, high-pitched laugh.

Beatrix walked between the five of us. "As cute as this little conversation is, we have things to do. Which vampire wants to go first?"

Amersyn put a finger on her nose, and Zeke quickly copied her movements. I had no idea what was happening, but whatever it was, Maciah wasn't impressed.

His gaze shifted upward, and he sighed heavily before stepping forward. "Seems as though I'm going first."

"Great," Beatrix deadpanned. "Follow me."

Behind us, there were the three rocks and a small table with jars and bowls on top of it.

Evelyn teleported next to us, a shimmer of energy disappearing around her form. "Are we ready?"

"Finally. Did you find the dagger at Spell House?" Beatrix asked while she poked inside one of the bowls.

Evelyn pulled a small three-inch blade from her back pocket. "Right where we left it last time."

Maciah held his hand out, wrist up, and without

hesitation, Beatrix sliced his skin open and positioned his hand over one of the jars.

Copper scent and heavy energy filled the air, and I took a step back, pulling Andie with me. Amersyn followed our movements and stood next to Andie when we were a few yards away.

"I met your aunt once—at least only once that I remember. I thought she gave me special abilities, but she was a tricky one. She instead stripped a concealment spell she'd placed on me when I'd been born. I didn't even know I was a vampire until Maciah found me." She nodded toward the vampire, and her eyes softened.

Andie relaxed her shoulders. "Interesting. That seemed to have been my aunt's specialty. I'm glad she was able to help you, though."

Amersyn's eyes landed on Maciah again and she smiled softly. "More than I think she ever realized." The vampire cleared her throat and nodded at me. "How'd you end up here?"

I shrugged. "Long story."

Amersyn's gaze trailed over me. "Got it. An alpha. No worries. We don't need to exchange stories. I'm just glad we can help. Beatrix did a lot for us a while back. Even if she won't ever admit it, she cares a lot more than people usually realize. When she reached out and asked for more blood, I knew whatever was going on was serious. That witch hates asking for help more than I hate dirty bloodsuckers, which, if you knew me, is a shit ton."

Andie tilted her head to the side. "You hate your own kind?"

Amersyn waved a hand. "Not at all. I just hate

vampires who think they're gods and that murder is cool. We can drink blood without killing people. It's super easy as long as you're not a grade-A douche."

I'd never met a vampire who gave a shit about anyone other than themselves. On the rare occasion, you could find one who at least respected their nest, but even then, I didn't trust them. They were the demons of the supernatural races, and there was a very good reason for that.

Maciah finished with Beatrix and was rubbing his already healed wrist when he joined us. "She's taking full jars," he complained.

"Then she must need them," Amersyn countered.

He raised a brow and cocked his head. "You didn't ask her why she needed more blood when she called?"

She smiled at him. "Of course not."

"What am I going to do with you, woman?" he grumbled, pulling her flush against his side.

Amersyn leaned against his arm and glanced at me and Andie. "He's going to love me for centuries, and he's going to enjoy every second of it."

"What the fuck, Beatrix?" Zeke screeched, garnering the attention of all four of us.

The old witch shushed him. "Maybe that will teach you to tell people I'm 'batshit crazy.'"

His shoulders hunched. "Oh, come on. That was before you ever helped us. I didn't know."

Beatrix pointed to the wrinkles on her face. "I might look old, but my memory is as sharp as ever."

Andie grimaced. "Should we help him? She's taking blood from both of his wrists."

Amersyn waved a hand. "Nah, he's tough. I staked him once and he didn't die. This won't kill him, either."

Andie looked up at me with wide eyes, and I just shrugged. Vampires were odd creatures. I wasn't about to try to understand them.

9

ANDIE

eeting the vampires was more interesting than frightening. I hadn't been afraid to meet them, but I'd expected them to be more intimidating. Instead, they were like any regular bickering family, which calmed any lingering reservations I'd had.

They left soon after their blood donations. Beatrix had disposed of the dark magic with some of the crimson liquid before Foster and I headed back to my house. I'd expected the process to be a big deal, but all she'd done was pour half a cup of the blood into a stone bowl, speak a spell, then funnel the dark energy into the bowl.

Billowing smoke rose several feet into the sky, and after a minute, Beatrix was done. She then stormed off once she found out that neither Foster nor I had bothered to check our emails to see what tasks had been assigned earlier that day.

Now, we were back at the house and both had our phones out, reading the email.

The only thing on my list was to practice magic. I was

mildly disappointed by that fact but also a little grateful. If I was going to help the coven and pack get my necklace back and prevent Moira from taking any more magic that she had no business having, then I had a lot of work ahead of myself.

"What's yours say?" I asked Foster when I glanced up.

His azure eyes met mine, and he set his phone down. "I'm supposed to make sure you're working on your magic at least six hours a day with only one day off a week and to be liaison between the coven and pack. Though, there was fine print that made it very clear my responsibilities could change at a moment's notice."

I sighed, not really surprised by Foster's tasks. "I wonder who's going to be helping me with the magic or if I'm supposed to figure things out for myself like I did earlier with teleporting? Though, it was Beatrix who told me how I could bring you back with me."

He reached for my waist and tugged me into his lap from across the couch. "I would bet that you'll be working with several people while also doing your own training. At least, that's what I would suggest if I were in charge. That will be the quickest way for you to learn. You'll especially want to work with people like Ava and Evelyn."

I scrunched my face. "Why? Neither of them seems like a good teacher. They're usually pissy about something."

Foster brushed a section of hair behind my ear. "Because you need people who won't take things easy on you. When you're with those people, I'll make sure I'm at the pack, so I don't interfere. While I want you to be pushed and be able to protect yourself against whatever we'll be facing, I'll still have a hard time seeing you knocked on your ass and not being able to do anything about it. Mate instincts are sometimes too strong."

I pressed my hands over his chest. "How are those mate instincts right now?"

His skin vibrated beneath my palms, and his eyes darkened instantly. "Pretty damn on point."

Since the night before, there had been a constant hum inside me. Like electricity searching for its source. Foster was my source. I'd thought the feelings growing inside me over the last month had been equally because of the bond and because Foster was an amazing man, but with our connection more solidified, I was certain that the pull I'd felt had only a small fraction to do with my initial attraction to Foster.

Our fated bond had only been lingering before I accessed my full magic, just enough to make me believe in its power, but now? Everything about how I felt was heightened. Though, I wouldn't give credit to the bond for all my feelings.

Not the way my stomach fluttered when his fingertips trailed over my arms. Or the way my core tightened when he gripped my hips and tugged me closer. Or the way I wanted to melt against him when he kissed me so reverently, as he was doing right then.

Everything about Foster was more than I'd ever imagined. He made my skin tingle. My heart race for more. My mind believe in the impossible.

After all I'd lost and how alone I'd felt the last few years, I hadn't thought it was possible to feel so alive again.

And I never wanted that feeling to go away again.

Foster leaned his forehead against mine, staring into my eyes. "You're feeling some pretty big things over there."

I pushed up on my toes and kissed him. "That's all because of you."

His left hand moved back up my side, his thumb brushing over my breast as he went, causing my breath to hitch.

I closed my eyes, soaking in the moment and the shared feeling. His hand raised to my cheek, and I leaned into his touch. I felt like I could fly if only I didn't hesitate to jump, because with Foster, anything was possible.

I was safe and cared for and admired and respected. All the things I'd ever thought I wanted and more.

When I reopened my eyes, Foster was grinning. He didn't do it all that often, so I cherished each and every time I was blessed to see it.

"I love you, Foster. So much that my heart might explode."

"I love you more than my own life. I have since the moment you nearly took me to my knees."

Our mouths crashed together, every stroke making me crave more of him, more of the way my heart soared when we were together.

I was still in Foster's lap until he lifted me back up and settled me on the cushion so he could lean over me, but he was too damn tall to make this work on the couch.

"Bedroom," I suggested.

The back of his hand stroked my cheek. "We don't have to."

I offered a slight grin. "If you want to keep my heart

from exploding, then we most certainly do. I meant what I said, Foster. I love you. I trust you with my heart, my body, my life. And that's not because of the bond. I thought it was part of it, but now? Feeling the pull toward you, the pulsing need inside me? That's only an amplification of what I already knew I wanted. And that's you. All of you, Foster. Now and forever."

His eyes darkened and glossed over, and he took a shuddering breath. "Shit, Andie." Foster gathered me into his arms and stood up. "I don't know that I'm deserving of all of that, but I promise I'm going to do my damnedest to try to be."

The guilt he still held inside him over his past hurt my heart, but talking about that now wasn't going to make anything better. Loving him and showing him how much I believed in him was what he needed and what I wanted, too.

Foster carried me into the bedroom, throwing back the comforter before settling me on the cool sheets. He leaned over and kissed me softly, pushing my arms above my head. "Let me love you tonight."

Hell. My whole body shuddered.

He moved down to my feet, sliding my socks and shoes off before his palms moved back up my legs, keeping even pressure over my jeans.

I lifted my head to watch him as he deftly unbuttoned my pants and gripped the waistband. My hips rose to help with his efforts, but regardless, Foster took his time removing the coarse material from me.

His lips pressed against each ankle and barely strayed from my skin while he made his way back up. Every touch was like fire. I was lightheaded, but I felt more alive than I ever had.

My hands ached to touch Foster, and I reached forward, tangling my fingers into his hair. His tongue dipped into my belly button before swirling around. "Shit, Foster."

He didn't relent. Instead, he moved over to my right hip, then left a blazing trail of heat until he reached the left.

Foster leaned up, resting on his knees, and cupped my center, still covered by my black underwear. "So eager."

"We've had weeks of foreplay. Do you blame me?" I countered, raising my hips into his touch.

He slipped his fingers under the damp fabric, sliding one over my slit until I couldn't stop myself from bucking beneath him.

His weight lifted off me, and I huffed before realizing he was undressing. He threw his shirt across the room, and the scent of sandalwood with a hint of citrus invaded my senses.

I closed my eyes and took a deep inhale. I'd thought I knew what Foster smelled like—an earthy tone—but this was something else entirely. I was thanking the bond for amplifying the scent so intensely for me to always remember.

Foster kneeled over me, pulling me back to the present. He was gloriously naked. It was a sight I'd seen on occasion before, but having my heart so open to him now was like taking him in with fresh eyes and feelings.

Every muscle thrummed with energy that called to me.

Every curve begged to be touched only by me. Every scar made me want to kiss it away.

His hands moved up my sides, taking my shirt with them as they rose up, forcing my arms to stray from where I wanted them.

Foster bent forward, kissing my lips briefly before creating a path of heat with his mouth down my neck, then to the center of my chest.

He nipped at the tops of my breasts while my back arched, and he unhooked my bra from the back with one hand. He tugged the restrictive material off my arms and threw it behind us before cupping my breasts and running his thumbs over each nipple until they pebbled.

My skin burned and thrummed, begging for some sort of release, but Foster didn't seem to be in the slightest bit of a hurry.

He moved back up, stroking my neck as he steadied himself above me. His dick throbbed right at my center, and I wiggled my hips until he pressed down, offering me the smallest bit of relief.

"Our bond will be complete if we do this," he said softly against my lips.

I'd already known that, but the fact that he seemed to be giving me an out, while unnecessary, was sweet.

"I'm ready, Foster. For all of it." My words were steady and strong when I stared into his eyes.

My fingers took hold of his cheeks, stroking the thin layer of hair there before I kissed him with everything I had. I didn't want him to doubt what I wanted or how I felt about him. He deserved more than that and needed to know the depth of my feelings.

He pulled back. "I love you."

"I love you, too." I smiled and wiggled beneath him.

He nodded, and any concerns I'd seen before were gone with a blink.

Foster removed my underwear faster than any other item of clothing he'd taken from my body since entering this room, and I had my legs resting against his waist when he positioned himself over me again.

His fingers dipped into my slit, his thumb pressing over my clit while another dipped inside me. I arched up, moaning and reaching for his face again.

He gave no resistance to me pulling him closer. Our mouths pressed together, opening for and tasting one another with an urgency unlike any I'd ever felt.

Foster replaced his fingers with the head of his cock, and I was more than grateful that I'd gotten an IUD just a couple of years ago. Having any sort of barrier between the two of us wasn't what I wanted in the slightest.

His eyes locked on to me, and with just one heated look, shivers raced down my spine. My fingers dug into his shoulders while he pressed into me. My muscles tightened in anticipation. It wasn't as if I hadn't ever had sex, but relaxing to make things easier seemed impossible when I knew what making love to Foster truly meant.

There were no second thoughts, but that didn't mean nerves of excitement hadn't ignited inside me.

Foster must have sensed that, because before my thoughts could spiral too far, he was kissing me senseless, demanding my focus to be solely on his mouth and nothing else. At least up until the point he was fully seated within me, and my pussy contracted so tightly, I thought I was already going to orgasm.

I was breathing so heavily, it felt like I wasn't breathing at all.

"You still with me?" Foster checked.

I nodded and pressed closer to him. "Always."

The pull I'd been feeling since last night intensified the moment he began to move again. Our eyes remained locked, and the heavier my chest became, the brighter Foster's eyes shone.

One of his hands tangled in my hair while he kept a steady pace, pumping in and out of me with reverent movements and never removing his focus from me.

My pulse raced, and the faster my heart beat, the faster Foster moved and the more on fire I felt. My moans grew louder, and I threw my head back when the urge to cry out in pleasure became too strong to ignore.

Foster stayed with me the whole time, never slowing or pulling back, even though I could sense an underlying layer of concern coming from him through the bond that was tightening between us by the second.

"Andie," Foster said, his tone one of warning.

I met his eyes again, and they had darkened from the light blue they'd been moments before to more of a violet color.

"You're glowing," he added when I was too interested in his changes to notice mine.

One glance to my left and right proved his words to be true, and my eyes widened in surprise. I was pulsing with the same violet color.

Foster must have mistaken my shock for fear, because

his movements slowed, but I quickly moved my hands to his ass, keeping him in place. "Don't you dare stop."

"Thank fuck," he nearly growled.

Within an instant, the slow and patient Foster was gone. In his place was the possessive alpha I'd already fallen in love with.

He gripped my hair tighter and angled my head before kissing me again. His pace increased, and my hips met his thrusts with eagerness while the connection between us exploded in a shower of emotion around us.

My chest expanded, and every muscle inside my body thrummed with energy. There was so much love inside my chest that I wanted to funnel directly into Foster until there were no doubts of his worth left in his delectable body.

"I…love…you…so…fucking…much." Each word he spoke was punctuated with even sweeter kisses.

I tried to return the sentiment, but I was too close to tumbling blissfully over the metaphorical edge to speak any longer.

Foster placed one of his hands under my ass, changing the position of his thrusts, and I nearly came undone right then.

With my eyes forced closed, the darkness I should have been surrounded in was diminished by a glowing tether I knew led straight to my soulmate. The one man I would always be able to count on. Who would love me fiercely— not despite my faults, but *because* of them.

Foster's pace increased, and the rumbling in his chest echoed through my mind. I gazed up at him, soaking in the love and protection and fear I could feel from him as if it were my own.

Sparks of magic flickered around us, and I couldn't fight off the heat wanting to claim me any longer. I cried out once more, my nails clawing at Foster's flesh, and I fell into the abyss, unafraid, because I knew he'd be there to catch me.

Explosions of euphoria began at my core and spread through the rest of my body while Foster slowed his pace and stiffened above me, grunting and lowering his head to mine.

Both of our hearts were racing, but in sync, and the connection between us soothed any of the worries I'd been holding on to.

I knew the moment I looked into Foster's eyes and the tether tying us together pulsed that no matter what else happened, as long as we remembered this moment, this bond, nothing could tear us down.

We wouldn't let it.

10

FOSTER

Whatever connection I'd thought I felt to Andie before was nothing compared to the sense of home I was blasted with while we made love.

For years, I'd thought "home" was a word that would never again hold meaning for me. Not even when the Moon Goddess told me that I had a mate had I thought that would change. But having the bond solidify between Andie and myself, feeling her heart and the depth of her emotions... That finally allowed some of my personal reservations to fade away.

I knew then that I had to be stronger and better and more capable for Andie. I wouldn't ever let her down. I would always protect her and support her by giving her my all.

She lay beneath me, her body quivering with aftershocks. She stretched and groaned, but a smile grew on her face. "That was...everything."

I stroked my fingers along her neck, realizing the

instinct to sink my teeth into her had never come, which was something I was certain had to be done in order to complete the bond.

Andie's magic took care of that, but that doesn't mean we can't mark her later, my wolf said, and I agreed with him.

One day soon, she would not only carry my scent mixed with hers, but she would also wear the mark of my bite.

I placed a soft kiss to Andie's lips. "And it's only the beginning."

She blushed and shivered.

"Forever my mate," I whispered.

Andie pressed her hand over my chest. "I can feel the tether, even though logically I know there isn't anything physically there."

"Just because you can't see something doesn't mean it isn't there," I countered.

She grinned widely. "Touché. Was that what you expected? I won't lie. I asked Charlie what would happen, but she didn't know, and there was no way in hell I was asking Beatrix."

I couldn't help but chuckle, trying to imagine that conversation with the old witch.

"I had no expectations." I paused, considering not broaching the biting subject just yet, but the thought of keeping anything from Andie nearly gutted me. "Though, I wouldn't have been sad if I'd marked you right here." My fingers rubbed the curve of her neck again, and her face scrunched.

"Marked? Like a hickey?"

I grinned. "No, Mate. Like a bite. One that would remind all others that you're mine."

Her cheeks flushed, and her chest expanded. "Oh."

"But that can wait until you're ready."

She nibbled on her lip, lowered her chin, and cast her eyes to the side. I nudged her head back up. "Or it doesn't have to happen at all. That would be okay, too."

The blush on her porcelain skin deepened. "It's not that. I was just surprised by how much the idea…turned me on."

She wasn't lying. I could smell her arousal, but I'd thought it was just aftereffects of our bond. As much as I'd love to mark Andie right now, I didn't want to hurt her.

"Then we'll try it soon." I withdrew from her, and she pouted. "You're going to be sore."

Andie glanced down, and her frown deepened for a moment before she smirked. "Probably, but it would be worth being sorer if we had a round two."

My head shook, and I picked her up. "How about we settle for a shower and see what happens?"

She nodded. "As long as you're under the water with me, then I can agree with that. For now."

For now. She was going to be the very thing that nearly killed me—yet kept me breathing all at the same time.

THE NEXT MORNING, ANDIE WAS GROANING WHEN SHE rolled over. "You were blessed in the dick department a little too much."

I glowered. "I told you we shouldn't have sex again last night."

Her lower lip popped out, and her eyes landed on my cock. "But he was asking so nicely."

I barked out a short laugh. "I didn't know he could speak."

She reached her hand for "him," but I snagged her wrist. "Tonight and no sooner, Mate."

Her shoulders shuddered. "I like when you call me that."

"Good, because that's what you are, and nothing will ever change that." I slid out of bed before she could change my mind. "You have training to begin—again— and I need to go to the pack."

I didn't want to leave her, especially after last night, but, at the same time, a part of me was more comfortable being separated because of the bond.

Assuming things were mostly normal compared to wolf standards, I'd be able to sense her emotions more clearly. I'd know the second she wasn't okay and, if I was in wolf form, she'd only be a few minutes from me.

Try talking to her telepathically, my wolf suggested.

Andie?

There was only silence in return.

I'm going to spank your ass if you keep tempting me.

I glanced back, and she was just getting out of bed, but there was no recognition that she could hear me, which was disappointing, but we'd survived the last five weeks without having that benefit. As long as I could sense she was safe, that was more than enough.

My wolf hummed but didn't say anything else.

He'd been unusually quiet over the last two days, but that was his prerogative. I trusted him to speak up when he was ready to talk.

We managed to take a shower without having sex, but there was plenty of touching and even an orgasm for Andie, which I'd been trying to avoid, but there was only so much torture I could put myself through when she stared at me with her tempting gaze.

I was in the kitchen making her tea when there was a knock on the door. Surprise filled me when I got a whiff of Charlie's spicy scent in the air and didn't hear the door open.

Maybe she wasn't alone and was trying to pretend she was respectful of boundaries. No, that wasn't it. I couldn't sense anyone else.

I opened the door to find her smiling at me with her arms crossed. "Good morning, Foster."

"Charlie." I moved to the side so she could come in.

"Is Andie up?" she asked, jumping over the couch and lounging across the cushions.

I nodded and headed back to the kitchen. "She'll be out soon."

"Great. I'll just wait right here."

Charlie was freaking me out a little with her polite demeanor. I grabbed the mug for Andie and went back to stare at Charlie until she told me what the hell was going on.

She ignored my intense gaze and stared up at the wall, whistling, like this was completely normal.

"Charlie," I grumbled.

She raised a brow. "Foster."

"What the hell is going on?" I demanded.

Charlie finally sat up and stared straight at me, then looked down the hallway before lowering her voice. "Don't tell Andie."

I took several steps closer to my mate's best friend, prepared to kill someone. "What?"

Charlie actually blushed, something I'd yet to see from her. "Um, last night…everyone in the coven, might have, um…"

"Spit it out, Charlie," I seethed.

"We know you guys had sex," she spewed, then covered her mouth, glancing to search for Andie again.

"How?" My voice was low and clipped.

"An explosion of sex-induced magic might have blasted through and probably turned on every member of the coven."

Fuck.

Andie chose that moment to exit the hallway. She glanced from me to Charlie and back, her eyes staying on me when she asked, "What's wrong?"

I couldn't lie to her. She'd know and I didn't want to, but I also didn't want to freak her out. Andie had lived a solitary life for the last several years. She wasn't used to sharing her business with others, and this was more than just normal "business."

Logically, I knew the coven and even the pack would know we'd had sex the moment they sensed our bond, but knowing we'd had sex and *knowing* the moment we'd had sex because of a rippling effect of magic were two totally different things. At least, they would be for my mate.

My long strides closed the distance between me and

Andie. I gripped her shoulders and directed her to sit on the couch next to Charlie.

Her mouth downturned. "What's going on? Was there another attack?"

I shook my head. "No."

Charlie was glaring at me. She didn't agree with my decision to tell Andie, but it was better coming from me than from some asshole who might say something to her unexpectedly.

I kissed her forehead. "Everything is fine, but Charlie wanted to warn us that the coven is going to know we bonded."

Andie let out a heavy sigh. "Oh. Okay. That's not really a bad thing, right? Unless we have to worry about the Supernatural Council more because of that. Oh, my God, I didn't think of that." Her eyes focused on mine. "What did we do?"

I shook my head and rubbed my hands up and down her arms. "This has nothing to do with the council."

Her gaze whipped between me and Charlie again. "Then what the hell is going on?"

"There was a surge of energy when we bonded," I said, hoping she'd come to her own conclusions with as little information as possible.

Andie glanced at Charlie. "Yep. A fact I wasn't really going to talk about publicly."

Charlie scoffed. "Right. Like I would have given you a choice."

I narrowed my eyes. "Not the point here, Charlie."

Andie gripped my chin and forced my eyes back to her. "Then what is?"

"That surge of energy we created, it expanded through the whole coven last night," I said softly.

She tilted her head to the side, then her eyes widened and she gasped, covering her mouth. "No-it-fucking-didn't."

Charlie fanned herself. "Oh, it sure did."

I growled, and she tried to edit her statement.

"I mean, it wasn't that big of a deal. Seriously. I'm sure nobody even really noticed," Charlie said.

Andie covered her face with both hands. "I'm never leaving this house."

Charlie grabbed her elbow, tugging her arm down. "We won't leave you alone until this blows over. If anyone says anything to you, Foster will bite their head off—literally—and I'll send magic right up their ass if he's not around. At least, anyone but Beatrix. She's the only one who can make my life hell."

Andie groaned. "Shit. Your parents. How am I supposed to face these people?" Her hands began shaking in front of her. "Oh, my God. Are they going to know every time we have sex?"

I shook my head, holding her hands between my palms. "Absolutely not."

"How can you be so sure?" she asked, a crease deepening between her brows.

"Because I will build us a cabin in the middle of nowhere if that's the case and you can teleport us there whenever we want. But let's hope that's worst-case scenario." Though, it didn't sound like a terrible idea to have Andie all to myself outside the coven. Maybe I'd make that thought come to fruition after the Moira mess was over.

There was another knock on the door, but this time, it opened without any of us saying anything.

"I hope you're not naked," Beatrix called out with closed eyes.

Andie hid her face again, and Beatrix cracked open an eye. "Oh, good. You're up and ready to go. Come on. You're late for training."

The witch shook Andie's shoulder from behind the couch, but my mate didn't budge. "I'm not leaving the house."

Beatrix sighed and rolled her eyes. "Because of last night? I knew you'd freak out, so I already took care of that."

I stared pointedly at the old witch. "What does that mean?"

"It means nobody even remembers it happened except for the four people in this room. I didn't bother including Charlie in the spell since I figured she'd find out anyway," Beatrix answered with a shrug.

I raised my brows and didn't know what to say, partially because I wasn't sure if we should believe her. Beatrix had been apologetic to Holden yesterday, and now she was saving Andie from embarrassment. Could Beatrix have changed *that* much?

"So, can we get to work? I didn't spend hours making schedules so they could be ignored." Beatrix reached for the door and waited for us to get up.

"Are you good?" I asked Andie.

She shook her head, but said, "Yeah."

I squeezed her hands. "That wasn't very reassuring."

Charlie nudged Andie. "She'll be fine. Are you staying here today?" she asked me.

Standing, I pulled Andie up with me. "No, I need to go speak with Holden, but I won't be gone long."

Beatrix snapped her fingers and pointed to her wrist. "We don't have all day."

Andie took a steadying breath. "I'll be fine. Have fun at the pack for both of us. I doubt much about my training will be fun."

Beatrix chuckled and muttered to herself, "At least she's smart."

I gave Andie a kiss. "I'll see you soon."

When I got to the door, I paused next to Beatrix. "Thank you for what you did for her."

She waved a hand. "I didn't do it for her. I did it so she'd focus better on what's important."

I nodded, not buying her bullshit. "You have my appreciation, nonetheless."

"Didn't really need it, but good to know," she said with a glint in her eyes.

I was beginning to realize the thought of never finding Andie had scared Beatrix more than anyone knew. Then, likely knowing Andie wasn't going to be a normal witch within the coven, well, I was sure that hadn't made matters easier for Beatrix.

Maybe I'd judged her too harshly before. Maybe she wasn't a psychotic witch. Maybe she was just a frightened woman doing whatever she could to protect those she loved, even if she was doing it all wrong at times—she was doing the best she thought she could.

Once I got onto the cobblestone street, I called my wolf forward and he surged to the surface, a little slower than I would have expected.

What was that? I asked my wolf.

He shook his fur out. *Just adjusting to the bond.*

I wanted to ask more, but Holden's voice cut into my thoughts. *Are you on your way?*

I am. Is everything okay?

It is. For now. We'll talk when you get here.

Shit. I didn't like the sound of that.

Let's run, I said to my wolf, and he was already sprinting before I'd finished speaking.

We arrived at the pack, and I was surprised that I didn't feel a tug back to Andie. Instead, it felt as if she were right there with me.

That made no sense to me. While I wanted to consider it a good thing, a part of me didn't feel like it was.

Before I could overthink things, I spotted Holden waiting for me at the road. He nodded curtly, and I shifted back to two feet.

He sniffed the air. "You're officially bonded to Andie now?"

I nodded. "Last night. Why?"

Holden's shoulders hunched, and he turned to walk farther into the trees instead of toward the pack house. "I called the Wolf Council yesterday, and they didn't return my call until this morning. Astor, the current head of the council, said that they've been in the process of disbanding the council for months. The idea was initially proposed under the wrong pretenses while the Supernatural Council was compromised, but they've since decided to continue with the process. They won't be helping us with any complaints received about your bond with Andie. They merely advised that you don't complete the bond yet."

My steps slowed the more he spoke, and I stopped fully at the tree line once he'd said that last bit. "Why?"

Holden nodded for me to keep following, and I did, but only once he'd started speaking again.

"Astor didn't really give a reason, but I don't think accepting the bond was the wrong choice. I have a good feeling that Astor was speaking out of fear and not because he knew what he was talking about."

My shoulders loosened slightly. "Why would the council leader be afraid?"

"He ignored a pack's plea for help. Completely disregarded them, and that came back to bite him in the ass in ways most of us will never know about. I can only assume, and I don't like to do that, so we'll move forward knowing that we're not going to have help from our own council. We'll need to handle any complaints as a pack."

We continued through the forest, getting farther from the pack. "Then why are we walking in the opposite direction?"

Holden glanced around. "Because I don't like the fact that one of my young was compromised, and, while I don't believe anyone in my pack would intentionally turn on us, I understand now that I can't be so open with everyone about what's going on."

I could have told him that to begin with, but he didn't need that kind of comment from me.

I took a step forward, and we kept walking. "Beatrix told me I'm going to be the liaison between the pack and coven. I assume this goes along with you not wanting the pack to know more than they need to?"

He nodded. "You coming and going is normal, but I'm almost always here and I'd never been inside the coven before yesterday. Beatrix has been here a few times, and each time drew attention. Right now, the less of that we draw, the better, until we figure out what the complaints are and where they're coming from."

My jaw tightened. Some people just didn't know when to mind their own damn business. "Do you have other packs you can trust?"

Holden stroked his chin. "I do. Several of them. And I've already sent out secure messages to the alphas asking for them to keep their ears open. We'll figure out where this mess is coming from and deal with it swiftly."

We stopped and looked around. There was nothing to see but trees out this way. "How far does your property go in this direction?" I asked.

"Farther than we'll ever use, but knowing the privacy is there? That's something we can't replace," he answered earnestly, then added, "How about a run before we go back to the pack and talk business more formally?"

My wolf perked up, and I nodded. I'd never deny him freedom when I had the opportunity to provide it.

This time, my shift came faster and the energy inside me was more charged than I was used to, but still, something about my wolf's actions felt forced, and I couldn't tell why.

Holden's grey wolf nudged me before the alpha spoke in my mind.

The bond changed you more than I suspected it would.

My wolf kept his head high, and I asked, *In a way that's going to be a problem?*

Not for me. I trust when you say you don't want to take over my pack, but for others? The kind of power that's pulsating off you would be enough to keep any smart wolf away from your territory.

Interesting he'd say that, because the longer we stood there, the weaker I felt, but maybe I just needed time to get used to the new energy.

This will feel normal soon, my wolf said, but he lacked the conviction I was used to hearing from him.

That worried me almost as much as Moira getting her hands on my mate.

11

ANDIE

Beatrix left Charlie and me on our own for a while. I would have thought that would be a good thing, that Charlie would take her time offering a recap of all the things we'd been working on before, now that I had the ability to use magic.

Except, that wasn't what happened. Not even close.

I was on my ass for the umpteenth time, and my face was beet red. I narrowed my eyes on my best friend and snarled. "Quit doing that."

She smirked. "Make me."

Oh, I wanted to strangle her. Badly.

Charlie had this little trick with her magic going. I had no idea how she was doing it, but apparently, it was one of her signature moves to send out an invisible bit of magic that smacked its target in the back of the head or legs or wherever Charlie wanted, over and over again, like a damn boomerang that didn't stop.

The energy felt like a dull blade slamming into my skin but never fully penetrating. Just distracting and painful enough that my muscles seized, and I had no idea how to stop her.

She bounced around me. "Come on, Andie. Where are those instincts you were bragging about earlier? You figured out how to teleport by yourself. You should be able to stop one tiny bit of magic."

I wanted to rip the grin right off her face. My fists balled up, and I called my magic forward—again—doing whatever I could to make her feel my annoyance.

With a deep inhale, I shoved my hands forward and exhaled, pushing energy out of my palms, directed right at Charlie.

Her eyes widened for the briefest moment before she attempted to disappear, but my power latched on to her shimmering form and slammed her onto the ground.

"Fuck, Andie." Charlie groaned.

I gasped and ran toward her, then fought back laughter when I realized she wasn't badly hurt. "Sorry. I mean, sorta. Mostly sorry. I think."

Her legs kicked out, and I suddenly found myself on the ground with her, still chuckling through the aches coursing along my body.

"I might be a little proud of you right now," she said with a groan when she rolled over to face me.

I raised a brow. "Is that so?"

She nodded. "I gave you an impossible task. One that was meant to break you. But you didn't let it. You pushed back, even when you were exhausted. That's the kind of strength that you'll need to get your magic back. It's not knowing all the tricks of what we can do; it's having the will to never give up."

I glanced up at the sky, focusing on the light-blue color. "What if I can't get my magic? What if I fail at becoming the witch I'm supposed to be?"

Charlie propped herself up on her elbow and looked down on me. "Everyone fails at who they're supposed to be, Andie. That's how you become who you were meant to be."

Tears pricked in my eyes. Charlie's words pierced my heart and found a permanent place there to always be remembered. A small part of me had felt like I was floundering with certain circumstances of my new life, but maybe my best friend was right. Maybe I needed to stop focusing on who I thought I was supposed to be and just see who I become.

As the day went on, the high I'd been experiencing the night before was fading. I thought it was the training and lack of sleep, but something more than that felt off and I couldn't place exactly what.

"Thank you for never giving up on me, even when I wasn't here," I said to her, then I frowned. "But what if who I'm meant to be isn't good enough? I don't want people to die because of me, and I feel weaker now than I have in days."

She grabbed my hand and squeezed tightly. "We'll figure everything out. I promise. In the meantime, we'll keep training, but you're done for the day. Tomorrow, you'll be with Evelyn, but I'll stop by and make sure she doesn't overstep."

I nodded and tried to smile, but I couldn't find the energy with which to do so.

Beatrix appeared out of thin air next to us, and she

looked down, grimacing. "Are we in preschool? Is this naptime?"

Charlie stayed where she was next to me. "Nope. In fact, we sailed past preschool and are probably in middle school right now. Andie just stopped a repeater spell."

Beatrix raised one brow ever so slightly. "Is that so?" Charlie nodded proudly. "Well, then I guess you can take a lunch break, but your day isn't over. Make sure to discuss spells and when to use them and when to rely on innate magic."

Beatrix reached her hand out to me, and I accepted, a little surprised when I nearly flew off the ground onto my feet. "Good job today, Andie."

Before I could offer my thanks, the coven leader disappeared into a shimmer of magic.

Charlie was on her feet and wrapped an arm around my shoulders. "Food sounds delicious. How about we grab some sandwiches and eat in the garden? It's too nice to be inside for the rest of the afternoon."

My head was already nodding before she finished speaking, and my stomach was rumbling. I needed food badly.

CHARLIE TOOK ME TO THE PART OF THE GARDEN THAT WAS ALL different kinds of colorful flowers and had a few picnic tables placed throughout. A few witches came and went while we ate the sandwiches we had brought with us.

Those who passed by us all smiled or waved, and none

of them made me feel as if Beatrix had lied about making everyone forget they'd known I'd had sex the night before.

Charlie kicked me under the table. "Why are you frowning?"

My face scrunched. "Ow. And rude."

She shrugged. "Don't ignore my question."

"I'm just glad people really don't remember what happened last night," I said with a sigh.

"You mean that not *everyone* remembers, because *I* certainly do and I expect details, woman. You can't have sex powerful enough to send a wave of magic through the coven and not share. That's just bad friend etiquette."

I laughed, crumpling up my garbage from the food. "Then I guess I'm a bad friend. I don't kiss and tell."

She tried to kick me again, but I was prepared this time and moved my shins out of the way. "You're no fun. A big stick in the mud."

I reached my hand across the table and grinned. "Because I love you, I will share that he was the biggest and best I've ever had. He was gentle and respectful, but then also demanding in what he wanted, even if the pleasure wasn't necessarily for him."

Charlie was fanning her face. "I need to find myself a soulmate or just a grumbly wolf to play with. Never considered it before seeing you with Foster, but maybe you can properly introduce to me the one with the wide smile and dazzling hazel eyes."

She gave me puppy-dog eyes, and an idea was already forming inside my head, one Foster would hate, but I would love it. "Mack? He's the beta and really friendly."

She raised a brow. "Friendly, huh? I can work with *friendly*."

"Maybe you can come to the pack with us next time," I suggested.

She grinned. "You know Foster probably won't like that."

"You let me worry about him. As long as Holden says it's okay, then you're welcome with us anytime. They have guest rooms in the pack house, and it's beautiful in there."

Charlie laughed and gathered up the rest of our stuff before we both stood. "Are you saying I can't stay in that small, one-bedroom cabin you've told me about with you and the wolf?"

"I love you, but not that much. And Foster would kill me," I said with a chuckle.

"No, he'd probably just punish you, but it wouldn't really be punishment coming from him." She waggled her brows.

I shoved her as we walked back toward my house. "I should probably be more concerned about the thoughts you have about me and Foster."

"Nah. I'll let you have the same ones when I land myself a sexy man, too."

There was little to no chance that I would be anything like she was once she found her other half, but I didn't need to tell her that. Charlie could have her fun for now. I knew she meant well.

Benjamin and his mother, whose name I'd yet to get, were walking toward us. He was grinning widely, and she was paying more attention to her hands than anything else.

Benjamin waved. "Hey, Andie and Charlie."

I smiled. "It's good to see you up and about."

They were within touching distance now, and Benjamin hugged me tightly. "Thank you for saving me."

"No thanks needed," I said when he pulled back. "I'm just glad I could help."

Charlie nodded at the woman. "Hi, Reah. I don't think you've met Andie yet." Charlie turned to me. "Reah and Benjamin joined the coven after you and your mom left."

"I saw her briefly, but it's nice to formally meet you," I said, but she still wouldn't really look up.

Benjamin nudged her. "Come on, Mom. It's okay."

Nerves assaulted me. "Did something happen?"

He shook his head, and his grin widened. "We have something to share with you."

Yeah, that didn't help ease the twisting of my insides.

Reah finally looked up after Benjamin whispered something in her ear. She had tears in her green eyes, and her lip quivered.

"Your mother? She was…" A hand covered her mouth as she sobbed.

Benjamin held her shoulders tightly. "It's okay, Mom. It wasn't your fault. Andie will understand."

I shared a concerned look with Charlie. Neither of us had any idea what was going on.

Reah took a shuddering breath and met my gaze again. "Your mother was my cousin, the only person I considered family until I met my Jeffrey."

My mouth opened, but no words came out as my stare bounced between her and Benjamin. My mind couldn't believe what my ears were hearing. Did I still have blood family in this world? How could this have been possible?

Charlie pinched my arm, but before I could get my thoughts in order, Reah continued. "We grew up together in Oregon, and I was younger by six years. She protected me and taught me everything she knew about magic and surviving in our family, but when I was a teenager, I thought I knew better than her. I met Jeffrey, and he told me about a coven who wanted his help, one that promised him all the things I could only ever dream of. One that would get me away from our oddly run coven."

"Moira," I muttered, and she nodded.

"Aspen tried to warn me off, but Jeffrey was my everything. I had to go with him. At the time, I thought if I let him go, then it would be the end of the world. My only saving grace was that Jeffrey was truly an amazing man. He protected me as much as he could after we quickly realized this new coven wasn't what we'd been led to believe it was. In the end, we were both stuck. There was no leaving once we were bound to Moira's terms."

"Except you did leave, when you had the right motivation." I glanced at Benjamin.

She nodded and squeezed her son's hand. "Jeffrey wouldn't let Benjamin be tainted by that woman. He gave his life so we could have one outside of the darkness, but I was so ashamed. I hid for months before Juniper found me. Apparently, Aspen had told her about me, and Junie promised to find me for her.

"When Junie did, I was so ashamed of my choices, I told her the only way I would come to the coven was if she didn't tell Aspen I was there and nobody else knew I was related to her. Aspen had already been through enough. She didn't need to feel guilty about coming back to fix my broken pieces, and I couldn't raise Benjamin beyond the coven. Not with his abilities. I needed help Aspen couldn't provide after giving up her magic."

My heart was breaking for this woman. I didn't know her, but hearing more of her story and knowing she was family, I wasn't going to let her hide anymore. We'd all been doing too much of that. It was time to break the family trait.

"I'm assuming Beatrix knew who you were, though, if she allowed you to stay in the coven," I said, urging Reah to continue.

She let out a quiet laugh. "Yes, she figured it out as soon as she saw me. I denied the help then, worried things wouldn't go how I felt I needed them to. That was when I tried to raise Benjamin on my own, but Beatrix found out about the troubles I was having and agreed to welcome me into the coven as just another witch with a son and a past we didn't want to talk about."

Charlie gasped and looked at Benjamin. "Beatrix didn't ask you to help only because you're an excellent tracker."

He shook his head. "I didn't know until after Andie saved me, but no, I think Beatrix thought my blood ties to Andie might help in the search."

My emotions were shaken. I didn't know what to do next. "I won't tell anyone what you've shared, but I would love to get to know you better if you're comfortable with that."

My phone vibrated, and I almost ignored it until I

realized Foster was the only one who would be calling me. I apologized to the others before answering. "Hey."

"Are you okay?" he asked quickly.

"Of course. Why?" I glanced around, making sure I didn't sense anything I might have been missing.

He let out a heavy breath. "The bond. I sensed your emotions changing."

"Oh. Well, I have some news to share, but it's not bad. We'll chat when you're back."

He grunted. "I'll be there as soon as I can be."

The call ended and I turned back to the group. "Sorry about that. I meant what I said, except for when it comes to Foster. I can't keep this from him."

Reah nodded, and there was a sadness in her eyes. "I understand, and I'd love to get to know you as well."

I bit my lip, not wanting to upset her, but needing to know. "Are there others out there? Who are part of Mom's family?"

"A few, but most of them split up after the kids grew and began to leave. We didn't grow up in a coven like this. It was family, but it wasn't safe. We stuck together as long as we had to, and then out into the world we went."

That was an awful way to grow up, but I was grateful they'd both found their way to Beatrix's coven. She wasn't conventional in the way she ran things, but this was a place of family and comfort. Nobody could deny that.

Well, except for my mom. She'd left, doing what she'd thought had been the only choice after the way she'd grown up.

I gave my head a slight shake. I couldn't fall into the past. There was nothing any of us could do to change things, but I could make an effort to know Reah and stay close to Benjamin.

"Thank you for coming to tell me," I said to both of them. "I've thought I was alone for so long, and coming back here has meant everything to me, but this makes it all that much better."

"Maybe Foster won't look like he wants to kill me when he finds out we're family," Benjamin joked.

Charlie laughed. "Good luck with that. I think that's his permanent facial expression."

Not long after that, we said our goodbyes and I walked back to my house with Charlie. My mood was lifted, and I was ready for the book part of my training that Beatrix had insisted we continue.

I just hoped Foster also brought good news home with him.

12

FOSTER

fter going over preparations with Holden and Mack for a few hours, I asked to see the boy who had attacked Andie. Holden had said he didn't remember much, but still, I wanted to hear it for myself.

I'd been tempted to race back to the coven instead, but Andie's emotions had been positive since I'd called her. Being an overbearing mate wasn't going to do me any good when she was safe within the coven.

"We've kept James in the pack house while we wait for him to recover. His mother is staying with him. She's more bite than she is bark, so tread lightly," Holden warned.

I nodded stiffly as we walked up the stairs to the second level of the house. We passed three doors before turning down a short hallway and cracking open the first room on the left.

Holden knocked first, then called out. "James? Lila?"

"We're still here, Holden," a woman droned.

The alpha smiled. "Yes, I just wanted to make sure we weren't interrupting anything."

"We?" she asked before noticing me, then she glowered. "What's he doing here?"

Holden stepped between Lila and me. "Foster is just here to chat with James. He means no harm."

She brushed dirty-blonde hair over her shoulder and crossed her arms while narrowing her light-blue eyes on me. "I think my son has done enough talking. He did nothing wrong."

I softened my face and nodded. "I agree, ma'am. But it was my mate who was the target and I'd just like to ask a few questions myself to have some peace about the incident."

"You nearly took his head off that night," she practically growled with darkening eyes.

"I did, but if you have a mate bond, then you'll understand I wasn't exactly in control over my actions. I didn't know he'd been spelled with dark magic," I replied earnestly.

She raised a brow. "And if you had, would that have changed what happened?"

I was tempted to lie but thought better of it. "Doubtful."

Surprising me, she smiled. "You can stay. For a few minutes."

For the first time, I noticed James propped up in the bed by several pillows. His skin was pallid, cheeks sucked in, and his brown eyes were dull. He might have even been trying to smile, but the action looked more like a grimace.

I stood at the foot of the bed with Holden right behind me. "Hello, James. I'm Foster."

"I know. I'm really sorry—"

I waved a hand, cutting him off. "Don't waste energy with an apology. I've seen what dark magic can do. You had no choice."

He nodded, and I continued. "Holden told me everything you shared, but I'm curious if you've remembered anything else since then. Like maybe how they got the thought into your head in the first place."

James shared a look with his mother, and she nodded. "We were going to tell you today, Holden."

"Tell me what?"

James cleared his throat and tried sitting further up. "The voice is still there, but it's quieter. I thought it was just a hum from being zapped by the witch, but it's getting louder…clearer."

I gripped the footboard, the wood creaking from my grasp. "What is it saying?"

"Kill the woman or kill yourself," he said, his voice trembling.

Holden patted his leg but looked at Lila. "Do you trust me?"

She nodded. "I wouldn't be here otherwise, and you know it."

"I'm going to bring Andie here to help James," Holden said.

Lila was out of her seat in an instant. "You *want* him to kill her?"

A snarl ripped from my chest. "*No.*"

Holden sent a wave of calming alpha energy through the room. "Andie can pull the dark magic out. Beatrix told me she did the same for the other boy, right?"

I nodded stiffly. "But that was different. Beatrix can help with this one. Or any other healer, for that matter."

Holden grimaced. "Beatrix already did help. We thought James was getting better, just slower than expected, but if he's still hearing a voice, whatever Beatrix did wasn't enough."

Fuck. This didn't make me happy in the slightest. Once Andie found out, she was going to want to help because that was who she was. I could keep it from her, but then I'd have to keep her from the pack and that wasn't going to work, either.

Holden clasped my shoulder. "Remember what I said earlier, Foster. We need to keep things minimal. Andie is who we need right now."

My wolf's growl echoed through the room while I turned for the door. I didn't even bother using the stairs. I leapt over the railing and landed with a thud on the first floor before storming out the front door.

James might have been a kid, but he still wasn't in control of his actions. Just the sight of Andie could set him off, and I was supposed to risk my mate being hurt just to save him?

I wasn't okay with this one damn bit.

WHEN I ARRIVED BACK AT THE COVEN, SOME OF MY IRE HAD fled, and I was a little surprised I hadn't heard from Andie. The bond should have alerted her to my mood change, but when I walked into the house, she was laughing with Charlie, acting as if everything were fine.

At least until she heard the door slam and met my eyes.

Her chair toppled over, and she was rushing across the house in the next second. "What's wrong?"

"You didn't sense anything before I walked in?" I asked first, because I couldn't let it go.

She shook her head. "But I can hardly breathe now that you're here." Her hand covered my chest. "You're hurting."

"No, I'm pissed off."

Charlie grabbed her stuff and stood from the table. "That's usually the same thing for men."

I didn't hold back my growl.

She held a hand up. "Easy, Wolf. I'm leaving unless there's anything I can help with."

I looked down at Andie, hoping Charlie would see herself out. "We need to go to the pack. Tonight."

Andie glanced back at Charlie, then up at me. "Can she come? I'd like her to meet some of the wolves, and it's been over a month since we've been going back and forth."

My jaw clenched. "Tonight's not really the night."

"What happened?" Charlie asked, all joviality gone from her voice.

I hesitated to reply, but she was going to know eventually.

"The kid who attacked Andie still has dark magic in him. Holden doesn't want to involve Beatrix, so he's asking for Andie's help." I met my mate's confused eyes. "He heard what you did for Benjamin."

She nodded. "Right. Well, I'm happy to try again. Is he awake?"

My grip tightened painfully at my sides. "He is, and whatever spell he was hit with is still telling him to kill you. And if he can't, he's supposed to kill himself."

Andie reached for her jacket behind me. "We need to go. Now."

I took a deep breath. I'd known she would want to help, but I wasn't ready.

Charlie met my fiery gaze. "Let me come with you. Andie will need supplies. Items I already have in my bag in case I'd needed them earlier while training. I can help her. She shouldn't do this by herself yet. You got lucky Beatrix showed up last time."

Charlie wasn't wrong. I didn't like the idea, but we didn't have much of a choice if we couldn't involve Beatrix.

Andie peeked her head around me. "I'm still here, in case you forgot while you were discussing what I can and cannot do."

Charlie winked at her. "Can't miss that pink hair of yours."

I cut off their banter. "If you come, you need to avoid as many wolves as possible."

She tightened the hold on her bag. "I'll follow your lead."

I narrowed my eyes, my voice deepening. "I mean it, Charlie. No games while we're there."

Charlie gave me a curt nod, and I turned for the door. Andie was smiling at me, but I couldn't offer one back. Not until she was safe from whatever she was about to do.

"Thank you," she said quietly.

I grunted. "Don't thank me yet."

She grabbed my hand and led me out the door. Charlie jogged ahead of us and turned around. "A quick lesson." She pressed her hands together and then pulled the right one away, facing it toward us and making a big circle. "Do that, but with your energy, Andie. While your palms are filling, think about where you want to be and how you want to get there. Picture the portal you want to open and what should be on the other side."

Andie gulped but nodded and released my hand before stepping forward.

I wanted to say we didn't really have time for even quick lessons, but I preferred this to teleporting any day.

Charlie moved to stand behind Andie, guiding her movements without actually touching her and offering short pieces of advice while Andie did her best to create the portal. The first few times, there were nothing but flickers in the air, but within five minutes, Andie had a portal opened in the forest, and I could see the dirt road leading to the pack house.

Andie let out a small *whoop* and hugged Charlie. "Thank you!"

Charlie smiled and squeezed her back. "That was all you."

This was a side to my mate's best friend that I'd yet to see, and I wasn't disappointed. Andie was in good hands with Charlie as one of her trainers. That made me feel only slightly better about this whole shitty situation.

I stepped forward and kissed Andie's temple. "You did great."

She blushed before grabbing my hand again. I could sense her pulse increasing, and that had my thoughts returning to the fact that she hadn't been able to sense me until we'd been in the same room.

Maybe our bond wasn't as complete as I'd thought it was, or maybe things were going to be more different between us than I'd been prepared for.

I waited for my wolf to pipe in with his words of wisdom, but there was nothing from him. That didn't me feel any better.

Charlie helped Andie close the portal, and we walked toward the pack house. I let Holden know we'd arrived, and he was waiting out front for us.

You didn't tell me you brought a guest, he said through the pack connection.

Andie is still too new to handle this on her own. It was either this or Beatrix. Plus, it shouldn't be out of the ordinary for her childhood friend to come visit.

He gave me a curt nod. *I guess not.*

"Good evening, Holden. This is my best friend Charlie. I hope it's okay that she came with us," Andie said, breaking the tension I'd created with the alpha.

Holden smiled. "Of course. I'm surprised you didn't bring her by sooner. Come on in."

Charlie stayed quiet, and we followed after Holden, who went straight up the stairs and toward the room James was in. I pulled Charlie and Andie back once we got to the top and kept my voice low.

"You're to remove this dark energy only. You're not responsible for healing him or anything extra."

Charlie patted my arm. "You got it. No need to worry."

My lip lifted, but Andie grabbed my chin and made me look at her. "I know you're nervous, but I need you to believe I can help this boy. Otherwise, I'm going to be distracted and this isn't going to work."

Fuck. Her words cut deep, and guilt nearly drowned me. "I'm sorry, Andie. It's not you I don't believe in. I promise. I just don't want you to get hurt."

She let go of my chin and offered a small smile. "Then stand by my side and make sure that doesn't happen."

I pulled her into my arms. "I can do that. I *will* do that. For you. Whatever you need."

The erratic feeling of keeping Andie safe had been changing over the last day. Ever since she'd gotten her magic back. Something wasn't right, and I was worried it had taken me too long to figure out, but there was nothing we could do about it right then.

Andie needed me to keep my shit together so we could help James. That was what I'd do. We'd figure the rest out afterward.

We walked the rest of the way toward the room and found Charlie waiting just outside the door with a grimace on her face. "Can you feel that?"

Andie placed a hand over her chest and nodded, but I had no clue what they were talking about. "What are you feeling?"

"The heaviness from the dark magic. There's more there than even Benjamin had," Andie answered quietly.

"A lot more," Charlie echoed.

Andie looked up at me. "We're going to need more jars just in case."

"I don't care what Holden wants. If we need Beatrix

here, then I'll get her here," I said before I considered heading to get the requested items.

Both Charlie and Andie shook their heads. "We can handle this," Andie answered.

They both entered the room with tense shoulders, but their heads were held high and smiles were pasted on their faces. At the same time, I felt like my heart was going to rip from my chest when I headed to get the needed containers.

What is happening to us? I asked my wolf.

He groaned. *Bond isn't right.*

What does that mean?

You bonded to Andie, but she didn't bond to us. I thought time would settle things out, but her magic isn't accepting us and it's making me tired.

Fuck. This was why he'd been so quiet. I should have known something wasn't right sooner.

How do we fix this? I asked him.

We still need Andie's necklace. Junie's magic isn't enough.

Will you be okay until we find it?

If my wolf was in danger, there was no more working alongside the witches—I'd be finding that necklace on my own terms and soon.

Just need to rest so I'm there when you need me. I'm fine. For now.

I was already in the kitchen and grabbing jars when I felt him fade away again. Whatever was happening wasn't okay, but we had to tackle one problem at a time, and Andie wasn't going to let me pull her away from this boy. Not when she felt responsible for his condition. Moira never would have messed with the wolves if my mate wasn't getting closer to the pack.

Racing back up the stairs, I entered the room to find James lying flat on the bed with his eyes closed, jaw tight, and light-yellow magic shimmering around him I assumed to be from something Charlie did. His mother Lila was backed into the corner, and Holden was standing with her while Charlie and Andie took positions on each side of the bed.

"I found three more containers." I set them at the foot of the table and went to Andie's side, settling my palm at the center of her back.

She shivered beneath my touch. "Thank you.

"What else can I do?" I asked, half-expecting them to tell me to stand to the side with Holden, which I wasn't going to do.

"Stay with Andie and hold on to her," Charlie said. "Share your alpha power, the connection through the bond, and anything else you've got swirling inside you once she begins pulling the dark energy out."

I wanted to tell her that the bond wasn't quite right, but Andie had already said she needed me to believe in her, so I kept that bit to myself for the moment.

Instead, I nodded and called my alpha power forward. It was easier than it had been any time before, and my skin tingled within seconds. I heard an intake of breath from behind me but didn't bother to turn around. The pack, including Holden, knew I was an alpha, but it wasn't my problem if they'd underestimated how much of my pack's power I still had inside me.

No matter how much I grieved and hated myself for failing them, their spirits never left me. I was more grateful for that than ever before as Andie's hands began to glow a bright purple and she placed them over James's chest.

"This might hurt a little."

13

ANDIE

My muscles were twitchy, and waves of hot then cold chills rocketed through me while I looked over James. He was only thirteen. Not even a young man. Just a boy who had been in the wrong place at the wrong time. He didn't deserve the pain he was experiencing.

Charlie had used a spell to secure him to the bed as soon as she'd walked into the room. At first, I hadn't understood why, but the darkening of James's eyes when they finally opened, and the baring of his teeth explained everything.

He truly wanted to kill me. At least, a part of him did.

I did my best to focus on the task in front of me, but it was made exponentially harder knowing that something wasn't right with Foster. He wasn't being possessive. Instead, he was almost out of control, which worried me more than anything.

When we left here, we'd be having a serious talk about the bond and possibly even asking for help from Beatrix and Holden together. We didn't know what to expect with a cross-race bond, but if we failed to figure things out, we were only asking for our own failure—and I wasn't going to let that happen.

"What do you remember about helping Benjamin?" Charlie asked me.

My hand hovered over James's chest. "I remember a pull toward him when my magic touched his skin. I couldn't stop myself from grabbing his hands and once I did, a connection ignited between us. More of my magic came out on its own and made a cocoon around him before the dark magic started soaking into my palm."

Charlie nodded and gave James another onceover. "Since he's not unconscious, this won't be as easy mentally. James is going to scream at you, but you have to ignore his words. It's not him who's talking. It's the dark magic."

I nodded. "Got it."

"Can't you knock him out?" Foster asked, the heat from his chest soaking into my body.

Lila snarled from behind me where Holden was keeping a hold on her arms. "You will do nothing of the sort!"

Charlie frowned. "We could try to force him to sleep, but I'd rather not. If his wolf can help us force out the energy, then we need to let that happen."

Holden gave Lila a pointed look, then he stepped to the end of the bed and placed his hand on the boy's foot. The alpha's pupils turned to slits, and his chest rumbled.

A wave of power rolled through the room, and I shivered.

"The wolf will fight as best he can, but he's not all there right now," Holden answered, his voice raspy, but his eyes were slowly going back to normal.

"Thank you," I said before glancing down at James again. "Are you ready?"

He snapped his jaws, and his eyes turned nearly black. He wasn't in control any longer. My presence had only continued to make things worse for him.

I could really use your help, Aunt Junie. I don't want this boy to die, I said mentally while calling my magic forward.

Warmth settled over my chest and spread through my arms, all the way to the tips of my fingers. Pressure settled over both sides of my shoulders and I smiled.

Mom.

I couldn't hear her, but I somehow knew she was there.

My throat burned with emotions I didn't have time to process. Instead, I focused on being thankful to have her there in whatever form she could be and that I was going to be able to help James, just like I had Benjamin.

My eyes met Charlie's, and she had a crease between her brows, but I shook my head briefly at her. She didn't need to worry. We had all the assistance we were going to need.

Energy pulsed around me, and goosebumps rose along my skin. I thrust my magic forward, and purple sparks shattered from my hands, landing on James, but unlike with Benjamin, James began to convulse and screech.

"You can't stop me. I'll find a way to get to you!" he roared.

I gritted my teeth and continued to push my magic out.

Moira wasn't even trying to disguise that she was taking control.

"I have what you want, and yet you hide away. What is it going to take to draw you out, Andie? That wolf of yours seems awfully useful. Maybe he'll be next." James spoke, but his voice was a higher tone than when he'd first yelled.

Lila began screaming obscenities about witches and burning them all, but I managed to ignore her rants along with Moira's attempts at conversation. If the dark witch could have gotten to Foster, she would have already. She couldn't take him from me. Not now and not ever. I wouldn't let that happen.

"You might think you're safe, but I know where to cut the deepest, Andie. I know you, because we're more alike than you realize. You want to help people you care about, and that's all I'm trying to do." The voice was softer this time, almost despondent.

I finally broke. "We're nothing alike. I'd never kill anyone else just to help another. Nobody's life is more important than another's."

Okay, maybe I might have considered a few people more important, like Foster or Charlie or Beatrix or...

I gave myself a mental shake. Moira couldn't deter me with her words. I had to focus on the task at hand.

My hands pressed harder against James's chest, possibly with too much force, but I had to get the shield to form over his body so I could make Moira shut the hell up.

James's body shook as Moira made him cackle. "Do you really believe that? If you could have traded your mother's life with a stranger's, wouldn't you have taken the opportunity?"

Was Moira hinting at her motivations? The answer to the question we'd said we needed to know just that morning? I wasn't sure, but I couldn't keep her talking. Not when James's life was at stake. As I'd told the dark witch, we didn't trade lives. Not even for information we needed.

I was almost there with the shield. I just had to focus. I pulled on energy from wherever I could, forcing it to aid in my efforts. Right when I was ready to collapse, Charlie called out.

"Done!"

As soon as I knew the dark magic would be contained within the shield I'd created, I began pulling it toward me. Except this time, I was replenishing all that I'd used to fight back against Moira's energy, and I didn't feel weaker because of it. This time, I was growing stronger from the dark magic.

Foster's palm settled over my spine, and I could sense his anxiety, but it was the least of my worries at the moment.

You can't stop me, Andie. I will get what I want, and the longer you prevent that from happening, the more deaths you'll be responsible for. Say goodbye to the child.

Moira's voice echoed inside my mind, and my body quaked from the invasion, but I couldn't let that distract me.

James's convulsions broke through Charlie's spell. His arms and legs began to flail, kicking Charlie in the face and nearly punching my jaw.

His eyes were all black, and he reminded me of the witch who'd disintegrated into the wall while we'd been in the attic.

"No!" I screeched, yanking fiercely on the dark energy. I wouldn't allow Moira to take this life. Not when I was so close to saving him.

Snarls, likely coming from Lila, echoed around the room, but I trusted that Holden could keep Lila out of the way for however long it took.

Blood trickled from James's mouth, and I fought harder against the dark energy, taking everything that I could from my connection to Foster and counting on my mother's presence to continue guiding my steps.

Black tendrils moved up my arms, heading right for my chest, and Charlie leapt across the table. "Not fucking happening," she snarled.

Her golden magic cut off the path of dark energy and she forced it into one of the jars before closing the lid.

My veins were darkening, but that wasn't any different than before, so I kept going.

Lila's screaming turned into cries for help behind us, calling for her son, wailing for the Moon Goddess to make this right. To help fix her son and bring him back to her.

I didn't know their Moon Goddess, but I was going to do my best to act on Her behalf.

Cracks formed along the boy's skin, fueling my desire to save him. Instead of trying to transfer the dark magic to the jars, I soaked up more of the energy into myself, expecting discomfort and instead feeling a high of power fill me.

Foster roared from behind me, and Charlie was saying

something, but I ignored them, intent to finish what we'd started. James deserved that, and so did his mother.

The boy let out an ear-piercing screech, one that I wasn't sure had come from him or Moira. And then, his body stilled.

Thudding sounded in my mind, and my legs could no longer hold me up. I was heading toward the ground, unsure if I'd accomplished my task or not, but there was nothing else that I could do. Not right then.

Cool arms caught me and held me tightly against a heaving chest. "Did it work?"

"Is my James alive?" Lila yelled over the first question.

I couldn't see what was happening, but I felt like death warmed over, so I hoped like hell my efforts had made a difference.

"Charlie," Holden warned.

"Just give me a damn minute," she snapped.

I wanted to smile, but I couldn't find the strength. If Charlie still had hope, then so did I. Moira hadn't won. We'd saved James. She hadn't taken him from his mother. She couldn't put another death on me.

Light-purple flickers fell onto the ground where my gaze was currently pointed, and Charlie let out a sigh. "Done. Holden, you'll need to help him the rest of the way."

Freezing hands touched my arm. "Andie?"

I groaned from the overload of magic and began to stand, but Foster wouldn't let me.

"She's burning up like last time, but the temperature is more controlled. Why do I feel like that's not a good thing?" Foster said with an underlying snarl.

"Because it's not." Charlie's voice quavered. "She took too much on, and the dark magic almost got to her core. We need to get her back to the coven to finish everything with Beatrix."

Foster's chest rumbled against my side where I was still cradled against him. "Let's go, then."

I broke the hold Foster had on me. "I feel fine. How is James?"

Charlie pointed to my arms. "Look at yourself, Andie, and tell me you're fine."

My eyes cast down and my veins were pulsating black. *Shit.* That wasn't at all what I'd expected to see.

I heard the door creak open and caught a glimpse of Mack's wide shoulders in the doorway, but he stayed quiet, and Charlie continued speaking while digging through her bag.

"On second thought. Holden, do you have a room we can borrow? I want to try something before we get her back to the coven and everything goes to shit."

Foster's chest was heaving as he stood next to me. "Why would things be worse if we went to the coven for help?"

Charlie nodded at James. "The controlling magic that was inside him is now inside our girl. We have no idea if Moira can force Andie to do something she wouldn't normally. You know, like unleash all that dark shit flowing through her veins on the coven members, creating mass chaos. I'd rather not risk it. I can do a few things to make sure that doesn't happen, but not in here."

The more my best friend spoke, the more I feared she was

right. I'd heard Moira in my head, and I didn't feel weak like before. There was a real possibility Moira was trying to make me a Trojan Horse, and I'd rather die than let that happen.

"I can help with that. Follow me," Mack said, his caramel eyes appraising the room while one hand rubbed over his buzzed dark hair.

I was so used to Mack's jovial personality that it was weird not to see him smiling, but hopefully this would all be over soon and things could go back to normal. Well, normal-ish.

Foster moved to pick me up again, but I pushed his hands down, afraid of him getting hurt by me. "I can walk."

His chest rumbled, and I knew he wanted to object, but we didn't have time for that. I strode forward behind Charlie, who was already following Mack into the hallway, and hoped my soulmate followed.

We went down another hallway and entered a smaller room without a bed in it, but there was a table. Charlie directed me to lie on top of the smooth, wooden surface.

"I need everyone to leave the room," Charlie said once I was settled.

Mack hesitated at the door, and Foster stood his ground. "I'm not everyone."

Charlie reached for his forearm. "Foster, you are hurting. I don't know what's going on, but you're too susceptible to what I'm about to do. I need you outside of this room for the three minutes it's going to take me to fix Andie enough that we can leave. Do this for her."

Foster growled, and his eyes darkened to a midnight

color. He bent down on his knees, level to the tabletop. "I'm sorry, Andie."

I tried to reach for him, but he was standing up and backing away before I could. "It's okay."

He gave his head a sharp shake from the door. "It's not, but it will be." His eyes turned icy, and he whispered, "I love you" before shutting the door.

Once it clicked closed, Charlie got right to work without warning me. Energy exploded around her and created a dome around the two of us while she muttered words I could barely hear.

When she was done, she circled the table, holding her hands over my supine body. "That wasn't very smart of you to do back there."

"But he's alive."

She nodded. "Because of you. Now let's make sure you stay the same."

Charlie bent down and brought a jar and three rose-colored crystals back up with her. The three stones were placed evenly around me, and an icy shiver traveled through my chest. My back arched and I cried out.

Charlie's lips turned down, but she started muttering a spell I couldn't hear over the roaring in my ears. The longer I lay there, the more I wanted to die. My hands itched to move, but I was frozen in place while agony ricocheted through me.

Finally, Charlie quieted, and she grabbed another empty jar. Her cold fingers moved my shirt out of the way, then she slammed the glass opening down onto my chest.

"Fuck," I groaned, sucking in air I didn't need.

Dark fog rose from my skin and into the jar. When I

glanced down at my arms, they were no longer pulsating with inky energy, and the high I'd been feeling before was easing by the second.

Charlie pulled the jar up and sealed it. "That's going to bruise, but you're going to live. Unless you feel like I missed something, I think I actually got everything. There wasn't much inside you, but what was there was strong and fighting against me."

My best friend was a badass. That was all I could think as she helped me from the table.

I wrapped my arms around her. "Thank you. I don't know why I took on so much when I didn't before with Benjamin."

Charlie frowned. "I don't know, but we'll need to talk to Beatrix, because when I was poking around, there was something else not...normal that I don't think has anything to do with Moira. It was likely the bond, so I didn't poke."

I was surprised by Charlie's comment, but I had too many other things racing through my mind to focus on any single one long enough to begin panicking.

Instead, I thanked her for doing as much as she had while she took down the dome around us. As soon as it was broken, Foster barreled into the room, followed by Mack.

Both men appraised us, and I was in Foster's arms within the next second. "You're okay."

My lips lifted into a smile. "I am, but I think we still have some things to figure out."

He grimaced. "We do, but not right now."

Foster's agreement wasn't making me feel any better.

Mack stepped forward and gave Charlie a slight bow. "I'm Mack Adams." He held his hand out, and Charlie returned his grin without accepting his hand. "It's a pleasure to formally meet you."

"You as well, Mack Adams," she replied coyly.

He raised a perfectly arched brow. "Do I get to know your name?"

"If you really want to know what it is, you'll figure it out." Charlie turned toward me. "We should get back to the coven."

Foster turned toward the beta. "This wasn't exactly subtle. What are you going to tell the pack?"

"We're going to tell them that James is officially on the mend and nothing else. For now, that's all they need to know. Lila will agree. She doesn't want the pack to look at her son any differently. They came here to escape a shitty situation, and I don't intend for them to be put back into one."

I'd briefly wondered where the father was, but with that bit of information, I could make my own assumptions without dredging up the past.

Charlie waved her fingers at Mack on her way out the door, following after me and Foster. Once we were outside and had confirmed no one was around, Charlie opened a portal that led directly in front of Beatrix's house.

Foster was at the front door first, knocking solidly. When we didn't hear anything, he raised his fist again, but I grabbed his elbow.

"Maybe we should just go home for the night," I said.

Before either of them could reply, magic rippled around us and the door opened, revealing a weary Beatrix.

Her long, grey locks were frizzy around her head, and wrinkles had formed deep creases around her face. "What's wrong now?"

"We just got back from the pack," Charlie said.

Beatrix stepped aside to let us through. "Tell me everything."

Charlie was describing in detail the events over the last hour before we'd even sat on the couch. The longer she spoke, the more my skin itched. The need to draw power was strong, and I didn't understand the sensations trying to control my actions.

"That's absurd. What was that alpha thinking?" Beatrix snapped when Charlie and Foster were done telling their versions.

Foster's chest rumbled. "He was thinking that he didn't want his pack to think they weren't safe within his territory and that the fewer people who knew what was happening, the less chance of information getting back to Moira. Just as you thought when you forced everyone in that room to keep what you shared to themselves."

Beatrix huffed and flicked hair out of her face. "Yes, but that was different. Regardless, we have another issue to concern ourselves with."

Foster narrowed his eyes. "What else should we be worried about other than Moira continuing to get close to us while we do nothing?"

"Andie sucking the life out of people. You, in particular," Beatrix deadpanned.

I nearly choked. "Excuse me?"

My stare went to Foster and Charlie, and only one of

them looked as surprised as me to hear her words. "Did you know?" I asked Foster.

He grabbed my hand. "I didn't know that exactly, but I knew something wasn't right, and not just because you're a witch and I'm a wolf shifter."

Charlie leaned forward and pointed at Beatrix. "How long have you known? Is that what I felt when I was pulling the dark energy from her?"

Beatrix nodded. "Since the day Andie saved Benjamin. Andie didn't just pull the dark magic from him; she took it for herself. Now, that in and of itself isn't abnormal, but the way her body reacted to the energy was. The overheating, the pulsing of her veins—that shouldn't have happened. I'd read stories of her kind, but I'd thought that family line was nothing more than fable."

Foster's hold on me got tighter. "And what kind would that be?"

Beatrix met my wide gaze. "Andie isn't just the last Bishop witch, she's also a syphon witch. Something I now realize Junie knew and she kept it to herself, probably because Aspen had forced her to. While things just got more complicated, they're also beginning to make more sense. Though, we're still missing a lot of the important pieces we'll need to understand what this means for Andie and possibly the effects the syphon part of her is having on the bond between the two of you."

Hearing all of that should have made me want to scream or cry, but I was tempted to laugh. After everything that had been happening, I was beginning to realize that I just needed to expect the unexpected and hope for the best. I knew I wasn't always going to feel so strong, but with the shitty evening, I was choosing to keep my calm front and center.

Beatrix paused, looking up, and closed her eyes. Her shoulders hunched and her lips turned into a frown. "I wish you'd trusted me, Aspie."

The old witch's words were a mere whisper into the air, but they nearly took my breath away. Beatrix cared so much more than I allowed myself to see.

I moved over and grabbed her hand. "You did all that you could."

She chuckled darkly. "I could have locked the two of you in the basement instead of letting Aspen leave with you after Henry was no longer around to provide the protection she knew you'd need."

"Well, yes. You could have done that, but I'm beginning to realize that's not who you are at all." I leaned my head against her shoulder.

Beatrix bristled. "Of course it is. When that's what the coven needs, then that's what they'll get, but enough about me. We need to stop what's happening with your magic. Like how it's trying to take from me even now, because it's nearly tapped out the wolf."

My eyes landed on Foster, and my breathing became shallow. So much for keeping my calm. "Is your wolf okay?"

He looked away from me, and pain emanated from him through our bond.

"I'm sorry," I said softly, afraid to go to him in case just being near him was causing things to be worse. How could I not have known what I was doing to him? Was I that oblivious to those around me? Or that wrapped up in my own problems?

Foster was on his knees in front of me and holding my hands in the next second. "This isn't your fault, Andie. You have nothing to be sorry for. There's a reason I'm here, and we're going to figure this out."

"He's right," Charlie said from across the room. "We didn't get you back only to lose you again."

I glanced at Beatrix. "What do we do?"

14

FOSTER

A syphon witch? I hadn't even known that was a thing. Outside of assuming Andie could take magic from whomever she wanted, I didn't know what else this meant for her or us—and I needed to know everything.

Beatrix answered Andie's question before I could ask any of my own. "We're going to harness your ability and use it to take down Moira. She's even more powerful than I realized if she can possess someone outside of her coven."

I moved back to the couch and turned toward Beatrix and Andie. "What risks will that come with for Andie? Even if this is who she is, taking on magic that shouldn't exist can't be safe."

My mate frowned. "I'm not really worried about me, Foster. We need to figure out how I can stop hurting your wolf before anything else."

Beatrix stood and went to a closet in her hallway that we could see from the living room. Though when she opened the door, the inside resembled a black void to me. She pulled out a book and brought it to Andie.

"This has always belonged with the coven leader," Beatrix said. "It has been passed through several generations of witches. I don't think we'll find what we're looking for in here, but it's worth reading. Your family spell books are where we should start tomorrow."

Charlie took a few steps forward. "Are they at Spell House?"

Beatrix nodded. "We can go there after everyone has gotten a good night's rest. It's been a long day for all of us."

Andie squeezed my hand. "Is Foster safe to still stay with me?"

"He should be, unless his wolf thinks otherwise," she answered.

Andie looked up at me with wide eyes, and her lips thinned. I brushed the back of my hand over her cheek. "I'm fine. I'm not leaving your side. My wolf is resting, and he's not concerned."

At least, he hadn't been the last time he'd spoken with me. I wasn't going to call him forward until we had a solution.

Her green eyes glistened with unshed tears. "Are you sure?"

I nodded. "I promise." I glanced at Beatrix. "We can take the book with us and go to Spell House in the morning, first thing?"

"Yes, but let me try something before you leave." She placed two hands on Andie, one on her thigh and the other on her bicep. "You're going to feel like you've lost access to most of your magic, but I'm only muting it. This should help reduce any draining you might be doing without realizing it."

Andie nodded, and a few tears finally slipped down her cheeks. "Whatever helps."

My heart was racing, and I wanted to put my fists through a wall, but that wasn't what Andie needed from me. I did my best to steady my breathing and push through the tunnel vision as I watched Beatrix cover Andie in silver magic.

My mate shuddered and, within seconds, I could hardly sense her through the bond. It was as if she were dying, and my rage returned in full force.

While Beatrix still worked on Andie, I stood from the couch and stepped outside. Charlie followed me and I swirled around, snarling at the witch to stop her from getting any closer.

"Leave me alone, Charlie," I snarled.

She put both of her hands up and took a single step back. "She's going to be okay. I just thought someone needed to remind you of that before you did something you couldn't take back. You know, like tear through the coven."

I closed my eyes and lowered my head. I knew she was right. At least, I *wanted* to believe she was right.

The need to pummel everything in my path was strong, and ignoring it wasn't easy.

"I can help if you'd let me," Charlie said with one glowing hand still raised. "Just a little something to get you through the night. Andie won't be able to rest if you're not capable of calming down."

I'd never trusted a witch before meeting Andie. Had never let one use magic on me. The thought of allowing Charlie to do so now was hard to fathom, but when I pictured Andie's tears and the terror in her wide eyes, I knew I didn't have much of a choice.

I gave Charlie a curt nod and unfurled my fists at my sides. She hesitantly stepped forward, keeping her magic-filled hand raised up so that she likely didn't have to get closer to me than necessary. Smart witch.

My eyes watched her every move, and the heat from her palm made a growl rip from my throat. She flinched but didn't back up. Within seconds, the rage began to dissipate.

I took a shuddering breath and met her stare. "Thank you."

Charlie smiled. "You're welcome. Now get back in there and remind Andie that everything is going to be okay."

That, I could do. At least, I could now.

What happened? my wolf finally asked.

Too much, but Andie's okay and we're going to figure out what's going on soon. Just keep resting.

He made a grumbling noise and disappeared again.

Shit. That was too easy. The wolf I knew never would have accepted that as an answer. We had to get through the books and find a solution sooner rather than later. I'd go through the one Beatrix had just given us while Andie slept, because even with Charlie's assistance, there would be no relaxing for me.

Not until Andie understood her powers and not until

our bond was fixed. What we'd shared last night wasn't going to be a one-time thing.

I'd have my mate. All of her. For as long as I walked this Earth.

ONCE WE GOT HOME, I'D LAIN NEXT TO ANDIE FOR AS LONG as it had taken for her breathing to even out, and then I was up and grabbing the coven book.

Hours went by as I sat up in the bed, switching between watching Andie and scanning pages for any bit of information that could help. Not only did I not find anything helpful, I also didn't find anything about syphon witches at all by the time the sun rose back into the sky.

Though Beatrix hadn't thought there would be anything inside the book, I had still hoped for something useful. My dwindling optimism didn't get better when I thought about the task ahead of us at Spell House, either. If Junie had known what Andie was and had worked to keep it a secret, I didn't assume she'd have left information that could clue people in where anyone could stumble upon it.

Sure, not all of the coven had access to the attic where I'd seen the books, but enough of them did. From what I'd been learning about Junie, she'd been a witch who would have taken precautions we weren't going to figure out until we really began digging for them.

I decided to get dressed for the day before getting back into bed and waited almost another hour before Andie began to stir. I ran my hand over her arms, enjoying the way her skin shivered beneath my touch.

Charlie's spell had worn off, but it had given me enough time to get my head right without murdering anyone. So when Andie rolled over and smiled at me, I was able to return the gesture without it feeling forced.

"Good morning, gorgeous," I said softly before kissing her.

She looked around the room. "You've changed clothes, but did you sleep last night?"

"Why would you ask that?" I countered.

Andie shoved against my chest. "Don't answer a question with a question. It's rude." Her tone was serious, but a grin played at her lips.

"I'm sorry, Mate. I rested and feel much better." None of which was a lie, but I still hadn't actually answered her question.

She eyed me, not buying my bullshit, but let it go. "Has Beatrix called?"

I shook my head. "Get dressed and I'll let her know we're up."

Andie rolled over and threw her leg over my hips. My dick perked up, but I regrettably shot down any ideas of things that could trigger our bond. That was when my wolf had begun feeling weaker. I wasn't going to risk his wellbeing, no matter how much I wanted my hands on Andie's delectable body.

"Let's get answers before anything else," I said as softly as I could, then I pressed my lips to hers.

Her lower lip jutted out, but I nipped at it and swept my tongue across the seam until she opened for me. My hands got lost in her hair while I tasted the sweetness of her mouth until she was panting beneath me.

I pressed my forehead to hers. "To be continued, just as soon as we know everything is okay. I promise."

"I'm going to hold you to that promise." She rolled out of bed with a huff, and I watched her ass until she closed the bathroom behind her.

Once I was up, I grabbed my phone to send Beatrix and Charlie messages. Both replied instantly that they were ready when we were.

Andie had been right the night before. Beatrix wasn't at all who we'd thought she was. The attitude she exuded was seeming more like a wall she used to keep her real feelings at bay. After what we'd seen last night, it fit as an explanation for her frequent mood swings.

By the time I was dressed, had a cup of coffee, and had tea ready for Andie, she came down the hallway. Her hair was in a knot at the top of her head, and she wore a loose, forest-green tee with black leggings.

She noticed my appraisal of her outfit and shrugged. "We're probably going to be sitting and hunched over reading all day. Figured I'd dress comfortably, at least."

I lifted her chin and handed her the tea. "Good choice."

She took the offered cup and rose onto the tips of her toes to kiss me briefly. "Where are we meeting Beatrix?"

"She and Charlie will be here..." A knock echoed through the room. "Now."

Andie drank her tea while I opened the door.

Charlie came through first, dressed nearly identical to Andie, but instead of a green shirt, Charlie's was pink. She gave Andie a high-five. "Great minds think alike."

Beatrix walked between them. "Let's hope that extends to your ancestors as well." She appraised me next. "You're in a better mood this morning."

I nodded at Charlie. "Thanks to her, you didn't have to kick me out last night."

She hummed. "That might have been fun. Is everyone ready?"

Andie finished her tea and headed to the kitchen.

"I'll go grab the other book from the bedroom, then we can go," I said.

Beatrix ignored me, and I quickly jogged to the room. When I returned with the book, the three of them were just walking out the front door, but Andie was last and looking back for me. She smiled, but the gesture didn't reach her eyes.

I made a silent vow to do whatever it took to find a solution to our problem that day. I wouldn't let my mate suffer. Not if there was anything I could do about it.

15

ANDIE

We arrived at Spell House, appearing in the yard first. I glanced around, and a sigh of relief escaped my lips at the realization that there was no evidence left of the battle that had taken place here just a month ago.

Beatrix walked along the front of the yard with her hands out and humming quietly before she followed us inside. "Everything is secure."

I wasn't sure if she'd done that for my peace of mind or hers, but either way, I was glad to hear it.

When we walked inside, guilt assaulted me. I'd been meaning to come back here and get the items from the room Junie had left for me, but I'd been so distracted by my magic not doing what I'd wanted that I hadn't yet made it back.

Beatrix headed right up the stairs with Charlie behind her. I hurried to catch up with Foster not far behind myself and as soon as we got to the second floor, my eyes went to the room that was suddenly consuming all of my thoughts.

Beatrix was busy opening the attic with Charlie there to help in case she needed any assistance with the stairs, so I took the opportunity to go back to the room Aunt Junie had left for me.

Foster continued to follow closely behind me, and I twisted the handle to the door and walked in, leaving it open for him to come in behind me if he wanted. Everything was just the way it had been before with the light-pink walls, twin-sized bed, and the dresser with the music box on top.

My fingers trailed over the box first, and I closed my eyes, soaking in the warmth of the room. A heaviness settled over my chest, and I let my feet continue to guide my movements.

I opened my eyes when I stepped away from the dresser and headed toward the closet. Sliding the wooden door open, I covered my mouth and let out a quiet sob.

Inside were clothes left behind from our old house, but not just mine. There were items from my mom and dad. Things I'd thought I'd never see again. Reminders of them I'd thought I'd never touch.

The wrinkled suit my dad hated but kept for special occasions because it had made Mom happy. Mom's blue sundress that she'd worn when she wanted to feel pretty, and the matching green one she'd bought me for my fourth birthday.

There were blankets folded at the bottom, and my sobs got louder. Why hadn't I come back here earlier?

A knitted white blanket from Aunt Junie was on top,

and I gathered the soft material in my arms and kneeled on the floor, holding the fabric against my tear-stricken face.

Foster sat beside me, staying silent yet present. I leaned my head against him and soaked in his strength. For just a moment, I let him heal the grief that I still held for my family, and then, when I realized what I was doing, I cried harder and scrambled away from him.

"I'm so sorry," I muttered, hiding my face with the blanket.

He pushed my hands down and stroked my cheeks. "You have nothing to be sorry for."

"I-I was taking from you to make myself feel better. Even if I didn't know what I was doing, I still hurt you," I sobbed.

Foster forced me into his arms, and my head rested against his chest. "I love you, Andie. That doesn't just mean that I get to do so when things are good. I don't care what you take from me. I'm not going anywhere."

Once the tears had started, I couldn't turn them off. The last few days had been like the world's worst roller coaster. I was desperate to leap off, not caring what happened when I landed back on the ground.

The attack at the pack, merging with Junie's magic, saving Benjamin, learning the council wasn't happy about Foster and I being fated mates, then bonding with Foster, only to find out the connection between us still isn't right, plus helping James

On top of that, I was hurting people. I was taking energy from them without knowing it, and I had no idea how to control my actions.

Foster's hands moved up and down my back until my crying ceased, then he held me tighter when I still shook from the overbearing emotions.

"It's going to be okay. We're going to figure out what this means, and you're going to get your magic back," Foster said, his voice even and sure.

I did my best to grasp on to his certainty. I wanted to believe him. I wanted everything to work out, but every backward step we took was chipping away at me.

Pressure weighed down on me again, but this time, it was comforting. I closed my eyes and relaxed my body against Foster's. Instead of taking strength from him, I allowed the presence of my ancestors to lift me back up, to reignite the flame I'd been ready to let go out.

I took a shuddering breath, wiped my cheeks, and whispered, "Thank you." Foster's grip on me loosened, and I pulled back, leaning my back against the bed. "We're going to be okay."

He nodded. "There's no other option that I'm willing to accept."

"Me, either. Just keep reminding me, okay?"

Foster got up and reached a hand for me. "Always."

When I was back on two feet, I glanced around the room. "I want to take this stuff back with us soon. Even the bed. We have the extra room it can go in. I don't want anything left behind once we have time to move it carefully."

"Then nothing will be," Foster promised, and we headed for the attic.

Before we got to the top of the stairs, I could hear Charlie and Beatrix arguing. I smiled.

"I just put those in the fridge like you told me to," Charlie huffed.

"Well, now I need them. Go get them."

"Get them yourself. I found the Bishop section, and I want to start pulling books for Andie."

I'd never heard Charlie tell Beatrix "no." Clearly, I wasn't the only one losing my shit thanks to all the stress.

"What do you need?" Foster asked when we got up the stairs.

Beatrix eyed him. "One vial of vampire blood."

Foster kissed the top of my head. "I'll be right back."

He disappeared back downstairs, and I headed toward the wall of books. "Where should I start?"

"I like him," Beatrix muttered. "I didn't think I would. I mean, I intended to tolerate him, but he's not as bad as I wanted him to be." She wasn't looking at either of us, so I wasn't sure if we were supposed to respond.

"You wanted Foster to be bad?" I asked anyway.

Beatrix blinked several times and met my amused stare. Instead of answering, she just shrugged and went back to browsing the pages of the book she had in her hands.

Charlie waved me over to her. "This should be the best place to start searching. All of the ones from the end of that shelf to where I've propped that book out are from your dad's side of the family."

My lips scrunched, then I asked, "What if this has nothing to do with my dad?"

"What?" Beatrix demanded and walked closer.

I glanced between them. "I know my original power

comes from Dad, but Mom had her own magical line, right? Couldn't I have inherited something from her?"

Charlie frowned. "We don't have anything from Aspen's family."

Beatrix lifted a finger, shaking it along with her head before turning and walking back to her spell book.

"What do you think?" I asked her.

The old witch looked up at me, eyes squinting. "Huh?"

Beatrix's lack of attention was the last thing we needed today. "What do you think about the idea of this syphon thing having come from my mother?"

"Oh. That." She paused, looking at anything but me. "I have thoughts, but I can't share them yet."

I sighed. We didn't have time for this. Instead, I went back to Charlie. Even if there was nothing about this syphon energy inside the Bishop books, there had to be something there I could learn, so it wouldn't be a waste of energy to give them a onceover while Beatrix worked her craziness into something the rest of us could understand.

Charlie handed me a stack of three-inch-wide books. "Start with these."

I lugged them to a table and took a seat. All three were bound with aged leather and the pages inside were tanned by time, but the black, handwritten ink was easy enough to make out, and there were even a few images here and there of my ancestors.

Flipping pages, I learned that Aldis Bishop was the original warlock of our family, and his wife had birthed Olivia, Delores, and Mikhael. All three had gone on to grow their families, and by the third generation, there had been over thirty members of the Bishop coven.

With every birth had come more power gifted to the family, though they didn't say where that power had come from exactly, only frequently talking about the Earth's core and how they'd strived to give and take with everything that they'd done.

Decades later, the family had spread out across the world, no longer only having children with other witches and warlocks, but humans as well. When this had happened, the magic line hadn't always carried on, so the number of remaining Bishop members had begun to decrease steadily.

Then the war for magic had begun. The Proctor coven had become jealous of the relationship between Jacobs and Bishop. They'd tried to form the same alliance with the Grimm family, but ultimately, that had been their downfall. The Howe coven had tried to stay on their own, not wanting to be part of any battles, but Grimm wouldn't stand for that. They'd slowly taken over Howe until there'd been nothing left of that group, either.

This had only tightened the bond between Jacobs and Bishop, according to the books, and I was beginning to see that had continued for many more years. Beatrix was the current Monarch of the Jacobs family, the oldest and most powerful witch of their family line, and while she didn't always do things the way others expected, she was fighting tooth-and-nail to keep us all together.

When I finally looked up from the first book, I'd nearly jumped out of my seat to find Foster next to me and two mugs placed between us.

"How long have you been there?" I asked, reaching for the tea and frowning when it was cold.

"About two hours," he replied with a grin. "You were really into the book. I didn't want to interrupt."

Well, shit. I stretched back in the chair and groaned. Yeah, my body was suddenly feeling the lack of movement.

"Has anyone found anything?" I asked, though I wasn't hopeful for a positive answer if they'd let me read for so long.

"Beatrix has been making a spell and stayed pretty quiet in her corner," Foster answered. "Charlie and I have been scanning books, but nothing about wolves or syphon witches has been mentioned yet. I figured we should look for both to see if there's any mention of cross-race soulmates."

I reached for his hand. "That's a great idea. I'll try to read a little less in depth."

He smiled. "Do whatever feels right. We'll find the information when and where we're supposed to. Remember, everything is going to be okay."

His reminder and permission to do things my own way was just what I needed as I picked up another book.

I had no idea what Beatrix was up to, but I didn't stress as I cracked another cover open, the pages calling to me as if my ancestors were rising from the paper with every word that I read.

16

FOSTER

We didn't find anything about my bond with Andie or her rare ability to syphon power from others. I wanted to be frustrated by that fact, but Andie was practically glowing with energy by the time we'd left the attic. Beatrix had even suggested that she take some of the books back with her, as long as she kept them inside her house and nowhere else.

When we got back to the coven, Beatrix took us to her place and presented us with a vial of the spell she'd spent most of the day working on.

"Are you going to tell us what that is now?" Andie asked when we all sat around the older witch's living room.

Beatrix nodded. "I was able to make twenty of these, which means we have less than three weeks to figure out the bond between the two of you."

Andie's brows pinched together. "What do you mean? What happens if we don't?"

I'd been starting to form my own assumptions, but I'd

tried to avoid the direction they'd been going. Though, it didn't seem like Beatrix was going to allow that any longer.

She stood and handed me the vial. "You need to drink one of these every day or you will lose your wolf. When that happens, I don't know if you'll become human or a warlock because of your bond with Andie, but it's not a matter of if. Only when. If we don't get Andie's necklace back, things will only continue to get worse. In the meantime, this will strengthen the bond between the two of you while protecting the wolf spirit."

Andie's grip tightened on my leg. "Can't you keep making more of that when we get low?"

Beatrix shook her head. "It took me all last night to find the spell I was looking for and I had to use some of the rarest ingredients on Earth. Unless we can find more of them, which isn't likely, then what I've made today is all we're going to have."

Charlie crossed her arms. "What about muting Andie's power like you did last night?"

"I could keep doing that, but eventually, the power will fight back and, again, things will be worse for everyone. Andie would turn into someone none of us recognized if I had to keep doing that for too long."

I opened the vial and looked at Andie. "We have a solution for now. One that doesn't put you at risk. That's most important."

She nodded, but she wasn't okay. Her heart was racing, and her nails were close to ripping through my jeans.

Tipping the liquid to my lips, I swallowed it down in one gulp. I hadn't heard from my wolf all day. He'd said he was resting so he'd be ready when I really needed him, but his silence was more than deafening.

It was slowly tearing pieces of my soul out as he slipped farther away from me.

The connection I had to Andie was keeping me intact, but as much as I hated to admit it, without my wolf, I wouldn't be able to be the mate Andie needed. Even if I became a warlock, I wouldn't be me. Not without my wolf.

The spell traveled down my throat, burning a path directly toward my heart before spreading along my chest. I took slow and steady breaths, waiting for my wolf's presence to reappear.

Seconds ticked by and nothing changed.

"What should I expect from this?" I asked Beatrix, trying to keep my voice even to hide my unease.

She pressed her hand on my chest and zapped me. I snarled at her, and the sound echoed in my head.

Wolf? I called

I'm here. What happened?

You've been gone all day. Beatrix gave me something to bring you back. A temporary solution to our problem.

I'm dying, he stated evenly.

A pit churned inside me, and my chest felt like it was being torn apart. *I won't let that happen.*

If it's between me or Andie, then you know we don't have a choice. I'd die for her without question.

His conviction pierced my heart, but I wouldn't let this news tear me down. I'd keep fighting. Beatrix had given us twenty days and I'd use every one of them to the fullest. We'd find Moira and get Andie's necklace back, and everything would be fine.

It had to be.

Andie's hand moved over my arm. "Are you okay?"

I nodded. "He's back." My eyes met Beatrix's. "Thank you."

"You're welcome. Now go home. I'm tired." She turned away and headed down the hallway.

Andie shook her head and got up, leading the way out the door.

I locked it behind us while Charlie and Andie said their goodbyes, then Andie teleported us to her house.

The moon and stars shone above us, and I tried to take solace in the energy coming from my creator, but tonight, there was no peace to capture.

Once we were inside, Andie headed straight to the bedroom with her books in tow. I followed behind her. She gave me a onceover, her face remaining neutral. "How are you feeling?"

I took a moment to answer. Something was still off, but I couldn't figure out what that was.

It's the bond. Beatrix's spell will make both of you stronger, but there's a wall between us and Andie that wasn't there before, not even in the beginning.

My wolf's words rang true, and my shoulders relaxed, glad to have his guidance back.

"Better than before." I closed the distance between us and set the books on our bed before grabbing her hands. "What about you?"

She pulled her lower lip into her mouth, then released it. "Indifferent. I don't like what Beatrix said, but today made me feel like we were on the right path. I just wish I could talk to my parents and Aunt Junie. They'd know what to do, and it's frustrating that there was nothing left behind to give me answers."

Andie stepped closer, leaning her head against my chest.

"I know they didn't mean to leave me, that their deaths were all unexpected, but that doesn't make any of this less frustrating. I can sense them here. I think I even felt my dad today, but I can't hear them like I did when I was getting Aunt Junie's magic."

My hand rubbed over her back slowly and with even pressure. "And Beatrix said there wasn't a way to connect with them? I thought that was a thing with the witches."

Her head shook. "Those beyond the veil aren't supposed to interfere unless it's absolutely necessary."

Her voice was taut, and I understood how maddening the rules of our supernatural life could be, but they were broken all the time. Just like when the Moon Goddess came to me and offered Andie's scent.

That never should have happened, and an idea occurred to me.

"Maybe I can try to reach out to my creator," I said. "She helped me find you. Maybe she'll help again."

Andie lifted her head. "How would you do that?"

"I don't know, but Holden might. I'll ask him tomorrow. Tonight, maybe we can read more about your family together."

I reached for one of the old books and paused when I sensed Andie's mood swing. "What's wrong?"

She was smiling, but her emotions were muddled.

Andie pulled out her phone from her back pocket and checked the time. "Damn. It's probably too late now. I can't believe I forgot to tell you. Or that I didn't think of this as soon as I thought my issues might be coming from my mother's side."

Her foot was bouncing rapidly against the ground, and she was tapping her palm against her side. I wrapped my fingers around her wrists, trying to get her to focus.

"What did you forget to tell me?"

She smiled, and there was a spark in her stare. "I have family still alive. Two of them. Right here in the coven."

A surge of adrenaline hit me right at my core. "Who?"

Andie's grin somehow got bigger. "Benjamin. Him and his mother, Reah. When you called from the pack because you could sense a change in me? That was when I found out. I was going to tell you when you came back, but we went to the pack and we've been so busy since, I somehow forgot. I can't believe this."

And to think, I'd wanted to murder Benjamin when I'd first seen him with Andie.

"This is great news, but it's after eleven. We'll have to wait until tomorrow morning to go see them unless you want to try to call, see if they answer."

Andie shook her head and placed her hands over my chest. "No, tomorrow is soon enough. We've had a long day, and I've missed you. Missed our connection. It's better, yet different in a way I'm not sure I like."

I brushed strands of her hair back and cupped her cheeks, soaking in her warmth. "My wolf said there's a barrier between us, one that allows the bond to stay intact but stops the connection from taking what it shouldn't."

She frowned. "Your wolf is really okay now? I bet he hates that you got stuck with a broken witch as a mate instead of a strong shifter."

My eyes bored into hers, hoping she would not only hear my words, but feel their truth as well. "We were not *stuck* with you, Andie. We were blessed the day we found you. He would die for you, as would I. There are no doubts or regrets or questions of *what if*. Having you is exactly what I want."

Her eyes glistened, and she licked her lips. "I don't want to lose either of you."

"You're not going to. I told you everything was going to be okay, and I meant it." I placed her hand over my heart. "I feel that right here."

I didn't like making promises to my mate that I wasn't sure I could keep, but I also didn't want to let doubt into either of our minds. We needed to believe this would work out or else we would give Moira even more power over us, and that wasn't acceptable.

Andie pushed up on her toes and kissed me. "I love you so damn much."

"And I love you."

I guided her onto the bed, easing her back. My intent was to be gentle and slow, but Andie gripped my shirt, her eyes pleading with me. "Make me forget everything except for you."

My lips crashed down onto hers and, in an instant, my body was on fire only for Andie. Energy flickered over my skin, and the need to claim her was stronger than even when we'd first bonded.

I scraped my teeth over her neck, then her shoulder,

and knew there was no getting around leaving my mark tonight. Maybe it wasn't the right time with our bond being tampered with by magic, but with this, I wouldn't ignore my instincts.

I ripped my shirt over my head and helped Andie with hers when I was done. I lifted off her long enough to kick the rest of our clothes to the floor and pull her to the edge of the bed.

Her legs fell open for me. She was trusting me with her body, and I wasn't going to disappoint. My hands trailed up her legs, and the higher they went up, the tighter they squeezed.

My head dipped forward, and I licked up her center, starting as low as I could until I reached her clit, where I sucked hard.

Andie gasped, and her hands grabbed on to my hair, tugging me closer. "Holy shit, don't stop."

I did as she commanded but also brought one of my hands forward, slipping two fingers inside her slick pussy. She contracted around them and cried out, encouraging my efforts.

My mouth and fingers fucked Andie until she was hardly breathing—until she was quivering beneath me. In and out, sucking and licking, all of it over and over to make her forget the shit we'd been dealing with.

Not only that, but to remind her that no matter what happened, I was going to love her in every way possible for as long as I could.

She began tugging on my arm, and when I lifted my head up, she shook her head. "You're not done down there, but I want the other half of you."

Fuck.

My balls tightened just from her words. I wanted to tell her "no," but there was no way that I could. Instead, I pushed her farther back onto the bed and complied with her request.

My knees rested on both sides of her head, and before I could take another breath, she had my cock in her hot mouth.

I groaned and lifted my hips to give her a better angle before pulling her legs toward my head. My fingers rubbed over her clit and her moans vibrated against my dick as she squeezed my balls.

Shit, she was going to make this finish before I wanted it to be if she kept that up.

I pushed two fingers deep inside her, curling them inward before tasting her delicious pussy again.

She shook beneath me, fighting her own release, but I wanted to hear her scream, and I wanted it right then.

My hand pulled back and I buried my face between her legs, my tongue ravishing her until I felt her tensing.

Her teeth grazed against the head of my cock. She licked and sucked, but her efforts were slowing while mine were increasing.

Andie's head jerked to the side, and she screamed while my dick twitched against her neck.

I didn't lift my head up until her hands gripped my thighs. When I turned around, her eyes were brighter than I'd ever seen them, and she wore a lopsided grin.

My lips captured her grin before I tugged her off the bed and flipped her over in one motion. Her hair fell to one side from the movement, and I grabbed as many of the thick locks as I could while raising her hips until she was on all fours.

She glanced back at me, lips glistening. "I love you. All of you."

My chest rumbled in response, more from my wolf than myself.

I pressed her lower back down, then moved my hand around her front. She was still dripping for me, and I slid inside her with one hard thrust, nearly coming when she contracted around my cock.

My hips moved until my dick was almost all the way out before I slammed back into her. She tried to drop her head as her moans got louder, but I still had a hold on her hair, keeping her right where I wanted.

"Fuck, Foster," she muttered, and I knew she was close again.

Our night was far from over, but I wanted her to remember this moment with clarity, so I let go of her hair and pulled her up as I settled back onto my ankles.

Her ass was sitting on my thighs while I was still buried deep inside her. She tried moving up, but I kept her closer.

"I'm going to mark you," I stated before dragging my teeth over her sensitive skin again.

My words weren't a question, but I gave her a moment to take them in. When she pushed her head to the side, exposing more of her porcelain skin, I took that as her acceptance to my wants.

Andie's hips moved from side to side, and I brought one of my hands forward to give her the relief she was searching for.

When she sucked in a breath from my touch, I used her distraction to extend my canines.

"Mine," my wolf growled, only the sound didn't stay inside my head.

"Always yours," Andie panted.

I sucked on the spot where her neck curved into her shoulders. She shuddered, and then my teeth pierced her skin.

If she were a wolf, she'd be doing the same to me now, but she wasn't, and while I worried I might feel like we were missing something, I knew as soon as her sweet blood trickled into my mouth that there was nothing I could have imagined better than this.

The separation I'd felt between us earlier was shattered, and heat spread from my chest. Andie's euphoria filled my mind in those few seconds, lighting everything inside me on fire. Energy sizzled over my skin, and my dick twitched inside her warmth. I wanted to stay this way forever, locked together, just me and her.

Andie's nails dug into my arms, her moans growing softer, and I pulled back, running my tongue over the bite. Between our bond and her natural healing abilities, the marks were already closing over, leaving two small puncture marks that were only a few shades darker than her porcelain skin.

She slid up and off my dick before turning around and pressing my shoulders back onto the bed while smiling softly. "That was almost as powerful as last night."

"Almost," I agreed.

A wicked grin grew on her precious face. "Now it's my turn."

I'd rested on my elbows when she pushed me back, but Andie wasn't having any of that. She wanted control and she'd have it.

Andie shoved me the rest of the way back, and I gripped her hips while she guided herself back over my cock.

She sank slowly, almost torturously so, until she was fully seated. Her knees spread, and she rolled forward, putting pressure right where she wanted.

I lifted up, timing my thrusts with the roll of her hips. She gripped my chest and threw her head back, her pussy already gearing up for another release.

This time, I wasn't far behind her, so I held her tighter.

Andie's head lolled forward, and she opened her eyes to find me watching her every movement. The way her breasts bounced as she moved over me, how her chest swelled from ecstasy, and how her skin glowed from the magic she was trying so hard to hold in.

"Let go, Mate," I demanded as I drove into her over and over.

She nodded, and her lips dropped open. Before she could make a sound, I sat up and captured her mouth, holding her to me while my dick twitched inside her throbbing pussy.

Minutes ticked by before she came back to me, but I wasn't done with her.

I wouldn't ever be.

17

ANDIE

Foster's touch had a way of making me forget every thought. He'd taken all of my stress and tossed it right out the window by reminding me what was most important: the time we had together.

No longer would I let the fear of losing him, his wolf, or even myself guide my decisions. I'd woken up this morning determined to keep a positive attitude. No more freak-outs, no more bouts of crying, and no being angry with the way things were going.

I had to believe that every step forward—or backward—and every bump in the road was guiding us toward where we were meant to be. As long as we kept fighting and trying, we'd get there, and we'd find the ending we were striving for.

And if we didn't? Well, then maybe it wasn't meant to be. At least not for us. Maybe our sorrow was meant to pave the way for someone else's happily-ever-after. To prevent another family from feeling the way we'd been. If that was the case, I'd find a way to accept that as well—I chuckled to myself—mostly because I had no choice.

"Are you ready?" Foster asked me when he came back into the bedroom.

I nodded and pressed my hand over my chest. "Though, I wouldn't mind going back to last night. The walls were down for a while there."

When Foster had bit me, the separation I'd felt had disappeared and it had been just me and him. No worries of magic or spells or necklaces. Just my mate and me. That moment had left a mark on my soul that I would never forget.

Foster's hand gripped the back of my neck. "I felt that, too. We'll get back there soon."

I wanted to believe him more than anything, but it was hard. Instead, I nodded and changed the subject. "Did you talk to Holden? Any thoughts on how to contact the Moon Goddess?"

He reached for my hand. "He didn't think it was possible, but that doesn't mean he's right. He's going to contact the East Texas Pack, who had the most communication with her recently, and see what they have to say."

Hope sparked within me. "Do you think they'll come here to help us?"

Foster shrugged. "Not sure. I know they had their own problems they dealt with, but I can't be sure the aftermath is sorted out. Alphas don't often like to leave their packs, either."

I still held on to my optimism. That was part of

believing everything was going to work out just the way it was supposed to.

"Well, since we've learned nothing this morning, let's hope Reah might have something for us that she didn't think to share before," I said, reaching for my jacket. It had been raining earlier, and I wasn't sure if Reah would want to let us in the house after how closed off she'd seemed before.

We might have been family, but we didn't know each other, and I wouldn't push myself on her. She'd kept her past a secret for a reason, and I wanted to respect that.

Foster pressed his palm against my lower back, and we walked outside. I caught sight of the clouds still looming above and decided to open a portal to Reah's instead of walking.

"Do you know where you're going?" Foster asked as he gave me some space. I was getting better with my magic, but I still needed to focus.

I nodded. "I texted Charlie for the information."

With practiced effort, I closed my eyes and pushed my energy forward, focusing on what I wanted. Since the portal didn't need to be secure, it wasn't necessary to use a verbal spell to get it opened. I was rather thankful for that, because all the Latin-esque speak wasn't easy to remember or pronounce.

On the second try, Reah and Benjamin's house came into view. It was a small cottage out in the trees. There were other witches who chose to live out there, finding safety within the coven without having to be part of the everyday activities. Though, according to Charlie, they were mostly elder coven members just living out the rest of their days in as much peace as they could find.

Reah was still young, though. She'd lost a husband and her family, but she still had so much life left to live. I hoped one day she would find a reason to come around again. Maybe Benjamin helping more within the coven would be the first step in making that happen.

I closed the portal, and when we were halfway up their short concrete pathway, Benjamin opened the front door. "Hey!"

He waved animatedly at us, his locks of red hair bouncing around above his ears.

I returned the gesture. "Morning, Benjamin."

"What are you guys doing all the way out here?" He leaned against the post holding up the small, covered porch.

"I was hoping to chat with your mom if she's up for it," I said.

Benjamin glanced at the door, then back at us. "She's up. Let me ask her real quick. Do you mind waiting right here?"

Foster answered first. "Not at all."

Benjamin nodded and darted back inside, closing the door behind him.

I sighed. "I had a feeling she might be leery of guests, even if I'm family."

Foster wrapped his arm around my waist. "Do you think she'll talk to us?"

"Yeah, we just might be doing so outside. Which is better than nothing. Well, as long as it doesn't rain on us,"

I said, looking up again. The sky was ominous, and I didn't like that my mood was trying to match the vibe.

Foster followed my gaze. "It's not going to rain."

I raised a brow. "And you'd know that because…"

"Wolf senses," he said seriously, and I laughed.

"That's an odd one, even by supernatural standards."

He pulled me tightly against him and lowered his voice. "Are you making fun of me, Ms. Bishop?"

My skin heated, and my pulse sped up. "Possibly. What would you do if I was?"

He leaned down, presumably to whisper the answer, but Benjamin came back outside, and we both straightened as if we'd been caught by our parents in the act.

Benjamin chuckled. "Come on in."

I blinked several times before Foster nudged me forward. Benjamin already had his back to us, leading the way, and I looked up at Foster, who just shrugged.

Clearly, I was the only one of us who thought we'd be standing outside.

Reah was in the kitchen. She was humming a soft melody I didn't recognize and putting some muffins on a tray. Orange juice and four glasses were already waiting on the wooden tabletop.

I glanced back at the living room, noticing only a couch with three seats, a small television, and a table between them with a halfway-finished puzzle that I was pretty sure was going to be a garden of wildflowers when it was done.

"Good morning," Reah greeted us, placing the tray of muffins in the middle of the table. When I met her gaze, she was smiling and more at ease than she'd been the day before.

"Good morning," I said. "I'm sorry to just drop in, but I had a few questions for you that were better asked in person."

Foster pulled a chair out for me, and I took a seat while waiting for Reah to respond.

I ended up between Foster and Benjamin and across from Reah, which I preferred since I hoped to be talking to her most.

Once she was settled, she placed one hand over the other on top of the table and sat up straight. "What did you want to ask?"

My eyes shifted toward Foster, and he nodded, pressing his hand on my jittery thigh.

I wasn't used to having family. I didn't know how to broach the subject, so I just dove right in, hoping I wasn't about to offend Reah or freak her out.

"I was wondering about my mom's side of the family. Did any of the witches or warlocks have special powers?" I asked.

Her lips pinched together at one side. "Not that I know of, but like I mentioned yesterday, we didn't really stick together as a coven. Information wasn't shared freely outside of immediate families. I only knew what I knew about your mother because she took it upon herself to look after me once I started going to the same school as her, even though she was years ahead of me."

Well, that wasn't really helpful, and I wasn't sure how much I should say. I hadn't told Beatrix we were coming here, and I didn't know how secret this syphon ability was supposed to stay.

"Did something else happen?" Benjamin asked with a mouthful of muffin.

Foster gave my thigh another squeeze, and I took that as a sign to be truthful. His wolf would have a better sense than I did if I couldn't trust them. Maybe this conversation would also begin building the bridge to having a real relationship with Reah one day.

"Well, I found out that even though I have Junie's magic now, I'm still not capable of bonding with Foster the way we should be able to. We thought maybe we'd found a loophole in the system, but it backfired. When I took on my aunt's powers and…" I paused, suddenly realizing I was about to talk about having sex in front of a seventeen-year-old boy who seemed more sheltered than others his age. While awkward, it was too late to stop.

"And when I accepted the bond with Foster, I began pulling energy from his wolf. If Beatrix hadn't found a temporary solution, the animal spirit might have died. Even now, we have less than a few weeks until we're out of options. Worse, we don't know the consequences for Foster if we can't figure out how to stop me from syphoning from him or we can't get my necklace back from Moira."

"Damn," Benjamin muttered.

Reah's narrowed eyes leveled on him. "Language, Son."

He cringed. "Sorry, Mom."

I cracked a smile until Reah frowned at me. "I wish I could say I've heard of such things, but I've never even met a cross-race couple. I was so young when I left with

Jeffrey, and once we entered Moira's coven, we never left until it was time to run."

"Is there anything you can tell us about her coven?" Foster asked. "Like where it's at or what kind of shield they have protecting it?"

"Beatrix already checked that out years ago. Moira had already moved by the time I found the courage to tell our story. I'd been afraid for so long that I thought it was better if I stayed quiet. I didn't want anyone else to get hurt." Her tear-filled eyes stayed on me. "I'm sorry I didn't speak up sooner."

I shook my head. "You have no reason to apologize. After everything that's happened, I have a feeling we'd have ended up right here, in the same position, no matter what."

She twisted her fingers together. "Maybe." Then her head perked up. "Wait. There might be something."

Reah stood from the table and headed toward the short hallway on our left. She opened a door, and there were shelves filled with blankets, books, and board games. She grunted through several rows of stuff before she made an "aha" sound.

Another few seconds later, she pulled out a black metal box with a silver handle and lugged it over. "Junie brought me this years ago. I'd completely forgotten about it. She said that she and Aspen had added items inside and that I wasn't to open the box until I knew when the time was right. Given everything that's been going on, I'm thinking this might be that time, but I don't think I'm the one who's supposed to open it."

Reah set the box in front of me. Its thud echoed around

us, and my hands hovered over the single latch. My hesitation only lasted as long as it took me to meet Foster's gaze. His blue eyes saw into my soul, lifting me up and reminding me that no matter what we did or didn't find out today, I could do this.

I nodded, more to myself than anyone else, and flipped the latch. Tingles rose along my hands and arms as the lid lifted on its own.

"Freaky," Benjamin whispered.

I absolutely agreed.

My head began to throb from the energy coming out of the box.

Reah stepped back to the other side of the table. "Now, I'm almost positive that I wouldn't have been able to open the box myself, even if I'd tried."

Foster sat comfortably next to me.

"Do you not feel that?" I asked.

He shook his head. "What am I supposed to be feeling?"

I looked back at the box. "A heaviness of some sort. There's lots of power in here. Like, too much for one little box."

Reah nodded. "I'd have to agree with you, but this is Junie we're talking about. She was the queen of magical tricks."

Reah's words triggered something that Beatrix had said before. When I'd merged with Junie's magic, Beatrix had said, "Sneaky, Junie," or something like that. I'd forgotten about it then, but maybe we needed to revisit what Beatrix had meant and soon.

When the initial wave of power calmed down, I pulled

the box closer. My fingers itched from the extra magic around the box, but it was manageable.

At the top were two envelopes, both with my name on the front, but in different handwriting. I pulled them out, and my throat burned. *Mom and Aunt Junie.*

I held them close to my chest and glanced at the rest of the box. There was a flat, palm-sized yellow citrine stone that called to me, and I was pretty sure that was where most of the power was coming from. Underneath that were piles of pictures from my childhood and a few trinkets I could remember from the house.

My attention went back to the letters, and I opened the one from my mother first. My shaking fingers tugged the sealed envelope open, and I nearly dropped the single sheet of paper when I pulled it out.

My Dearest Andie,

If you're reading this, then I want to apologize for leaving you in whatever manner took me away. I'm doing my best to keep you safe, but I worry every single day that I haven't made all the right choices. When I took us away from the coven and had your memories stripped, I didn't realize what I would be taking from you. I only knew that my heart couldn't stay in the same place where I'd loved your father so fiercely.

Selfish as that was, I still believed that was what was best for you. Now, I'm wondering if it was wrong, but when I see your light-green eyes, so full of life and safe from the magical mayhem of the world, I pray that I wasn't wrong.

You are a special witch, Andie. If you haven't already figured that out, then I hope this letter will help you understand. You are made from two strong families. One that stayed in the shadows and one that shined amongst their peers.

Mine was the former and for good reason. The women in our generation learned long ago that we couldn't trust others with our secrets. We ran and separated ourselves as best we could from the world, but then I met your father, and running was no longer an option for me.

I fear you've been born with an ability that could cost you your life. One that others will hunt you down for, not only because you're one of the last Bishop witches, but because you're an Abbott witch.

My family history has no rhyme or reason to it. For years, every woman born was cursed with this ability, then it began to skip generations until there was no way to tell until the witch reached full maturity.

I begged Juniper to take your magic because you began showing signs of syphoning even human objects at such a young age. I don't know what this means for your future, and I hope like hell that I'm there to help guide you, but if I'm not, your aunt will help you, and if she can't, show this to Beatrix. She'll know what to do. She'll remember the Abbotts.

Tell them I'm sorry. Most importantly, I hope you know how much I love you and that I would do anything to be with you right now. Just the thought of knowing I might not be there in your future takes my breath away, but I know you're going to do great things, Andie Bishop. You are the light and soul of our family. Always remember that, no matter what obstacles you face, and don't ever settle for less than you deserve.

All my love,

Mom

My hand was covering my mouth while I attempted to choke down the sobs raging through my body. I should have known better than to read something so special in front of other people, but I'd been so eager to find information that I hadn't thought my actions through.

Foster was standing behind me and holding me together with his embrace. He stayed silent, even when I set the letter down.

That was when I looked up to find we were alone at the table, possibly even in the house. I gave myself the permission to fall apart one last time, to miss my mother, and be angry at all I'd lost. Every tear shed helped ease the pain inside me, helped me to feel renewed, and I kept them coming until I couldn't breathe any longer.

When I was done, I turned sideways in the chair and Foster moved to meet me. He kneeled in front of me, holding my hands. "Better?"

I swiped at a few stray tears. "Oddly, yes."

He nodded toward the front door. "They went outside when the tears first started to fall."

"We should bring them back in," I said, but Foster handed me Aunt Junie's letter instead.

"Maybe read that first. Just in case."

Damn. I wasn't sure I was ready for another emotional tornado, but it was better to do now instead of prolonging the inevitable.

I took the envelope and chuckled at the dragon stamp on the backside.

My Little Dragon,

When I recommended your mom write one of these letters to

you, I didn't realize what I was asking of her. I never wanted to picture a world where I wasn't helping you reach your full potential, but I see now that things aren't going to work out the way I'd like.
Knowing you, you've read your mom's letter first. If not, go back and do that. I'll wait.

I laughed so hard, I snorted and had to hold my stomach. God, I missed her so much.

Now, I love you, Andie, so I'm not going to pull any punches. You're an adult now. Your mom is gone and you're probably feeling pretty alone in the world, but you need not to worry. We're always going to be there for you. Just not when you're with company behind closed doors. No auntie or parent needs to see that.

It was Foster's turn to laugh now. "I can see why she and Beatrix were best friends."
Smiling, I nodded and continued reading.

As you've just learned, after I'm gone, you'll be the last Bishop witch, and you're also an Abbott descendant. Your mother and father only ever told me, and it was the only secret I've ever kept from Beatrix. Please tell her I'm sorry, but I had no choice. We tried to prevent things from happening, but life doesn't always go the way we want.
Don't try to hide from your powers. Use the citrine stone to control them. Pull your magic out of the moonstone and show the world who you are. Don't be afraid of what's coming, because your light shines too bright to be diminished. Trust Beatrix.

She'll guide you through what's coming next, and I'll be there as much as the afterworld will let me.

Lastly, enjoy the items I've left for you. Most are from your mom and dad, but there's a candle in here that I hope you'll never use, but remember it in your darkest moments. When you bring life to the flame, things will seem a lot brighter.

Love you always, my not-so-little dragon.

Your Auntie Junie

I was still smiling by the time I finished. My heart was full, and I was ready for whatever came next. This was the closure I'd needed, the kind that would allow me to believe in myself and those around me.

I turned to Foster. "We need to go see Beatrix."

He reached a hand to me. "Then let's go."

18

FOSTER

ndie was somehow holding everything together better than I'd imagined. Sure, she'd cried while reading the letter from her mother, but with every tear shed, I'd only sensed her resolve growing. She wasn't afraid any longer.

Then again, fear wasn't always a bad thing. I hoped Andie wasn't pushing hers to the side, thinking she needed to be brave for the rest of us.

With our bond, I should have been able to read her better, but after last night, the wall was back up, stronger than ever, it seemed. I hated but appreciated it all the same, since it kept my wolf from disappearing on me.

We're going to figure this out. We haven't come this far for everything to fall apart, he said.

I fought a smile. I'd missed his optimism.

I sure hope you're right.

After thanking Reah and Benjamin for their help and saying our goodbyes, Andie and I arrived at Beatrix's house. She was waiting at the door, staring at me. "Is the spell still working?"

"It is. Thank you again," I said, squeezing Andie's hand tighter.

She glanced between us. "Well, if you're not dying, then why aren't you sticking to the schedule? Nothing has changed. We still need to be preparing."

Andie stepped forward, handing the letters from her mom and aunt to Beatrix. "Except something *has* changed."

Beatrix plucked the papers from Andie's fingers. "I can read these?"

Andie nodded. "I think you need to. Come to my house when you're done."

Beatrix's eyes glistened. The first sign of softer emotions I'd seen her display. She nodded and promptly turned around to shut the door in our faces.

I looked down at my mate. "That was kind of you."

"I might not have minded breaking down in front of others, but Beatrix deserves to do that in private. Those letters weren't addressed to her, but the apologies and answers were for both of us."

My lips pressed against the side of her head. "Let's go home, then."

Andie teleported us back to her house without giving me any warning. My stomach churned, and the ground shifted beneath my feet for a moment. "I don't like that."

She grinned. "Well, I won't always have time to make a portal and if we need to leave somewhere in a hurry, it's better you get used to doing so now."

I wanted to argue with her, but she made a valid point,

one I should have thought of before. "We'll use that method for now. Until my wolf stops complaining."

He growled. *Not cool throwing me under the bus like that when I can't correct you.*

I'd say I'm sorry, but I'm not.

Andie and I entered the house, but before I could make it to the couch, my wolf stopped me in my tracks.

I'd like a moment with her.

Andie had seen his physical form. She'd touched him and talked to him, but he'd never requested to have her attention before. Not like this.

Of course, I replied, then I grabbed Andie's hand. "Do you mind if we go to the backyard?"

She tightened her jacket around herself. "As long as it doesn't rain, then let's go."

I laughed. "I told you it wasn't going to."

She gave me a "yeah, right" look, then headed to the back door. I followed after her and walked out into the grass. "My wolf wants me to shift."

Andie's smile pierced my heart. "Then what are you waiting for?"

Taking several steps back, I called my wolf forward, shuddering as the magic of the shift overcame my body.

The change was slower than even the day before, and I attributed that to Beatrix's spell, but once he was on all fours, a surge of energy rolled through us, allowing me to ignore any unease.

He stepped slowly toward Andie, and she met him in the middle of the yard, sinking her hands into his thick coat. "Good morning," she cooed.

He rubbed his head against her stomach, and a shock

moved between them. I worried for a moment when Andie gasped, but as their eyes locked, I only saw the joy radiating from hers. I continued to sit back and let them have their moment.

"How did you do that?" she asked, tears falling from her eyes.

He nudged her again, and she wrapped her arms around his neck.

What did you do? I asked.

You biting her last night created a new connection, one that allows her to feel me separately from you. I still can't talk to her, but she knows I'm here in a way she didn't before.

"Happy" didn't even begin to describe what I felt for him. I'd known there was a sliver of disappointment he'd had when accepting that Andie wouldn't have a wolf for him to bond with, but seeing how they could share something like this, that was an option I hadn't known would exist.

Andie continued to talk to him, and she seemed to accept his changing emotions as answers that had her laughing and crying all at the same time.

He lay in the grass, and she snuggled right into him, gazing up at the cloudy sky. We stayed that way until Beatrix showed up an hour later.

"Well, this is different," the old witch muttered.

Andie glanced up, grinning widely. "I don't think anything is supposed to be normal around here."

Beatrix scoffed. "Not with you around." Then she held up the letters and Andie got off the ground, walking toward her.

Thank you for that, my wolf said just before I shifted back to two feet.

She's as much yours as she is mine. You never have to thank me for spending time with our mate.

She's even more special than I thought.

I know.

I just hoped that "special" wasn't going to be our downfall.

Andie and Beatrix were hugging, so I stayed back. I hadn't thought I would ever care for the old witch, even after she'd apologized, but seeing her walls lowering, proving she wasn't a heartless bitch, changed my opinion.

They parted, and I expected Beatrix to go back to being guarded, but she met my stare with unguarded eyes. "I'm glad it was you. I don't think anyone else could have been trusted with her."

"Thank you, Beatrix. That means a lot coming from you," I said sincerely, and I stepped forward finally.

Beatrix held Andie's hand and glanced between the two of us. "I know what we need to do, but it's not going to be easy. We still need Andie's magic back first and we still only have nineteen days left to get it."

Andie's shoulders straightened, and she stood a little taller. "We can do it. Moira doesn't stand a chance against us."

I nodded, pulling on her resolve. "She's right. We have the pack and coven and each other. Moira only has herself."

Beatrix shook her head. "She still has two family members locked away. One I've learned today is her sister.

We don't know how keeping these two people hidden benefits Moira, but there must be a reason why she's going to the trouble to do so. Though, with the restraint she's shown, the witch doesn't know that Andie is also an Abbott witch. Otherwise, this would have been a bloodbath weeks ago."

A sinking feeling hit me in the chest. "Why? Besides this syphon ability, what does being an Abbott witch mean?"

Beatrix glanced around. "Let's head inside. I've already said too much out here."

Andie waited for me and grabbed my hand, whispering, "I have a feeling about the sister. She's the key to all of this. Moira told me we're more alike than I knew, and I had a feeling she was talking about wanting to save her family. Only, at the time, I didn't know I had family to keep safe, so maybe my thoughts are just grasping at straws."

"Try not to overthink things until we hear what Beatrix has to say," I said, more because I needed to hear it, but I knew Andie did as well. Maybe things would seem brighter once we knew what Andie was supposed to be capable of. Then we'd know what defenses we had going up against the dark witch.

Not that I was okay with Andie being the one to face Moira, but I also knew my mate. She wasn't going to let anyone fight this battle for her, and I wouldn't try to take that from her.

Beatrix was sitting in the chair in the living room when we walked in, so we took the couch. Her expression was calm, and I wasn't sure that was a good thing.

She closed one hand into a fist, muttered words I didn't

understand, and then spread her fingers out. A cloud of silver magic formed over her palm before quickly expanding and covering the walls of the room, then disappearing seconds later.

"A privacy spell," Andie said to me, and I nodded.

Beatrix smiled and folded her hands over her crossed legs. "Now for story time. The Abbott family was rumored to be the sixth original family, but they remained elusive from the other five. They spread out and hid amongst the humans instead of banding together like most covens did at the time. Because of that, there is very little information available, but Junie prepared me more than I realized for this day."

Andie tensed beside me. "How so?"

Beatrix snapped her fingers and a small book appeared in her grasp. "With this. She gave this to me as a gift three years ago. Not too long after we found out about your mother, in fact. I didn't think anything of it then. I didn't even really care to read the words, but Junie said it was one of her favorite tales and that I needed to give it a try."

She brushed her fingers over the aging tan cover.

"It's supposed to be fiction. A book written by a human for entertainment, but after learning what I have about Andie, I can see the truth in the words. Do you have the citrine stone with you?" Beatrix asked Andie.

My mate got up from the couch and grabbed the box we'd dropped off before going to Beatrix's house earlier. "Right here."

She raised a brow. "And I assume the candle is there?" Andie nodded and handed over the box, and Beatrix smirked. "You're still one-upping me from the grave, Juniper."

Beatrix dug through the box and Andie sat back down next to me. "What are we supposed to do with the candle and stone? Junie said she hoped Andie would never have to use it," I said wearily.

The old witch muttered to herself for another minute before she answered. "Yes, but Junie didn't know that Andie's necklace was going to be stolen. She's only half the witch she's supposed to be, and without her whole self, she can't control what's inside her on her own. The candle and stone will help provide another temporary solution. One we couldn't rely on without knowing what I know now."

Beatrix grabbed the candle, book, and stone and handed them to Andie. "You're going to cast your first official spell, and it's something you have to do on your own, but I will guide you as far as I can."

Andie bit her bottom lip, looking over the three items. "And we're doing this now?"

The witch raised a brow. "Would you rather wait?"

My mate's head shook furiously. "No."

"I didn't think so. Let's head to the power stones, and we'll get this started." Beatrix was headed toward the door, but I stopped her.

"What exactly is 'this'?"

She turned back to me. "Andie is going to unleash her full syphon power. She has to control the energy before it controls her. Only then will she understand who she truly is. My words can't do that for her."

I looked down at Andie. "Are you ready for that?"

She gripped my hand. "A part of me doesn't want to be, but I know this is right." She placed her other hand over her chest. "I can feel my family here, feel them guiding me in this direction."

I stroked her cheek. "Then I'll do whatever I can to support you."

Andie leaned against me as we walked toward the door. "Just you being here is more than enough."

19

———

ANDIE

Thirty minutes later, I worried Foster was going to destroy the book Beatrix had given me. Even though it was supposedly fictional, and we mostly only skimmed until we got to a certain chapter, the words often hit too close to home, making both of us overly tense.

When we read the chapter together about unlocking my syphon power and it mentioned the heroine's energy being "ripped to shreds" in order to unlock a "great power," Foster's jaw ground tighter and tighter together.

"Are you sure this is the only way?" he asked Beatrix.

She was setting the candle up in the middle of the three stones that would serve to contain the magic I was going to unleash.

When she glanced back up, her eyes were bright, and she nodded. "I wouldn't risk Andie's life if I thought otherwise."

Foster snarled. "Are you saying she could die?"

I grabbed his hand and pulled him toward me. I placed both hands on his chest and waited until I had his full attention. His breathing was heavy, and his eyes were darker than normal.

"I'm not going to die," I stated.

His left eye twitched. "You don't know that."

"Yes, I do, and so do you. We have everything we need, and this is the only path forward."

His glower deepened. "I don't like it."

"I know you don't, but I appreciate you being here anyway and not asking me to stop doing this." I didn't think I would have gone through with the spell if he had walked away. I needed his support more than anything else.

Foster let out a heavy sigh. "I'm not being helpful. I'm sorry. It was harder to read those words than I thought it would be."

Beatrix peeked her head between us. "Want me to make you not worry so much?"

I chuckled. She seemed a little too excited about her offer.

"Not fucking happening," Foster bit out.

Beatrix huffed. "Well, then. Let's get started. We need the full sun for the citrine stone."

My hands pulled Foster's head down until I could reach his lips. "I love you," I murmured before kissing him.

"I love you," he replied, his words less edgy than before.

Before he could get worked up again, I stepped away

and headed toward the power stones. The citrine stone was next to the candle on the small, wooden table. Both exuded heavy energy that had my pulse racing and skin feeling like it was being poked by a million needles.

"Start with the spell," Beatrix said from outside the stone circle.

I nodded. I knew what I was supposed to do. The words from the book had penetrated into my mind, and I had them on repeat. I wouldn't screw this up. We only had one shot at getting it right. The candle only burned once.

I took a steady breath and soaked in the love and support I could feel through the bond from Foster even with the barriers between us. He was terrified, but he was doing his best to support me, which was more than enough.

Our gazes locked for the longest second of my life. My heart filled with his affection, easing the last of my anxiety, and I closed my eyes.

My hand rose and hovered directly over the candle that I didn't need to see with my eyes. Its energy was so powerful that there was no way not to know where it was.

I pictured the flame I wanted to light the candle, and magic traveled down my arm and out of my palm until heat started coming back to me. I pulled my hand back, holding both arms at my sides, and kept my eyes closed with my head tilted down.

I repeated the spell in my head once more before saying the complicated words out loud.

"*Luxis confractem trans sepermindus. Reliquous corpiem animen.*"

With every word spoken, the heaviness around me intensified until I felt as if the stones were closing in on me. My eyes stayed closed, and lights began to dance behind my lids. My legs swayed, and I was certain I'd fallen over, but then the ground disappeared out from under me. I hoped it was just the spell taking effect and not something that was actually happening to my physical form.

The freefall lifted my spirits, and I realized I wasn't falling at all. I was rising up, though to where, I had no clue.

"Andie Bishop, daughter of Aspen Abbott Bishop and Henry Bishop. You are entering into a realm in which you don't belong. We will grant you access only this once. If you attempt to return here again, we will not send you back to your earthly form. Do you understand?"

A multitude of high-pitched voices echoed around me, but I still couldn't see anything, and the book didn't mention anything about traveling to realms that I didn't know about.

"I understand," I said with a steady voice, even though my insides were churning like a tornado.

As soon as the words had left my lips, I fell to the ground again and lights blinded me. I blinked rapidly until a form came into view, one I thought I'd never see again.

"Mom?" My voice was a whisper while I fought back tears, trying to be sure I was truly seeing her and not going crazy.

She bent down, her red hair falling just past her

shoulders and her bright-green eyes filled with so much love that bored into my soul.

"Hi, baby girl." Her hand reached out, and I placed mine in hers. Her skin was fair, almost translucent, and cold compared to mine.

"Where am I? How is this happening?" I asked, glancing around. We were surrounded by white fog, and I couldn't see anything else. I couldn't even sense anyone else, not even Foster.

"You're in the witches' ether. A place where we can communicate with those still living, but we're only allowed here on rare occasions, and the living almost never enter. Today is special, though."

She smiled at me, and I couldn't contain myself any longer. I threw myself at her, wrapping my arms around her neck and squeezing tight. Her form was solid, and her returning hug felt so real.

My throat burned with rising emotions, but I kept the tears at bay. "I've missed you so much."

She stroked my back. "I'm sorry I left you. I wish things could have been different, but I'm so proud of the path you've chosen and the woman you've become. Seeing you with Foster has made your father and me so happy to know you have him watching out for you. Not that Beatrix and Charlie wouldn't have done a great job. It's just different with a soulmate, as I'm sure you've grown to understand."

I nodded, grabbing and squeezing both of her hands after pulling back from the hug to see her face that was so much like my own. Her fair skin, the subtle slope of her nose, high cheekbones, they were all reminders of myself when I stared at her, missing her more than ever, even though she was right in front of me.

"Not that I'm not grateful to see you, but why am I here? Why isn't Dad or Aunt Junie with you?" I glanced around again, double-checking I hadn't missed anyone.

"Only an Abbott is allowed to help you through this process. Just like Juniper helped you receive her magic, only those who are needed get to interact with the living in such a way that we've been blessed to do."

I bit my cheek. "Will I ever get to talk to Dad?"

She smoothed the crease between my eyes with her thumb. "I don't know, but I hope you know how much he loves you and how sorry I am that I took all of your memory of him from you."

"I know, Momma. It's okay."

She sighed and nodded. "We don't have much time. We must finish the spell before the flame goes out on the candle. Are you ready?"

My head shook, and tears burned in my eyes. "When we're done, I'm going to have to leave you and might not ever talk to you again. Not like this."

Mom held my face between her hands. "I'm always with you when you need me, baby girl. We all are. And one day, a long, long time from now, we will see each other again. Don't you worry about that. Just concern yourself with living—because the world needs your light in it."

A few tears leaked down my cheeks. "I love you."

"I love you, too. More than the moon and stars."

My heart soared. "Tell Dad and Aunt Junie I love them, too."

She nodded. "Though they already know. Now, shall we?"

Mom's hands lay palm-up in front of me. I took a shuddering breath and placed mine on top of hers. "Ready."

"You're going to do exactly as you read in the book. It might not have told everything that was going to happen, but it prepared you for the steps that need to be taken. Your physical form will do what it's supposed to as long as your mind doesn't fight the magic. And when we're done, you'll open your eyes to find yourself back where you belong. Okay?"

My gaze traveled over her face again, memorizing every angle and blemish and freckle. I never wanted to forget her or this moment. "Okay."

"Close your eyes and expel the magic from your body. Every ounce you can find, send it into the ether," she said softly, her hands vibrating beneath mine.

I did as she asked, searching every crevice inside myself and forcing the energy out. The more I let go, the weaker my legs became, but the gentle connection with my mom kept me upright and anchored in place.

"Press the stone to your chest with your left hand," Mom whispered.

My mind pictured the table in front of my physical form, and I reached out, grabbing the citrine.

"Very well. Now, drain the stone. Replace what you've given to the ether with the power you feel inside your hand."

This part had been in the book, and this was where I was supposed to be "ripped to shreds" before being turning into an all-powerful being. I tried to tell myself I wasn't afraid, but that was a lie.

Fear tore through me, but it didn't control me. I knew what I needed to do, and I trusted my magic to keep me alive.

I pictured a tether between my chest and the citrine. I latched on to the stone, wrapping the tether several times around its smooth surface. Once the connection was secure, I yanked hard until it felt like the stone was penetrating my skin.

The rock was a part of me now. I pulled on its energy, taking whatever it had to offer, even when my skin began to burn and flames licked around the glowing, yellow stone.

Everything seemed like it was going fine until the rock began to crack. The more fissures that began to form on its surface, the more they began to appear over my skin.

My insides burned, and I wanted to force the foreign energy from my body, but my mom was right there, reminding me to be strong.

"This will not break you unless you let it. You are more than this spell. You are mightier than the sun, my daughter."

I squared my shoulders and forced my head back, staring up into the sky, not actually seeing anything other than the bright light of the magic tearing me to pieces.

Suddenly, I felt the need to spread my arms apart, breaking the connection to my mother. When that happened, the sun's full strength blasted into my chest. I cried out.

My soul shattered into a million glass shards, blasting across the ether.

I was lost in the world that I didn't belong in, but I wasn't gone. The ether couldn't claim me. Not today.

With renewed determination, I called my magic to me. I brought my power to where it belonged, and with every strand of energy that came back, a piece of my soul returned with it.

Different, but still me.

Mom's voice echoed around me in a whisper that smoothed the last of my cracks. "You did it, baby girl. Just like I knew you would. Remember, we're always with you. Whenever you need us. We love you more than the moon and stars."

I tried to respond, to open my eyes and see her one last time, but I was sucked from the ether without warning. My body felt like it was folded in half, and I wrapped my arms around myself until I could hear shouts.

Slowly, I unraveled myself and forced my eyes open. The world above me was dark, and I was lying on the ground with the candle beside me. There was maybe a half-inch left, and the flame flickered out just as soon as I reached for it.

"Andie?" Charlie's hoarse voice called.

I turned until I could see her, confused as to why she was there and I couldn't see Foster.

Then I heard the howl. A mournful one that pierced my chest.

I got to my knees just as Foster appeared. His eyes were wild and nearly black.

Beatrix stepped in front of him. "You can't go in there

until she comes out on her own. We've already been over this."

"I'm okay, Foster," I said, practically shouting since he was snarling at Beatrix. "Just give me a second to find my feet again."

Beatrix didn't seem afraid, but Charlie was side-eyeing my mate as if he'd done serious damage while I'd been out.

When I got to my feet, I nearly fell back down, but I reached out to steady myself on one of the stones. My palm felt like it was on fire, and I yanked my arm back. "Rude."

"Those three rocks saved your life. I wouldn't insult them," Beatrix said.

Speaking of rocks, I couldn't see the citrine stone anywhere, but that was something to worry about after I went to Foster.

I forced my feet to move forward, and when I exited the perimeter of the stones, a wave of energy washed over me. The Earth, Beatrix, Foster, Charlie. Each one had a different taste and called to me. I wanted to inhale them all, but I knew that I couldn't. I didn't want to hurt my family. I wouldn't let myself become a monster.

"Very good, Andie." Beatrix praised me, moving out of the way.

Foster closed the distance between us and had me in his iron grip. "I thought you died."

"I think I did for a minute there," I said lightly.

Beatrix chuckled. "Or hours. It's been almost twelve hours since you lit that candle."

Holy shit. It had felt like twelve minutes, not *hours*, with my mother.

Foster didn't let me go and his rough voice whispered in my ear. "Where did you go?"

I tried to pull back so I could see him, but he wouldn't let me budge. Charlie and Beatrix came around the other side, keeping a distance, but I could at least see them with my head turned against Foster's chest.

"The book left out a few key parts," I explained. "I went to the ether. My mom was there. She helped me fill in the missing pieces."

Foster tensed beneath me, and his hold loosened ever so slightly.

"And Junie?" Beatrix asked.

I shook my head. "Mom said only an Abbott was allowed."

Charlie swiped at her cheeks with ferocity. "If you could quit almost dying, that would be great."

My heart felt for her. "I'm sorry, but I think I'm done now."

I went on to tell them what had happened with my mom and the ether, all while Foster stayed silent, holding me against him.

By the time I was done, his heart was at least beating normally, and I could breathe a little easier within his arms.

"So, what now? We go after Moira?" Charlie asked, glancing between me and Beatrix. "Andie can just suck the life out of the crazy bitch, and we can all go home."

I shuddered at the thought of killing someone, but it

was a real possibility that I needed to consider—and soon, if things started going in the right direction.

Beatrix shook her head. "Now, we keep what happened here today to ourselves and we revisit our plan. Only when Andie feels comfortable with her new abilities and when we understand the workings of Moira's coven will we go to New Orleans and face her together."

Foster finally pulled back from me and jerked his head toward Beatrix. "You know where she is?"

"I do and that's my secret to keep until we're all ready as a team. The only way we win is by working together and making sure we're all mentally and physically prepared."

I expected Foster to try to bite her head off—with his words or possibly even literally—but he merely nodded and kept me flush against his side.

Charlie smiled at me, still keeping her distance, likely to keep Foster calm. "I'm glad you're okay. I love you."

"I love you, too." My chest tightened at Charlie's words. While I'd already known she loved me, it wasn't something we'd ever said when we parted ways for the day.

When she and Beatrix teleported away, I looked up at Foster. "I feel like I should be sorry for whatever happened while I was gone."

His touch became gentle, and his eyes were finally returning to their normal blue. "Your body rose into the air and shattered into tiny pieces that floated within the three stones for hours. My wolf had to force a shift to keep me from leaping inside with you. Beatrix swore you were fine, but I thought you were dead. I couldn't feel you, and I…"

"I'm so sorry, Foster," I muttered before wrapping my arms around him. "I didn't know. The book…"

"Told us what we needed to know. It's okay. I can see that now, but I couldn't before. All that matters is that you're back and you're safe." His words soothed some of my guilt, but not all of it.

I just hoped this was the last time either of us had to feel this way.

20

ANDIE

Eight days had passed painfully fast. Every hour closer to the deadline we were up against—thanks to the amount of potion left for Foster—made my skin crawl, but that wasn't the only thing.

The energy inside me was a constant battle. If I lost too much focus, I latched on to the nearest person and tugged on their magic, ever so slowly, sometimes not noticing until they couldn't stand on their own any longer.

Thankfully, only Charlie and Ava had been subject to that mishap, and they weren't holding my actions against me, but still... I didn't like knowing that I was harming people without realizing it.

Today was a better day, though. I was beginning to understand the energy better and know when to feed my inner beast in order to prevent that part of me from lashing out at my friends and family.

Feeding a part of myself sounded insane, but that was how I looked at the syphon ability. And doing so wasn't all that much of a hardship.

I was sitting in the forest beyond the cottages and pressing my palms to the Earth, calling on nature's energy and soothing the jagged edges of the voids inside myself.

Beatrix assured me that this wouldn't be an issue when I got my born-magic back, but until then, I'd at least found a moderate solution that didn't require everyone except for Foster to stay away from me.

With our bond, I still pulled on our connection, but thanks to the potion from Beatrix, Foster said there was nothing draining that he could feel between the two of us any longer.

We'd both grown exponentially tired of the barriers between us that were necessary to keep him safe, though. Waiting out the next eleven days wasn't ideal, and I hoped to be going after Moira sooner rather than later.

After an hour of becoming one with Mother Earth, I teleported myself back to the house, ready for another day of grueling training.

Only, when I arrived, Charlie and Foster were inside the house, not dressed for combat practice.

"What's going on?" I asked when I closed the door behind me.

Charlie looked up at me from the couch. "I was just making fun of Foster. Nothing new."

I glanced down at her skinny jeans and bright-yellow tank top, then raised a brow. "Are we training today?"

She nodded at Foster, who was already walking toward me. "Ask the big guy."

His arms wrapped around me, and he placed a kiss on my forehead. "Good morning in the woods?"

I nodded. "It's getting easier every time I'm out there."

He squeezed my hand. "Good. Holden invited us out to the pack, and I told him we'd come as soon as you were done if you were feeling up to it. We haven't been there all week."

"You mean, *I* haven't been there all week. Is there something wrong?" I asked, glancing between my mate and best friend.

Charlie answered first. "Nope. When I heard Foster on the phone while I was waiting for you, I thought a day off would do you some good. Things seem to be getting easier, and it's better if you don't overwork yourself. Let's go have some fun. My time at the pack before was too short."

She waggled her brows, and I peeked up at Foster. "You said she could come?"

He shrugged. "She started to whine when I first said no, and I knew you'd enjoy having her around, so I told her it was fine."

"You realize she's going to hit on Mack, right?" I pressed, hoping he was fully aware of what I already was.

"The beta and your best friend are of no concern to me. *You* are all I care about. Plus, Gemma might have asked Holden to call me."

Excitement immediately filled me. "Did she have her baby?" I squealed, feeling bad I hadn't thought to check on her since the night of the new moon.

Foster nodded, fighting his own grin. "She wants you to meet her son."

I glanced at Charlie. "Are you good with visiting a friend with me before we go to the pack house? I'm sure Mack won't mind."

The last bit was meant to be a joke, but honestly, I wasn't sure it was.

Charlie was up and off the couch before I'd finished asking. "Let's go. I already told Beatrix we were taking today off, and she agreed it would be good for you to be around more wolf shifters to see how your syphon ability reacts."

I chuckled. "So, in her eyes, I'm still training. Got it."

Foster nudged me toward the hallway. "Go get dressed and we'll be ready to go whenever you are. I'll let Holden know all three of us will be there soon."

I pushed up onto my toes and kissed his cheek. "Thank you."

When I tried to dart off, he grasped my hand and pulled me back for a real kiss that had Charlie gagging. "Oh, come on. Can't I go one day without seeing the two of you eating each other's faces off?"

Foster looked over at her. "Sure, if you can go one day without coming over to our house."

Charlie scoffed as I headed for the bedroom to quickly change. She'd never stay away, even for a day. At least, not until she had her own reasons to be distracted.

Within minutes, I was changed into loose jeans and a black tank top since it was warmer than normal out. I headed back to the living room, but I didn't see Charlie. "Where'd she go?"

Foster shrugged. "Charlie decided to wait outside."

I sighed. "I swear, the two of you were meant to be brother and sister."

He intertwined his fingers with mine and kissed the

back of my hand. "In a way, we are, since you consider her the sister you never had."

He wasn't wrong about that. Charlie was so much more than my best friend, and she always would be.

We went outside to find Charlie balancing on a rock, humming to herself and not seeming to have a care in the world.

She met my stare and grinned while hopping gracefully off the rock. "Ready?"

I nodded and laughed. "You know, if I tried to do that, I'd probably break a bone."

"Want to give it a try?" Charlie joked.

Foster grumbled and I shook my head. "Not today."

I opened a portal this time since I hadn't quite accomplished teleporting with multiple people and we stepped through, arriving in front of the pack house.

There were three shifters walking by, and they all froze at our sudden appearance until they noticed Foster's glower. Then they scampered off without another word.

My fist quickly found Foster's ribs. "That was rude."

"So is staring. Are you going to punch them as well?" he countered. I couldn't really argue, though the wolves had every right to be curious after all the shit that had been happening.

The front door opened, and Mack practically pushed Holden out of the way when he rushed forward to greet us. Or more accurately, Charlie. An action that had me raising a brow at the beta.

Holden merely shook his head and continued forward.

Mack slowed his pace and stroked his fingers over the beard he was attempting to grow.

"Charlie Wildes. It's a pleasure to see you in our pack again," he said with a slight bow of his head.

She smirked. "I see you did some asking around."

He looked her up and down and returned her saucy grin. "Of course, I did. I need to know who's going to be visiting my pack."

Holden cut dark eyes to Mack. "*Your* pack? Watch your words, Beta. You don't want to say the wrong thing and have Charlie find out that you sing in the shower to nineties boybands every morning."

Oh, how I adored this alpha.

Mack's jaw tightened, and he stood straighter, keeping his mouth shut. Charlie, however, was covering her mouth in a weak attempt to silence the laughter.

"Right. Well, how about we give Charlie a tour and make our way to Gemma's?" I suggested when the men just stood there.

Holden glanced at me. "I was hoping to chat with you and Foster for a minute. Do you have time to do that? Charlie can join us."

Charlie opened her mouth before I even had the chance to think of my answer. "Mack can give me a tour and the three of you can talk privately."

She was a woman who knew what she wanted.

Mack, on the other hand, was fighting a grin when he looked to his alpha for permission.

Holden sighed. "That's fine, but stay close. I'm sure Andie would like to know where her guest is when we're done."

Mack nodded once. "Of course, Alpha. Let me know

when you're finished, and we'll be waiting on the back porch."

Charlie hugged me. "I love you for bringing me here."

"I hope I still love you when we leave. Be good."

Foster made a rumbling noise behind us. Yeah, Charlie would *be* whatever she wanted, and I had a feeling Mack wasn't going to encourage "good" behavior.

The beta held his hand out, gesturing for Charlie to join him, and she did so with a skip in her step and a wide smile on her face.

Holden narrowed his eyes on me. "If this ends badly, I will hold you accountable. Regardless of how much I like you."

"She's harmless." My grin slipped. "Mostly."

"Right. Well, let's get inside." The alpha turned around, and I looked up at Foster.

"That was okay, right?" I asked quietly. "Encouraging Charlie to spend time with Mack?"

Foster nodded. "He would have said more if it weren't. Don't worry about it. I'm sure they'll tire of each other's company soon enough."

Oh, poor Foster. If he thought that, he had another thing coming. Outside of them not being fated mates, Charlie and Mack were a perfect match.

We entered the house and headed toward Holden's office on the first floor. He had wide windows on the back wall that were tinted, keeping prying eyes out of his business. The wood walls and floors extended into this room as well, but the ceiling was a cream color, bringing much-needed light into the room.

Holden's desk was at the center of the room, and he

was leaning back in the black leather chair by the time we entered. "Have a seat."

Foster pulled the cushioned chair out for me first and only sat beside me once I was comfortable.

Holden steepled his fingers beneath his chin. "How are you feeling, Andie?"

"Much better today," I answered. "While it's not a simple task to keep things in check, it's all getting easier. I spend a lot of time outside to help with that, connecting with the Earth's energy instead of those around me."

The alpha looked to Foster. "And your bond? Do you still require the walls to be up in order to protect the wolf spirit?"

Foster's brow creased. "No offense, but how is that relevant?"

Holden leaned forward. "Your wolf is part of my pack. I don't mean to pry, but you've told me about the timeline, and I'm not sitting idly by, waiting for your wolf to die."

I flinched hearing his blunt words. Foster and I had avoided most conversations about his wolf unless it was checking on how he was doing. As long as there was nothing to immediately worry about, then I preferred ignoring the fact that he could die in eleven days and the only reason we hadn't acted to solve that problem was because of me.

"We've been doing everything we can on our end to make sure that doesn't happen," Foster said gruffly.

"As have I. I've reached out to some of the other packs and have news to share that the two of you and Beatrix might find resourceful," Holden said, relaxing back into his seat.

"And what would that be?" Foster asked hesitantly.

"Moira's remaining family members? One is indeed her sister. And the other? He's her soulmate, not her blood relation—and he's dying."

My eyes widened, and I looked at Foster, blinking rapidly and trying to keep my heart from racing out of my chest.

Moira had been right. We *were* more alike than I'd realized, because if she wanted my magic to save her soulmate, then I was going to have to disappoint her.

Because I needed it for the same damn reason.

21

FOSTER

eavy air within the room pressed down on me, but I fought back. This wasn't terrible news. Though, judging by Andie's grip on the chair she sat in, she thought it was.

"Moira will do anything to save her soulmate. Just like I would," she said, her voice filled with certainty.

I reached for her arms. "Yes, and we're going to win."

"But at what cost?" Andie asked me with wide eyes. "We're supposed to kill her just because she's trying to save the one she loves more than her own life?"

Shit. I hadn't thought of it like that.

"We don't necessarily have to kill her," Holden said.

My eyes met his and I shook my head. "She won't stop until she *is* stopped. We can't be naïve enough to think otherwise. Not after all she's done. Do we know what's wrong with this soulmate of hers?"

Holden frowned. "No, not yet, but I'm working on it. Maybe he can be saved, and Moira can be…rehabilitated."

That was a thought to consider for a utopian life, but that wasn't the world we lived in.

Andie looked at me. "I need to tell Beatrix. She has to know as soon as possible."

The door opened before I could respond, and in walked Piper. Her auburn hair rested over her shoulders, and her pale-green eyes appraised the room. She hadn't been around the pack much lately. Holden said she had things to do in town at their other ventures, but I had a feeling he just wanted her as far away from potential threats as possible.

"Alpha, I'm here to go over the books," she said, then she nodded at me and Andie.

My mate glanced between the two of them, then at me, but stayed quiet, even though I could tell she had a question.

"Please, wait right outside. I'm almost done here," Holden said, standing from his chair.

Piper nodded and backed out of the door.

Andie pointed at Holden, then behind us. "She's your…"

Holden grinned proudly. "My daughter, but she prefers not to be addressed as such when we're handling pack business. She wants to pave her own way amongst the shifters, and I respect her wishes."

Andie let out a breath. "Wow, that's impressive and admirable. Unsurprising that she's your daughter."

Holden chuckled. "Is that a compliment, Andie?"

She grinned. "Yes, it would be. Now, if you'll excuse me, I'm going to make a call." Andie looked up at me and squeezed my hand. "I'll wait out front for you?"

I stood to give her a quick kiss. "I'll be there soon."

"Actually, head to the back deck if you want to find your friend," Holden said before Andie left the room.

She nodded, and my eyes watched every move my mate made until she closed the door behind her. When I turned back around, Holden was watching me.

"Do you have something to tell me?" he asked with a raised brow.

"Do *you* have something to ask me?" I countered.

He gestured to the chair. "Why don't you sit for a minute longer?"

I sighed. "Your daughter is waiting."

"And she'll keep waiting. This is important." His sharp tone left no room for negotiation. "Your wolf. How is he? Are Beatrix's potions still helping like before?"

I nodded. "He's still quiet, but he says he's better. I trust him to tell me if something is wrong that I can't sense."

I would tell you, I promise, my wolf confirmed.

"Very well. I just wanted to make sure there was nothing more we needed to worry about besides this deadline of when the potions run out. Your alpha power is still strong, so that's reassuring." He twisted in his chair and kept staring at me.

"Is there something you'd like to share?" I asked, leaning forward with my elbows resting on my knees.

He drummed his fingers over his thighs and thought for a moment. "Maybe, but it doesn't have anything to do with your mate or this dark witch, so it can wait for now."

"Okay." I took his word for it and stood up again. "Are we good here?"

Holden nodded. "We'll meet for lunch shortly?"

"I'm sure Andie would like that."

Holden walked me to the door. "But would you? Has the pack not grown on you yet?"

That wasn't a simple answer, and it wasn't something I was quite ready to talk about. Time hadn't been on our side, and thinking about the changes in my life outside of finding my mate had been low on the priorities list.

I couldn't deny that running with the pack during the new moon had been reinvigorating. Connecting with the other members, soaking in our creator's energy, and letting my wolf enjoy the life he had always been meant to have, reminded me of not only what we'd lost the day my pack had been attacked, but what we still could have had if only I hadn't let fear guide my choices.

I finally answered Holden. "The pack is fine. It's just taking some getting used to."

He grasped my shoulder. "I figured, but don't forget: You're not in this alone anymore. If you need someone to talk to, I'm here."

His sincerity punched me in the gut, and I nodded, twisting the handle on the door to end the uncomfortable conversation.

"Thanks, Holden."

Piper was still waiting outside when I stepped into the hallway. She nodded at me, and her green eyes darkened. I got the feeling she didn't like me very much, but that wasn't my problem. I hadn't interacted with her outside of a few brief meetings with minimal shared words. I'd done nothing wrong. Whatever bothered her was her problem to concern herself with. Not mine.

Using the weak connection I had to Andie, I made sure she was still on the deck before I headed that way. When I arrived outside, she was sitting on the wooden patio furniture with Charlie and Mack. Her head was tossed back, sending her pink hair cascading down her back as she laughed at something Charlie had said.

I watched them for a few moments, just soaking in the calmness. This was what we were supposed to have. Not constant chaos and questions about whether or not one of us was going to die at a moment's notice. I hated that I couldn't give Andie a simple life filled with love and laughter, but I hoped that would change one day.

Andie loves us, regardless of what we can give her, my wolf said quietly.

But she deserves so much more than what she's gotten.

He hummed in reply before fading away again, and I finally walked forward to join the others.

I lifted Andie up and sat in the chair she'd just been occupying before letting her get comfortable in my lap. "What did I miss?"

"Just Charlie pretending she's stronger than a shifter," Andie answered.

Mack barked out a laugh. "I would love to wrestle with you and let you prove yourself."

Charlie lowered her eyes on him and smirked. "I'll take you up on that one day."

"Why not now? We're both here. Lunch isn't for another hour," Mack challenged.

Charlie stood slowly from her chair, but Andie raised her hand. "If you want to join me in visiting Gemma, you will not accept that wolf's challenge, Charlotte Wildes."

Charlie cut her gaze to Andie. "What did you just call me?"

Andie winked at me before getting up. "Now she doesn't want to 'wrestle' Mack. Diversion successful." She grabbed Charlie's arm. "Oh, calm down. I'll race you to the cabins to make you feel better."

Charlie glowed. "Just like the waterslide."

"Minus the water, sure." Andie chuckled, then leaned back down. "You have fun with Mack. I'm going to see Gemma and the baby, and we'll be back for lunch."

I accepted the quick kiss she offered. "You don't want me to go with you?"

She cupped my chin. "Gemma moved to stay within the shield—Mack already told me where to go—and Charlie is with me. We'll be fine. I promise."

A rough noise left my throat, but I let her walk away. I couldn't keep her in a bubble, no matter how much I wanted to.

Charlie waved at Mack, and he grinned foolishly.

"You're not really going to entertain that, are you?" I asked once Andie and Charlie were far enough away. It wasn't that I didn't think Charlie was worthy, but Mack's mate could show up any day, and then what? Charlie would be left hurting, and that would also hurt Andie. Hell, the same could happen to Mack if Charlie met the one meant for her.

Mack's expression turned serious. "Did you know that nearly all shifters, who are going to have a mate in this lifetime, meet their match by the time they're fifty. I'm fifty-one, and while I'm sure there's a miniscule chance I could still find the one, it's not likely. I've accepted that, as has my wolf."

He sighed heavily. "After almost four decades of hoping, I'm done waiting to live my best life. I'm happy here, but I'd love life even more if I had someone to share it with."

"And you think Charlie is that person for you?" I asked, because I really hadn't expected him to feel so serious about the witch.

He smiled, looking up at the blue sky. "No clue, but I enjoy her free spirit and the way she likes to challenge me in her own ways. Not many I've crossed paths with have ever done the same. So to answer you, I don't know, but I'm intrigued. More importantly, I'm fully aware of the risks, and I'll make sure she knows them, too, should she agree to see where things might go between us."

I didn't entirely agree with his thought process, but I had to remember that Mack wasn't me. He and Charlie were adults who could make their own decisions. It wasn't something I needed to involve myself in. Though, I suspected Andie would be keeping her nose in things until she was certain her best friend was happy.

"So, do you want to sit here for an hour? Or do you want to head to the gym and beat the hell out of some of the other shifters who're training?" Mack's eyes held a glint in them that told me the latter was a favorite pastime of his.

"How about we beat the hell out of each other and make it a fair fight?" I asked, because an alpha didn't normally train with the other wolves unless he knew their weaknesses and strengths. I wasn't the alpha here, but the notion still applied. I wouldn't risk hurting one of the other shifters with my stronger energy.

Mack, however, was a beta, and he could handle it if I unleashed my true power.

He jumped out of the seat, vibrating the wooden deck from the force of his landing. "You're on, Kline."

I chuckled and stood, reaching a hand to him. "May the best shifter win."

22

ANDIE

Charlie and I ran so hard that my chest burned before we hit the trees. When we'd been little, we would race to our waterslide made out of black plastic that ended in a kiddie pool. Whoever had gotten there second had to hold the plastic and hose in place for the other and then suffered through their own, not as fun, trip down the plastic.

We'd been five. Bragging rights and a smoother trip to the waiting kiddie pool had been a big deal back then. Though, if Charlie's rough breathing and grunts were any indication, racing was still a big deal to her.

I kept my pace even, and she passed me right at the end, raising her arms into the air. "I am victorious!"

I laughed. "Congratulations. I'll be sure to make you a gold medal when we're back home."

She pointed at me. "I'm going to hold you to that."

I had no doubt she would.

"So, where to?" Charlie asked once we'd both caught our breath.

I nodded to our left. "Should be two cabins down that small path. Look for the blue ribbon that Mack mentioned while we were waiting for Foster."

We walked through the trees, and I inhaled deeply. I really did love the woods within the wolf shifter territory. I didn't know what it was about being in the pack, but there was always a sense of home when I was here. I wanted to attribute that to my bond with Foster, but something told me that wasn't the case. Maybe when I had my magic back, I could figure things out.

Charlie pointed. "That has to be it."

There was a small wooden cabin ahead of us, and there wasn't just a blue bow on the door. No, there were balloons and lights and a banner that hung over the front window reading, "Congratulations" with cute little pawprints all over it.

My heart warmed seeing how celebrated the new birth was. Wolf shifters were strong and could be ruthless, but they still cared deeply about each other. Every member of the pack was family. This was merely another reminder of that truth.

I went to the door first and knocked. It cracked open from the slight pressure. "Gemma?" I called.

"I gotta swap out my diaper. Be right there." Her voice echoed from the hallway.

Charlie snorted. "A diaper? Seriously? Why would she need that? Unless she meant for the baby…"

Gemma came strutting down the hallway, pulling the top of her black yoga pants above her much-smaller bump. She had the biggest maxi pad I'd ever seen in her left hand —thankfully, a new one—and raised it in the air. "This is a new mother's diaper. When you give birth, your body expels gallons and gallons of blood. It's like your worst period on steroids. We're not supposed to talk about things like that, but like I told Andie before, I don't like to keep most of my thoughts to myself when I don't have to."

Gemma winked and then walked into the small living room that was covered in baby items, but the one I zeroed in on first was the white bassinet the shifter went to.

Charlie shoved me. "Why haven't you brought me here sooner? I love these people already."

I shrugged. "You never asked. Now, be quiet before you wake the baby."

Gemma shook her finger at us. "Be as loud as you want. Little Bryson Joseph needs to get used to the noises if he's ever going to nap properly."

Charlie stepped forward and waved. "I'm Charlie. Andie's best friend. Hope you don't mind that I tagged along."

Gemma laughed. "If I did, you'd already know it. Want a souvenir?" She waved the oversized pad in the air.

Charlie scrunched her nose. "I'll pass, but thanks for the information. Kids have officially gone in the *no* column for me."

Gemma rubbed her hand lightly over her son's blue blanket that he was swaddled in. "It's worth it. Every stretch mark, every time I peed my pants, every contraction that made me feel like this little blessing was coming out of my asshole instead of my vagina." She sighed. "All worth holding him in my arms."

Charlie's face was pale by the time Gemma finished, and I just shook my head. These two were going to be trouble around each other. I stepped closer to the bassinet. Bryson's lips were suckling on nothing, and his eyes were closed. Only one of his arms was free from the blanket, and his little fingers were so precious that I couldn't stop myself from rubbing one of my own over his hand.

"He's perfect, Gemma," I cooed.

She grinned widely. "I know. How about we sit before he wakes up in five minutes because the smell of my milk is too alluring to sleep through?"

Charlie shuddered and sat on the couch first. "You're a brave woman for bearing children."

"Eh. I was braver for taking a mate. Men are way more work than babies. I can assure you of that."

I laughed. I wasn't there with Foster yet, but I had no doubts she was right.

"Charlie has a crush on Mack," I said with a smile.

Gemma's jaw dropped. "Our Mack? The beta? It was the dreamy hazel eyes that did you in, wasn't it?"

Charlie blushed, an action I wasn't used to seeing on her round face. "Might have been that."

"Once you go shifter, you never go back. Be careful what you're asking for," Gemma warned, and I choked on my own spit.

"Is that a legit thing people say?" I asked once I could breathe right again.

Gemma shrugged. "It's what I say and I'm people, so yes."

Bryson chose that moment to start fussing, but Gemma stayed put.

"Aren't you going to do something?" Charlie asked hesitantly.

"I already am. I'm seeing if he's awake or just making noise. If I get him out of that bassinet every time he makes a peep, I'll lose my sanity."

Bryson quieted a few seconds later, and I looked over at a triumphant Gemma. "This is your first kid and it's only been a few days. How do you know so much?" I asked.

"I have two sisters who are much older than me," Gemma answered. "They've popped out three each of their own. One set of triplets and then twins and single for the other. I helped a lot before I met Joseph. I learned from their mistakes, as any smart younger sibling should do."

Bryson let out an ear-piercing scream.

"And that's the kind of sound I don't ignore." Gemma was on her feet in less than a second, and she unbuttoned her loose top before grabbing the baby.

"Momma's here, sweet boy. No need to yell like a banshee." She sat back down and popped a boob out like a seasoned pro. Within seconds, Bryson was content as could be.

Charlie leaned closer, curiosity in her eyes this time. "Maybe it's not all that terrible to have a kid."

Yeah, maybe not, I thought.

We both watched Bryson eat and Gemma smile down at her son for several minutes before she engaged in more conversation. "How are things at the witch coven? People aren't talking as much as they were before, so I hope that means good things?"

That was a relief. That meant Holden's plans of keeping things quiet were working.

I nodded. "We've been hard at work trying to sort out

this mess with the dark witch, but I think we're getting closer. We'll know more in the next few days."

I hated that I couldn't tell her the whole truth, but I wanted to respect Holden's wishes.

"That's great to hear. It would be nice to move back home with the baby, but at least we had somewhere private to stay in the meantime," Gemma said.

Bryson startled and Gemma stroked his cheek, trying to calm him.

While she tended to the baby, I glanced out the window. Birds were flying low in the sky and making all sorts of noise. My gaze cut to Charlie, who was looking down at the rising hairs on her arms.

"That's not normal," she muttered.

Before I could respond, a force pressed down over us, and I covered my ears until my head found some sort of relief from the energy.

"Either they're changing the shield or someone is trying to take it down," Charlie said.

Gemma's wide eyes glanced between the both of us. "I thought the shield would keep us safe. Can they really break through?"

She held Bryson closer to her chest, and I turned to Charlie. "Teleport her and the baby to the coven and tell Beatrix. I need to find Foster."

"I'm not leaving without Joseph," Gemma said, tears filling her eyes as Charlie stood.

I reached for her hand. "Joseph would want Bryson safe, wouldn't he?" She nodded numbly. "Then let us make that happen, and I will make sure Foster tells him where you and the baby are as soon as I get back to the pack house."

A thundering crack echoed around us, and this time, the windows rattled. Gemma stood up and went to the table across the room, picking up a black bag. "I can tell Joseph through our bond. He won't want to leave unless I go out there and make him."

Her words held no conviction. There was no way Gemma was going out there, especially when we didn't really know what was going on. I waited a few seconds for her to accept that as well.

She sighed. "I need to grab a few things, but I'll be quick."

Gemma darted off into the bedroom she'd exited from earlier, and I turned to Charlie. "This has to be Moira."

"Or at least the horde stupid enough to follow her," Charlie replied with a sneer.

"Make sure Gemma and the baby are safe. Don't take them to my house. Use yours in case someone goes to mine who shouldn't. I'll stay as close to the pack house as I can so you can find me easier."

Charlie wrapped her arms around me. "Be safe, and don't be afraid to unleash every inch of the kickass-ness inside you. She's not stronger than you, Andie. None of them are."

I nodded against her shoulder. "I love you."

"I love you, too. Now, go find Foster and I'll take care of these two." She shoved me toward the door, and I didn't hesitate to run outside.

The blue sky was gone, and in its place were what looked like ominous clouds that sparked with lightning above me. With every bright strike, the shield lit up, and small fissures could be seen forming along the top of the normally invisible barrier.

Howls sounded off in every direction around me, but I didn't stick around to figure out where they were coming from. I ran faster than ever toward the pack house, hoping like hell Foster was still there.

23

FOSTER

I slammed Mack so hard to the ground that the floors shook, but instead of being fazed, he merely laughed. "Again."

With a sigh, I reached down and helped him up. "You're a glutton for punishment."

He gave me a shove. "Nah. I just don't get to work this hard very often. This is invigorating." He nodded to the other shifters trying to pretend they weren't watching us on the mats while they worked out with the gym equipment across the room. "Plus, they get their panties in a twist when I win. There's little joy in pissing them off."

I slapped his back and chuckled. "You're a good beta, Mack."

I looked around for my water bottle and stumbled unexpectedly. Then the walls shook and, this time, it had nothing to do with us wrestling.

The hairs on the back of my neck stood, and my wolf rose to the surface.

Andie.

"Someone's here," I said to Mack. "I need to find Andie. Where's Gemma's cabin?"

His eyes darkened. "Is that the shield?"

"Highly possible. Where is my mate, Mack?" I asked one last time before unleashing my wolf.

"About half a mile out. What are we supposed to do?" he asked me, and my alpha power surged forward without thought.

"You find Holden and put any plans you've been concocting in the event that someone attacks the pack into motion," I said, jogging toward the door, ignoring the furrowed looks from the other shifters as I paced by.

"Is that what's happening?" he called out.

I didn't bother to turn around. "We're about to find out."

After nearly ripping the door from its hinges, I stepped outside to find the sky covered in dark, swirling fog and flashes of lightning striking through the sky but never touching the ground.

The air was heavy and pressing down on my chest. My skin tingled with energy, and my wolf senses were fully awake for the first time in days.

Andie's getting closer. We need to wait for her here, my wolf said.

Before I could respond to him, Holden came racing toward us in his wolf form. He leapt and shifted back to human midair before landing on his feet. If I could have thought of anything other than Andie, I'd have been impressed.

"I've been calling for the pack, but nobody is responding," he growled just as Mack stepped outside.

"I just told the shifters inside to wait there for me. But what do you mean we didn't respond? I must have missed your message, but I told you I was headed to the pack house," Mack said, not understanding what Holden was saying, but I did.

"Moira cut your ties to the pack like she did with James." My fingers tightened at my sides, and my insides burned with fury. "Holden, she was testing us when she used him. The kid wasn't the main event. Whatever this is? She's coming to destroy us."

Holden's chest rumbled loudly. "I need to figure out a way to warn the pack and get those who can't fight out of here. We have pups and mothers who don't need to be anywhere near *that*."

Holden pointed up and I agreed. The darkening sky was bearing down over the shield, and I suspected it wouldn't be long before our layer of safety was broken.

Andie's pink hair appeared in my peripheral vision, and I whipped my head around to see her. She wasn't hurt, but she was alone.

"Where's Charlie?" Mack asked.

Andie stopped and sucked in a breath. "She took Gemma and the baby to the coven. Is the pack ready for whatever this is? Charlie will get the witches here as soon as she can."

"Holden can't reach the pack, but maybe Mack can?" I glanced at the beta, doubtful, but it was worth a try.

He closed his eyes, and his jaw tightened. "No."

Andie's lips thinned. "What do you mean? What about your mind speak? Did Joseph even hear Gemma before I forced her to leave?" Her words began running together as she spoke faster.

I grabbed her shoulders. "We'll find Joseph to make sure, and we'll help the pack." Then I turned to Holden. "Where do we start?"

Mack stepped back. "I know where Joseph is. He's with the group we'll want here fighting. I'll go get them and then circle the perimeter of the pack, but how are we going to get people out of here?"

Andie raised her hand. "I'll do it. More witches will be here soon to help. I can open a portal right here and send them to the coven. Just point the pack in this direction."

Holden let out a heavy breath. "That will be a huge help. I'll head the opposite way of Mack and begin sending people here. Thank you, Andie."

Mack was already gone before Holden had finished speaking, and the alpha shifted as soon as he was far enough away from us.

Andie was still breathing hard, and her face was pale. I pulled her into my arms as another pulse of energy vibrated around us.

She pushed me back. "Standing here, just waiting for people to show up doesn't feel like enough."

I nodded. As much as I just wanted to keep Andie safe and run away with her, this was our fight. Moira wouldn't have attacked this pack if I hadn't come here for help.

"But it is. Until that shield fails, this is the most helpful thing we can be doing. You work on the portal and maybe open it on the backside of the coven so the witches who don't know what's going on yet don't freak out. While you're doing that, I can shift. My wolf's howling should draw pack members in as well."

Andie pointed up. "That should be enough to make people worry, but howling will give them a sound to follow instead of wandering around, not sure what to do since they can't communicate."

She made a valid point, and I was thankful she wasn't panicking.

While she worked on the portal opening, I shifted to my wolf form. *Are you ready for this?* I asked him.

I am. There's a reason I've been reserved. I knew our fight was far from over.

We have to save as many of them as we can.

It won't be like before, he promised.

It can't be.

My wolf's howls cut through the air, a signal to the pack that I hoped they wouldn't ignore. We kept that up for several minutes before a small family sprinted around the corner of the pack house.

I transformed back to two feet when they did the same. It was a mother with her two children. A teen boy and a young daughter.

"We're going to get you out of here," Andie said, the portal nearly big enough for people to walk through.

I went to the mother, whose name I didn't know. Her blue eyes were wide, her light strands were haphazardly sticking out from her ponytail, and she was shaking. "It's going to be okay. My mate will get your family to the coven."

"Why can't I reach Holden? Where is our alpha?" she begged.

"He's here and he's trying to bring in the pack members so we can get them out of here. A dark witch has silenced our communication, but we're going to help as many as we can."

She glanced behind me. "My mate. He's with the guard team training. I told him I was coming here. He can hear me, but neither of us could reach Holden. He told me he'd meet here as soon as he could get some answers."

That was good to know, and I was sure a relief for Andie since she had felt guilty about sending Gemma away without being sure their mate connection still worked.

"Tell your mate to stay where he is and to let the others know that if they haven't already, then they need to tell their families to do the same as you. Come here as quickly as they can."

She pressed a hand over her chest and closed her eyes. I glanced at the kids. The little girl was clinging to her brother's neck, nearly choking him. He met my stare and didn't seem the least bit scared.

"Gerald is taking care of what you asked. He said Mack is also there and helping," the woman said, and I nodded before looking back at Andie.

"Good. The portal is ready. This leads to the forest within the coven territory. You'll be safer there and more will join you soon."

The shifter reached for her son's hand and pulled him toward the opening. Andie stepped out of the way and to my side.

Her eyes were bright, and her skin was glowing a faint purple. "Are you okay?" I asked.

She nodded. "I'm ready to face Moira."

"How do you know she'll be here?" I asked since the dark witch herself hadn't shown up when her group had last attacked.

"I just know." Andie's hands curled into fists. "What did you mean when you mentioned the communication with the pack being cut off before?"

I sighed. "I think what happened to James was only a trial run. Holden hadn't been able to feel the pup when he went after you. If you hadn't electrocuted him, there would have been nothing we could have done to stop him unless we'd really hurt him. I can only assume now that Moira has figured out a way to cut off all contact with the pack except for mates, but let's hope she's not controlling any of the wolves this time."

Andie's shoulders slumped. "I hope like hell not. We can't kill our own."

I wanted to agree with her, but I stayed silent instead, because my words would have been a lie.

More wolves began showing up and they didn't question the portal. Thankfully, they took their children and moved on through, spreading out into the trees.

After nearly thirty pack members had made their way to the coven, Charlie finally returned. She wrapped Andie up in her arms and then looked up at the sky.

"The shield is only going to last another few minutes. Then, that dark sky is going to let in witches and warlocks who want to kill us all until Moira gets what she wants."

I thought back to the last attack at Spell House and tried to remember anything helpful. "Moira's coven is connected somehow. How can we use that to our advantage?"

Charlie kept her eyes on the sky. "With each member who dies, their strength weakens. Since the coven is joined mostly by dark magic, they don't get to recoup the power from their deceased like we do. They'll slow down with every death, but it won't be noticeable until we've eliminated more than half of them."

Andie shuddered next to me.

"Just remember, they're not giving you a choice," I whispered. "It's your life or theirs, and it was their choice to attack us."

She nodded, but the action lacked conviction. "I'll be fine." Then she looked at Charlie. "Where are Beatrix and our coven members?"

Andie was right. They should have been here by now.

Charlie's response was cut off when Benjamin's head peeked out of the portal. "Are there more coming?"

"More wolves? I don't know. There could be," Andie answered.

"Beatrix asked me to stay here and make sure everyone got through and then to close access so none of Moira's witches sneak through. I'll leave it open as long as I can. Do you need anything?" he asked, glancing at all three of us.

Before any of us could respond, screams cut through the air around us, and Benjamin took a step back.

The barrier has been broken, my wolf warned.

I grabbed both of Andie's hands. "I'm going to shift again, but I won't leave you during this fight."

"If I'm hurting you or your wolf, then you're going to

have to," she begged. "It might be the only way to win this."

My wolf growled, and I echoed him. "That's not possible."

Her hands cupped my face, and she pulled me closer. "We don't have any other choice, Foster. We both need to know the other will be safe, and if that means we need to be separated, then we need to be okay with that. Right now."

I jerked away from her and gripped my hair tightly. "Fuck!" We didn't have time for me to be indecisive. I understood what she was saying and, shit, I even agreed with her, but I couldn't lose Andie. I couldn't fail to protect another person I cared about.

I wouldn't survive that.

The fog from above the clouds began shooting toward the ground. We were out of time, and I would not let my last conversation with Andie before we entered into this fight be one that had ended in disagreement.

My hands gripped her hips, and I lifted her up, devouring her mouth with my own for just a second—one I knew we didn't have to spare. "I love you so fucking much," I murmured over her lips.

"I love you, too. We're going to be okay."

Her forehead pressed against mine, and I slowly let her back to the ground. I was terrified to let her go, but I also knew we didn't have any other choice. Time had run out. It was time to protect our pack and coven.

When we pulled apart, Benjamin was guarding the portal with glowing, green hands that matched his eyes, and Charlie was bouncing on her feet. "The witches have begun arriving. Looks like the fight is beginning behind the pack house."

She started running that way, and Andie took a step to follow her. My hand flinched to pull my mate back to me, and she paused for the briefest second. "Believe in us, Foster. That's all we can do if we hope to win."

I nodded stiffly. I could do that. I had no other choice.

Andie moved farther ahead, and I let my wolf push forward.

We'll keep her safe for as long as we can, he said.

But will that be long enough?

He howled into the air. *It will have to be.*

24

ANDIE

oster's darkening eyes, clenched jaw, and increased breathing were hard to ignore and caused my anxiety to rise, but there was nothing either of us could do. Running wasn't an option. It was a death sentence.

With the last crack of thunder, I knew Moira had arrived. She wasn't close, but my magic recognized her energy. If she was here, then she meant to take what she wanted, which I assumed was me.

With the pack's communication down and all of us feeling so separated, Moira had the upper hand, but I hoped it wouldn't stay that way for long.

At least Benjamin was watching over the portal. He was only a teenager, but he had heart, and that meant a lot when it came to protecting the innocent.

I considered teleporting, but I didn't want to appear somewhere less than ideal, so I followed Charlie's path and continued to race around the back of the house.

When we arrived, witches were teleporting in from our

coven—though not as many as I would have expected—while dark witches were forming out of the shadowy fog from Moira's.

My eyes scanned the crowds, searching for her. The witch was nowhere to be seen, but she hadn't gone far. I was as sure of that as I was that Foster's wolf was snarling next to me.

I bent down and gripped his fur. "Don't let him stay with me if I'm hurting you. I'll be fine."

The wolf's warmth soaked into me, and he nudged my stomach with his massive head.

I moved to place my lips on his coarse hair, but the wolf was out of my grasp and jumping over me in the next second.

A warlock had been coming up behind us, and Foster's wolf now had him by the neck. Within seconds, the unknown man was lifeless on the ground. I tried to process what I'd witnessed, but there was no time.

Our arrival was being noticed, and they were coming toward us in hordes. Witches, warlocks, and wolves alike.

Foster had hoped none of the wolves within the pack were being controlled, but as they sprinted forward with black eyes, I knew that hope was lost.

His wolf jumped in front of me, and I readied my magic, saving my syphon power for when I needed it most.

Charlie appeared at my side and moved to stand so that our backs were touching. "They're searching for you and Foster both."

I wanted to be surprised by that, but I wasn't. Moira would know that if she took my soulmate from me, I'd be more willing to comply with her demands. I just hoped that wasn't a situation we found ourselves in.

A wolf leapt at us, and I sent a stream of the same magic I'd used on James straight into its chest. There was a loud yelp and then the beast crumpled to the ground, but it didn't stay there like the boy had.

"They're stronger than James was," I warned Charlie and Foster, wondering once again where the hell Beatrix and the rest of the coven were.

Holden's wolves who weren't being controlled were helping as much as they could, but from where I stood, most of them were only able to get a bite or two in before they were zapped with dark energy.

We were quickly losing numbers and running out of options. I had a thought on how I could help in a bigger way, but I needed Foster to get as far from me as possible first.

His wolf was busy snapping at incoming pack members when I noticed three witches dressed in the same robes that I'd seen that day at Spell House. Their glowing, silver eyes were the only thing I could make out beneath the hoods, and I stepped forward.

Charlie called out a warning to me, but I ignored her. This was what I'd been training for. If these witches wanted me, then they were going to get me. All of me.

I began to jog forward and pushed magic into my palms. My left hand created a shield that I held in front of me, and the right was packed with a punch powerful enough that it should put all three of them on their asses if I timed my hit correctly.

Except they separated at the last second, a black tether of energy connecting them as they circled me.

Shit. I was trapped, and they were chanting something that didn't sound like it was going to be good for me.

I glanced at Foster's wolf. He wasn't far enough away, but I had to do something before these three captured me.

Dark magic began pressing down on me and I dropped to my knees, digging my fingers into the ground. As I called energy to myself, whips covered with black magic lashed at my back. I stifled my cries and began to push the energy I'd collected back out.

It took concentrated effort to stand again. Every muscle inside me ached and the witches were only a few feet away now, but I wasn't giving up. They wouldn't take me. Not today. Not ever.

I pressed both of my hands together, charging them up before I thrust them out and spun in a circle. Light-purple magic began to darken and hit each of them in the chest.

They faltered, but their connecting tether didn't break.

I was going to have to get closer.

Foster's wolf howled, but I didn't look back. I only acted on instinct and closed the distance between me and the nearest witch.

My hand slammed into their chest, but it went straight through the cloaked figure. There was no body mass to absorb my hit.

Charcoal-colored magic traveled up my feet, swiftly moving up my legs and bringing me closer to the ground.

I choked on the energy. It was taking the air from my lungs, and my vision was fading.

Another howl cut through the air, but this one was a reminder. I couldn't give in. I couldn't let them win.

I'm sorry, Foster, I thought before I began sucking in the black magic. I had to take from them what they never should have had and what I most certainly didn't want. Then, I'd destroy them with the very thing they thought made them invincible.

My fingers reached for the robes, searching for anything to latch on to. Once I had a hold, I pulled, first absorbing the magic that was preventing me from breathing and then focusing on the soul before me. They may not have had a physical form, but there was still a source of life inside the shadows, one that I could take and end before they caused any more damage.

The first witch dissipated into the air, and their energy source was gone from the tether that flickered when I stood back up.

The two remaining witches were throwing everything they had at me, but I was glowing a dark midnight color and growing stronger by the second, thanks to their friend.

I launched myself at the next target but was blasted back by the other. Charlie looked down at me, blood trickling from her nose. "There are too many and I don't know where Beatrix is."

I glanced back, keeping one eye on the two robed witches still coming for me. Bodies lay on the ground, blood covered those still standing, and wolves were fighting each other like they were lifelong enemies.

Foster was right there in the middle, staying as close as he could, but every time he tried to get nearer, another witch or wolf cut off his path. They were purposely trying to separate us.

Charlie groaned, then snarled. "Keep fighting, Andie." Then her body shimmered, like she was trying to teleport, but she didn't move from her spot next to me. "Shit! There's a block around us. That's why the rest haven't shown." Charlie grunted while she began fighting another witch.

I barely had time to comprehend what she was saying before the two robed witches were on me again. I'd broken their circle, but they were still powerful.

One of them barked out a word I didn't understand, and I was forced to the ground, putting my face right in the dirt.

"That hurt," I muttered as I pushed myself back up.

When I whirled around, my hands were already filled with energy, and I blasted my two attackers with enough magic that it should have fried them to ash.

Except, as their forms started to crack from my hit, they disappeared from sight entirely.

I turned to look for Charlie, and she was still standing, so my gaze traveled to Foster, who wasn't faring nearly as well as he had been when I'd last checked.

His wolf was missing a chunk of skin from his front flank, and he was breathing too hard. Three wolves were taking turns swiping at him while a warlock stood there watching.

They could have killed him already and, while I was more than thankful they hadn't, I didn't understand what the point of the torture was. It was going to end right fucking now.

I charged forward. With every stride I took, I drew energy from the Earth and every supernatural being I could reach.

By the time I'd closed the distance, I was once again glowing with energy that I intended to slam into the other wolves, hoping like hell I didn't hurt Foster too badly in the process.

Except, when my feet lifted off the ground to jump forward the rest of the way, I was yanked back by an invisible force.

I landed on my ass and elbows, groaning from the impact. I tried to turn around, but hands grabbed my hair and jerked me up.

Once my feet had purchase, I twisted until I could see who was behind me, coming face-to-face with a woman I knew immediately to be Moira.

She was wearing my necklace, which was floating over her chest, almost like it was trying to get to me.

"Hello, Andie," Moira jeered before she grabbed onto the front of my shirt. "It's nice to officially meet you. Let's chat."

I thought she was going to bring me closer. Instead, she bent her arm only a couple inches, then shoved me farther away from Foster and Charlie.

This time, I landed on my feet with my knees bent and one hand pressing into the ground, taking one last boost of energy as I watched Moira come for me.

She waltzed forward wearing dark skinny jeans, a black leather corset top, and bright red heels that matched her thin lips. When she grinned, her cheekbones protruded and slight wrinkles formed around her charcoal eyes.

I scrambled back but didn't get to stand fast enough before she was kneeling over me, her long, sleek, brown hair creating a curtain around us. "You're coming with me, or my friends over there will kill your pet."

I wanted to call her bluff, but I knew she wasn't wrong. Foster was all alone and weakening, possibly because I'd used my syphon ability. Beatrix and the others not showing up had been the final nail in our coffin. Naïve as it might have been, I still wasn't willing to give this particular witch whatever she wanted.

My fingers rose and I reached for my necklace, but she pulled away, shaking her finger at me. "I don't think so. This is mine until I get what I want out of it."

I raised a brow. "To save your soulmate?"

She sneered at me. "Don't you speak of him."

I leaned forward slowly, but she backed up just as much. "Why? You're the one that told me we were alike. I wanted to know just how true that was. I see now."

Her eyes roamed over me, and her lip lifted. "You see what?"

"I see that we both want to save our soulmates. Yet we're at an impasse. You want something from me, and I can't give it to you—for the same reasons." While I had her momentarily distracted, my hand shot out again, this time faster, and my fingers touched the moonstone. As soon as they made contact, a light exploded inside me.

My magic.

I pulled on the energy, but Moira's fist punched me in the cheek, breaking at least a bone or two.

"Don't touch that unless I tell you to!" she screeched.

I held my hands up, then pressed one over my cheek,

sending some healing vibes where she'd hit me. All the while, my palm still facing Moira was reaching out to my magic. I didn't have to touch the stone to get what I wanted. Maybe Beatrix had been smarter than I'd realized, not acting before I'd been ready. Everything I'd been doing the last eight days had prepared me for this moment.

"Moira, you need me, and I need my magic. Why don't we come to an agreement we can both live with?" I asked, lying my ass off to keep her interest in my words while I lowered my arms but left my palm facing the dark witch once it rested at my side.

"You'd work with me?" she asked, her tone tight and rightly suspicious.

I shrugged. "I'll do whatever I have to in order to save the most lives here today, including my soulmate's. Why don't you tell me about yours?"

A glossy sheen covered her eyes before she blinked, shaking her head. She took a step forward, then paused.

"What, Moira? What has you hesitating?" I taunted, needing to keep her distracted.

The tether inside me, the one I'd felt when I'd been in the ether, I'd been drawing on that part of me, focusing on making it stronger throughout the last week.

With practiced effort, I sent the invisible tether out of my palm and toward Moira's chest where my necklace still floated. The clear thread circled around the necklace before halting instead of doing what I'd hoped it would.

I didn't know what the tether didn't like, but I didn't care. I drew the energy back and tried again. As much as I'd have preferred to have the whole necklace back, I was okay settling for only what was inside before blasting Moira into the next world.

Moira scoffed at my previous question. "I'm not hesitating, I'm assessing, as any smart witch would do. You're different than I expected, but I also didn't foresee you having a wolf shifter for a soulmate. He's tainted your energy."

I cocked my head to the side. "Has he? Or was that your doing when you took what wasn't yours?"

She shoved her hands forward just as my tether finally wrapped around the stone, pulling taut and holding strong. Instead of focusing on protecting myself, I concentrated on keeping the connection to the necklace secure, which was how I ended up slammed into a tree from Moira's hit and bashing my head so hard, I saw stars.

Moira was on me again before I could stand, but I didn't care. I was drawing my power back and she had no damn clue.

"You will do as I say, or you will die. They will *all* die," she spat in my face.

I shook my head. "You won't kill me, Moira. You said too much before. You need me."

She backhanded me and blood flew out of my mouth. "You need me, too."

"No, I don't. I'm already getting what I want."

The stone was almost drained. While I probably looked like death, I was growing more powerful by the second. My insides felt like lightning, and I was ready to strike.

Except before I could do so, hellfire rained down on all of us.

Magic pierced my skin. At first, it was burning, but

then the sensation melted away for me within the next second. Though that didn't seem to be the case for those under Moira's control.

Screeches sounded off all around us, and witches I recognized finally began to appear. I didn't know how Beatrix had done it, but she'd finally broken through whatever block Moira had had around us.

And not a second too late.

Moira stumbled back, and as much as I wanted to go to Foster, I wanted this nightmare to be over. I had to finish removing Moira's hold over us. I needed all of my magic.

I launched myself at her, but her form was already dissolving into mist, and I stumbled right through her. Her transparent form turned and glared at me while she raised her arms into the air. Her misty body swirled until there was nothing left but a tornado of dark fog.

Moira's voice echoed around me. "Our time is up for the day, but we're not done yet, Andie. And I'll be taking a few friends with me to make sure of it."

My eyes immediately cut to Foster.

His wolf was on the ground, and I was too far from him.

Wolves and bodies began rising into the air, carried by the dark fog from which Moira's witches had appeared. They were retreating, but I didn't believe we'd come close to winning.

Inky tendrils wrapped around Foster, and his head hung limply when he was lifted off the ground.

Without thinking, I thrust my arms toward the black magic covering him. Midnight energy blasted out of me, but instead of just attacking whatever was trying to take

Foster, the power spread out and targeted every ounce of dark magic around us.

I pulled on the energy, forcing it to come toward me, commanding it to obey my command instead of Moira's.

Only that wasn't all I was doing.

There was light magic being mixed in, and the witches from our coven began dropping to their knees. Even though I knew what was happening, there wasn't a single part of me that wanted to cease my actions.

I needed to do this. I needed to take all that I could from Moira before she could steal anything else from me.

Beatrix stepped in front of me and grabbed my wrists. Her body was covered in an opaque shield, and she didn't seem at all affected by my magic. "Stop it, Andie. Control yourself before you kill all of us."

My head shook. They'd tried to take Foster from me. I couldn't let them get away.

The wall between myself and Foster cracked as I used more of the dark energy. A small part of me knew to listen to Beatrix, knew to stop before anyone else got hurt because of me, but I was no longer in control. I couldn't slow the momentum of my power.

The protection Foster was supposed to have from me shattered inside my mind. Our bond flared like a beacon in my mind, and I finally fell to my knees.

My soulmate. My Foster.

I tried to stop pulling on the bond. I tried to stop taking on more of the dark magic remnants, especially since Moira and her people were already gone, but I was no longer calling the shots.

Beatrix smacked me across the face, and I merely

chuckled. "You can't stop me," I snarled, my voice not entirely my own.

Her silver-covered hand pressed over my forehead. "Actually, I can."

My eyes widened, and the world around me went black. When I could see again, I was looking up at a clear sky with a pounding inside my head unlike I'd ever known.

"What the hell was that?" I asked with a groan.

Beatrix leaned over me. "That was me stopping you from killing half the coven and your mate all at the same time. Now get up."

Foster.

I searched for the bond, but the light I'd pulled on just moments before was gone. I could still feel him, but it wasn't the same. *We* weren't the same.

My throat and eyes burned, and I covered my mouth with both hands to hold in the sobs I wanted to let rip from inside me.

The wall between us was all the way gone. I'd broken through Beatrix's potion, and I'd begun pulling energy from all around me in hopes of… I couldn't think of the reason. All I knew was that I'd screwed up, and Beatrix was right.

I'd almost killed people.

She helped me onto my feet, and my stare immediately went to Foster's wolf. Only my eyes couldn't see the rise and fall of his chest that I hoped for.

He was lying on the ground, unmoving, and only a faint hint of energy pulsed from him.

When I got to his side, I dropped to my knees and hovered my hands over his bloodied fur. "Is he…"

Beatrix kneeled next to me. "He's alive, but he took on dark magic when the barrier between the two of you broke."

Holden raced toward us. He was covered in so much blood that I couldn't tell whether it was his or someone else's. "Foster!" he roared.

"What can we do?" I asked Beatrix, afraid of trusting myself.

Except it was Holden who answered.

"You need to stay away from him until he can shift back to his human form. In fact, until we have all of our wolves back, it might be better if you just stayed away altogether."

My chest constricted and stomach twisted until I was certain I was going to throw up. I recalled watching the shifters and witches' bodies being raised into the sky. I hadn't recognized any of them, but I also hadn't been in my right mind.

My hand still held on to Foster, but my eyes searched for Charlie. "Where is she?" I demanded.

Beatrix pulled me back. "We haven't found her."

No, no, no. This couldn't be happening. I'd just gotten most of my magic back. Moira was gone. There was supposed to be a victory here, but instead, my best friend had been taken, and my mate was possibly dying… because of me.

"What did I do?" I muttered, more to myself than anyone else.

"I'm sorry, Andie, but you need to leave. I have to

focus on the wolves, and you're still pulsing with dark magic." Holden moved between me and Foster's prone wolf form.

My lip quivered. "But I didn't mean to…"

He nodded stiffly. "I know, but it still happened. Someone will be in touch if he wakes or anything changes."

I gripped Beatrix's arm but stared at Holden, trying not to completely fall apart. "*If?*"

Holden closed his eyes for a brief moment. When he reopened them, they were no less furious. "I won't lie to you, Andie. I mean *if* he wakes up. Now go. Before he gets any worse."

Beatrix pulled me up and forced me back. "We're going to fix this, Andie. I promise."

I badly wanted to believe her, but with every step I was forced to take away from Foster and every thought that reminded me my best friend was also gone…

I didn't see how anything could be fixed.

My steps faltered, and I wanted to turn around and go back to my soulmate, but Beatrix yanked hard on my arms. "Let Holden heal his pack, Andie. We'll come back just as soon as it's safe."

Ire exploded within my chest, spreading throughout my body in seconds and extinguishing all prior thoughts of doubt, self-pity, and woe.

Safe? Nothing would be safe until I saw Foster's blue eyes again and held him in my arms.

And if that didn't happen quick enough?

The world would feel my wrath—and soon.

Want to know what happens next? Preorder Forged Magic today!
Want to chat all things Fated to the Wolf? Join my reader group Heather Renee's Book Warriors!

Also, a quick note, if you did not download the ebook version of this book from Amazon, or you were not gifted it directly from the author, then you are reading a pirated copy of this book. Please, delete this copy and grab one from Amazon so you can help support the creation of more books in the future! Thank you!

STAY IN TOUCH

Find Heather on Facebook:
Reader Group:
Want to talk all things books and get updates before anyone else? Come hang with me in my reader group!
Heather Renee's Book Warriors

Author Page:
Teaser and big updates are also posted here!
Heather Renee Author

Newsletter:
I send this out sporadically. Don't worry. You won't ever be spammed by me and you get a couple goodies when you sign up!
http://smarturl.it/HeatherReneeNL

ABOUT THE AUTHOR

Heather Renee is a USA Today Bestselling author who lives in Oregon. She writes Paranormal Romance and Urban Fantasy novels with a mixture of romance, humor, and sass. Her love of reading eventually led to her passion of writing and giving the gift of escapism.

When Heather's not writing, she's spending time with her loving husband and beautiful daughter, going on their own adventures. She loves to hear from her fans, so visit her website: www.HeatherReneeAuthor.com and check out the Contact Me page for ways to connect.

ALSO BY HEATHER RENEE

Fated to the Wolf

An abandoned witch. A rogue wolf. Can the two save each other or will their bond only lead to destruction?

Scorned by Blood

A complete New Adult Vampire series featuring a not-so-human leading lady and the sexy vampire bound to protect her no matter the cost.

Luna Marked

A complete New Adult wolf shifter series (dual POV) featuring a strong-willed leading lady and a patient, yet fierce alpha male.

Broken Court

A complete New Adult Urban Fantasy series featuring an unconventional and anti-heroine leading lady, a broody love interest, and a fae kingdom with a vile king.

Royal Fae Guardians

A complete Young Adult Urban Fantasy series featuring fae, magic users, a sweet romance, along with snark and humor.

Shadow Veil Academy

A complete Upper Young Adult Urban Fantasy Academy series featuring shifters, elves, witches, and more.

Elite Supernatural Trackers

A complete New Adult Urban Fantasy series featuring witches, demons, a smart-mouthed female lead, alpha males, and a snarky fairy sidekick.

Raven Point Pack Series

A complete Upper Young Adult Paranormal Romance series featuring wolves, witches, vengeance, and fated mates.

Blood of the Sea Series

A complete Young Adult Paranormal Romance series featuring vampires, open seas adventures, and the occasional pirate.

Standalone

Marked Paradox - A complete Young Adult Fantasy fae story about a realm divided and one fae to bring them back together.